Overcoming

Volume 1: Adapt

Jade Green

DEDICATION & ACKNOWLEDGEMENTS

This book is dedicated to a group of the most amazing, loving, and supportive people I have ever had the honor of knowing—my Fannibal Family. Without you all, this would not have been possible. I would like to extend special thanks to Sabrina Ripperger and Alexandra Slater for their support and advice while creating this story. Sabrina has done an audio book of this story's original form. It can be found at https://soundcloud.com/sabrina-ripperger/sets/overcoming-a-hannibal-will.

The artwork contained in this volume was created by TheSeaVoices, whose talent has brought this story to life. Due to the constraints of printing, I was unable to present them in color, or even show all of the created pieces. I encourage you to visit https://theseavoices.tumblr.com/tagged/myart to view the full pieces in all their glory. Thank you so much to Cheryl, and to the anonymous patron who commissioned these pieces.

For my muses, Mads and Hugh, and for Bryan, who made it all possible.

Chapter 1

Twenty-five years ago, the Earl of Reddig entered into a contract with the Duke of Westvale to give one of his grandchildren of marriageable age to the Duke's grandson, the Marquess of Clarges, at a time when it suited him to one day marry.

He had happily put that contract behind him and did everyone the disservice of dying without mentioning said contract to his son, Statton Grant, who became the new Earl quite ignorant of his father's machinations until now.

Dumbfounded, he stared at the man who came in the Duke's stead, one Mr. Linden Stammets, and said with no little fear, "I have never in my life seen this document, nor did I agree to it."

Linden Stammets considered himself a man of some distinction, a man of note in the ducal household, entrusted with the most private and dearest of instructions from the Ledford family. He was not about to be dissuaded by anyone who was *not* of the esteemed Ledford family, be they Earl or Alpha or any combination thereof.

"I am sorry," he said, the words careful and polite, his features schooled into calm despite the rising tide of inner offense. "I fear I was not clear. Perhaps you would like to take a moment and reread the contract once more?"

"I don't *need* to reread it!" Lord Reddig said, incensed, his round cheeks filling with color. "I am telling you now, I am not abiding by a contract which I have not signed!"

"I am afraid I have the necessary legal paperwork to the contrary," Linden said, cautious to be gentle as if pressing the point were to change his mind. "The previous Earl signed it some twenty-five years ago, clearly agreeing to give one of his grandchildren in marriage in exchange for an alliance with the Ledford line; more specifically, one of *your* eligible children to wed the Duke's grandson and heir."

"His grandson who has been missing from this country for the past ten years," Lord Reddig said, speaking loudly enough to be heard in the hallway. "The same grandson whose arrogance and stubbornness and previous marriage are the subjects of gossip to an unending degree? The very same grandson we *all* assumed would gladly give up his inheritance to spend his days as a country doctor when he retired from the military—*that* grandson?"

Linden stiffened at hearing the Ledford family spoken of in such a way. "Are you attempting to tell me, Lord Reddig, that you consider the contract null and void?"

"No, you twit, I'm saying in the meantime I unknowingly married my daughters off to men who are wealthy enough to care for them and very much on this country's soil, sir! I have no daughters left!"

Mr. Stammets was not a man who would willingly return in defeat nor be easily put off of his given task. Patiently, he said, "I am aware that you *do*, in fact, have a daughter of marriageable age. She is some eighteen years now, is she not? Not yet Out? She will do quite nicely, I am sure. His Grace desires me to return at once with a report of the child, so please have her presented."

Lord Reddig stared at him once again, his blue eyes wide and unblinking.

"It is a longstanding agreement, my Lord. It is *Expected*," Linden said, reminding him of his duty.

"Mr. Stammets," Lord Reddig said, his mind working quickly to find a way out. "Hannibal Ledford is notorious in his temper. He already stands condemned in the public eye as a murderer of his late wife. What guarantee do I have that my daughter will not be mistreated?"

He looked down at the contract and read it twice. Nowhere did it say that they had to be female, only that they must be of childbearing age and capable of providing the expected Alpha male children to continue the Ledford line. While Lord Reddig was not willing to part with his youngest daughter to a murderous and intolerable future Duke, he was more than happy to be rid of the Omega born alongside her.

"The former Lady Clarges died of unfortunate natural causes and your daughter is a noblewoman," Mr. Stammets said, shocked and embarrassed at his lack of discretion. "I assure you, my Lord, that no one in His Grace's household would treat a gently-bred lady with anything other than respect and delicacy."

Lord Reddig snorted and stood. He caught the eye of his butler, and said loudly, "Blake, fetch me Willia."

Blake started at the unfamiliar name, but rapidly gathered himself, taking his cues from his master's wide-eyed glare.

"Of course, my Lord," he said, nodding. "It will take some time, however, as she is..."

"Reviewing cook's menu," Lord Reddig filled in, clearing his throat. "It will take a short while to let her ready herself, Mr. Stammets. You know how particular females are about their appearance."

"I am in a hurry," Mr. Stammets said, displeased. "But I wish to see her at her absolute best. I am content to wait."

Lord Reddig gave him a wavering smile and rang for tea, hoping his plan would work.

⌘⌘⌘

"What's happening?" Will asked for the thousandth time, confused by the flurry of activity around him. So far, in between the estate office and the house, he'd only been told he must hurry, he must look presentable, and he must mind his manners. "Has something happened?"

He was shuttled into his sister's suite without further explanation and was confronted by all manner of dresses being flung about in such haste that the maids all looked fit to faint.

Blake was giving quiet, clipped orders to Mina's maids. Mina herself was pale and wide-eyed near her dressing room, quite bloodless and shocked. Concerned for his twin sister, Will called her name and she gave him a half-smile that meant something terrible had happened and he was to make sure she didn't suffer for it, as always.

"Will," she said, sweetly and with wheedling intent that he was immediately worried by. "Father has a great favor to ask of you."

Will tensed, knowing his father asked very little of him but his absence, since Will had the temerity to be born Omegan rather than a "full" boy.

"Mr. Grant, his Lordship has indicated that he wishes you to meet a visitor," Blake said, frowning softly. "Please, Mr. Grant, if you could undress?"

"Undress?"

"Will, darling, there's really no time," Mina said, hastening towards him, wringing her pale little hands before her, the picture of worry. "This visitor is not patient and you don't wish to upset Father, do you? You know how it goes if you upset him."

Mystified and frightened, Will started to do as he was asked despite the many people in the room. No one in this household had ever been particularly thoughtful of him for the past eighteen years and he did not expect them to start now, but it was still terribly embarrassing to take his clothes off in front of so many critical, assessing pairs of eyes.

Apparently he moved too slowly for the moment, because in a trice no less than four of Mina's maids lit on him and stripped him down to his skin.

Flushed with mortification, Will covered his groin with his hands, protesting softly as they tugged at his limbs to dress him. His objections were overridden, unheard by his sister, who exchanged heated conversation with Blake.

"What is *happening*?" He reached a volume that made both of them look at him, annoyed. Beseeching, he quieted somewhat as the maids began to dress him in Mina's clothing and asked again, "Please... what is happening? Why are you dressing me in your clothes?"

"Will, Father wishes you to play a role in my stead," Mina said, deciding her best means to success was his acceptance and collusion. "*Willia*, you will answer to. Do you understand?"

Will cringed as he was corseted and encased in silk and satin from stockings to throat. He was, luckily, as slender as his sister and her healthy bust gave allowance in her clothing for his broader shoulders, but they were otherwise quite alike from their riotous dark curls and limpid blue eyes to the tiny crook in their pinky toes.

"Mina," he said, unused to nay saying his sister because it had always earned him his father's wrath for the past eighteen years. "Father has always threatened to hang me should he ever find me in a frock!"

"Mr. Grant—Lady *Willia*," Blake automatically corrected, overseeing the transformation with a critical eye. "It is your place in this household to make life easier for your family, is it not? Your grandfather entered into a very surprising contract with the Duke of Westvale which would require your dear twin sister to marry a man who simply does not suit her. You shouldn't like for that to happen, should you?"

"Will," Mina put in, watching them arrange his curly locks into a modest hairstyle to hide their lack of length. "You would never want me to be given away to some stranger, would you? You know how long I've been waiting for Timothy to come 'round, don't you? Surely you wouldn't rather see me packed off to the Duke of Westvale's snobbish heir?"

"You would be a Duchess one day," Will said, bewildered and uncomfortable as they slid his feet into her little slippers, which were too small and far too tight. His anxious blue eyes flicked from Mina's closed face to Blake's own hard one. "Mina, why would you wish me to be shown in your stead when you stand to gain a duchy?"

Mina's sideways glance to Blake warned him there was a very good reason, indeed. He fleetingly wondered how they could ask him to take her place and show mercy to her when none of them would show mercy to him, but the thought was gone before it fully formed. He had been a burden to them for the whole of his life, as his father said; the least he could do was be silent while wiser heads than his took charge.

"Darling," Mina said, as she always did when she wished him not to argue. She even stroked his face, a rare kindness she knew he craved. "Father has already promised me to Timothy. It would be so embarrassing now to break things off, hm? Still, he cannot breach a contract with a *Duke*."

Will trembled. His voice was unsteady when he said, "They will murder me for this deceit, Mina."

That seemed to touch her when other things would not. She pet him again, careful not to disturb the job her maids were attempting on his curls. Gently, she said, "They would not dare, Will. Trust me, will you? By the time they realize you are an Omega they will be forced to accept you or risk a very damaging scandal. *Please*, Will. Please, do this for me? You could be a Duchess, if he is favorable to your feminine side as Father is not. At any rate, you will be marrying up, which is more than the dismal future Father has planned for you."

Will shivered a little, uncertain but still convinced of one thing—his father's dislike of him would ensure he would not long survive Mina's marriage and passage from their house to her husband's.

"And just imagine, Will," she went on, pressing her advantage, a lively and beautiful mirror of himself whom he loved absolutely. "There is every chance you will find a happy home there. You will have status, power enough to protect you from Father, and you might even find that Hannibal Ledford is tolerable to deal with. You *could* be happy, darling, hm?"

5

"Perhaps this is for the best..." he whispered, the corset making him even more breathless than his sudden hope.

"Mr. Grant, you know better than to question your father's decisions," Blake scolded, uniformly disapproving of the way he was dressed. "He is an Alpha, after all. Alphas always know what is best for creatures such as you."

Will ducked his head, a scarlet flush climbing his cheeks.

"You look so much like me," Mina said, tipping his chin up again to look at him. "It's like looking into a mirror when I'm very sad and fragile."

"We have no more time, I'm afraid," Blake said, nodding that the getup would do for now. "Come along, Mr. Gr—er, *Lady Willia*."

Will followed him, moving with ease despite the unfamiliar clothing and too-small shoes, his natural Omegan grace adapting quite nicely, his heart fluttering with excitement and fear. A thousand worries assailed him, a thousand tells that he was not what he claimed. How on earth could he hope to fool this beta, let alone the Alphas which must abound in the Duke's household?

He started to voice this fear to Blake, but they arrived at his father's office and a knock on the door forbade him from asking more questions. His father called entry from within and Blake announced him, holding the door wide, saying, "Lady Grant, my Lord."

Nervous, Will stepped into the room and greeted his father, a rosy pink blush on his pale cheeks. He nodded meekly at the stranger in the room whom Blake introduced as Mr. Linden Stammets, a servant in the employ of the Duke of Westvale. Will inclined his head again in greeting, tensing when his hand was swept up and a kiss was grazed across his knuckles.

"This is my only remaining available child, Lady Willia Grant," Lord Reddig said, the flush on his face betraying his irritation at seeing Will got up as a woman. His anger coiled around Will like a vise, plucking at his instinct to deflect the potential violence of the Alpha who had control over him. Self-preservation won that round, as he still bore the marks of the last time he'd dared to soothe his father's temper and found it turned on him instead. "As you can see, she is very modest and sheltered."

Mr. Stammets released his hand, showing no curiosity over the fact that it was less soft than he might have expected. Instead, he gestured for Will to sit and waited until he had done so, arranging his skirts around him as he'd seen his sisters do countless times before and tucking his feet back out of sight to hide how ill-fitting the shoes were.

"Lady Grant," Mr. Stammets warmly said, pleased with what he saw. "What an exquisite jewel you are! My Lord, His Grace shall be very pleased at the quality of the spouse you are providing his heir. This will be a great alliance, indeed. Now, tell me of your education."

Will hesitated, gathering his thoughts before he answered, keeping his voice deliberately soft. "I have had the same education as any young lady expected to run a noble House. I am afraid my instruction does not differ from that of other ladies my age."

Mr. Stammets nodded and made a small notation on the paper he was holding.

"I can surmise, then, that you are more than capable of keeping household accounts and directing staff," he said, taking from it what he would. "But what of other ladylike accomplishments, Lady Grant?"

Will wet his lips. Mr. Stammets' eyes lingered there and his father bristled, sensing his interest.

"I am very well-versed in the harpsichord," Will told him, quietly doling out those accomplishments which his father had always belittled for being too feminine. "I am a tolerable singer and a very good rider. I am an ardent reader and prefer to keep my own company. I am, however, a very good listener."

His father cleared his throat, and Will subsided, falling back into his seat as if he'd been chastised.

"Well, my dear, it sounds as if you will make Lord Clarges a biddable and agreeable wife," Mr. Stammets said, almost rubbing his hands together with glee. "Yes, Lady Willia Grant, I believe you shall do quite nicely."

"So, we are agreed, then?" Lord Reddig cut in, eager to be done with it.

"The final decision will rest with His Grace, but I cannot see any reason why two such lovely people should not marry, as per the contract," Mr. Stammets said, his mind already made up. "I shall carry my observations to His Grace and return with his answer."

"I have one condition," Lord Reddig said, flushing. "Should His Grace agree, I wish him to send his solicitor and a proxy so the marriage can be performed here. I will have Willia leave this house secure in her new place."

"I am sure those terms will be more than acceptable considering Lord Clarges is still some time out from arrival," Mr. Stammets said, making another note with a smile. "He has not, of course, learned of the gracious way in which His Grace has arranged for his return, but I am confident he will be home to take his place as soon as the news is delivered."

"Blake," Lord Reddig called, and the office door opened immediately. "Please see that Mr. Stammets is refreshed and set out with fresh horses."

"Yes, my Lord," Blake said, escorting the Duke's man out.

Will sat very still, his chest rising and falling slightly beneath the tight silk and starched, ruffled neckline of the dress. He waited for his father's anger, for his loathing, perhaps even for a slap for his audacity. Will had very quickly been beaten out of his proclivity for pretty and soft things, shamed for his interest in dolls, his love of seemingly feminine things pruned out of him with such savagery that the memories still woke him from terrified sleep.

"Will," his father said, and he twitched, drawing in, defensive postures which usually only incited his father to more towering rages. He did not, however, decide to indulge in one at present. Instead, he cleared his throat and softened his tone to say, "If His Grace agrees, you will marry the Ledford heir."

"Yes, Father," Will whispered, not looking at him, not daring to meet his gaze.

"Your sister's clothing fits you," Lord Reddig observed, a thread of displeasure coloring his words. "You will be packed off with her things. She is due a new trousseau for her wedding."

"Father," Will said in the subsequent silence, daring to steal a glance up. "They are an Alpha family. Will they not realize I am Omegan?"

His father frowned, irritated to have it pointed out to him. "Do you think yourself so clever that you have considered things which I have not?" he questioned, the sharpness of his voice cutting. Will dropped his gaze in haste, desperate not to issue an unbidden challenge. "The marriage will be signed, sealed and delivered before *you* are delivered to the ducal household. By the time anyone realizes you are not, in fact, your sister, it will be too late to do anything about it."

Will schooled his face to show none of his nervous tension, but it was clear in his voice when he asked, "Will they not despise me for deceiving them?"

"Whether they do or do not is no matter to me," Lord Reddig answered. "They are, however, a distinguished family and the contract did not specify a beta female. They wish to have another generation to secure the line of succession and you are capable of providing that, confused creature that you are."

Will's hands pressed over his flat belly, hard as stone beneath the cinch of the corset and bone stays. He had no choice but to answer, "Yes, Father."

"William," his father said, resting his forehead in his hand, his skin pale and taut. "I never dreamed a day such as this would come. Fate has worked in our favor on this count, however. At least I can spare your sister a terrible fate thanks to you. I never counted on your Omegan nature being anything other than a curse."

"I know, Father," Will said in a tone of apology, familiar guilt washing over him. He had tried all of his life to be the son his father wanted, disappointing him daily with his very existence, with his penchant for beauty, with his love of things his father considered emasculating, like his fascination with his sisters' dresses, baubles, and activities.

"The fact of the matter is that despite everything, you were never the son I desired," Lord Reddig sighed, rubbing his face with weary resignation. "At least in this you will have a use."

"I am sorry, Father," Will said, his voice soft and small.

His father lifted his head to stare at him, gruff and embarrassed when he admitted, "I haven't done right by you, William. I've bent your nature to suit my ends and it may go the worse for you when it comes down to it."

"I have always been glad to please, Father," Will said, his father's admission chilling him as no icy water ever could. It frightened him to hear his Alpha speak with such uncertainty. It upset the balance of his world to realize that his father might have made some mistake with him, that he had *not*, in fact, been acting in Will's best interests by bullying him to more masculine pursuits.

"It's that damned Omegan nature of yours!" Lord Reddig said, and Will flinched. "Of *course* you were glad to please! But here you are, about to be married off to a future Duke and the one good thing I could have done for you probably ruined by my desire to have a real son."

"I *am* your son," Will said, his stomach clenching with nausea, with deep fear. "If they send me back unwanted, Father, I will continue to be your son."

"No, Will," Lord Reddig said, looking at him with something like regret, but it quickly became the familiar dislike that had greeted Will from his earliest memories. "No, you were never my son and you never can be, no matter how much I wish it was otherwise."

Will flinched again, ducking his head as hot tears formed in his eyes. He willed them away, fingernails biting into his palms as he fought not to cry in front of his father. Tears had been lovingly soothed from his sisters and followed by coddling and indulgence, but Will's tears had always been thoroughly chastised and berated, resulting in his standing alone in a corner of the nursery until he could get himself "under control". He had learned with time. Everything his father had taught him, he had learned because he could *see* things as his father did. It was an unspoken, unacknowledged talent he had, this strange perception of his. It was the reason that his father—rapidly understanding that proximity affected it—had insisted Will be separated from other company at an early age lest he be too much like them and less so the son he wished Will had been.

"That habit of yours," Lord Reddig said, the only way in which he ever addressed Will's helpless ability to take the perspective of those around him. "You will need to control it."

"Yes, Father," he murmured.

"*William*, understand that you cannot allow it to overcome your good sense!" his father insisted, scowling. "They won't stand for such nonsense! Do you understand?"

"Yes, Father," he said again, staring steadily at his hands fisted in his lap, the cold wings of panic fluttering in his heart.

"This man I'm giving you to," Lord Reddig said, not remarking Will's distress anymore now than he ever had. "He has a reputation for being high-handed and stubborn. Do *not* give him any reason to be unkind to you."

"I will not give him reasons, Father, to the best of my ability."

"Do as he says," his father told him. "Whatever he wants of you, you give him. Do you understand me?"

"Yes, Father."

"*Whatever he wants*," his father repeated, as he always did when he felt Will wasn't absorbing what he was being told. "If it's dresses and frippery, then so be it. If it's being shut away at a distant estate bearing children in succession, then so be it. There is no room in the ducal house for the creature I raised, understand? Serve your purpose and keep them from complaint with this family."

Will shivered, at a loss. Helpless, he looked up at his father with fear brimming in his bright blue eyes and said, "I don't know how to be the person they want, Father."

Something passed in Lord Reddig's gaze, then, some slow understanding or even compassion, overdue as it was. "I know that, William. Perhaps in such a setting your natural instincts will guide you better than my necessary correction ever could."

Will frowned and looked back at his lap, trying not to tremble with nerves.

"Go to your room," his father said. "Tell Blake to have the servants start packing."

"Yes, Father," Will said.

It was the last time in a very long time that he spoke thusly with the man who had loathed him from the moment of his birth.

11

The Ledfords were an esteemed family, a family with a long and noble history of service to the throne for which they had been remarkably rewarded with titles and holdings. They were one of the oldest Alpha families in the whole of the Empire, blue bloods bred and true.

It was only within the last century that the mighty had fallen, so to speak. The family fractured beneath the weight of its dignity and power, offshoots flung to the four corners of the Empire, and new and startling notions became the norm.

The most startling of which was the fact that the Ledford heir, Hannibal, Marquess of Clarges, had studied to become a medical doctor and actually *practiced*.

It was often overlooked that he did so on the battlefield as his duty to the Crown. Overlooked, of course, by a Society quick to gossip; *not* overlooked, however, by a bevy of concerned relatives dreading every day of combat that sought to take their Duke-in-waiting away from them, thus leaving the lines of inheritance in question.

"Another letter, m'Lord," Berger said, pushing into his master's tent with the missive held in front of him, a look of acute dread on his face.

Hannibal took it, leaving bloody fingerprints on the ivory-colored paper, his face already falling into a grim frown which his valet knew all too well from his years of service.

He opened it, brown eyes flicking over the paper, and sighed on a soft laugh, rolling his eyes heavenward.

"Berger."

"Yes, m'Lord?" was the immediate response.

"Do you find thirty to be an unusually great age?"

Berger froze, uncertain. "Not terribly so, m'Lord," he decided was safe enough.

Hannibal smirked. It was not a pleasant smirk, all things considered, but it was about as close to humor as he got these days and it relieved his valet to see it.

"Apparently," Hannibal said, tipping his head back on another sigh. "I have been given an ultimatum."

Berger perked up, attentive to any conditions which might involve them going home to their own blessed country.

"My dearest grandfather has bought my commission," Hannibal said, his voice tight and dark and vastly unhappy. He handed the letter to Berger, who read it quickly, eyes widening. "I either return immediately or forfeit my place as his heir."

"He surely wouldn't..." Berger began, though he read it twice, disbelieving.

"My grandfather is not one to make idle threats and the lines of succession must be secured," Hannibal said, annoyed. "It is perfectly reasonable to act as he has, just incredibly annoying and overbearing because he knows I would never forfeit."

Berger finished the letter, swallowing hard at what he'd read there. "And the other, my Lord?" he asked, his voice a near whisper.

"On the matter of my wife?" Hannibal inquired, the polite menace of his tone making Berger wince, doubly so when those humorless amber eyes landed on him, sparkling with ire. "That matter, too, depends on my answer. Should I give up my place why, then, the young lady he has chosen will be given to my successor."

"His Grace has already chosen," Berger said, somewhat mystified but not entirely surprised. The letters over the years had become increasingly short and to the point. More than once the subject of a wife had been broached without answer.

"He, unfortunately, has taken my silence as assent," Hannibal said, glowering. He waved his bloody hand in a dismissive gesture and said, "It matters not. I am sure, as the daughter of a noble, she will be perfectly capable of providing the Alpha son he desires, as any other woman. She will serve her purpose and be rewarded with a title. No gently-bred woman would wish for more, would she?"

"Oh... of course not, my Lord," Berger agreed. "...no *woman* would ask for more."

Hannibal laughed mirthlessly, his eyebrow arching over one piercing dark eye. "Believe me, Berger," he said, shaking his head. "My grandfather would never dare hand me an Omegan wife."

"...because they are spoken for so young, m'Lord?" Berger asked, hesitantly touching on his master's single blind prejudice, unable to resist his curiosity about its source.

"Because they are useless irritants incapable of rational thought and I'd rather marry a mule than be saddled with an Omega," Hannibal told him, his mild tone only putting a sting in his words. "And my grandfather knows that well enough. That aside, there is that damnable contract of his with the former Earl of Reddig. No doubt his insipid little granddaughters will be clamoring over who is to be a future Duchess."

Berger stayed silent for a long moment before tentatively asking, "So... what will you do?"

Hannibal sighed heavily again, shaking his head hard enough that the short locks of his brown hair whispered back across his forehead.

"I suppose you must pack, Berger. We are going home."

Chapter 2

Over a month passed before the ducal coach returned bearing several ministers of law with the marriage proxy riding alongside it.

Mina, well warned of their approach, watched with wide eyes from behind the drapes as Will was once more polished to appear in her place.

"My, what a fine seat your proxy has," she sighed, blushing on a smile. "It is too bad *he* is not the heir. I should not mind being a Duchess if he were the Duke."

Will scowled at her, asking with ill humor and sharpness borne of pure, dreadful anxiety, "And what of Timothy? Or are your affections so fleeting?"

Mina laughed, a floating and lovely sound, and left the window to look him over.

"That is my favorite day dress, don't get anything on it. Though I suppose it doesn't matter now."

Will didn't dignify that with a response. His father's influence was such that he felt ridiculous in her beautiful dresses, though the maids all assured him that he wore them with the same grace and charm as his sister. Still, he couldn't imagine continuing this farce for long. According to his father, he wouldn't have to.

The coach rolled to a stop and Mina ordered the servants to start loading her trunks. Her new wardrobe was already commissioned, no few pieces presently in her keeping. She was eager to clear out her old gowns to make room and continue the illusion that Will was nothing more than the lovely young lady he seemed.

A part of him *wanted* to be, the part of him his father had all but gutted him of. He hoped they would be content with him, that he might be able to make a life that was, if not happy, at least a little less miserable than his life here at home. He had amused himself with daydreams that had grown with time, silly imaginings that left him smiling with possibilities despite the fury that would no doubt follow his deceit.

He just wanted to be part of a proper family. He wanted to be useful and important to someone, to have some small trace of the love his sisters had enjoyed growing up and from their respective spouses.

He would gladly bear the Ledford family's ire if only they would choose to be kind to him in time.

Blake came for him. The moment Will stepped out from Mina's room he caught the scent of an unfamiliar Alpha mingling with his father's own, overridden by the sharp taint of fear.

Dismayed and frightened, Will hurried after Blake to the receiving room where the two solicitors, the proxy, and his father were already waiting. His father's wide blue eyes betrayed his stark concern, and Will immediately knew what they had planned was impossible.

The moment the Alpha proxy turned to face him, startled recognition crossed his handsome features, and he frowned, knowing without a doubt what they had done.

"Willia, this is Anthony Diment, Viscount du Millau, Hannibal Ledford's cousin and proxy," Lord Reddig said, as if keeping to manners might somehow prevent the inevitable realization that he was trying to foist an Omega off on them. "My Lord du Millau, this is my daughter, Willia Grant."

"*Lady* Grant," Anthony said, approaching Will's trembling form with the lithe grace of a cat, amusement and wonder dancing in his blue eyes as he swept Will's hand up for a kiss.

Will managed a small curtsy, averting his gaze, hyper-aware of the way the man's nostrils flared and uncomfortably certain his own scent was changing in the presence of a virile Alpha youth.

"Gentlemen," Anthony said, addressing the room. "Lady Grant needs some air."

"I will have a servant—"

"I'll take her for a turn about the garden," Anthony said, cutting Lord Reddig off. He subsided with indignant, frightened fury, but did not protest. Anthony looped Will's arm over his elbow, graced him with a cat-like smile, and escorted him straight from the house to the garden without saying another word.

Will clutched his arm in a stupor of dread, barely aware of the warm material beneath his spread fingers, but uncomfortably aware that an Alpha male had hold of him. His pulse raced like mad from it and from the fear that he was caught. He was sure he was being led out here for some terrible purpose or harsh scolding that would only precede the one his father would give him.

Instead, Anthony pulled him to a bench within sight of the receiving room windows and settled him there, asking, "Do you mind if I smoke?"

Not trusting his voice, Will shook his head and directed his gaze at his lap, fidgeting.

"Look here at me, please," Anthony asked, and Will tipped his head up to find the man looking at him intently as he rolled a cigarette, his blue eyes critical. "You are lovely, Lady Grant. I suppose you hear that quite a lot?"

Will shook his head again, managing, "I am not allowed visitors or visiting."

Anthony chuckled and licked the paper on his cigarette, sealing it tight before lighting it and taking a deep pull. He blew smoke out, picked a small bit of tobacco from his tongue, and asked, "What game is your father playing at, hm? I had wondered why he was so beside himself when I showed up. What say you, *Lady* Grant?"

Will shivered, but did not answer. Every instinct he possessed urged him to throw himself at this man's feet and beg for mercy, to somehow save himself whatever retribution was to come. But the memory of his father's beatings were stronger than any instinctive urge and he sat still, caught like a deer at dawn, eyes wide and mouth parted.

Anthony laughed softly, shaking his head. "Did he think he could fool another Alpha with this?" He gestured at Will's person with his free hand. "It wouldn't make a difference if he hadn't deliberately put to Mr. Stammets that you were a beta female, but the crux of the issue is he *has*. So, I suppose the question is, why has your father presented you as *your sister*?"

Will began to tremble, uncertain how much he knew of that contract or how Mr. Stammets had represented him to the Ledford family.

"I had wondered when they said your name was Willia," Anthony said, smirking. "I could have sworn the charming minx I'd seen was named Wilhelmina and answered to Mina, not Willia. Are you twins? You look so much like her it's uncanny."

Will swallowed hard and nodded.

"An Omegan twin," Anthony mused, busying himself with his cigarette as he thought. "Is there some reason your sister doesn't want to marry my cousin? Mind you, I can think of a thousand reasons why any sane woman wouldn't,

17

considering, but Mina surely hasn't that much knowledge of him, young as she is."

"Lord Rathmore just settled with our father for her hand," Will admitted, his voice soft and wavering with nerves. "There was no way to break with him without hard feelings."

Anthony blew out a cloud of smoke, amused and smiling. "And then along comes Stammets with a decades-old contract and your father has a brilliant idea to settle both?"

Will dropped his gaze again. "He seemed certain it would sort things."

"Yet, I imagine your father has a *very* good idea of the man my cousin is," Anthony said, moving to sit next to Will. He searched Will with jaded blue eyes, looking for some crack in his composure, for something he could use. "Your father dislikes you immensely."

Will looked off the other direction, baring the long column of his throat as he did so, a combination of movements created to beg clemency and to be left alone, performed by instinct rather than design. "Yes," he whispered. "Immensely."

Anthony was silent for a long moment, contemplating. "I have half a mind to go back to Grandfather and have him settle this."

Will made a low, distressed noise at what that statement conjured—images of Mina dragged unwilling to wed her ducal heir, heartbroken and bereft. Lord Rathmore's family siding against his father, incensed at the indignity they'd been dealt. His own father blaming him for giving it all away and ruining his plans. Will shuddered to think of what would happen to him.

"Then again, this could be fairly interesting," Anthony said, more to himself than to Will. "*Strictly speaking*, your father did not breach the contract. You are capable of bearing an heir so there should be no complaint on that count. Though I do feel somewhat a cad handing you to Hannibal, now that I think of it."

"Please," Will managed, turning to him to plead, more terrified of his father than he was of a stranger he'd never met. He went so far as to grasp Anthony's hand, his blue eyes wide and beseeching. "*Please* pretend all is well. Then I will be your cousin's problem to deal with and I will swear you knew nothing!"

That made Anthony laugh, thoroughly amused, and he squeezed Will's small hand in his. "You fetching little thing! Ah, but they will never believe I did not know. Your father has done you no favors, darling. The moment you set eyes on me your scent changed, and I am but half the Alpha my cousin and grandfather are. You are quite obviously and delightfully an Omega, and there will be no hiding that fact."

Will all but wilted, sickly thinking of his life to come.

"However, I *can* claim that I assumed you were, in fact, the one on offer," Anthony said. "And Mr. Stammets can confirm that, bless his beta heart. With all of the legal aspects put into place the family will be loathe to take action against your father, leaving your sister quite in the clear for Lord Rathmore."

Will's relief emerged as a breathless laugh and he tipped his head back, drawing a breath eloquent of delighted release of tension.

"Lord du Millau," he said when he could speak at last, his fingers clenching on the large, strong ones in his grip. "I owe you my life, sir!"

Anthony's blue eyes held an unholy gleam Will was utterly unaware of. Smiling, he said, "I will hold you to that, Lady Grant. Shall we have ourselves a wedding?"

Will, insulated within his own naive experience, nodded vigorously, pleased and relieved he would not have to face his father's wrath.

He had no idea there could be ever so much worse than his father's vitriolic hatred awaiting him.

⌘⌘⌘

The ceremony, such as it was, was quick and to the point. Lord Reddig printed Will's name on the document as Willia M Grant and Will signed his name as he always did. There would be no escape on a technicality on the documents themselves which declared William Grant the proper and legal spouse of Hannibal Ledford via proxy.

The trunks were loaded by the time it was all legally accomplished. The two solicitors took a hired hack back to the Capital to file the paperwork, and Will was bundled into the ducal coach to be taken before His Grace without any fanfare or word of goodbye from his family.

"Have you wrapped your mind around it all?" Anthony inquired, choosing to ride inside the coach with Will instead of alongside it.

"Yes, my Lord," Will answered, prompting the man to laugh with delight.

"Ah, no, you're a Marchioness now and my better, Will—may I call you Will? I got the impression that female clothing is not to your taste and you've a preference for male address," he remarked.

Will blushed lightly, fingering the fine dress he'd been given away in. Mina's favorite no more. "It isn't precisely *not* to my liking," he said. "It is only that it has been soundly disallowed in my father's house."

"Disallowed?"

"Yes," Will said. "Father says a young man must not make a spectacle of himself with color and cut. He says a young man must at all times be serious and attentive to his work and not be distracted by frivolous things."

Anthony sat and pondered that before venturing, "You are an Omega, Will. Do you have nothing of color in your keeping besides your sister's wardrobe?"

"No, sir, I have not," Will answered, blushing. "I have no desire for such things."

"Is that yourself speaking or your father?"

Will fidgeted, wishing Anthony would not look at him so closely.

"I can assure you that my grandfather will overhaul any deficiencies you arrive with once he accepts you," Anthony said, making the soft hue of Will's blush turn a vivid, embarrassed red. "Your father forced you into a rather unconventional lifestyle. I do hope you gleaned enough skills to make our heir a good match."

"They are more than welcome to send me home," Will said, appalled at his own temerity but lacking any other recourse. He had no Alpha to guide him and no previous experience to draw from, so he was left to fend for himself.

Anthony laughed and said, "Alas, no. Your father was most insistent on that point. You, my dear, are an unbreakable commitment. Should you fail to meet expectations, you are remanded to His Grace's custody for disposal as he sees fit."

Will let out a trembling breath but evinced no surprise.

Anthony's brows rose at his reaction. "He must truly dislike you indeed to offer such a thing. Perhaps he thinks he has ruined you, forcing you into a male role. I know very few Omegas who live only as full men do. So very few, in fact, that I cannot call any name to mind. Prospects are better for females when it comes to marrying up, I suppose."

"I was content," Will said, swallowing hard. His allegiance to his father was so deeply rooted and powerful that he could not speak a word against him. Instead, he wet his lower lip with the tip of his tongue and looked out at the unfamiliar scenery passing by. "I lived as I was told to live by my Alpha. I was content to obey him."

Anthony snorted, clearly not impressed with this reasoning. "Hannibal is going to chew you up and spit you out."

Will started, shocked, a sudden bolt of fear rocketing him. He turned his wild eyes to Anthony, who merely smiled at him, and clenched his fingers in the soft folds of Mina's dress.

"Or, perhaps if you look at him like *that*," Anthony remarked, chucking him under the chin. "He may be content to swallow you whole. Ah, don't be so frightened! There is nothing to be done for it, now. I did, however, have the foresight to ask that insufferable Blake to pack your usual clothing. Considering the colors his face turned, he did as he was bidden."

"Wh-why would I need such?" Will asked, his voice thready with panic.

"Call it a hunch," Anthony said, winking at him, and would say no more on the subject.

⌘⌘⌘

Hannibal drew in a deep breath of tangy country air and sighed, eyes sweeping closed as a knot of anxiety unraveled inside of him. After nearly a decade, he was home again on the soil of his homeland, riding down familiar roads on his very own horse while a ducal coach rolled along somewhere behind him bearing his trunks and his disgruntled valet.

He caught sight of Hartford House and tapped his stallion's rump with his crop, clicking his tongue to urge him into a trot. He felt a keen desire to see his grandfather again, the worry for him that Hannibal had suppressed all this time finally rising to the top. He was no young man anymore, the Duke, and no doubt it was far past time for Hannibal to settle and take over the running of the estate so Grandfather could enjoy his retirement.

Which brought to mind what manner of wife his grandfather had picked from those on offer in Lord Reddig's household. The Grant daughters were all beautiful, he'd been told; enchantresses with good health and genteel pursuits and no head for harshness.

Which, Hannibal knew too well, meant they were somewhat stupid and easily entertained, but at least physical beauty might make the task of getting an heir less onerous.

A missive had been waiting for him at the port saying Anthony was to marry her by proxy. She would be registered officially as his spouse and the various entitlements would be put into place by the time he arrived home. Hannibal was surprised at their rush, but could only assume some hurry had been in order. Then again, perhaps his grandfather merely wished her to be waiting for him on his return, ready to provide the longed-for children that would keep the Ledfords a solid presence among the nobility.

"Or perhaps she is simply unpleasant," he murmured, frowning softly as he rounded the bend and hit the lane for Hartford House. He found himself searching the place as he rode up, refreshing his memory with its sparkling windows and intricate embellishments. He saw staff milling out front as a coach drew up at the house ahead of him. Someone spotted him, which sent them all into a flurry of activity. He slowed the stallion despite his anticipation, giving them time to prepare for his arrival.

⌘⌘⌘

Will was awoken from his broken, uncomfortable slumber by the sudden shift of the coach as they pulled into the drive of the sprawling estate belonging to the Duke of Westvale, commonly known as Hartford House, according to Anthony. He fought not to tremble at the thought that this could be his future home. It was far more stately and vast than his father's estate. He began to imagine the number of rooms from the number of windows and the amount of staff such a place would require just to keep it livable. That calmed him somewhat, enough to make his breathing even out and his heart slow a touch.

Anthony watched him carefully, amused by his reactions.

"You're remarkably poised for being so far from your father, Will," he said, careful not to touch him or startle him in any way, cautious of him as only an Alpha could be.

"Father was insistent I learn to do without him," Will quietly said. "He said it was unseemly that any person be unable to function without someone else to decide for them. He wanted me to be able to deal well on my own if I managed to outlive him."

"It isn't natural for anyone to be on their own," Anthony said, disapproval tingeing the words. "You will be much more comfortable here, I hope. We'll see what happens when Lord Clarges arrives. Until then, I am sure you will find grandfather's presence far more stabilizing than that of your father. The Ledfords are one of the oldest Alpha lines in the realm, after all."

"I am aware of their history, sir," Will said, blushing.

"Ah, here we are," Anthony breathed, a sigh of relief leaving him as the coach rolled to a stop. "Brace yourself, it looks as if my cousin has just arrived, rather sooner than we all expected, too."

Will felt low, stark anticipation and fear blossom in his belly and looked back to find a lone rider heading towards them at a gentle trot, his erect carriage and tight control of his horse unconsciously indicative of great personal power and confidence.

"Shall we?" Anthony urged, amused by his discomfort.

Swallowing hard, Will emerged to a silent audience of Westvale servants turned out in their starched and pristine uniforms, watching him with curious eyes. He felt their interest like the tickle of fingers over his skin, uncomfortable and close.

Their attention, however, was mitigated by the arrival of Will's husband and, indeed, his own attention shifted to take in the man dismounting before the staff. He felt Anthony at his shoulder, a curious and amused presence watching the both of them.

Hannibal Ledford was nothing like Will had imagined. He was older, far older than Will had thought he might be, which was the only impression he could garner before the travel-dusty and weary man's amber-bright eyes fastened on him and bloomed fire.

Hannibal locked eyes with the slender, alarmed little Omega next to his cousin, pale but for a rosy tint to their still-round cheeks, wide blue eyes framed in long, curling lashes, head topped with a riot of glossy-dark curls and a sweet scent wafting his way that was a mouthwatering mixture of youth and fertility which momentarily struck Hannibal dumb.

But only momentarily.

"Hannibal," Anthony said, grinning. "You are just in time for our arrival."

The staff waited, uneasy and bewildered by the sudden tension even their dulled beta senses could feel, unwilling to insert themselves into an unseemly family matter.

"I should say *you* are just in time, cousin," Hannibal said, his critical eyes traveling once again to the undeniably beautiful and delicate little creature now trembling at Anthony's side. The scent grew stronger when the breeze shifted, bringing him the sweet-hot spice of an unmated Omega that, once discovered, could never be ignored. Glowering, he sharply asked, "Why did you bring that thing here?"

Will flinched, the bottom dropping out from his stomach. He clenched his hands in the folds of his skirt and trembled with the urge to hide.

"Why, for *you*, cousin," Anthony said, his grin positively wicked. "May I introduce your new wife?"

The silence was stifling.

It was broken soon enough by Hannibal coldly ordering, "*Into the house! Now!*"

⌘⌘⌘

It was chaos from there.

The servants scattered in every direction, scrambling to get out of the path of their silently-enraged, newly-returned master.

Hannibal grabbed Will by his elbow and bodily hauled him into the house with Anthony a laughing third, shouting over the sound of Will's distressed cry, "Don't do any harm, Hannibal!"

"*Grandfather!*" Hannibal bellowed, dragging the frightened Omega alongside him into the Duke's office where the elderly Alpha was working, a ferocious frown on his own spare, lean face. Hannibal flung Will hard at the desk and he fell against it, catching himself on his hands, briefly eye-to-eye with the Duke before he jerked back and fell into a deep curtsy.

"Cease your nonsense this instant!" Hannibal said, turning his fierce glare on his calm, unmoved Grandfather. "Would you please explain to me how *this* has happened?"

Will bit his lower lip, his trembling knees almost refusing to hold him up. It was too much all at once for a boy who had never been in any company other than his father's and now found himself drowning in the presence of three Alphas at odds.

His Grace's eyes flicked to Anthony, who moved to take Will's elbow and deposit him into the chair near his desk where he sat stiff as a board, trying to adjust.

"Hannibal," His Grace said, his vibrant voice as deep as his grandson's and filled with the same Alpha power that turned Will's legs to jelly. "Welcome home."

"Welcome home?" Hannibal echoed, and laughed without humor. "Welcome *home*? Grandfather! Please explain to me how your intention to procure a wife from a proper family resulted in Anthony bringing home this..." he gestured at Will and settled for, "*mixed abortion of genders*?"

The Duke's gaze hardened on Hannibal, disapproval in every line of his face. He looked at Will, who shivered in the chair but did not shrink. He inwardly retreated from the lash of their anger and Hannibal's harsh words, fear and hopelessness rolling off of him in waves. The depths of his anxiety agitated all three Alphas in the room even more so than the situation itself. Anthony hovered near him, uncertain what to do but driven to care for an Omega who was in such telling and gut-wrenching distress, even if not one whit of it showed on his impassive, young face.

"Hannibal, you are my heir and a gentleman. Must I remind you to watch how you speak?" the Duke asked, his cold stare enough to bring his grandson's sharp tongue under some form of control. Taking a deep breath, he pulled the bell cord behind him and they waited in silence for the butler to arrive. When he did, His Grace said, "Mr. Hawkes, I believe Mr. Stammets is still on the premises. Fetch him here, if you please, and have Cook send up tea and cakes."

"Yes, by all means, let us compound this insanity with tea and cakes," Hannibal scoffed, pinching the bridge of his noble nose with weary exasperation.

"Anthony," His Grace said, ignoring him. "I expect you have some explanation for this?"

"I merely did as I was bidden, Grandfather," Anthony replied, straightening his waistcoat with renewed satisfaction, his hand falling to Will's nape without him being aware of it. "I went to the Reddig household and married Willia Grant in Hannibal's stead, as instructed. I had not thought the fact that Willia is Omegan was of any consequence, as she had been vetted by Mr. Stammets."

Will trembled under the touch, almost as frightened by the comfort it brought as he was by the tempers of the men around him. His Gift, heightened by his fear, forced him to feel their anger acutely, to instantly understand why Lord Clarges was so angry, why the Duke was impatient, why Anthony was bristling and unpredictable. It was painful to have such clarity and it left him mute in his chair, heedless of anything but the men around him.

"Did you not, indeed?" His Grace softly asked, his cold brown eyes on his other grandson.

"This is outrageous!" Hannibal pointed out, looking from his grandfather to his cousin, his face tight with fury. "You sent word you had married the Earl's *daughter* who, I am told, is a very fetching creature with dark hair and blue eyes and is the sum of every feminine beauty one could desire!"

Anthony's cat-like grin returned when he said, "I *did*, my dear cousin. I went there and married a very fetching creature with dark hair and blue eyes who is the sum of every feminine beauty one could desire."

"Anthony," the Duke said, clear warning in his tone.

"Then perhaps *you* should take it," Hannibal suggested, pinning his cousin with his fierce brown gaze, ignoring the pained noise Will made. He did not care what discomfort the Omega was currently in because it was not his concern to tend to it, no matter how its distress dragged at his nerves. There had been an awful and costly mistake and he was determined to set it to rights. He leveled a pointed stare at Anthony's soothing hand and snapped, "It certainly seems to like you well enough!"

"*Sit!*" the Duke shouted, the lash of his Alpha presence stinging even the stronger of his grandsons. "This is *my house* and I *will be obeyed!*"

They sat, Anthony pale-faced and shaken from his cruel humor, reluctantly removing his hand from Will's nape; Hannibal stonily silent and tense but doing as he was told, though his resentment was thick enough to taste.

"Give me the documents," His Grace ordered, and Anthony offered them from his small satchel, all of them silent while they were thoroughly examined.

Will made himself as small as he could manage, eyes closed and head tipped down in token submission, vibrating with tension that threatened to spill over into tears. He knew better than to expect mercy from any Alpha, but he had hoped in some strange way that life here would be less fearful than facing his father's daily disgust with him. Now all he could wish for was to be home again, hard at work at some menial task given to him by Blake, ignored and largely undisturbed.

"William," the Duke said, not unkindly. "William, look at me when I speak to you."

Will looked up, but his eyes stayed unfocused and distant with the blank readiness for retribution that his life at home had trained him for. He had little hope otherwise with three Alphas in the room and all of them varying degrees of angry, the two strongest scents overpowering, deadening Will's senses to anything but dread and his awful, unwanted Gift.

"Yes, your Grace?" he said, his voice so small and soft it was barely better than a whisper.

"I see you signed these documents with your own legal name," His Grace said, ignoring Hannibal's chuff of disdain. "William? Is that how you choose to be called?"

"Yes, your Grace," he admitted, having no other recourse. "Will, if it pleases you."

"And was there some valid reason why your father chose not to send us your sister, Wilhelmina?"

Will swallowed, reluctant to repeat what had been said to him. He wet his lips and stared into the middle distance, offering, "Mina is only just promised to Lord Rathmore. Father could find no reason to break their engagement and engender hard feelings when he had me to spare."

He felt Hannibal's eyes on him, boring holes into him with their heat. Will nervously turned away, caught between the stark stares of three Alphas with no escape in sight.

"Except that he was in clear breach of contract, the bounder," Hannibal informed him, glowering at the Omega across from him, vastly annoyed that it lacked the good grace to leave of its own accord.

"Far from it," His Grace responded. "The contract was that House Reddig would provide a spouse to my heir who was of bearing age to secure the line of succession. Will is an Omega. They are notoriously prone to fertility as well as producing Alphas nearly consistently. There was no stipulation in the contract whatsoever that the spouse be a beta female."

The Duke fell silent again, looking at what was before him. He finished, stacked the papers in his long, pale fingers, and tidied them before drawing a deep breath. The tea and cakes arrived and were set out by nervous staff keyed to the tension in the room, which they quit as quickly as possible.

"It is difficult for me to think, Anthony, that you did not intend harm to your cousin in this matter," His Grace said, settling back into his chair to turn his icy gaze on his younger grandson. "Knowing what you know about Hannibal makes it almost impossible to believe otherwise."

"I did—"

"As you were told, yes, you have already said so," Hannibal interrupted, fingers drumming a restless rhythm on the wooden arm of his chair. "The question is how do we undo it?"

"There will be no *undoing it*," the Duke flatly announced, holding up his hand in a staying gesture before Hannibal could protest. "No, Mr. Buddish has submitted the necessary paperwork and the news will be printed in the papers come morning, as per my arrangements. No, there is no undoing it, Hannibal."

"I refuse, then," Hannibal said, his anger transmuted to deadly calm. "I refuse to have it."

Will shrank slightly into the chair, almost vanishing inside a froth of silk and lace, his stomach a churning lump of self-disgust and sickening fear. Only years of his father's belittling and beatings kept him from tears of hopelessness; that, and an unyielding streak of pride which stiffened his spine like a steel rod, neither beating nor punishment ever quite able to peel it out of him completely.

The Duke leaned forward and very carefully said, "If you refuse, Hannibal, then you will forfeit your place as my heir."

Dead silence greeted his remark. Anthony's gaze shifted quickly from his grandfather to Hannibal, thoughts moiling in his eyes.

"My terms were very clear—return at once to claim your bride, father a son, and secure your inheritance," His Grace said with deadly calm. "If you defer the spouse I have chosen for you, you defer your place as my heir which, I suppose, is precisely what young Anthony here hopes to have happen."

"Grandfather!" Anthony protested, shutting his mouth with a snap when the elderly Alpha looked his way yet again. He subsided, meek in the face of his grandfather's disapproval.

"Are you putting this thing's interests above the interests of your family, Grandfather?" Hannibal coldly asked, his stare matching the elder Alpha's. It was clear where he got his temper from as well as his formidable strength of will.

"I am abiding by a contract which you will accept if you wish to one day be Duke of Westvale in my stead," he said, matching his icy tone. "No one is forcing you to do anything you do not wish to do, Hannibal. The papers are signed, everything is in order. If you reject Will and choose to disgrace the Ledford name for the sake of your own pride, then I would venture to say that *you* are the one choosing other interests above those of this family. And if that is the case then you cannot be entrusted with either my title or the responsibility for our family at large."

Hannibal's mouth thinned into a tight line of displeasure.

Mr. Stammets arrived then, ashen and sweating and hoping not be noticed. He jumped when Mr. Hawkes announced him and immediately fell into a low bow which the Duke ignored.

"I have but one question for you, Mr. Stammets," he stated. "Is this the child you met and recommended?"

Mr. Stammets took one look at Will and vigorously nodded, saying in a rush, "Yes, your Grace! She most certainly is! I was taken immediately by her modesty and beauty, so becoming in a young lady her age. And her accomplishments, as I have already offered—"

"You may continue to extol its virtues until the cows come home," Hannibal said, transferring that terrifying stare to him, and pointed at Will's slender, motionless form with one imperious finger. "*That*, however, is not a woman. You gave me the wrong one, you imbecile."

Mr. Stammets paled even more, on the verge of a swoon from fright.

"Mr. Hawkes, take Mr. Stammets to the parlor and get him a brandy, please," the Duke ordered. "Anthony, go home."

"Grandfather—"

"Hannibal, go refresh yourself, you've had a long trip and your temper is not all I could hope for," he said, utterly ignoring his other grandson, who skulked from the room without another word. "As for you, Will."

"Yes, your Grace?" Will responded, some small measure of anxiety abating with one less Alpha in the room.

"Please do me the pleasure of pouring for me."

"Yes, your Grace," Will responded, roused somewhat from his terrified daze.

Hannibal wrinkled his noble nose at him and snapped, "No better than a boy in a dress! How little this family respects itself!"

With one last telling look at his Grandfather, he quit the room in a simmering temper, leaving Will alone with the aging Alpha.

"What is your preference in address?" His Grace asked, a polite opener for conversation with an unfamiliar Omega.

"Male address is my preference," Will answered, thinking of how ridiculous that sounded when he was dressed in feminine clothing. "It is how my father raised me."

His Grace nodded, adding that to his knowledge of Will. His calm effected a returning calm on Will's part, the shift in his scent from acrid anger to warm age like a fine old book soothing the Omega's frayed emotions.

"Mr. Grant, then," he said, careful not to use Will's married name as yet. "Did you take instruction with your sisters?"

Will hesitated before nodding, admitting in a small but steady voice, "Yes, I have had the same instruction as any Omega of a noble family. It was my mother's dying wish that I should be educated as such."

"But it does not interest you?" the Duke prodded, frowning.

"I am not precisely disinterested," Will said, unwilling to answer with half a truth. "I have merely been born into a household with seven sisters before me who were expected to wed and do their duty. It was never expected I would follow in their footsteps."

"But you possess the necessary understanding of households to run one from either direction," His Grace clarified, nodding softly when Will did. "Tell me, Will, do your true talents lie in paths your sisters were not allowed to pursue?"

Will hesitated only slightly before nodding again.

"Well, you are less inclined to the feminine than some Omegan children I have encountered," the Duke said at last. "But not for lack of charm and you are certainly pleasing overall."

"I was once told that when it suits me I am more than a competition for my sisters," Will stammered, flushing with embarrassment to relay the praise that had bolstered him through the entirety of his puberty, a kindness he had hoarded. "I... it simply does not suit me, Your Grace."

Will straightened a little, hoping he didn't seem terribly shabby to the man who held his fate in both aristocratic hands.

"Goodness, you *are* a sight for sore eyes," he was told, and lifted his gaze in surprise. "Stand up, Mr. Grant, let me look at you."

"Yes, Your Grace," Will murmured, straightening at once for the aged Alpha before him. His scent was stronger without the others to confuse it, triggering a primal response in Will's young Omegan body. His eyes dilated and his heart rate jumped. His clothes shrank two sizes too small and the fine hairs all over his body lifted. Faced with an unknown Alpha without others who might stymie him, Will's entire body seized on survival—ally or flight, and Omegas had always formed alliances through flesh. It was an unaccountable and unknown response that left him bewildered and rather frightened, all of which was immediately conveyed without his meaning it to be.

"A sight for sore eyes, indeed," the Duke said, a stately and handsome man who must have been very breathtaking in his prime, Will thought now that he had a chance to look at him without fear clawing at his insides. Even now, with his hair gone silver-white with age and his skin lined with experience, he was intimidating and impressive. "Bless your soul, Mr. Grant, your father did you no favors keeping you from polite company. I can nearly taste you from here, my dear."

"I am... mortified, Your Grace," Will whispered, blushing furiously, embarrassed. He dropped into another curtsy more to hide his flaming cheeks than to offer respect.

"Nonsense! You've nothing to be ashamed of," the Duke said, shifting to wheel his chair out from behind his desk, his legs hidden behind a light blanket across his lap. "I'm flattered and terribly pleased. A response that strong means you'll breed well for my grandson."

Will's uncertainty stayed him. His confused and raw instincts pushed him to make a submissive gesture, but it ran counter to everything his father had taught him, so he stood there in the center of the room trembling with indecision and growing panic that something was terribly and irrevocably *wrong* with him.

"Come here, Mr. Grant," the Duke said, sensing his unease. He brought his wheelchair close to the armchair nearest the tea set and patted the cushion. "Come have a seat. You've gone quite pale. I don't wish to distress you. Your upbringing has been very unusual, indeed."

Will did as he was told, unable to do anything other than obey an Alpha with such presence. When he sat, he took a soft breath to accustom himself to the Duke's scent, surprised when the old Alpha gathered his hand up and briskly rubbed his palm with his thumb. It was strangely soothing, as Anthony's touch had been, and Will relaxed, a shiver running out of him with the gentle motion. His father had but rarely touched him with kindness. Though heavy-handed with his correction, Lord Reddig had been entirely spare with his distant affection to the point that this touch went straight to Will's starved heart.

31

"There, there, that's better, hm?" His Grace said, smiling at him, his sharp teeth bared behind his full beard. "My cousin on my mother's side was Omegan. He lived entirely as a male, but he was such a nervous little creature. He always said nothing calmed him like a warm touch."

Will nodded, growing used to the scent of him, making the connection between the elderly Duke and the kindness being shown him.

"It's a pity you're so young, Mr. Grant," the Duke said, pleased when he relaxed. He didn't stop rubbing Will's palm, which seemed to be soothing the both of them. "My grandson has twelve years on you. A peculiar, prickly beast, that boy, as you've unfortunately discovered for yourself."

He gazed out of the window, lost in his thoughts, his movements stilling until he simply sat there, Will's hand wrapped in his.

"Wondrous creatures, Omegas," he mused, giving Will a warm squeeze. "I'd quite forgotten how comforting it is to be near one. This family has done itself a grave disservice going without for so long."

Will sensed he was not expected to remain silently attentive, and ventured, "Shall I pour, your Grace?"

"Ah, yes, Will, please," His Grace said, releasing his hand with another soft squeeze. "Anthony certainly had an agenda bringing you as he did, but as I told my grandson, it is all perfectly legal and binding. I am certain Hannibal will see reason once his temper has had a chance to settle. War has no good effect on anyone and has done nothing to improve his disposition."

Will poured for them, still trembling, but managing not to spill. He adjusted it to the Duke's preference and waited for him to take a sip, only then pouring himself a cup. The soothing heat comforted him and helped ease the knot that had formed in his belly. But he couldn't keep the image of Hannibal from his mind for long, the utter contempt and disgust on his face when he looked at Will. To distract himself, he asked, "Will it matter that I am not as feminine as some Omegas are?"

The Duke studied him, his dark amber eyes assessing. "No, Will. It may serve you well where my grandson is concerned. Perhaps the fewer reminders he has that you are Omegan, the better. He is a peculiar boy."

Will considered that. With great reluctance, he asked, "Would you still want me to remain? I have no grounds to dissuade you should you send me home, considering I have deceived you."

"Your father is the one who deceived us, Will. But would it surprise you if I did want you to remain? Perhaps for selfish reasons," the Duke admitted, smiling sadly. "Knowing my grandson as I do, I can say with some certainty that he will do his duty by you until you give us an heir, and then he will leave you to your own devices as he pursues his own."

"That sounds rather similar to most marriages between great families," Will said, weighing his options.

"Yes, it does," the Duke said, chuckling. "You will remain here with your children, naturally, and ease me through my dotage with your presence and the joy of little feet pattering through these halls again. It is, perhaps, not an ideal life, but there is a chance for happiness in it which might rival what your life could offer if you remain in your father's house."

Will considered it, a thoughtful frown bowing his mouth. What remained for him in his father's house was not pleasant, if the past eighteen years were anything to judge by. Without Mina there to stand as an inconstant shield between them, Will wasn't entirely sure he would last another year in his father's questionable care.

"I have never given much thought to children but I suppose I should like to have one or two," he said, surprising himself with the truth. "I would have a place here, and your protection."

"Mine and my grandson's to follow," His Grace said, reaching out to pat him again, a compulsive act of calming when confronted by Will's doubts. "When I do eventually die, he will know where his place is and take it accordingly. He will treat you with the respect and consideration you are due."

Will absorbed that in silence.

The Duke smiled kindly at him and said, "Finish your tea, Will, and then I will have Mr. Hawkes see you to your room. I am sure you need to rest up some and prepare yourself for supper, as we shall all be in attendance."

"Yes, Your Grace," Will said, managing a hesitant, uncertain smile. "I should like that very much."

Chapter 3

There was no instruction, no familiarization when Will was led away, weary and resigned. The butler, Mr. Hawkes, had his orders to take Will straight to the relative safety of his suite and deposit him there and that was precisely what he did. Will moved in his wake, eyes wide and frightened and taking in the vast house, too tired to sort the various scents that vied with those he had already learned.

"Here you are, Mr. Grant. The houseboys have brought your luggage in," Mr. Hawkes said, opening the door to let him into a lovely suite made up in neutral, pleasant colors, soothing and quiet. "Has your father sent a servant to assist you?"

Will shook his head, cleared his throat, and softly said, "No, he did not. I have never had need of a servant to assist me. I am the youngest child in my family."

"If I may be so bold, I would like to pick a member of our staff to assist you now that you are here with us," Hawkes said, giving him a kindly look which brought Will's uncertain smile to the surface. "Would you prefer female or male?"

Will, vague with too much happening at once, roused himself enough to say, "I would be more comfortable with a male assisting me. My wardrobe is both female and male so it would be more convenient to have someone familiar with such things, if there is any such person who can deal well with an Omega."

"Of course, you are quite right," Hawkes said, nodding a little. "I shall send someone up directly to unpack for you while you take some rest. The suite is yours to use as you wish, the washroom is there through that door. The House has all new plumbing the family is quite taken with, I'm told. Please, feel free here. After all, Hartford House is now your home."

"Thank you very much, Mr. Hawkes," Will said, relaxing to be away from any prying, interested eyes.

He retreated to the window and looked out at the grounds, smiling to see the carefully tended gardens and statuary, the small fountains and shade trees beckoning long walks and quiet inspection to sate his boundless curiosity. He was left alone until a short while later when there was a soft knock on the door and a smooth, even voice that called, "May I come in, please?"

"Yes, come in," he said, moving hastily away from the window and straightening his dress, feeling awkward and fairly caught out.

A man somewhat older than him came in, pleasantly plump and blond and smiling. He had the strange absence of true scent all betas had, lacking any artificial scent that could upset their Alpha employers, but he smelled good all the same, clean and wholesome like laundry drawn in fresh from the line.

"Mr. Grant, I'm James Prince," he said, inclining his head a little, his smile never slipping. "I would prefer you call me Jimmy, as everyone else does."

"Of course, Jimmy, if that's what you prefer," Will said, relaxing in the face of his comfortable manner.

"Mr. Hawkes has informed me you prefer to be called Mr. Grant? And you have need of a valet?" he made it more of a statement than a question, moving to the dressing room to check the status of the trunks. "I'd be more than happy to operate in that capacity if you wouldn't mind it."

"Ah, no, please, I... that would be fine," Will said, his smile hesitant. "I'm afraid I was sent with quite a lot of female clothing but my preference is male, if that is acceptable?"

"Oh, whatever you like, I can work with!" Jimmy's nose wrinkled on a wide smile and he asked, "Little bit overwhelming isn't it? All this?"

Will nodded, his smile easing and his shoulders relaxing.

"Well, you're in good hands with me, Mr. Grant," Jimmy informed him, opening the nearest trunk and getting to work. "I had the pleasure of working for the Raleighs before being engaged here. Are you familiar with the Raleighs?"

"Ah, yes, I am," Will said, returning to the window to look out, chasing the curve of hills and trees to the village proper far in the distance. "My father kept company with the Raleighs. I spent several summers with their children when we were very small."

It had, in fact, been his father's determination that exposure to other Omegan children was to Will's detriment and had started the escalating habit of isolating him to cultivate the son he desired rather than the Omega that threatened to emerge unbidden.

"Well *I* was the personal attendant of Samantha Raleigh," Jimmy said, blue eyes sparkling.

35

"Sam?" Will asked, surprised and pleased. "You're familiar with Omegas, then."

"Heavens yes!" Jimmy said, deftly plucking his clothing free and shaking out the wrinkles, sorting them according to need. "I was with Samantha from the time when they still went by Sam. It was quite a surprise to the family when they decided to embrace their feminine side; they were always so adamant they be addressed as male. *I* say it was that Dartson boy, don't you?"

Will laughed shyly and nodded, saying, "I would say so, considering they're married now."

"Such a handsome little devil, that Lord Dartson," Jimmy commented, drawing things from the trunks with an illusionist's flair. "I'd have swapped, too, in their place, though Lord Dartson prefers them however they go, be it Sam or Samantha. The two of them spend all their time running about hunting and sporting together, quite in love."

"He was quite the catch," Will admitted, put at ease by Jimmy's chatter and carelessness. It was nice to be close to someone who wasn't alarmed by or wary of the fact he was an Omega. "I remember when father read the announcement. I was very happy for them both."

"Well, I'm simply delighted to be in your service, Mr. Grant," Jimmy said, no artifice just plain good humor and understanding. "I'll take excellent care of you! *Which*, speaking of, why don't I draw you a bath, hm? A good soak can do wonders and I'm sure you'd like to get all that travel dust off of you, wouldn't you? Such lovely hair you have, Mr. Grant! You must be the envy of your sisters!"

He moved swiftly to the washroom to draw a bath, chattering like a magpie, which suited Will just fine. He had nothing much to say and appreciated a break in the silence and the good intentions it implied. He had a good soak, washing up with a pleasant soap which complimented his own natural scent, and dressed in the clothing Jimmy had chosen for their coming supper. Will had requested the clothing he was used to, hoping to feel less vulnerable in male attire.

"The whole household has been fair chomping at the bit to finally lay eyes on you," Jimmy confided, deftly helping Will into his underclothes. "Everyone is very excited, you know. It's been quite some time since they've had an Omega marry in. I think His Grace is hoping to get a few little Omegas of the Ledford extraction to offer on the marriage market."

Will blushed, silently yielding to Jimmy's sure hand. The man dressed him expertly in snug breeches, smoothing them into his shiny boots. The shirt was one of Will's more fitted ones, the cinch of his waist emphasized by his jacket drawn tight at the small of his back to compliment the slight curve of his hips. He lacked the full chest of some Omegas, the budding breasts some elitists declared were the distinction of a true Omega, but his own physique was supple and trim enough to lend delicacy to the clothing Jimmy had chosen. The watered silk jacket was dark in color but light in weight, a stark frame for Will's pale skin and dark curls. Jimmy exchanged Will's usual knotted neckerchief for his mother's coral-pink brooch pinned at the throat of his shirt, leaving his neck mostly bared.

"They'll expect to see you," Jimmy murmured, adjusting the brooch with a discerning eye. "You understand, of course, as they're Alphas."

"Yes, I understand," Will said, realizing that exposing his throat was going to be his new norm in a household of Alphas. "It's just very strange to do so."

"You don't show your throat?" Jimmy gently inquired, no judgment in his question.

"No, my father dislikes it," Will said, fingering the brooch. It was his single memento of his mother and the only piece of jewelry his father had allowed him. "Proper young gentlemen dress accordingly. Bare necks are for ladies and slatterns, he always told me."

Jimmy's brows drew together in a slight spasm, but he nodded to put Will at ease and slipped Will's pocket watch into place, ensuring the chain dangled just so.

"Thank you, Jimmy, for taking care of me."

"It's my pleasure," Jimmy said, beaming. "Now, follow me, okay? We're heading to the dining room."

There was no one else anywhere along the way, as if there was a tacit understanding that Will not catch sight of anyone on his path to the dining room.

"Okay, here we are," Jimmy said, pitching his voice low as he drew to a stop in front of a pair of closed doors where two footman waited at the ready to open up for him. He fussed with Will's light jacket, brushing imaginary lint from his shoulders before nodding. "You feel alright?"

Will nodded, the sudden strengthening of Alpha scents making him dizzy.

"Deep breaths, okay?" Jimmy urged, smiling in soft understanding. "It'll be easier as you become accustomed to more Alphas in the future, but this will take some time. Just breathe through it and don't panic."

"Yes."

Will entered to find the Duke at the table and Hannibal at the windows, staring out at the grounds. More footmen were arranged along the wall like furnishings, doing their best to remain unnoticed.

Hannibal turned, the force of him stinging Will like a lash. His fingers clenched so hard his nails bit into his palms, but he forced himself to relax, even as every fiber in his being focused in on the Alpha surveying him. He could feel Hannibal willing him to look up, to meet his gaze so it could be interpreted as a challenge, a good excuse to make his displeasure known.

Hannibal frowned, glaring at the delicate young Omega who refused to look up at him. Someone had dressed him to please, using every artful drape of clothing to display his trim figure, an androgynous beauty in dark watered silk which made the most of his striking blue eyes and dark hair. He was moderately more composed than he had been earlier, but Hannibal could still sense his unease and guessed the cause—up until his arrival the little minx had attached to his father, no doubt using every weapon in his predictably vast arsenal to wheedle what he could from the besotted old codger. Now, however, his Omegan instincts pushed him towards Hannibal, who made no secret of his dislike or refusal to indulge the vapid trivialities of a witless Omega.

"Will, please join us," His Grace said, waving off Will's automatic bow. "Hannibal, you as well, please."

Will moved around to the Duke's left, causing a baffling ruckus when one of the footmen attempted to seat him even as Will seated himself. He blushed, embarrassed that the duality of his gender caused such confusion among the uncertain staff, aware of Hannibal's low chortle of mocking laughter.

"I trust you are comfortable in your suite?" Grandfather asked, at the head of the table as was his right.

"The suite is fine, Grandfather," Hannibal said, seating himself across from Will, scrutinizing the top of Will's head when the twit stared down at his empty plate. Irritated, he said, "I still find myself astounded that you would allow this creature to sit at your table."

Will's head tipped up and Hannibal saw a flash of temper in those blue eyes. He smirked, congratulating himself on unmasking him even a crack.

"Will is not a *creature*, Hannibal," Grandfather said, affronted. "He prefers to be addressed in the masculine and you will respect that, thank you."

"Ah, but how was I to know?" Hannibal lightly asked, lifting his glass as soon as it was filled. "They are such confused beings, are they not? Unable to decide between male and female on a given day?"

"You would know by asking, my Lord," Will ventured, his voice the soft velvet of sexless youth, neither deep nor high, simply clear and lovely. He raised his glassy, unfocused blue eyes with a shadow of his prior meekness. "Much as I ask if you are happy to finally be home in the bosom of your family?"

Hannibal laughed, waiting until the footmen had delivered their first course before saying, "I have been nearly a decade in a country not my own, fighting to save the lives of men who fight for the sake of those who cannot be bothered to fight for themselves, and I return to the *bosom of my family* to find an intruder has been installed in the place meant for my wife."

He took a taste of the *consommé* before him, nodded to the hovering footman, and turned his attention to the Omega across from him. He was, tellingly, not attempting to eat. His small shoulders were squared with determination, but his hands remained in his lap and his eyes stayed half-lidded and staring, seeing nothing while giving the impression of attention.

"I wonder what your father was thinking, pulling such a stunt," Hannibal continued, aware of his grandfather's growing irritation. "I imagine by now you've realized I am not going to roll over and fall dead at your feet, as your father undoubtedly led you to believe? Or are you planning on amassing a small fortune from my grandfather, instead?"

"I will take nothing from your grandfather without his insistence," Will said, drawing in a deep breath, becoming accustomed to his unwilling husband's scent. It was strongly earthy with the tinge of anger, but absolutely indicative of primacy of experience and virility. It was difficult for Will not to respond to it, but he did the best he could within the confines of his meager experience.

In this moment of relative ceasefire, he was able to look at the man he'd been thrown at and found himself thinking that Hannibal's personality quite matched his looks. His resemblance to his grandfather was great, having his same high, stark cheekbones and deep eyes. His mouth, however, was entirely his own, full lips curved in permanent disapproval above a chin that owed allegiance to ancient Greek statuary. Will found him much like a statue of Apollo he had seen as a child—cold beauty, removed and dignified and carved by a masterful, incautious hand. Even his ashen brown hair refused to be out of place with the threat of his displeasure. Every part of Hannibal Ledford's appearance lent credence to Will's growing understanding of him. His dignity was his shield, his esteem of self a boot he used to grind those lesser than he to dust. He knew well his own worth and knew well that Will was *not* of worth.

Will twitched, stung by it all over again, the view of himself through Hannibal's eyes reopening wounds left by his father's heavy hand that had barely begun to heal. It was nothing he could control, it simply *was*. Without meaning to, he found himself echoing Hannibal's coldness and steely reserve.

"Ah, yes, I suppose you will get nothing from us. Nothing but a match to make any sane person weak with envy, access to a fortune you have had no hand in amassing, and luxury to rival even the King's lauded concubine," Hannibal said, irritated when he continued to sit there, placid and calm, giving Hannibal that damnable Omegan stare. Empty-headed, vain little opportunists, the lot of them. "Yet here you sit, unable to hold conversation in polite company, waiting for some gracious Alpha to tell you that everything will turn out just as you wish and you never need worry for any lack. I am unprepared, Grandfather, to be burdened with something so useless and ineffectual."

"You will moderate your speech, Hannibal," the Duke warned. "Will is neither a burden nor an inconvenience! He is your spouse and he is here by *my* decree and you will treat him with the respect he is due!"

"And what respect is that?" Hannibal snapped, by now all of them uncomfortable, down to the footmen. "Tell me, dear grandfather, what feats this confusion has performed to lie so heavily in your esteem? Or did you simply look at him and lose your wits, as he no doubt considers is normal?"

The Duke slammed his hand down onto the table so hard the silverware jumped. Will jumped, too, a distressed noise breaking from him that he tried to bite back. The two Alphas bristled, a contest of wills that had no clear good ending. The Duke won by habit of power rather than strength, saying, "I will not subject Will to your nasty temper, Hannibal. Will, if you please?"

"Your Grace, my Lord," Will said to them, standing up on shaky legs, trembling as he quit the table and moved towards the doors.

"He's a lovely young thing and he will make you a beautiful spouse—"

"I don't *want him*," came the clipped, sharp reply, so cutting that Will flinched and hurried his step, his mouth pressing tight to hold back his hurt sound. As the door swung closed behind him, Hannibal clarified, "You said you had chosen my *wife*. Will is not a woman, Grandfather, or need I point that out? You *gave me the wrong one*."

"Hannibal, please see reason—"

"My Lord," Mr. Hawkes softly said, trying his best to draw Will away from the door where he stood in shocked, wide-eyed silence, straining to hear. "Please, my Lord—"

"If you like him so much then why don't *you* take him?" Hannibal suggested, the anger in his voice carrying through to Will's trembling heart. "Hm? Take him off of my hands before I arrange an accident for him."

Will gasped in horror and fled, shocked at what he'd heard and heedless of Mr. Hawkes' well-meaning, soft assurance drifting from behind him that things would be much better come the morning.

But Will knew better than that. His strange Gift of *knowing* had never been so thoroughly tested as it had this day and it was telling him now that Hannibal meant every word. He wasn't indifferent to Will, but actively hated him—not for anything he'd done but for what he was. He was not welcome in this house, and everything the Duke had told him now tasted like lies.

There would be no doing one's duty. There would be no overcoming of Hannibal's bone-deep contempt for the sake of an heir; in fact, his brain screamed at him to run, to go home, to seek the dubious protection of his father because he was absolutely not safe with Hannibal Ledford and he knew to the very core of himself that this was blatantly, irrefutably true because he could see it as clearly as he could see himself.

"What have I done?" he moaned, curling into the corner of his suite into the smallest ball he could manage, tears rising and overflowing with such force not even Jimmy's patient, sympathetic soothing could stem them.

⌘⌘⌘

Roland Ledford, current Duke of Westvale, sat awake in his bed long after the staff of Hartford House had retired for the night. It was not only age which kept him wakeful, nor mere sleeplessness, but a deep concern whether he was doing the right thing.

Twenty years ago, he had lost his only son and his little granddaughter in an accident that had been entirely avoidable. Hannibal, ten years old at the time, had come to live with him thereafter, quiet and withdrawn and frighteningly intelligent, surpassing most adults in reason except for one area where he would not bend.

Omegas.

Hannibal, whose mother had died delivering him, had grown under the care of his father's Omegan concubine, a notorious creature even among concubines, and ten years of such tender care had hardened the boy to the worst possible impression of the human race's blended gender. When one factored in that the entirely avoidable accident which killed Hannibal's father and sister was the full fault of the Omega who had so thoroughly ruined him, his contempt was more than understandable.

Roland's thoughts turned to Will Grant, a sweet and intelligent little mite whose father had done him serious harm, one could tell just from seeing him. Jimmy had reported the boy bore unusual scars was skittish as a wild creature, speaking to a life not precisely comfortable before his arrival here. It was apparent that Will had no defense against Alphas and that Hannibal fully intended to intimidate him as much as he humanly could. It was Roland's fervent hope that the inner steel which had helped Will survive thus far, as well as his youthful adaptability, might help him penetrate Hannibal's armor deeply enough to make his hard-headed grandson see that there was more to an Omega than tricks and demands.

But he worried. Oh yes, he worried. The direct Ledford line was too thin to leave anything to chance and he wanted this so very, very much.

He delved into his nightstand and withdrew an aged and fading miniature portrait, smiling at the sight of his own young face and that of the older, more somber man next to him.

"He has your features, Charles," he murmured to the memory of his dearest companion. "He is you in Omegan form, save for his height. You would like him very much, I think."

He touched the picture, memory replacing the rough texture of paint with warm and soft skin. Though brief and forcibly ended by familial obligations, theirs had been a passionate affair near on madness. Not even time and distance had settled it. They had been unable to enjoy a formal union between them, but had hoped their progeny could someday realize the mingling of their lines—his through his grandson and Charles through one of his own numerous granddaughters. It would please him immensely to see this delicate, Omegan version of himself walk the halls of Hartford House with the full approval of the law to bear sons of the Ledford line.

"Now to convince them this was meant to be," Roland sighed. "He married once without my approval, now he is married without his own. I will see our blood united, Charles. I swear it."

Feeling more determined, he rang for his night servant and requested pen and paper. After scrawling instructions, he sealed it from prying eyes and sent it to Jimmy's capable hands with instructions to be given to Will.

Reassured on that count, the elderly Duke shifted his weary bones in his bed and closed his eyes, thinking with pleasure of what lovely little great-grandchildren he could expect from the union of Hannibal and Will.

⌘⌘⌘

The next morning Hannibal avoided the breakfast table in favor of going riding. He was darkly amused that he was so eager to escape the home he had been yearning to return to. But then, nothing in his imagination had prepared him for his grandfather's choice in spouses.

They had talked, finally, all grandstanding set aside. Grandfather had given him a variety of reasons they should have an Omega in the family and Hannibal had accepted his explanations before giving those of his own—they were fickle, inconstant, scheming little nuisances lacking the brains to save themselves from drowning. It was a wonder the whole lot of them hadn't died of their own ineptitude.

Will, he was told, was not like that. Nor, he was told, were other Omegas. Hannibal had just been badly exposed and that was all Roland would hear on the subject.

He drew up short when he caught the now-familiar scent of his supposed spouse, a sweet sharpness like well-aged wine and sugary treats, warmly inviting any Alpha with a pulse to come calling.

He scowled, confronted with the interloper himself, dressed for riding in a bleak and frayed black jacket and worn dark breeches, soft kid gloves on his small hands and tiny, cracked but polished riding boots hugging his equally slender legs. It was a wonder they even made them so small. Hannibal peevishly wondered if it was used to having everything specially made to suit its tastes.

Will, to his credit, did not turn or acknowledge Hannibal in any way. He'd been warned by the turn of the wind that his husband had arrived, but he lacked any recourse of escape except the one he was currently saddling.

"Where is the stable boy?" Hannibal demanded by way of greeting, looking around for someone to fetch his stallion's saddle.

"There is no one here but the two of us," Will said, his tone even and calm. He checked the girth strap and patted the mare's rump, willing his pulse to slow. He was achingly aware of those flashing eyes on him and blushed to be so keenly watched.

"Well, who saddled your mount for you?" Hannibal demanded, sourly passing him to reach the tack room and look for his saddle.

"I did, my Lord," Will said, surprising him so that Hannibal actually snorted a laugh.

"How amusing," he said, unable to picture it. He hefted his tack down and moved into the stallion's box, saying, "I should like to see that."

"I have just finished," Will said, refusing to engage in verbal sparring, still off-kilter and wary of him from last night. He had, after all, spoken of arranging an accident. It was not so far from what Will's father had promised him in the aftermath of his perceived infractions. "Perhaps another time."

"Grandfather insists I get to know you," Hannibal informed him, expertly dressing his restless stallion despite its help. Will merely stood next to his mount, waiting for a dismissal so he could escape. "He tells me you enjoy sports. He did not, however, inform me that you were in the habit of riding in the morning, as is a habit of my own."

"I will change to suit, my Lord," Will said, hoping to please him in that, at least. His absence was a gift he was very happy to give right now, unsettled and frightening as things were. He did not trust his own safety with a man who had everything to gain by hurting him.

"That is precisely the heart of the problem with Omegas," Hannibal said, disdain dripping from his even, calm voice. "Inconstant as a breeze, flitting to whatever catches your attention next. Colorful little butterflies with the intelligence and purpose to match."

Will's mouth thinned, but he wisely stayed quiet. When Hannibal looked over the stallion's back at him, he looked away, doing his best to appear meek, to give him no reason to find fault.

"Do you think yourself handsome, Will? Pretty, perhaps? It must be upsetting to realize you are not as pretty as you think you are," Hannibal informed him, the coy glances aside not fooling him in the least. "When I was told I had a wife waiting for me, I did not expect someone so particularly plain as you."

"Of course, my Lord," Will said, mortified. He never thought himself pretty or anything close, though he had wondered once the staff made over him whenever he was dressed in Mina's clothing. He had looked in the mirror to see if there was something there they found which he did not, but it was the same face staring back at him, same blue eyes and pale skin, an agreeable combination in sum that hardly rescued him from being passable in his own eyes. His husband's assessment of his appearance merely piled wood onto the fire of his self-doubt and he averted his face, trying not to offend.

Hannibal finished gearing his mount and led the stallion out into the strengthening sunlight, telling him, "You'll ride with me until I approve of your seat. I won't have you ruining the ducal stable with ineptitude."

"Yes, my Lord," Will said, apparently one of only two answers he was capable of speaking.

Hannibal turned to give his slender spouse a leg-up, but Will was already up in his saddle, seated comfortably with the reins in a soft grip and his crop angled over his thigh. Hannibal huffed, irritated that he'd intended to assist it and grimly thinking that it must assume he was already becoming addled by it.

He swung up easily and took up the reins, guiding the stallion out to the park and onto the worn, dirt lane where the sun was beginning to spread its glory. He wanted to have a look at the village and see what changes had come in his absence, something he'd intended to do while alone.

When Hannibal chanced to look back, he saw Will looking at the tree line, handling his mount with easy grace and care, lids half lowered against the slight wind that tossed his long curls around his head in a flurry. He rode well, Hannibal could give him that, and he wasn't an incessant talker. In fact, he'd barely said more than two words, riding near silently behind Hannibal with his blue eyes restlessly searching, though for what Hannibal couldn't hazard a guess. Escape, maybe. He hoped so. If his unwanted spouse fled and got himself killed, it would make things so much easier.

"Are you afraid to ride alongside me or is riding behind some type of subservient Omegan nonsense?" he asked, irritated for no other reason than he was spoiling for an argument.

He glanced over at Will, who looked the opposite direction, the pale column of his throat flashing in the morning light. It was a delicate throat, as far as throats go, and Hannibal found himself straining to catch his scent. Irritated by it, he pressed, "Well?"

Will wordlessly nudged his horse up abreast of him, keeping his head angled down, turned away, unable to make himself look up at the man who looked back with such open and impatient contempt. It burned him like a brand to feel such blatant disapproval from the Alpha who had so much control over him and his impulses were in a frenzy of overdrive, pushing him to submit, to pay obeisance, to please him in any way possible because the alternative was something he simply couldn't control. This was tempered by his fear, by his knowledge that Hannibal was capable of disposing of him for his own aims, but even that could not overcome biology or his father's dire warning to do anything his husband asked of him.

"What did you scheme with Anthony to land yourself here, hm?" Hannibal asked, wondering with irritation if he was going to be forced to look at the back of the little twit's empty head the whole time.

"There was no scheming, my Lord," Will answered, his tone neutral and soft. "My father acted according to the terms of the contract."

Hannibal laughed, a short bark of humorless noise that made Will start slightly in his saddle. When the man looked back at him, Will looked away again, not sure if he could withstand another attack on his looks so soon.

At first, Hannibal thought Will was avoiding his gaze, but when he did it continuously he realized he was doing something else entirely—flashing his throat in an age-old Omegan ploy to inspire an instinctive Alpha reaction.

Had Will any idea of such things he still wouldn't have been stupid enough to attempt them. He was simply doing his best to remain unobtrusive and polite in Hannibal's company, tuning him out as best he could to glean some small enjoyment out of his morning ride. Assuming he was as good as invisible to

Hannibal, when he saw a rabbit at the edge of the tree line start to groom its face in the morning light, he felt safe enough to smile a little in response, his soft laughter husky and unintentionally seductive.

Hannibal glowered at him. "Such naive innocence, Will. Is it difficult to summon in times such as these?"

Bewildered, Will skated a glance his way, unsure what he'd managed to do to earn such a strange remark. His lashes swept up in time with the turn of his limpid blue eyes to find his husband staring at him with something Will couldn't put a name to.

Hannibal could, however, and decided to put a halt to it at once.

"*Stop it*," Hannibal sharply said, the biting intensity of his voice startling Will so much his horse sidestepped, sensing his sudden nervous tension. Will's blue eyes widened, etched with growing fear that only made Hannibal more certain of what he was seeing. Hannibal reined his horse to a stop and seized Will's slender arm in a tight grip.

Will winced, shocked when Hannibal's fingers bit into his arm, painful and dangerous. Hannibal shook him until his perfect white teeth rattled, saying in a low growl, "Don't waste your efforts in trying your Omegan tricks on me! It would take a powerful imagination indeed to believe I would ever look at something like you and be ruled by a lust which you cannot even manage to inspire!"

Will made a low, distressed sound that only angered Hannibal further because it goaded him to offer comfort, another one of their helpless tricks. Wiles and lies with the only goal of living like a parasite, useless for anything other than debauchery.

Will had no idea what had provoked this sudden ferocity, but his instincts kicked his Gift into overdrive. He was flooded with the urge to flee in terror, but Hannibal's restraining hand wrenching him back and forth prevented it. The only other option was to submit, to cower, to abjectly accept and hope to survive and he did it without meaning to, every word like a blade piercing his soul. He felt like he was pouring out of the holes they left, draining away until his sense of self was replaced by Hannibal's version of him, startlingly clear and believable when he looked at himself through Hannibal's angry amber eyes.

"Creatures like you are repulsive," Hannibal said, his careful, low tone making the impact of his words all the more harmful, flung as they were into Will's open and malleable mind, absorbed by his Gift and sharpened by it. "Vain and empty-headed and thinking all you need to do to be comfortable in life is to seduce your way into someone else's. Stupid, silly creatures no better than children, falling to tears at a sharp word and helpless in the face of even the most simplistic of troubles. It's *sickening*."

Heart thrumming with the panicked need to submit or escape, one, instinct overcame all sense of self and Will quietly sobbed, "*Alpha*," helplessly bonding to the man before him in frightened self-defense, a last-ditch, desperate effort to deflect perceived deadly intent.

Hannibal curled his lip at him, finding his theatrics repugnant. He didn't let go of Will so much as give him a shove that nearly unseated him. Will's death grip on his pommel kept him upright. His blue eyes were huge and swimming with mingled fear and horror, but mostly shame at his rejection, the denial of something so deeply ingrained in him that he couldn't quite process the negating of it.

"*Omegas*," Hannibal said, disgusted, looking away as if he couldn't bear the sight of his young spouse trembling beside him. "Weak and needy and only good for whorehouses."

He glanced back down at Will, completely unmoved by the devastation on Will's face and the terrible understanding that came with it. Unable to resist twisting the proverbial knife, he murmured, "Your father should have sold you to a brothel, Will. Your nature would be much better served there."

Will didn't follow when Hannibal spurred his horse ahead, but his tear-filled blue eyes followed his erect, dignified carriage as he rode off towards the village. His Gift and the bond pressed those words on him, and for the longest time he sat there atop his mount, the tears in his eyes slowly drying as he critically examined what Hannibal had said to him. His urgent terror drew back like a wave, looming over him and waiting to crash again, sucking away what his secret heart had told him was true about himself and leaving only something wretched and hateful in its place. The terrified bond he'd formed to Hannibal left Will open and vulnerable to his preferences over and above that of his strange Gift.

It was an Omega's place, after all, to be all their Alpha desired.

And Hannibal Ledford desired him to be absent, if not simply dead, reinforcing those lessons his father had taught him so painfully and so clearly.

Trembling, Will closed his eyes against the beautiful day, feeling Hannibal's esteem settle on him like a heavy, dragging cloak, rendering his talents meaningless, his thoughts pointless.

Plain and unneeded, burning with shame at the sliver of hope he'd had the gall to invest in this marriage, Will turned the horse around and headed back to the house, feeling the very definition of repulsive that Hannibal had so callously called him.

Chapter 4

"Your Grace, Mr. Grant will not be joining the family for dinner tonight," Mr. Hawkes somberly said. "Mr. Prince says he is taken somewhat ill and out of sorts."

"Out of sorts?" Hannibal blandly echoed, disgusted. He waved Hawkes away, telling him, "No matter, he is contrary to good appetite."

"Send him up a tray, please, Mr. Hawkes," Roland said, settling to eat. "I had hoped to have a better meal this evening than last, but that is not to be."

"Thank that overly dramatic Omega you married me off to," Hannibal said, attacking his plate with more gusto than he actually felt. "Pouting in his room, no doubt."

"He has little reason to be in your presence when you behave so terribly towards him," Roland pointed out. "You have never in your life been so rude to another. That is hardly the conduct of a gentleman."

"There is no reason to be polite to an Omega, Grandfather," Hannibal said, leveling a hard look at the old Duke. "It only encourages them to take advantage. Besides which, they haven't the capacity to remember anything for very long that is unpleasant to them. If he's even half as brainless as others I've met, he'll forget we're married by morning and my problem will be solved. And good riddance to bad rubbish, I say."

"That is more unkind than you are wont to be," Roland remarked, eyeing his grandson. "I had imagined the war would make you more sympathetic rather than less so."

Hannibal glowered, focusing on his food, though he hardly tasted it. He had spent an altogether unsatisfying afternoon avoiding the house and his grandfather's potential displeasure only to return and find that his pretend-spouse had retreated immediately to his suite without a word to anyone. He couldn't decide what irritated him more, the fact that he'd avoided the house all day for nothing or the fact that Will hadn't run to his grandfather to tell tales as Hannibal had assumed he would.

"Flighty little thing," he complained under his breath. Will had probably forgotten all about it already and gone back to his room to play dress up. "Why is he dressed in male clothing now?"

Grandfather did not react to this apparent and strange change of subject. Instead, he told him, "Will prefers male clothing. Apparently, his father armed him in his twin's clothing and sent him along with that. Anthony, fortunately, requested of the staff that they also pack Will's usual clothing so he could be more comfortable."

Hannibal scowled, recalling the shabby riding clothes he'd seen earlier in the day. "It will cost a fortune to dress him."

Roland did not betray himself with a smile, merely said, "He is very small. He will not cost all that much to outfit properly."

"His clothing at supper was not that worn," Hannibal said, glaring at his plate as if it had some hand in things.

"Mr. Prince has informed me Will's formal clothing has had little use," Roland told him, though he did not mention what else Jimmy had said about Will's threadbare and pitiful wardrobe. "I have asked for Mr. Avery to come at the end of the week to measure and fit him."

"Already indulging him, Grandfather?" Hannibal asked, his tone nasty. "Don't think to spoil him. I'm not keeping him."

"I believe you are, and I will do as I please with Will," Roland said, unperturbed. "It costs nothing to be kind, Hannibal."

"It does with *Omegas*," Hannibal darkly said.

"Hannibal, you cannot afford to reject him," Grandfather said, nearing the end of his patience with his stubborn grandson. "Even the lure of being a Duchess would not be enough to tempt any good family into marrying with ours!"

"And why is that, pray tell?" Hannibal bit out, annoyed. "Remember, Grandfather, I have been near a decade away from home."

"Yes, and in that decade there has been much speculation about poor Melinda's tragic end," he was told, and Hannibal stilled at the mention of her name. Sighing softly, disliking the pain he caused his dear grandson, Roland said, "You fled to the front the day she died, Hannibal. You did not even stay for the funeral."

"I had little reason to," Hannibal said, returning to his meal with such stiff dignity it was almost painful to witness. "She was already gone."

"According to Society gossips, you had every reason to leave," Roland said, sipping his wine with caution. "And your haste lent credence to their supposition. It is generally accepted, Hannibal, that *you* are the cause of Melinda's death."

Hannibal abruptly stiffened and looked away, a muscle in his jaw jumping with tension.

"Despite my attempts to handle the situation quietly, the rumors still abound and they have greatly limited your potential matches," Grandfather said, firm with him now. "We are *lucky* House Reddig was contractually obligated to provide you with Will! You have precious few prospects otherwise! Had you not married so hastily to avoid it in the first place, you—"

"You and that damned *contract*," Hannibal said, shaking his head. "It plagued me then and it plagues me now! I will not deal with him, Grandfather, necessary evil or not, and you would do well not to press the matter."

In the face of his rising and unpredictable temper, Roland quite wisely did not continue. They spoke instead of the changes in the village and the future of Hartford House, all while avoiding the inevitable need for another generation to be added to the line of succession.

Pleading weariness, grandfather forewent after-dinner brandy and retired to his room, sending for Jimmy with near immediacy.

The pleasant and bright young man arrived in due time, all smiles as was usual for him and absolutely delighted to help however he could.

"How is Will?" Roland asked without preamble. He had very specifically assigned Jimmy to Will in the full knowledge that he would inform him of Will's needs without sacrificing discretion.

Jimmy hesitated, cocking his head slightly and looking off to the side as he searched for words. "Your Grace, he's... grieving, I think would be the best word."

"Did he tell you what happened?"

"No, your Grace," Jimmy said. "He went out riding this morning and came back rather sooner than I expected, white as a ghost and refusing to say anything. He went straight up to his suite and hasn't come out since."

Roland heaved a sigh and said, "Hannibal rides in the mornings."

"I had no idea, your Grace, else I would have dissuaded Mr. Grant," Jimmy said.

"It was no fault of yours *or* his," Roland said, scowling at the unpleasantness that occurred with every interaction of his grandson with his spouse. "Did he eat?"

"I could only get him to eat a little," Jimmy said, wringing his hands. "Your Grace, I hesitate to say it but I believe Will was more mistreated at his father's house than we knew."

"Mistreated?" Roland echoed, eyes sharpening. "In what way?"

"I have no desire to betray his confidence, your Grace," Jimmy said, ever vigilant of his charge, which was why Roland had chosen him. "Just please understand that he was neglected to an alarming degree and dealt with far more harshly than any child his age I've ever met, especially considering his family's position."

Roland heaved a sigh, fondly saying, "So in other words, Jimmy, do my best to keep Hannibal's sharp tongue between his teeth?"

"I would never presume—"

Roland waved away his apologies, "Presume, Jimmy. Always presume. I want no further harm coming to Will here. I *do*, however, want a great-grandchild sooner rather than later."

"Yes, your Grace," Jimmy said, nodding. "I received your message, of course. Would you like me to talk to him tonight?"

"I think you'd better," Roland said. "Hannibal is an Alpha in the end. It should take very little to fan a flame between them."

"Very well, your Grace, I'll see what I can do," Jimmy said, and quit the room when Roland nodded at him.

He only hoped it went as he wished and not as he knew it could go, given Hannibal's terrible temper. All he could do now was wait.

⌘⌘⌘

Will was hardly aware of the time when Jimmy came to dress him for bed. He was surprised to see his valet arrive and even more surprised by the darkness beyond the windows.

"His Grace has asked me to discuss something with you."

Will struggled to pay attention to Jimmy speaking as he was dressed for bed. He'd been fighting a strange numbness all day that had eventually overtaken him. Now that it had, he wished he'd given in earlier because it certainly felt better

53

than the raw, aching disgrace of his own personal truth that everything his father had said about him was true.

"Mr. Grant?"

"I'm sorry, Jimmy, what?" he asked, his voice faint.

"I said His Grace has asked me to discuss something with you," Jimmy repeated, helping Will into a pair of light linen pants he preferred to sleep in. "It's rather personal so I want you to know it's alright to be embarrassed, okay?"

Will's stomach clenched in response, empty and tight.

"Okay, so, here, have a seat," Jimmy said, settling Will on his bed and sitting next to him. "*So*, has your father ever talked to you about intimacy?"

Will's cheeks bloomed with heat and he shook his head, speechless with shock and embarrassment.

"I figured not," Jimmy said, sympathetic. "Well, let me give you a little crash course, okay? So, you know about Alphas and how Omegas are made to fit them?"

Will nodded. He was vague on the details but figured he knew enough to get by.

"Well, the truth of the matter is, an Alpha finds it rather difficult to resist an Omega under certain circumstances, especially one like yourself, unmated and near your first heat," Jimmy said, his easy manner of speaking keeping things from being too painfully upsetting. "What His Grace would like, Mr. Grant, is for you to go to his grandson and let Nature take her course, so to speak."

Will blinked. "What?"

"His Grace wants you to do everything you can to get Hannibal to claim you," Jimmy said, squeezing his hand in something like sympathy. "He's going by the Once Bitten law and all, hoping his grandson will mark you and settle after the fact."

"Hannibal hates me, Jimmy," Will said, his voice cracking when he thought of the things Hannibal had said to him. He hadn't spoken of it to anyone, refusing to confess to how unacceptable he honestly was, but he was willing to say that much.

"His Grace is hopeful he'll indulge in what you're offering and the two of you will prove to be compatible," Jimmy said. "He sent me personally to ask you to please try, at least."

"But I don't know what to do!" Will said, anguished, heart pounding at even the idea of what it meant.

"Just... let Nature take her course," Jimmy said, patting his shoulder gently. He looked like he didn't believe a word he was saying and that only made Will's stomach plunge harder.

Will swallowed hard, his gaze drifting to the door. He couldn't imagine Hannibal ever looking at him with anything other than disgust. Yet, he clearly recalled how his father enjoyed humiliating him, took no little relish in causing him pain. Surely after his show of force this morning, such an overture on Will's part would elicit a similar reaction. Perhaps a humiliating, painful coupling would be preferable to Hannibal, a suitable substitute for the kindness and closeness Will had so stupidly dreamed he might find here.

"Just... *try*," Jimmy said, gentle with him as if he might shatter like a teacup dropped on the floor. "It's all he asks."

"I can hardly deny the request of a Duke," Will said, the words thready with fear, a fine tremble coursing through him.

Bracing himself, Will got to his feet and slowly made his way to meet his fate.

⌘⌘⌘

Hannibal had no sooner settled into an armchair before the fireplace in his room with a snifter of brandy and a good book than he heard a soft knock on his door.

Eyes narrowing, he put the book down and called, "Enter."

A pale, small form moved quietly into his room in a waft of sweet scent.

It was Will. Of *course* it was Will.

Hannibal's mouth curled in sardonic humor when he saw him, every Omegan aspect of him working overtime to enhance his appeal. He was wearing only a pair of linen pants that exposed the slender sweep of his belly and the hollows of his hip bones. His arms were crossed in front of him, hands clasped at his shoulders with his head down in a mockery of shyness. Hannibal could see faint lines on his skin, shinier than the white skin around them, but could not make sense of them in the shadows.

"What do you want?" he asked, though he knew. Of course he knew. It had occurred to Will at long last that if he consummated their marriage then Hannibal couldn't have it annulled or otherwise be rid of him without a lengthy, embarrassing scandal.

Will took a few steps forward, toes curling with nerves, white limbs shaking as he moved into the firelight, even the scent of him working towards seduction despite its underlying tang of fear. Indeed, the tang of fear was only a spice, making his sweet scent more alluring.

Hannibal laughed, tapering to a sigh, watching Will's blue eyes chase the room from corner to corner, anywhere and everywhere but at the man he'd come to bed.

"I already told you I despise what you are," Hannibal murmured, watching a shudder course through him that was eloquent of shame. It pleased him to see it, atonement for being what he was, *mortification.* "Yet here you are, unable to resist your nature, armed and ready with Omegan wiles to do what you creatures do best."

Will's hands fisted at his shoulders. He swallowed hard but said nothing. Hannibal could scent the faint salt of his unshed tears and felt a sudden desire to shake them free, to sharpen the smell of fear and panic riding beneath his desperation.

"What do you plan to do, Will? Strip before me and hope I'll be overcome? Trust in your deceitful nature and pray for the best? My grandfather contracted yours for a *wife.* Instead he gives me *you*—a construct of meager appeal housing a vapid, empty mind and a lack of true purpose outside of getting bedded. I want a partner in life, not something else that demands more of my attention than I can spare."

Will hung his head and softly offered, "I can give you an heir—"

"I don't want one from you," Hannibal quickly overrode him, leaning forward in his chair to scrutinize his trembling spouse. "I cannot, in fact, think of anything I want less than the possibility of you giving me something exactly like yourself, Will. Ruled by heats and impulses, needing an Alpha for every little decision, unable and unwilling to lift a hand to save itself because its very nature requires its dependence on something stronger and better than itself. I'd feel compelled to drown it at birth rather than sentence it to live in such a demeaning and debasing way."

Will flinched, arms dropping to cross protectively over his belly as if Hannibal's threat might somehow be heard within by a child yet undreamed of.

"Your father should have been so kind," Hannibal told him, and turned his attention back to the fire, dimly aware that his anger was making him much crueler than he had a right to be. "You are vile to me, *disgusting*. Get out. Out of my sight. Out of my house. *Out*."

There was a soft, near soundless whisper of feet on the carpet, the mute thud of footsteps pattering lightly over the wooden floor and the careful, quiet click of the door closing.

Hannibal looked back at the space where he'd been and drew in a breath damp with his spouse's salty tears. Even he could admit he'd been much harsher than he should have been considering Will's tender age, but the hard, ugly coil of resentment inside of him refused to be sorry for it.

He reached for the brandy bottle and poured a steeper drink, staring into the fire with sightless eyes, his thoughts on his father's concubine and how thoroughly she had destroyed his entire life, as easily and thoughtlessly as Will would if given his way.

He tossed back his drink and grimly imagined how different his world would be if there were no such things as revolting Omegas.

⌘⌘⌘

"My Lord, His Grace wishes to see you immediately."

It wasn't the first thing Hannibal wished to hear in the morning, but he wasn't surprised. Will had probably fled directly to Grandfather last night, eager to bear tales of Hannibal's cruelty.

"Is he up already?" Hannibal asked, flinging back the covers and emerging to the cool air while Berger stirred up the fire. He stretched, yawning, brushing his hair back from his face.

"He is, my Lord," Berger said. "The shaving water is ready."

"Thank you, Berger, I'll do it myself," Hannibal said, already annoyed that his day would be so disturbed. This had not been the homecoming he'd wanted, and it irritated him that the Omega was causing friction in his family. If only they'd done the sensible thing and chosen a wife for him, a *proper* wife.

Even as a grandson and heir, Hannibal was not at liberty to keep his grandfather waiting. He made short work of shaving, bathing and dressing and headed down to his grandfather's study, unconsciously seeking the sweet scent of his spouse, only aware of what he was doing when he realized it was particularly absent.

He knocked and entered when Grandfather called out. Without preamble, he seated himself in front of his grandfather's desk and blandly said, "Berger informs me you wish to speak with me."

Roland was pale with quiet fury, something Hannibal hadn't seen since he'd been very young and his father had managed to incense him. He pushed a paper across his desk to Hannibal, who took it up with a frown to peruse it.

"What on earth is this, Grandfather?" he asked, growing livid when he read the contents, which gave full and legal ownership of Hartford House to none other than Will Grant unless and until there was an Alpha male child born of their union.

"*Incentive*," Roland answered, his voice as hard and sharp as Hannibal's own, his anger palpable. "After last night, I feel compelled to offer Will some form of compensation for what I've done to him."

"For what he's done *to himself*," Hannibal reminded him, hand tightening on the damning paper. "This cannot be correct, Grandfather! Have you *any* idea what you've written?"

"I am quite aware of what is written there, Hannibal, as I wrote it this morning," Grandfather said. "If you cannot restrain yourself from ordering your spouse from Hartford House, then I will make a gift of it to him."

Hannibal stared at him, outraged and disbelieving, then laughing with scorn. "I see. So the little minx ran straight from my bedchamber to yours? Hm? And no doubt listed the various ways in which I rejected him—"

"To the contrary, he was nearly a quarter of the way to his father's estate before he could be overtaken and returned," Grandfather said, cold fury sparkling in his amber eyes, "and only said upon hard pressing that he was ordered out of the house and, lacking anywhere else to go, he wished to return to his father."

Hannibal was silent, wondering how the Omega had managed to yet again pass on a chance to reveal his behavior. "You should have let him," he said, his voice deceptively soft. "I don't want him. He is entirely unappealing to me in every respect and I wish to be shed of him."

"I am the head of this family," Roland reminded him. "You are my heir and, as such, will do as I tell you for the best of our line. To that end, Hannibal, this agreement stands. Hartford House will belong to William Grant in its entirety. The only way in which you will regain control of this estate is by fathering an Alpha son on him, at which time ownership will revert back to my heir, to *you*.

Those are my terms, and as I am an old man, I expect you should get started rather quickly."

Hannibal stared at him, aghast that the home which had housed the Ledfords from time immemorial would be given part and parcel to that little interloper for no good reason he could see.

"Will Grant is an accepted part of this family, Hannibal," Roland said, grave and angry. "There will be no annulment, no dissolution of this joining. I want a child of his line; indeed, I want several, including Omegas, and if I have to strip you of Hartford House in order to get them, *so be it*."

Hannibal frowned, reining in his temper with difficulty. In a quiet, dangerous voice, he asked, "Why do you persist in this, Grandfather? What manner of spell has he cast that you cannot turn loose of him?"

"I am solely concerned with the continuance of the Ledford line," Grandfather reminded him. "Will Grant's breeding is impeccable and he is rich in his own right, or will you turn your nose up at the dowry he arrived with? There is no viable reason not to pursue this except for your petty refusal to see him as the person he is rather than what you perceive him to be."

Hannibal put the paper back down on the desk, chewing his lower lip with anger, fair trembling with it.

"There is another way I am hopeful you will not insist on," Grandfather said, taking the paper back.

"And what is that, pray tell? Please don't underestimate my desire to be rid of that thing, Grandfather."

"The option, of course, is to make Anthony my heir," Roland said, freezing Hannibal's blood in his veins with outrage. "He was your proxy in marriage to Will and would have no qualms becoming Duke of Westvale in my stead. They deal very well together and will, no doubt, make charming children. It would be simple to amend the documents to remove the proxy from them."

Hannibal just stared at him in disbelief. With quiet shock, he clarified, "So I am either disinherited in part or in full on the whim of an Omega?"

"Hannibal," Grandfather sharply said, reminding him that, though aged, he was a fierce Alpha in his own right. "Do you believe me so feeble that I lose my sense in the presence of an Omega young enough to be my own great-grandchild? If you cannot bring yourself to understand that Will hasn't a cruel or manipulative bone in his body, then trust in my judgment!"

"I trust in your judgment, Grandfather," Hannibal growled, standing and straightening his jacket.

"Then what will you do?"

"*Pack*," Hannibal snarled, stalking from the room and shouting over his shoulder, "You can insist that creature have this house, but you cannot insist I stay here! If he stays, then I will go!"

"Hannibal!"

Fuming, Hannibal stomped up the stairs, roaring for Berger to pack his things, his mind a white-hot flare of anger that refused to be swayed.

Chapter 5

Six years later...

⌘⌘⌘

Lord Clarges

I am writing to you now in the full understanding that you have formed a new life since last we met. Though I am loathe to intrude upon it, I am compelled to inform you that His Grace, the Duke, your own grandfather, has fallen to ill health, and desires your company as there are issues of estate yet unresolved between you. Please make haste and return to Hartford House at your earliest convenience for his sake.

Sincerely,

Will Grant

⌘⌘⌘

Hartford House had not changed any more in six years than it had in the time he'd been away at war, Hannibal found. Not on the outside, at least, save for the cobbled road that now fed in from those that led on to the Capital.

The passing of six years' time had dulled his anger somewhat, but he still felt uneasy returning. He had not quit this place in any good form and was not proud of how he had behaved since, but he would face what needed to be faced in order to bring peace to his grandfather.

Hannibal sighed, dismounting to walk his horse up the lane towards the house, idly noting the manicured lawn and the thriving growth of saplings planted within the past few years. So, some changes, then. Will would have changed, too, no doubt. Hannibal had heard a stray story of his unwanted spouse from time to time, whispers in ballrooms where he danced with women who were not his own, tittering and laughter about the unacceptable wife left pining away at Hartford House or, more scandalously, dealt with the same as Hannibal's first wife had been. Less often he had heard tales from his cousin, Anthony. He had written Hannibal first shortly after he'd gone to ask him why he was not in residence at Hartford House, and again some time later to tell him both grandfather and Will refused to step foot off the grounds, his grandfather due to his failing health and Will due to the very public disgrace brought on him by Hannibal taking a mistress the moment he landed in the Capital. Anthony, never one to mince words, had managed to prick his conscience without offending him —a rare talent indeed considering his traitorous acts—and wrote now only on the occasion it happened to strike him. His own letter of their grandfather's declining health had reached Hannibal a scant few days after Will's had, prompting him to return to the ducal seat at long last.

Life as the Westvale heir apparent was comfortable, to say the least. Hannibal lived in luxury in the Townhouse during the Season where he excelled in his medical duties to his fellow elites. He rotated among his other estates to ensure they were running properly and summered at Galley Field, where his mistress was currently installed, thick with their next child. He had no desire to lose the inheritance that afforded them their lifestyle and that was compounded by his refusal to allow that Omega the joy of seeing him stripped of everything. He only hoped he could prevail upon his grandfather to legitimize his bastard son, should this next child be born male, because there was certainly no chance of a child with Will Grant and he wished his grandfather would see reason.

"My Lord," Hawkes said when he arrived, the usual army of servants turned out to greet him. He was older and grayer but still stiff with his own dignity, beaming at the man who had been like his own son. "Welcome home at last."

"Hawkes," Hannibal said, nodding a greeting and glancing around for his spouse. "How is Grandfather?"

"Ailing, my Lord," Hawkes said, concern thickening his voice. "He is very distraught by the circumstances. He wishes you could find a place here."

"Ah, but this is not my place, is it, thanks to that damnable Omega," Hannibal said, a scowl flickering over his features. He handed the stallion off to a footman who took it away. "No matter. I've come at Grandfather's request to do as he bids me. What's to be done after is entirely up to me."

Hawkes quailed, murmuring, "Yes, my Lord."

"Take me to him, then."

"Ah, he is sleeping right now, my Lord," Hawkes said, hastily opening the doors to admit Hannibal. "The medication he takes for his arthritis tires him."

"And the Omega?" Hannibal asked, voice taut as he stepped inside and looked around. There were all manner of changes inside the house proper, updates that had been long overdue. He imagined his spouse had a grand time prancing about ordering staff off their feet to cater to its whims. After all, Hartford House had been handed to it on a silver platter, and all it had needed to do for it was play the victim. There was no doubt in Hannibal's mind that if he had not been summoned first, he'd have been barred from the House altogether for the sake of its pride.

"Mr. Grant is overseeing some business, my Lord," Hawkes said, his voice warming considerably.

Hannibal laughed, thinking Hawkes was making a joke. The butler offered an uncomfortable smile, changing the subject by asking, "Should you like to refresh yourself, my Lord? I have it on good authority that Mrs. Pimms has made some pastries just for you."

"Ah, trying to fatten me up already, Hawkes?" Hannibal asked, willing to be put in good humor even if his damned spouse wasn't bright enough to realize he should be here to greet him for the sake of appearances. "Yes, that will do fine. I'm going to have a bath. Send Berger up when the coach arrives."

"Yes, my Lord," Hawkes said, watching him scale the stairs with athletic grace.

The changes extended to the upper levels, Hannibal saw. New rugs and runners, new furnishings, new upholstery on heirloom pieces. There was a soft touch to it that suggested the Omega had instigated such changes. Hannibal sourly wondered at their debt now that it had been unleashed to spend to its heart's content in his absence. Perhaps six years had been a bit mulish on his part. He'd be lucky if there were two pennies to rub together.

He did realize that while he saw the influence of Will Grant in the house, he did not find his scent. There was a distinct lack of Will's sweet smell, in fact, enough so that he let himself through the shared washroom of their conjoined suites to open the door to Will's room.

It was there, but faint, like a memory from years before, a cobweb of fragrance clinging here and there. It was strongest at his bed, an indistinct lingering perfume that was hard to trace. Curious, Hannibal moved to the vanity, an item that had served Duchess after Duchess over the course of its lifetime. He expected baubles and pearls, boxes filled with jewelry bought on impulse and quickly abandoned. He found instead a single plain jewelry box with a handful of modest, jeweled pins, each one accompanied by a note of birthday congratulations from Grandfather and nothing else. A silver hairbrush and comb lay neatly to one side, other than that, the vanity was quite empty save for several mysterious glass vials of liquid and the blush-pink brooch Will had worn at their ill-fated supper.

"Grandfather must have put his foot down on that subject," Hannibal murmured, moving to the dressing room. Instead of the overblown wardrobe he expected, Hannibal found a somber sum of clothing suitable for funerals in its color and lack of embellishment. Hannibal himself was no fop, but even his clothing had more life to it.

"I hate to greet you with correction, my Lord, but you are in the wrong suite."

Hannibal turned, armed with a frown, his hands clasped behind him as he faced Will Grant after a six-year absence.

He had not spent much time with Will during his failed homecoming six years ago, but even so short an exposure hammered home the realization that Will Grant had changed considerably since. He was taller, still trim even in his layers of disguising clothing, watching Hannibal with unsettling blue eyes that neither flinched nor acquiesced. His dark curls were somewhat tamer, shorter than they had been, and his face had hollowed slightly, his square jaw a perfect foil for the excess of his delicate, full mouth.

He'd lied and called this creature plain once upon a time, not nearly pretty enough to get his way.

Hannibal very much doubted now that there was anything in the world Will Grant could ask for and not receive immediately just by fluttering his ridiculously long eyelashes, and no doubt he well knew it.

"I am the future Duke of Westvale," Hannibal reminded him, aware that he was testing the air for Will's scent, still strangely elusive even so close. "Every room in this house is mine."

He clenched his teeth once he said it, realizing it was not true in the least. Hartford House belonged to Will Grant, no matter who happened to be Duke at the time—at least, until he bore an Alpha son for Hannibal.

Will inclined his head with a slight, wry smile, arms crossed over his chest and pale, small hands tucked out of sight. Hannibal noted with irritation he wore a neckerchief, thick and properly knotted as per the fashion but entirely covering this throat. He had no means or reason to protest or complain, but he felt an instinctive frustration rise at the Omega's refusal to be seen. Hannibal had never before met one that did not flaunt its neck like a prize, daring any Alpha with strength enough to try laying their mark for all to see.

"The ownership of Hartford House notwithstanding, your grandfather has assured me I have a place here, though I have never claimed it is a permanent one," Will said, moving to his vanity to slide the brush to one side. It was less a tidying than it was an excuse to give Hannibal his back, though that, too, was a provoking sight. His shoulders had stretched along with his height, but his waist had slimmed even more, all traces of baby-round softness whittled away to leave the clean lines of pure symmetry.

Hannibal was profoundly flustered.

"I assume you are going to remind me that this House is no longer mine?" he asked, recovering enough to deliver the barb with true heat. He saw Will's face reflected in the mirror, his dark brows drawing down and a soft frown curving his full mouth.

"I have not heard that you forfeited your inheritance, Lord Clarges," Will said, his gaze lifting only slightly to reach Hannibal's in the mirror, a fleeting contact lost almost at once. "Your grandfather will be beside himself to hear so."

Hannibal stared, his own features schooled to hide the resulting bewilderment of that particular statement.

"I am by no means forfeiting my inheritance!" Hannibal said, scrutinizing his slender mate despite himself. "I am speaking of the fact that Hartford House belongs to you! Little though you deserve it!"

Will tensed, a subtle shift of muscles along his shoulders, a slight tightening at Hannibal's insulted tone.

"Hartford House is the ancestral home of the Ledfords," Will softly said, though his voice was stiff and offended. "I have no intentions of taking that from you, Lord Clarges, but I will not be berated for something which I have had no hand in."

"Hartford House is yours from turrets to foundations less than three days after your arrival and you expect me to believe you had no hand in it? Ha! The very nerve!" Hannibal huffed, shoulders back and chin tilted slightly, unconsciously highlighting his Alpha qualities in instinctive reaction to Will's continuing disinterest. "That is why I am here, to discuss things with Grandfather so that we may sort this entire mess. It is nothing you would understand or have any interest in."

The silence that followed was thick and Hannibal fidgeted, uncomfortable and strangely uneasy with their conversation, as if Will had the intelligence to realize what his return actually meant—find a way to pry Hartford House from his grasping, greedy little hands, finger by finger.

"I am relieved you read the letter and did not burn it out of hand," Will murmured, tactfully changing the subject, or else losing interest, one. He moved so that Hannibal could no longer see him in the mirror, but still was faced with his shoulders sweeping into his narrow waist and the flare of his coat that served to emphasize rather than disguise the slight curve of his hips.

"And why would I burn it?" Hannibal asked, annoyed that Will would believe him to be so petty when Omegas were notoriously so. "You had never sent a letter even once in six years. I assumed there was some purpose behind it."

"Well, you're here, at least," Will said, turning to face him, his arms crossed again, defensive postures that only served to irritate Hannibal. While he did not expect a warm welcome, he *did* expect Will to behave as an Omega alone with an Alpha among Alphas. He did expect the usual sort of trembling, wide-eyed excitement he often elicited from courtesans who remained free and willing. He did expect self-aggrandizing chatter meant to endear, the sly looks and coy smiles of a creature that could not help its own nature.

Will watched him, cautious but unaffected, his solemn blue eyes weighty and far older than his smooth face allowed for, trapping a peculiar melancholy out of place in one so young.

"If you would like to change rooms," Will slowly said, a mocking smile curving his pink mouth, his head tilting slightly to one side as if Hannibal was a bemusing novelty. "Then I will have Jimmy pack my things."

Hannibal stiffened with affront, mouth pursed in disapproval of his cheek. In a haughty, hard tone, he said, "I came to see if you had gone by now, knowing that I was arriving in order to take my place at last. Imagine my disappointment to find you still here."

"Imagine," Will blandly agreed, his white teeth flashing in a wry grin. When he said nothing more, Hannibal's frown intensified.

"Do you always dress as if about to attend a funeral?" he asked, his amber eyes flicking over Will's clothing—black coat and black breeches, black knee boots, all dark except for his white shirt and knotted neckerchief. He made Hannibal's own tastefully embroidered coat seem positively peacock-like in comparison.

Will's brows rose in mild amusement.

Hannibal found it vastly unsettling.

"Are you trying to *insult* me, Hannibal?" he asked, sounding ever so faintly disapproving and amused. The sheer *gall*. "Or are you frightened I've spent your fortune on clothing and somehow managed to hide it all from you?"

Hannibal glowered at him, eyes narrowed. He would have said there was some mistake and Will Grant was a beta, but even so faint his scent was undeniably that of an Omega... however little he behaved like one.

"Ah, I apologize," Will said, feigning understanding of the cause for Hannibal's sudden, stiff affront. "You would prefer I call you Lord Clarges, would you not? Very well, Lord Clarges. I shall wait downstairs until you are satisfied with the contents of my wardrobe and return to your own suite before I intrude on you in my own again."

"You'll do nothing of the sort!" Hannibal snapped, flushing in consternation, uncertain how something as diffident in nature and fawningly submissive as an Omega had somehow managed to subtly scold him. "I have no interest at all in your wardrobe, damn you!"

"Of course, my Lord," Will murmured, watching him with amused, mocking blue eyes.

"Don't call me that, for the love of the gods!" Hannibal ordered, jerking on his coat to settle it, consumed with the desire to groom himself in the face of Will's obvious yet elusive disapproval. "The servants will have a field day!"

He realized how silly it sounded the moment it left his mouth, saying something like that to the spouse he'd abandoned six years before and then proceeded to publicly make a fool of in polite Society.

Frustrated and feeling off-center, Hannibal gruffly told him, "Call me by my given name."

He stalked purposefully towards the door of their shared washroom, bristling at the soft utterance that followed him out.

"Of course, *Hannibal*..."

⌘⌘⌘

Will released a deep, relieved breath when Hannibal left. He slumped against the door, his hand trembling when he lifted it to brush his curls back from his heated forehead.

Seeing Hannibal again after six years was like a punch in the gut. Secluded here at Hartford House with only the aging Duke, Anthony, and beta servants for regular company, Will had forgotten what an Alpha in his prime could do to him. Rather, what this *particular* Alpha in his prime could do, as he had no such issue with Anthony Diment during his visits.

But then, he hadn't bonded to Anthony as he had to Hannibal, and there wasn't a day that passed that he didn't wish otherwise.

Hannibal loomed behind his closed eyes, tall and fit and watching him with the stoic, effortless beauty of an uncaring god. Just the thought of him keyed Will's nerves tightly. His pulse raced, his nostrils flaring to gather the heavy scent of him. His heart pounded and he thanked every god he could recall that the scent blocking products and repressive tonics he took were able to hide the extent of Hannibal's effect on him. He could only imagine how the haughty Lord Clarges would react had he any inkling of how Will's instincts responded to his nearness.

"He won't stay," Will assured himself, moving to sit at the vanity before his weak knees gave out on him. He propped his elbow up and dropped his head into his palm, drawing another breath that was easier than before as Hannibal's scent faded. "He'll leave. He'll settle things with His Grace and he'll leave..."

Six years ago, he'd been cautiously told by Jimmy that his husband had packed his things and gone. Will had been stricken with guilt, anxiety, and panic, knowing he was the cause of his defection, frantic at the thought that he would be held accountable for breaking the Ledford family's main line with his unsuitable presence. The sudden and absolute loss of the Alpha he had instinctively bonded to had devastating consequences for Will, who was left picking up the scattered, shattered pieces of himself without the ability to put them back together again.

So he'd adapted, as Omegas were designed to do. He'd adapted to Hannibal's perspective, which Will's Gift had made his own. He'd adapted to the Alpha desires he had bonded with in a moment of duress and emotional distress. He'd sent Mina's wardrobe back to their father and refused the tailor's recommendations for soft colors and light fabrics. He'd ordered the bare minimum, opting to live like a renunciate, rejecting anything his nature found pleasing. His place in and ownership of Hartford House had been bought with a lie, and Will was determined they shouldn't suffer for it. He'd taken charge of the house and estate to spare Roland and, after a few short months of oversight, His Grace had been content to leave things in his hands. For the past six years Will had lived like a ghost in this house, barely seen, rarely heard, and ruthlessly efficient at making the estate run like clockwork.

Now it was all about to end, he knew. Hannibal had returned and he was no more inclined to accept Will now than he'd been six years ago, nor was Roland any more inclined to pack Will off back to his father and pretend the whole sordid event had never taken place.

"Mr. Grant?"

"Yes, Jimmy?" he asked, looking up to find his valet peeking in the door at him. By all rights he should be addressed by his title, but Will refused it. His insistence that they call him "Will" had been met with scandalized refusal but "Mr. Grant" did well enough for everyone.

"Was that him?" Jimmy mouthed, pointing towards the washroom door.

Will cracked a weary smile and nodded, softly saying, "As agreeable as ever, I'm afraid. He was checking to make sure I hadn't invested his inheritance in my wardrobe."

Jimmy pulled a face, knowing better than anyone how spare Will was with regards to himself.

"Has something happened?" Will asked. "Or were you just curious?"

"Well, you know me," Jimmy chuckled, waving his hand. "*But*, I'm actually here because Lord du Millau is downstairs asking after you."

"His timing is uncanny," Will said, not surprised in the least. "I doubt Lord Clarges will be glad to see him again. Thank you, Jimmy, I'll be down directly."

Jimmy left with a soft smile and nod, leaving Will alone again.

He looked in the mirror, staring at his own blue eyes. A stranger looked back at him, pale and lifeless and plain. Certainly no match for a future Duke, as he'd been told countless times over the years by overheard gossip repeated below stairs, carried in by the servants who felt the need to defend him against his justified detractors, even if only among themselves.

Sighing, Will pushed to his feet and left, hoping Hannibal was satisfied by what he had found and would keep to his own suite for the time he was here.

Anthony was in the salon, a younger and more amiable companion than Hannibal could hope to be, the resemblance between them less strong now in six years of growing. Will never imagined he could forgive Anthony for his part in what had happened, but he actually found him very agreeable and amusing. The fact that he was an Alpha rarely if ever came up—Will never felt moved to respond to him thanks to his bond to Hannibal, and Anthony had mentioned on more than one occasion that the suppressants made Will a beta male in all but truth. They had become unlikely friends over the years, the close proximity of the Diment holdings at Fernhill allowing for fairly frequent visiting during the off-season, though it only went one direction.

"Ah! There you are! I wondered what had happened!" Anthony called, turning with crackling energy, tapping his riding crop against his boot in a rattling rhythm. "You weren't in your office."

"I was informed by the servants that Lord Clarges had returned," Will said, noting the surprise on Anthony's face. "You didn't know?"

"No, of course not," Anthony said, aghast. "I would have gone the other direction if I had. Well, I guess that puts a damper on my plans, then."

"What plans?" Will asked, idly straightening a pillow on the settee where Anthony must have been sitting before he came down.

"I thought we'd go for a ride," Anthony said, delighted with himself. "Have Cook pack us a lunch and go fishing? You've been cooped up in your office for weeks now. You need a break."

Will laughed, shaking his head a little.

"Actually," Anthony said, casting a searching glance at the salon door. "If we hurry, we could get away before Hannibal knows I'm here."

Will opened his mouth to say he couldn't possibly escape, then thought better of it when he recalled how Hannibal had spoken to him upstairs. He nodded at Anthony and told him, "Yes, let's go. He would prefer me not to be here at any rate; I doubt he would complain over the absence of either of us."

Anthony's grin widened, his similarity to Hannibal giving Will a pang of discomfit, and he rang vigorously for Hawkes, who appeared as if by magic.

"Lord du Millau and I will be going on an outing to the dock, Mr. Hawkes," Will said, aware of the butler's disapproving silence directed Anthony's way. "If you could ask Mrs. Pimms to make up a basket for us and have my fishing gear packed?"

"Of course, Mr. Grant," he said, his sonorous voice carrying almost as if he hoped Hannibal or Roland would hear him and come investigate. "My Lord du Millau, will you stay for dinner?"

"Yes," Will said for him, and quirked an eyebrow at Anthony's indignant huff. "If I'm going to get into trouble for this, you're going to get into trouble with me."

Anthony's grin returned in full force. "Partners in crime, then! Yes, I'll stay, Hawkes. And get a move on, old boy, will you? I want clear of the house before my cousin comes to box my ears. I haven't danced out of his reach for six years just to be caught *now*."

The hamper was brought directly and Will's horse was brought around, saddled and loaded with his gear bound on its rump. He mounted up and sighed as he settled into the saddle, already feeling the tension of Hannibal's arrival loosen inside of him. He had few pleasures he rarely partook of and a day at the riverside was one of them.

"So, is there some devastating piece of news you wish to throw on me?" Will asked, giving Anthony an assessing look as they rode at an easy pace towards the estate's mill.

"What? Why would you ask that?"

"Because you rode over today wanting to take me on a picnic," Will said, laughing softly, "*and* take me fishing. The last time you did that you brought me news of Hannibal's daughter having been born."

"Ah, yes, that," Anthony said, shifting uncomfortably, those high Ledford cheekbones stark in the afternoon light but his mouth more that of a Diment. "No, nothing so terrible as that."

"It wasn't *terrible*, just..." Will said, troubled by the memory of it. "It was just... *informative* of my place. I'm glad they both did well and thrive. Hannibal's mistresses deserve no blame for my situation."

Anthony frowned his direction, mouth pursing.

"Your sister is becoming quite the talk of Town," he said, the neutral caution of his voice alarming Will more than the content.

"Which one? I have several sisters," Will said, though he knew which one. His twin, of course. She had married her Lord Rathmore as planned and in the past six years had behaved with the same outrageous arrogance their father had encouraged in her. When Lord Rathmore had taken a mistress, Mina had publicly thrown a fit and tried to have the poor woman's house burned down. There was truly no telling what she had done now. The last Will had heard, she was threatening divorce and had taken up with an actor, making no move to hide her own affair.

"Will, honestly," Anthony scolded, shaking his head. "I saw her weekend last and she asked about you."

Will felt cold fingers trail down his spine and shivered, wondering if it was his father's doing.

"Considering she has never once tried to contact you in all these years, I was understandably taken aback," Anthony went on. "She wanted to know what Hannibal's plans were in regards to you."

"She could have asked him herself," Will said, his voice subdued. "I am sure they have seen much of each other these past six years."

"Actually, no," Anthony corrected him, guiding his horse onto the trail down towards the mill. "She was justifiably terrified to go near him considering the part she played in your marriage. They have not once crossed paths that I am aware of. She's damned near as good at it as I am!"

"I suppose that is for the best," Will said, thinking of what that meeting would have ended up as. "I cannot imagine how she would react to being called ugly."

"Ugly?" Anthony asked, laughing. "Why would anyone call your sister ugly?"

"I have always been told my resemblance to Mina is frightening to every detail," Will said. "Hannibal would find her every bit as unappealing as he finds me."

Anthony laughed and shot a sideways glance at him, shaking his head. "He is alone in that estimation, Will. What few of my fellows who have seen you think you quite lovely and attractive, with pleasing manners and a faraway sadness that begs relief."

"You should not associate with such fools," Will said, dismissing it. "Nor with an Omega, Anthony."

"Bollocks," Anthony pronounced it, laughing. "My prospects are being discussed back home and a few Omegas number among them, rare as they are." He turned his twinkling gaze on Will and winked at him when he happened to look up, saying, "But not a one to compare with you."

Will laughed, chalking it up to more of Anthony's ridiculous nonsense.

They rode a ways down the riverside from the mill to a small fishing dock that Roland had ordered built for Will as a birthday present when he found out that

Will loved to fish. Will would never cease being grateful to the aging Alpha for all of his many kindnesses, even if most of the affectionate gifts he attempted to lavish on Will were refused.

"Shall we fish first or after?" Anthony asked, swinging down to take the basket from the back of Will's mount.

"I'd rather fish for a while, unless you're famished?" Will said, deftly dismounting and loosening the straps which held his fishing gear in place.

"Fishing first, then," Anthony said, already peeling off his boots and stockings while Will put the poles together and strung them with line. "Are you worried now that he's back?"

"No," Will said, focused on finding suitable hooks and sinkers in the modest box Mr. Hawkes had given him to hold his small loose pieces.

"You know this won't end well," Anthony said, picking his way barefoot to the patient horses to take their gear off. He hissed when his mare shifted, dancing a cursing jig to avoid his bare toes being stepped on.

Will laughed at his antics, saying, "You should have done that before you took your boots off."

Anthony scowled at him but finished anyway, piling the gear up in the shade of a nearby tree and letting the horses wander.

"You didn't say anything," he said, tired of waiting for Will to address his statement.

"I wasn't aware you had asked a question," Will pointed out, finished tying on the hooks, corks and sinkers. There was a small oilcloth packet of side pork to use as bait tucked into the top of the picnic basket and he gathered it up, offering one pole to Anthony to take. "Hannibal has come to claim his place, Anthony. It's no business of mine how he does so."

Anthony took the pole and packet, frowning softly as he watched Will strip off his own boots and stockings.

"You could lose everything, Will," he said, sounding genuinely concerned, "if he convinces Grandfather to allow an annulment. If he doesn't, Hannibal won't stop trying, not so long as Hartford House belongs to you."

"I know that," Will said, his voice quietly carrying over the sound of the river. He stood steadily when he got to his feet, all the long years of his life preparing him to have strength in the face of adversity. It was dangerous, after all, to show any weakness before an Alpha, no matter how friendly they might seem. "One way or another, he'll manage to be rid of me. Even after I was told of His Grace's decision, I never imagined my place here would last."

Anthony frowned, finding more in that statement than he cared for.

"Let's not speak of unpleasant eventualities," Will urged him, summoning a smile that was brittle and worn thin. He headed to the dock and plopped down at the end, dangling his bare feet in the water with a sigh.

With no other recourse, Anthony joined him, both of them threading their hooks with bait and leaving more complicated conversations behind them.

⌘⌘⌘

By the time Hannibal was properly refreshed, stuffed with pastries and tea by his overeager staff, and summarily outfitted in fresh, clean clothing, Grandfather was awake and asking to see him.

Hannibal steeled himself for what was to come, no doubt some awful row like the one they'd had the last time he was home. He dearly loved his grandfather but they were two Alphas cut from the same stubborn cloth and that caused no little friction between them.

He was not prepared, however, to see his grandfather lying frail in his bed, looking haggard and spare and much older than he should.

"Hannibal," he said, smiling to see his grandson, holding out one trembling hand which Hannibal grasped immediately. "I wasn't sure you would come."

"Of course I came, Grandfather," he said, wondering where all his strength had gone. Then again, six years was nearer a decade than it wasn't, and Roland had not been young for a very long time. "I had no idea you were so ill. Will should have written me sooner!"

"He wanted to, but I wouldn't let him," Roland said, squeezing his fingers. "I had hoped you'd come home on your own."

Hannibal drew up, scalded and slightly ashamed. He'd thought often of his grandfather once the anger at his machinations had burned out, but his damnable pride had prevented him from reaching out. It had, as always, gotten the better of him in that regard and this was the price of it.

"Hannibal," Grandfather said, bringing his thoughts back to the present. "I am not well at all these days, my boy. I have no time to dance around subjects or spar with you—I want that child, Hannibal. I want a child to carry on the Ledford line."

Hannibal stared down at him with wary calculation before telling him, "My mistress is pregnant once more. Should it be a son—"

"I'm not legitimizing your bastard," Roland snapped, the effort forcing a coughing fit that left him breathing hard. When he had recovered somewhat, he went on with less force to say, "You are very much in danger of losing this estate, Hannibal. All I ask is a child."

"No, you ask for *an Alpha son*! *With* the Omega you foisted off on me," Hannibal reminded, frowning. "There could be any number of children born before that lauded child! I refuse to be trotted out like a stud to a broodmare!"

"I have changed my arrangement," Roland said, pointing weakly towards his roll-top desk. "There, on the blotter."

Hannibal retrieved what he was asking for, reading the elegant, precise handwriting with growing surprise.

Addendum to a Previous Declaration:

Let it be known that the previous Declaration of Ownership of Hartford House is now Amended. As such, Hartford House will no longer belong to William Grant until the time that he bears an Alpha son. From this day, it shall be legally of consequence that on the delivery of any sound, living child of Hannibal Ledford by William Grant, ownership of Hartford House will immediately revert to Hannibal Ledford in its entirety and a legal separation will be filed on his behalf should he so desire. William Grant and his child will remain as guests of Hartford House until the death of Roland Ledford, current Duke of Westvale, after which William Grant's continued occupancy of Hartford House will be strictly by the invitation of Hannibal Ledford.

All Hannibal needed to do was get Will pregnant and Hartford House would be his again. Rather, *would* be his upon the child's first breath in the world, but nothing more than that. No sharing Will's bed through countless children until meeting that Alpha son requirement, no enforced cohabitation in the misplaced hope a bond would form. Just one child, and once he took his place as the Duke of Westvale, he could see Will thrown out on his ear for his insufferable scheming.

There most certainly had to be a catch.

"All you require is a single pregnancy?" he asked, sure that his grandfather would never be so incautious where he was concerned. "Even if the child was to be female or, gods forbid and strike me dead, an Omega?"

Grandfather nodded unsteadily.

Hannibal reread the document, asking as he did so, "And Will would only remain here until the time of your death?"

Again, Roland nodded, managing to make it infinitely sorrowful.

"I have asked far more of him than I have had a right to," Roland admitted. "He has wasted the best years of his youth shut away in this house with only an old man and your cousin for company. One child is all I ask, and then the both of you can seek whatever design best suits you. But I will have that child, Hannibal, Alpha, beta, or Omega, there will be a Ledford of House Reddig extraction, even if your heir is eventually the bastard get of your shoddy wigeon in the Capital."

Hannibal took a deep breath. "Does Will know you have contrived to turn him out homeless into the streets the very day you die?"

"No, he does not know," Roland said. "Nor should you tell him if you have any intentions of making this come about. And I never indicated that Will would be turned out with nothing. I have made provisions for him in my will which Mr. Buddish and the Diments are all very aware of. He will be comfortably settled when my time comes."

"Yet with a child, Grandfather, there would be no annulment, only this... *separation* you write of," Hannibal said, placing the Addendum back where he had found it.

"Separation has never seemed to prevent you from finding affection and companionship where you please," Roland said, wry humor coloring his voice. "Under these circumstances, it will not keep Will from such, either. You will be shed of him, Hannibal, treasure that he is, and I will have the comfort of his company until death finally claims me."

"Death will hardly claim you, you stubborn old menace," Hannibal said with a fond smile. "Stop speaking with such certainty!"

Roland smiled, chuckling softly, his breath rattling in his lungs. He sobered after a moment and said, "If you agree, Hannibal, then sign that document."

Hannibal frowned, considering all the myriad ways this could backfire on him. As it stood, he would not have control of Hartford House again in his life, not fully. He was a powerful Alpha in his prime and there was a very good chance he could get Will with child in one attempt. It seemed little enough of a sacrifice to see his Omegan spouse tossed from Hartford House like the unwanted baggage he was with all of Society snickering at his shame.

His mind unhelpfully provided him with a clear picture of Will in his suite, leaning against the door with a cat's own lithe grace, his head tilted slightly so that his long curls fell to one side, his sad blue eyes secretive and amused at Hannibal's expense, his full mouth parting on a smile as he asked, "*Are you trying to* insult *me, Hannibal?*"

His back stiffened with instinctive affront and offended dignity. He impatiently returned to the desk and added his signature beneath his grandfather's, tossing the quill down with rather more force than was necessary at the recollection of his mate's cheeky comment.

His grandfather watched him with naked disappointment in his amber gaze and Hannibal wondered if he should not have agreed, if there was some other option which would bring the light of pride back to the elderly Alpha's eyes. Instead, he fanned the paper in the air and murmured, "I will have Mr. Stammets file this in the Capital with all haste."

"Yes," Grandfather said, closing his eyes in resignation and sinking into his pillows. "You do that, Hannibal."

Chapter 6

Once his grandfather dismissed him, Hannibal decided to ride down to Mr. Stammets' office in Hartford Town to set eyes on the bustling village again. The road between the estate and the town was properly paved now as well, a simple pattern of plain cobblestone that followed the worn old dirt lane. He wondered at how industrious they'd become to put such a thing in and thought them all very clever for it, making it far easier for them to move from the village proper to the various places on the estate that employed them and on to the greater roads to the Capital.

Mr. Stammets' office was above the bakery, the little sign proclaiming he was in. Hannibal dismounted and idly fastened his bad-tempered mount to a free ring on the plaster-coated wall, his amber eyes flitting around to take in the changes he'd noticed.

There were new shops, new faces, of course. In fact, the town had grown substantially in his absence.

Hannibal meandered down the main street, noticing that even the side streets were paved, albeit with less fanciful designs. Everything had a fresh air about it, scrubbed clean and newly whitewashed, enough so that he wondered if his grandfather had ordered Hartford Town made ready for his visit. He considered this as he roamed about, nodding here and there to others on the walkways. Very few recognized him, only those old enough to remember him from his misspent youth, one of whom owned the bakery he ended up back in front of after his unplanned walk around town.

Mr. Woodward was still holding his place at the counter, spectacles dusted with flour and his graying hair wisping every direction. He caught sight of Hannibal coming through the door and grinned, calling, "As I live and breathe, if it isn't Hannibal Ledford, Lord Clarges himself! Come here, my boy! Come here!"

Hannibal gladly greeted him, not minding the familiarity of the hug he was drawn into.

"You were no taller than my chin the last I saw you! Where've you been, boy?" Mr. Woodward asked, and immediately called, "Katie! Bring tea and a few tarts to the front!"

"Ah, I shouldn't stay," Hannibal said, smiling. "I'm on an errand for Grandfather and got distracted. I wanted to see how much the village has changed."

"Greatly, Lord Clarges! Greatly, indeed! Come, here's some tea, have a seat and chat a moment," he was told, and had no polite way to refuse. He was guided to a small table near the window and bundled into a seat while Mr. Woodward's daughter brought out the requested refreshments. The tea was hot and strong and suited him very nicely, however, and he nibbled the tart politely despite having been stuffed back at the house fit to burst. "Ah, you must be very surprised by all the changes, Lord Clarges! Have you met with Mr. Grant?"

Hannibal stiffened and managed to say with admirable neutrality, "I have not had the occasion to deal much with him."

"Well, you are but newly home, yes," Mr. Woodward said, sipping his own tea and smacking his lips. "I'm used to seeing him of a morning. He likes to ride over and watch the town wake up."

Hannibal frowned, settling his cup in its saucer as gently as he could. "I had not realized he was so familiar with Hartford Town."

"He's been here a solid six years, now," Mr. Woodward said, nodding. "Of course, you've been trying to arrange to come home. My compliments to His Grace on his choice, Lord Clarges; he's a well-spoken and bright little fellow, to be sure. He spent near on an hour in the fields when he first arrived here, watching the threshing machine at work and asking all sorts of questions. I sent him to the foreman for his answers."

He uttered a good-natured, pleased chuckle as if it had been a moment of true fondness. Hannibal frowned, subsiding in his chair and thoughtfully finishing his tea.

"I imagine he spends quite a lot of time amusing himself in town," he ventured. He pictured Will's slender body in his dark, solemn clothing and the embarrassing scarcity of his wardrobe and inwardly cursed, knowing he had been no spendthrift in the case of clothing, at least.

"Oh, he comes down now and then to purchase for the House, my Lord, for Cook's sake or at Mr. Hawkes' request," Woodward amiably said, pushing another tart towards him which Hannibal found quite menacing to his overstuffed stomach. "But he does spend every moment of his time attending to the estate with Lord du Millau since Mr. Vorgert's... departure. He is a very dedicated young man, indeed!"

Hannibal's frown deepened at the thought of his younger cousin showing off his spouse, however unwanted he was. Anthony had married Will by proxy and had always been partial to him in letters. Hannibal's suspicious nature seized on the niggling idea that perhaps the reason was that Anthony himself had designs on Will. It would be a sure way to best his elder cousin, stealing his spouse from under him. Anthony was an Alpha, after all, and if he was seduced by Will into bonding, why then nothing could be done about it. He knew without a doubt that the reason Anthony had never married was in case Grandfather decided to annul Will's marriage to Hannibal and hand it all over to his cousin in one fell swoop.

It annoyed him to think of Will seducing Anthony and making a fool of him, but it would solve one of his problems. At least if Will wound up in Anthony's bed, he'd be out of Hannibal's hair and someone else's problem and there was nothing his grandfather could say about it. He would no doubt vilify Anthony for his conduct and no longer consider him for the line of succession, leaving Hannibal quite secure.

"Yes, a clever little fellow, indeed," Mr. Woodward said, beaming. "I wish there were three more just like him!"

"Well, much to my misfortune," Hannibal intoned, standing to take his leave. "There is only the one and he is my problem to deal with. Good day, Mr. Woodward."

It was only once he scaled the stairs to Mr. Stammets' office that his brain brought up the other statement, that of Vorgert, the estate manager, being gone. Frowning, Hannibal pounded on the door and let himself in without a greeting, finding Mr. Stammets quite alarmed and pale behind his desk.

"Ah! Lord Clarges! Er..." His nervous eyes shifted and his pale hands groped over his desk in search of salvation, a pitiable display of ineptitude.

"Pray do *not* fall into a faint or I will be forced to find myself truly contemptuous of you," Hannibal warned, tossing down the envelope which held his Grandfather's addendum. He ungenerously noted that Mr. Stammets had attempted to grow a mustache in the past six years, and it had the sad look of an overused shaving brush clinging to his face. "Grandfather wants this sent to the Capital immediately. Changes to the ownership of Hartford House."

Mr. Stammets' hands trembled as he picked it up, hesitantly offering, "There is no seal—"

"It is an addendum only," Hannibal reiterated, moving to the window to look down at the street below. "Mr. Buddish will find it all quite tidy, I am sure."

"Yes, Lord Clarges," Mr. Stammets said, rallying. "I will send someone tonight to deliver it in the morning. Does His Grace wish a copy for his own records?"

Hannibal waved that away, saying, "Whatever you usually do in cases like this, Mr. Stammets, shall suffice well enough."

He heard papers being shuffled and studied movement behind him as the addendum was prepared. Abruptly unable to control his curiosity any longer, he asked, "What has happened to Mr. Vorgert?"

Mr. Stammets uttered a soft "eep" of surprise behind him and Hannibal very studiously did not turn around to glare at him as that would in no way help his current line of inquiry. Instead, he patiently waited until the beta man said, "It was discovered that he was fleecing the estate, Lord Clarges, of quite a large sum every year. Nearly the whole of Hartford House's profits, I believe, meager though they were."

Hannibal did turn then, scowling, and asked, "How was this theft discovered?"

Mr. Stammets paled, if such was even possible for a man of his anemic complexion, and softly offered, "Mr. Grant checked his books and reported it to His Grace immediately."

Hannibal's brows drew down in a grim glare. "Am I to assume that the Earl of Reddig somehow found himself poking into the business of my estate manager, Mr. Stammets, or are you trying to tell me that an Omega was able to identify a mathematical error? Because they are equally unbelievable to me, sir."

"Mr. Grant, as in your spouse, my Lord," Mr. Stammets corrected, too nervous to be lying.

"It must have been a very obvious ploy, indeed, for him to find it," Hannibal mused, wondering why in the seven hells Will was bothering the estate manager anyway.

"Actually, my Lord, it was very well hidden," Mr. Stammets said, seeming much more relieved on the count that Hannibal would not strangle him out of turn for mentioning his unwanted spouse. "His Grace's accountants were quite dismayed when Mr. Grant brought them to confirm. Mr. Vorgert is now in jail serving a sentence for fraud and theft."

"And who, pray tell, was hired in his stead?" Hannibal asked.

"N-no one, my Lord," Mr. Stammets answered, petting his heavy mustache, which made him look like a woeful walrus with a nervous condition.

Hannibal heaved a sigh, adding that to his mental list of things to tend to while he was home. An estate the size of Hartford House required constant attention, hence the estate manager. With no one to tend the books all this time, things were surely falling to rack and ruin, just as he had feared since Anthony was hardly a stand-in. He could not fathom why his grandfather had not contacted him earlier with things in such a deplorable state!

"Is there anything else of crippling importance I should know of before one of the townsfolk sees fit to tell me? Hm?" Hannibal asked, arching one brow in a haughty, scathing glare.

"No, Lord Clarges," Mr. Stammets said, swinging back towards faint again.

"Very well," Hannibal sighed, annoyed with him but feeling like a bully thanks to the man's insufferable pandering to the Ledford family. "Good day, Mr. Stammets."

"Good day, Lord Clarges." It sounded every bit as relieved as Mr. Stammets had attempted to prevent it from sounding.

Out of sorts and brimming with tea and pastries, Hannibal retrieved his horse and took the road back to Hartford House at an easy trot, squinting against the sun as it angled across the sky towards the horizon. He slowed the horse to a walk when he reached the shade of old trees sheltering the greatest extent of the road, allowing the breeze to cool his irritation.

It immediately flamed again as he arrived at the house and spied Will and another figure approaching from the other side of the estate, leading their horses and talking with their heads pressed together, thick as thieves.

Hannibal drew the horse to a stop and dismounted, leading it towards his troublesome spouse and what turned out to be his bounder of a cousin, Anthony. Neither one of them had shoes on and their pants legs were rolled up to their knees, jackets loosened. Hannibal could see their boots slung from their empty saddles, tied by their neckerchiefs along with all manner of mystifying gear.

"Is this how you've spent your time in my absence?" he asked, startling both of them. Will looked up at him and the mischievous smile on his full lips vanished at once, replaced with wary tightness that irked Hannibal to see. Anthony looked guilty as sin, as well he should.

"Will has been working nonstop the past couple of weeks," Anthony said, rising to his defense as stupid Alphas were so often wont to do for their Omegan counterparts. "I decided to break him out and take him fishing."

"Fishing?" Hannibal echoed, as if he'd never heard of such a thing before. He spied the picnic basket and pointedly asked, "And lazing about eating as well?"

"Lord Clarges," Will said, careful to keep his voice calm and even despite the sudden spike in his awareness. He fretfully lifted one hand to his open shirt collar, regretting the loss of the neckerchief that usually helped to shroud his scent. "I am sure you have more pressing business to tend to than questioning either one of us."

Hannibal's eyes narrowed, noticing how Will touched his bare throat with slender fingers, brushing the pulse that ticked visibly beneath his white skin. He could scent him, now at last, faintly—sweet-hot and edible, even more compelling than the baker's delightful confections. It prickled at Hannibal's nerves, and he resented it, which only made him more inclined to view his spouse with greater affront.

"I can only imagine the gossip about you when the servants see you in such a state," Hannibal said, his gaze dropping to Will's bare, muddy feet. He noticed the fish dangling from a cord in Will's hand, the same hand he was leading his mount with. It was quite a large fish. Hannibal wondered how he held it so easily, weak as Omegas tended to be.

"The servants are used to my oddities, and are very forgiving, considering I am possessed of only half a mind," Will said, rapidly growing angry with the sudden critical interest Hannibal was taking in him after six years of relative freedom.

"Hannibal," Anthony said, attempting to ease the sudden tension that sprang between them. "It was just a little fun—"

"I suppose that's all it ever is," Hannibal said, dragging Anthony into his judgmental gaze.

"Hannibal," Will said, drawing heavily on his patience, reminding himself that he was calm, even-tempered, and difficult to agitate.

"Running about barefoot like some sort of hoyden," Hannibal continued, ignoring him in favor of berating his cousin.

"*Hannibal*," Will said again, blowing out a breath of frustration when he continued to be ignored like a brainless child.

"Now see here—"Anthony cut in.

"As an Alpha, Anthony, you should at least have tried to correct him," Hannibal said, heedless of the dangerous spark in Will's eyes.

"*Hannibal*! I am standing *right here*!"

"They are malleable creatures, cousin, easily swayed to unbecoming behaviors —"

He was quite suddenly and shockingly smacked in the face with the cold, slippery side of Will's catch, hard enough that he stumbled sideways, unprepared for the force of it. Aghast, he stared in open-mouthed shock at Will, whose cheeks were blooming with pink fury, looking very much like a Valkyrie on the wing.

"How is *that* for *unbecoming behavior*?!"

Utterly at a loss for how a diffident, silly Omega could manage to channel such shocking temper, Hannibal mutely stared after him as Will turned on his heel and marched towards the house without a backwards glance, the unfortunate trout swinging like a pendulum from his tight little fist.

Anthony recovered faster than Hannibal and darted after Will with both horses, his throaty laughter enough snap Hannibal out of it.

Unwilling to chase after them for the sake of his pride, Hannibal contented himself with saying, "Utterly unstable and ridiculous things, Omegas."

Which in no way dismissed the fact that Will had, against all of Hannibal's expectations and directly contrary to the truths as he saw them, coshed him with a fish almost as big as he was.

It was massively unsettling.

His smarting cheek smelling unpleasantly of trout, Hannibal tipped his chin up, stiffened his back, and hastily handed his horse off to a stable boy so he could go to his suite and have another wash.

⌘⌘⌘

It took Will a very long time to calm down and he blamed *that* on Hannibal, too. He knew well enough how his Gift worked by now and resented that his bond to Hannibal meant he reflected his unwanted husband so quickly and with such effect.

He had just been so *angry*!

"I've worked too hard to be spoken to in such a way!" he said, feeling his temper rise again, so rare in him until he was well and thoroughly put out.

Jimmy nodded vigorously, straightening Will's cuff to fasten it at his slender wrist.

"'*Malleable and easily swayed to unbecoming behaviors,*' he said!" Will quoted, fire rising in his eyes. "I can't remember when I've ever been so offended!"

85

"Lord Clarges is a man who values his own opinion rather higher than most," Jimmy said, the most unfavorable comment he'd offered so far.

Will's eyes glazed slightly with the memory and he said, "I slapped him in the face with the fish, Jimmy."

"I'm sorry, Mr. Grant, you did what?" Jimmy asked with delicacy, looking up with the hint of a smile playing around his full mouth.

"I slapped him in the face with the fish," Will whispered, a burble of laughter escaping him. He clamped both hands over his mouth before he could dissolve into giggles, tears of mirth escaping him when Jimmy sucked his lips in and bit down to keep from unseemly laughter.

There was no stopping it then, their mutual amusement. Jimmy cackled like a laying hen with delight, eyes wide, and Will stifled his own horrified laughter with his pillow.

"I don't know what came over me!" he gasped, now shocked at his own behavior without Hannibal's expectations to skew him. "He ignored me like I wasn't even there and... I was so angry!"

"If anyone needs to let out a little anger, Mr. Grant," Jimmy managed, hitching with laughter, "it's *you*. Oh, *besides*, it's not as if you *hurt* him. It was a trout, for the gods' sake, not a hammer."

"I have no idea how I'll get through dinner," Will admitted, standing when Jimmy gestured so he could be helped into his dinner jacket, both of them still fighting amusement. "I just keep seeing the look on his face. I think his horse could have spoken to him in French and he'd have been less surprised."

"Well, he *is* rather unusual in his assumptions about Omegas, a sexist of such caliber that other sexists cringe in embarrassment," Jimmy said, buttoning him swiftly into his jacket and taking up his neckerchief to spritz it with scent killer. It was an added precaution as all of Will's freshly-washed clothing was soaked in the stuff before being left to dry, as per his request. "Especially considering he's only ever really known *one*."

"One?" Will echoed, tipping his chin up for Jimmy to layer and knot the cloth for him. "Jimmy, you must tell me now that you've mentioned it."

"Ah, I shouldn't have said anything," Jimmy said, concentrating on his task. "His Grace has forbidden us to speak of her and there's nothing worth mentioning anyway."

"Except that she ruined Hannibal on Omegas?" Will asked.

"Well *that*, if the rumors are true," Jimmy conceded, fussing with Will's coat and cuffs. He finished and put both palms on Will's shoulders, warmly squeezing him and telling him with earnest concern, "Don't think about it, okay? It won't do you any good and certainly won't endear you to Lord Clarges."

"Worse than coshing him with a trout?" Will meekly asked, feeling the dangerous return of laughter threatening to steal his calm.

"Worse than coshing him with a whole *river* of trout. Come on, it's time," Jimmy said, patting him again before heading for the door. "*Lovely* night you're in for, Mr. Grant—you, Lord Clarges, and Lord du Millau. Lucky for you I think His Grace is feeling well enough to command the table tonight."

Will exhaled softly in relief and headed down to the formal dining room, pausing on the stairs when Anthony called down to him from the landing.

"United front," he said when he caught up to Will, dressed in one of the few sets of formal wear the staff kept secreted away for him in one of the guest rooms. "Partners in crime and all."

Will smiled, walking in stride with him down to the dining room. His humor evaporated abruptly at the sight of Hannibal already seated, his fine mouth pursed with irritation and murderous thoughts lighting his amber eyes.

"Where's Grandfather?" Anthony asked, deflecting the tension with his question and using it to give Will time to take his seat without being set upon.

"He declined to join us," Hannibal said, gesturing for the footmen to begin serving. He noticed Will's formal dinner clothes were as bleak and plain as his day wear and felt a twinge of annoyance, feeling as if the world must think him a jealous miser for keeping his spouse in such dour, plain clothing. "I am glad to see that you remembered to dress for dinner, Will, though wearing shoes must no doubt pain you significantly."

"And I am glad that you remembered to wash beforehand," Will said, his voice as mild and calm as Hannibal's, exercising what he considered exemplary self-control to keep from laughing at the memory of Hannibal's surprised expression. "Trout is such a pungent fish."

Hannibal's lips twitched in a quickly-repressed smile, and he cleared his throat, regaining his former frown when he sternly reminded himself that Omegas were far too ignorant to express such humor on purpose.

87

"I had not expected to you to show your face here, Anthony," he said, shifting his attention to his cousin, who looked quite amused and relaxed when he had no right to be.

"Oh, well, I'm here rather a lot recently," Anthony said, volunteering the information with a grin as he took up his silverware. "Will tends to pine."

Hannibal's noble nose wrinkled. He didn't justify that with a response except to warn, "Don't be crude."

The appetizer was ladled neatly into waiting bowls, hot and fragrant.

"Eel soup?" Hannibal inquired, tasting a spoonful and finding it delicious, as all of Cook's recipes were.

"It's Anthony's favorite," Will said, taking a tentative taste of his own. "I had Mrs. Pimms alter the menu."

"What on earth for?" Hannibal asked, annoyed for no reason he could fathom except that Will had gone out of his way for his cousin and he did not like it in the least.

"Because it was no trouble and I had already planned a soup starter," Will said, giving him a quizzical look.

"You set the menu?" Hannibal asked, confounded. "But Cook always sets her own menu."

"Not for some six years now, Lord Clarges," Will said, a hint of a smile playing about his red lips.

Hannibal found himself staring. It was unconscionable, he knew, that someone should have such a mouth and smile with it in such a way. There must be laws to protect gentlemen from such smiles, surely. He was visibly startled from staring when Will added, "I have taken up the duties of the absent Duchess for your Grandfather's sake."

"That isn't all he's taken up," Anthony cut in, putting away the soup with ungodly haste.

"Other than coshing perfectly innocent gentlemen in the face with trout?" Hannibal asked, noting the way Will ducked his head, which was certainly more akin to amusement than shame. "I cannot imagine."

"He runs the estate, Hannibal," Anthony said, practically crowing about it.

"I beg your pardon?" Hannibal asked. "I'm afraid I didn't hear you correctly. Omegas can hardly choose their own clothing without an Alpha's approval. How on earth could Will manage to *run an estate*?"

"You're absolutely right, Lord Clarges," Will said, overriding Anthony's indignant response. He took a delicate taste of his soup, his spoon sliding between his plump lips with smooth ease. Hannibal found it shockingly obscene and fought not to tell him so as Will removed his spoon from his mouth with equally unsettling grace. He wet his lower lip with the tip of his pink tongue and added, "I imagine the entire place has fallen to ruin."

"I can only think so, considering there's been no estate manager," Hannibal said, glaring at the spoon in Will's hand, idly thinking that perhaps he should have the silver changed. It was simply defective tableware to blame.

"The house is practically falling down around us," Will said, glancing down at his spoon, where Hannibal's glare was directed. He tucked it into his soup against all good manners, mystified when his husband's amber eyes tracked the movement.

"Isn't it just?" Hannibal responded, lifting his gaze to find Will's blue eyes on him, sparkling with amusement, and he cleared his throat again, annoyed because *surely* Will was not intentionally baiting him?

"Why, I cannot imagine we are even able to dine in here, shoddy as things have become," Will said, wondering how far Hannibal would allow him to go before he realized what he was agreeing with.

About that far, apparently. He glared at Will and gruffly said, "You are perverse."

"Then we have something in common after all," Will meekly told him, and took a sip of his wine to hide his smile.

Anthony looked from Will to Hannibal, his blue eyes flicking back and forth. Whatever he thought of the situation, he wisely kept to himself and finished his soup.

Their bowls were cleared away and replaced with the meat course accompanied by a slew of very lovely vegetable dishes. It was a lavish enough dinner for just family, though Hannibal irritably thought it should be more grand in honor of his homecoming.

"I can hardly contain my curiosity about what main course an Omega will choose when left to its own devices," Hannibal said, turning his ire on Will himself when that salacious spoon was removed as a target.

Will lowered his head again. Hannibal had the feeling once more that he was only barely containing the urge to laugh. He raised his head, his lovely face set to studious serenity as the lid was lifted from the platter.

Hannibal stared in at the contents in consternation as Will mildly told him, "*Trout*, my Lord."

Hannibal looked from the platter to Will's tranquil, suspiciously blank face and ruefully admitted his spouse was a rather unusual example of Omegan nature, especially the way his blue eyes twinkled with amusement that chased away his usual sadness.

It was incredibly unsettling, to say the least.

"Is that the same fish you slapped Hannibal with?" Anthony asked, all innocence.

Will's voice was even and prim, betraying nothing more than polite calm when he said, "Yes."

Anthony laughed, waiting for the pieces to be served before saying, "I never dreamed to see you so taken aback, Hannibal!"

"I believe anyone would be taken aback," Will said before Hannibal could retort, taking his silverware into his dainty white hands, "were they slapped with a fish."

"I'll thank you not to make excuses for my state of being when you are the one responsible for it," Hannibal said, deciding to eat the creature that had so offended him as eating Will was certainly not an option. At least not in such a literal way as this.

"I do apologize for defending you, Lord Clarges," Will said, amused by Hannibal's beleaguered expression as much as by the presence of the fish. "I will not, however, apologize for my behavior. You were being provoking."

"You behaved like a savage," Hannibal pointed out, and glared at Anthony to still his snickering.

"You refused to listen to me," Will softly countered.

"So you settled on a violent assault with a trout?" Hannibal asked, and Anthony's snickers turned to chuckles.

"You had *agitated* me," Will said, taking a small bite of his trout.

"I will show considerably more caution in the future!" Hannibal said, looking down his noble nose at Will's slight smile. "Lest I next be coshed with something more dangerous than a fish."

"Then I believe I have made my point," Will said.

"Your preference for settling things with violence is not a *point*," Hannibal said, and, to Anthony, "*You* will control yourself, sir, or remove yourself upstairs."

"I can hardly do either," Anthony said, helpless with laughter, looking from one to the other. "I would never forgive myself for missing this!"

"Have a care, Anthony, lest you agitate Will," Hannibal warned, gesturing around the dining room with his fork. "There are any number of items at hand for you to be brained with."

"I believe this conversation has run its course," Will cut in, gesturing for more wine. "Everyone, let's please enjoy dinner, dangerous as it may be."

Hannibal began to argue, but abruptly cut off, unsettled by how much Will's sparkling blue eyes could convey when his face was schooled to show so little. Had any other Omega even a pinch of Will's beauty they would be deadly with it, he knew. He was very lucky that Will was not excessively smart, even if he was frighteningly pointed in his humor.

Will glanced up and caught Hannibal's assessing glare and cocked his head slightly. *Sickening*, Hannibal had called him that day so long ago, and wondered if Hannibal was even now cataloging his deficiencies, thanks to the reminder of the trout. In a voice so low he risked Hannibal not hearing him, he said, "Forgive me, Lord Clarges, if I have inadvertently ruined your appetite."

Hannibal heard him, reluctantly realizing Will's presence had indeed robbed him of his appetite, but not for reasons he was willing to admit.

"Yes, well, I shall strive to enjoy as I can despite it," Hannibal said, and was strangely disappointed to see the amusement in Will's eyes give way to cool reserve.

⌘⌘⌘

The heavy courses were broken up by a refreshing citrus shaved ice Hannibal found quite to his liking. Luckily, nothing more dangerous than the trout made an appearance through their meal, which passed in idle chatter initiated and sustained by Anthony.

Hannibal found himself quite annoyed by the easy familiarity between them, but could readily admit that if he had stayed these last six years, then he might have managed a similar rapport with Will.

He was confoundingly unlike any other Omega Hannibal had been exposed to and certainly nothing even vaguely like the Omegas his father's concubine had surrounded herself with. Hannibal had never in his life met an Omega who would dare to make him the butt of any joke or give him such mulish, sharp looks as if *he* had somehow done something wrong. He wondered if he might not buy Will something sparkling and distracting; surely then he would be amenable to Hannibal's advances?

"What do you think, Hannibal?" Anthony asked, forcefully proving he had not been paying any attention in the least to anything other than his spouse's tranquil face.

Hannibal cleared his throat and said, "I think I have far too many issues with the estate which need addressing to pay much attention to such trifling things."

Anthony seemed vaguely affronted by that, and Will's chin tipped up, cheeks pinkening with sudden color that was quite becoming on him.

"Hannibal," Anthony said, but Will lifted his hand to hush him.

"No, Anthony, do not trouble Hannibal's mind with issues which are beyond him," Will said, his voice cold enough to keep the citrus ice frozen and his words bringing a dark flush to Hannibal's cheeks. Before he could scold him for being so pert, Will airily overrode him with, "Lord Clarges, you went to the village today. Can I assume you've settled your business with His Grace?"

Hannibal frowned softly, thinking of the agreement they'd struck, what he'd decided to do to wrest control of Hartford House from Will's unknowing hands.

"Yes," he said, seeing the almost imperceptible sag of relief fall over Will's slender, straight shoulders.

"Then you will not remain overlong," Will said, glad to be rid of him. Hannibal was a dangerous presence, however little Will allowed it to show. Six years ago, Will had bonded to him instinctively during Hannibal's vicious tirade in a frightened attempt to submit to him, to somehow prevent his anger, to keep from being shattered from the inside out.

He *had* been shattered, however, and quite thoroughly, but the bond had stuck fast. All Will knew was that he was vulnerable to Hannibal in ways he was indifferent to other Alphas he had the occasion to meet over the years. He was sensitive to his scent, drawn to look at him, attuned to his words and the sound of his voice in a way that made him impossible to ignore.

In short, it was hell having Hannibal near him reinforcing those ugly truths that Will had fought so hard to change for himself over the lonely, endless days and nights of the past six years.

"I had not intended to stay any longer than necessary to settle our business," Hannibal said, watching Will's subtle responses, wondering why he inexplicably could not catch anything more than a faint trace of his scent again. Perversely, he added, "However, I have decided to remain for the foreseeable future."

Will's face fell to stony, smooth stillness, his blue eyes half-veiled by the thick fan of his lashes.

"This is your home, no matter what your Grandfather has put to his solicitor," Will said. "I am sure you will be comfortable here however long you decide to stay. Excuse me, my Lords. Mr. Hawkes will serve brandy in the Red Drawing Room for you both."

He rose with the same dignity and grace as a ruling monarch and left the dining room, both Alphas looking after him.

"Well, that was badly done of you," Anthony said, drumming his fingers on the table before standing.

"I cannot be held accountable for the fickle nature of an Omega, Anthony," Hannibal reminded him, rising and straightening his jacket fretfully. "I am surprised he survived a dinner with two Alphas without falling to tears or fainting dead away."

Anthony snorted, dogging his steps as he headed for the drawing room where a cheery fire was laid and two wing-back chairs were waiting.

"Will? *Faint*?" Anthony scoffed, choosing a chair before Hannibal could and propping his feet up with a sigh. "You have no idea who you've married."

"I have no idea who *you* have married," Hannibal said, taking the other chair with more grace and dignity than Anthony had mustered. "He is an Omega. That is all anyone ever needs know of a person."

"Good gods, man, your prejudice makes my teeth ache," Anthony said, shaking his head. "I remember her a little, you know. Your father's mistress? She was frightening, and a dangerous influence on your father, but she was just a *human*, Hannibal. We're all just humans. You judge every other person in your world by virtue of their character; can you not extend the same courtesy to Will?"

Hannibal frowned, taking the brandy offered by Mr. Hawkes, who moved with the silent stealth of a cat despite his bulk.

"You shouldn't have dismissed what he's done here, Hannibal," Anthony said, taking his own brandy and settling in. "It was incredibly rude of you to call it trifling."

"What, that he had the estate manager fired so that the place has run on its own steam for six years?" Hannibal laughed, taking a sip. "Frittered away Grandfather's fortune to keep Hartford House afloat without proper, skilled management?"

"No, updating the house," Anthony countered. "Bringing in new businesses and adding tenants, converting the fallow fields to raise livestock—Hartford House is more than self-sufficient, cousin. Hartford House is *productive*, thanks to his efforts."

Hannibal pursed his mouth to hold in an automatic denial that an Omega couldn't possibly manage to do such. Instead, he said, "I have seen no evidence of Will's hand in such things and you are outwearing your welcome, Anthony."

"I will always have a place here while Will is in control of Hartford House, though I suppose now that might not be for much longer," Anthony said, and when Hannibal glared at him, he added, "*No*, I haven't told Will. Grandfather asked me not to, though I cannot imagine why he has stooped to such deceit."

"Then you know of the changes he's made?"

Anthony nodded, unhappy. "It's churlish and cruel considering how much has been taken from Will already, but he is determined to have that child and you are too stubborn to agree otherwise. Had he not promised me that Will would have a home here until his death and made provisions for him in his will, then I would have warned your mate not to fall for it. Instead, I find myself complicit in my silence regarding your plots to oust him from his home after everything he's done to make a life here. I am more a cad than you are."

"To being insufferable cads, then," Hannibal murmured, and Anthony toasted to that with a twisted, unhappy smile.

⌘⌘⌘

Will had a terrible time getting to sleep knowing Hannibal would be sleeping in the room next to him. It worried him, not so much because he feared Hannibal's intentions in regards to his marital rights, but because Will knew he couldn't trust himself. He'd spent his entire life denying his Omegan nature, and

94

less than a full day in Hannibal's company had him doubting his own ability to control the threat of his instincts.

He eventually fell into restless slumber, his dreamscape transformed to an ocean side cliff jutting up into the velvety night sky. He was perched there atop it, naked and trembling and terrified because he could hear the rage in the waves crashing on the rocks below, hungry and demanding tribute.

'Do as he says. Whatever he wants of you, you give him. Do you understand me?'

'Yes, Father,' Will said, hearing his voice from somewhere behind him. Hands shoved him forward, towards the black shadow of a man there at the summit.

The roar of the furious ocean terrified him but his father kept pushing him, telling him over and over to do whatever it took, to give whatever he needed to give, down to his blood and bones.

Will took a step toward the cliff's edge, something deep inside of him telling him that it would be for the best, that the comfort he sought was there. It scared him almost to the point of freezing and he wanted to turn back, but the more scared he got, the more steps he took until he was so near the form at the edge that he could smell the salty ocean.

Hannibal was the person there before him, a murky, indistinct shape wavering between shadow and the starlit night.

'Come here,' he said, and opened his arms in welcome.

Frightened and desperate for comfort, seeking his Alpha for protection from his father's shoving hands, Will flung himself forward only for Hannibal to step aside.

Will plunged from cliff towards the swelling, angry waves, the sound of Hannibal's amused laughter becoming the noise of his own gasping sobs as he spilled from his bed, trembling and terrified.

Sweating and wracked with shudders, Will pressed his hand to his galloping heart and buried his face against the side of his bed, willing reality to return.

"It was only a dream," he breathed, the words shortened and stuttering with the force of his panting. He wiped his tears on his sheet, swallowing back his sobs until he had them under control, grateful that his half-awake attack of nerves had gone unnoticed by anyone else.

But the image of the cliff would not leave him. It stayed there in the back of his mind, threatening and dangerous as his father's snarling voice, a stark reminder of what awaited him if he ever tried to pretend his bond to Hannibal Ledford was anything other than an unwanted miscarriage of instincts brought on in a stress-induced bid for escape.

Chapter 7

Hannibal woke the next morning rather later than he intended, but though he had gone to bed at a decent hour, he had lain awake several hours after thinking of Will Grant.

Unusual was too paltry a word to use to describe the Omega his cousin had married him to. In less than a day he'd been subtly dressed down, made to look a miser by the state of Will's belongings, smacked with a fish in a burst of unexpected violence, and honest-to-gods *teased* at his own table.

Teased!

Antithesis of everything Hannibal knew was true might be a better description, all things considered. Hannibal had seen for himself the changes in Hartford Town and in the house itself, the updates to the fixtures and plumbing that brought it back on par with modern homes, the cottages and new businesses in the thriving town adjoining the estate. If he gave credit to Anthony's nonsense, then Will had done a passable job attempting to keep Hartford House afloat in the absence of a true estate manager. It was very difficult for him to think a lone Omega had been able to mastermind such things without racking up a mountain of debt, but Grandfather would never allow such flagrant spending for long and Will had shown he was a tad more than unusual in most regards. Hannibal knew firsthand how difficult it was to manage a holding this size, having watched his grandfather bear up under the burden for the years he had lived here with him. It gave him a curling tendril of admiration for Will that he had attempted such a task on his own despite what Nature had stacked against him in terms of sense, reliability, and motivation.

Yes, he was willing to concede Will was not *entirely* bereft of brains.

But he could put all that nonsense behind him now and turn his curly-haired head towards his own interests, which no doubt included watercolors, gossip, and an extraordinary amount of embroidery.

Feeling rather proud of how understanding he was being of his mate's inherent faults, Hannibal got out of bed and readied himself for the day with

Berger's assistance, wondering if Will had managed to acquire more trout for breakfast.

Will, however, was not present for breakfast, he found.

In fact, he was quite alone in the large dining room that seemed very vast and empty to him in that moment.

"I trust you are well, my Lord?" Mr. Hawkes politely inquired as breakfast for one was situated on the table for him.

"Ah, yes, Hawkes," he said, frowning softly. "I'm afraid even after so long away from war, I'm still an early riser."

"I hear it has begun anew, my Lord," Mr. Hawkes said, instructing the staff with subtle, almost imperceptible gestures. "And with greater fervor."

"Indeed, it has," Hannibal agreed, his frown deepening as there was still no sign of his spouse. "Definitive this time, I hope and pray. But tell me, Hawkes, where is my spouse this morning? Commanding breakfast in bed, I suppose? Or is the hour still too early?"

"Mr. Grant is in the estate manager's office, my Lord," Mr. Hawkes answered, delivering the paper still warm from the house maid's iron, footmen ranged along the wall as if an army waited to break their fast instead of one slightly disgruntled Marquess. "As he usually is this time of day once he finishes his ride to the village."

"When does he normally rise?" Hannibal asked, surprised. His father's Omega had slept until well after noon and complained if awakened earlier.

"Before dawn, my Lord," Hawkes said, gesturing a footman to bring over his tray. "Usually around ten minutes to five is when he has his breakfast, my Lord."

Hannibal frowned, saying, "Good gods, how industrious."

"He is often very busy, my Lord," Mr. Hawkes said, his voice never wavering from solemn monotone as Hannibal was served, "and is usually occupied until dinner."

"And my cousin?"

"He left for Fernhill early this morning after sharing toast and coffee with Mr. Grant, my Lord," Mr. Hawkes somberly told him. "It is somewhat of a tradition of theirs these past years."

Hannibal didn't like the sound of *that* one little bit. He angled a glance at the lined and proud man who had served the Ledford family since he'd been nothing more than a coal boy, knowing if anyone would give him the truth of things, it would be old Hawkes.

"What is he like, Mr. Hawkes?" he asked, taking up his silverware, an image of Will sliding his spoon into his mouth reminding him violently that he must have the tableware changed out.

"Very competent, my Lord," Hawkes said, standing to one side with dignified grace. "Mr. Grant is exceedingly meticulous. He has a very quick and curious mind that has become quite an asset to Hartford House and His Grace relies on him heavily."

Hannibal nodded slightly, mouth pursing with thought.

"What is the village summation of him?" he asked.

"I'm afraid he is rather reclusive, my Lord," Mr. Hawkes easily answered. "He is often not recognized as your spouse."

That brought an unbidden chuckle to the surface and Hannibal asked, "I assume he sets them to rights?" He rather hoped a trout or two had been involved.

"On the contrary, my Lord, he does not claim any ties to the Ledford family at all," Mr. Hawkes said, a faint note of disapproval threading its way into his voice. "It is a mistake he insists on fostering in order to do his work without distraction. But he is very kind to the staff when he is not required to be, and takes personal interest in all of us."

Hannibal mulled that one over, digging into his breakfast with sudden appetite. He recalled his conversation with Mr. Woodward and realized with some surprise that the old baker had been speaking of Will as an employee, not as Hannibal's spouse. It was quite a curious thing. Mystified, he asked,"Is that why you all refer to him as *Mr. Grant*?"

Hawkes cleared his throat, uncomfortable, and said, "He was quite insistent, my Lord, that you would find it distasteful otherwise. He seems to be unshakably convinced his place here is only a temporary one."

Hannibal frowned, idly swallowing the bite he'd taken. He honestly had not expected Will to think much of any of it, flighty as Omegas were. He imagined Will had been quite happy here at Hartford House, lording his position over Hartford Town, buying all manner of nonsense and spending his days painting watercolors no one cared to see and singing songs no one cared to listen to. He never dreamed he would hear that Will had not only *not* done just that, but had actively encouraged people to assume he was no one of consequence.

It was entirely unusual.

"Yes, well, I suppose it suits him," he said. "I cannot imagine anything an Omega would like more than being fawned over with a bevy of 'my Lords', but he is a rather unusual creature."

"He is thoughtful, polite, and unassuming," Hawkes said, rising to sudden and surprising defense of Hannibal's spouse, "and we would all very gladly drown him in 'my Lords' if he would stand for it. Perhaps, my Lord, you might have a word with him on that count. It is not entirely proper that a Marquess should be spoken to in such a common way. It is entirely beyond the pale that a noble should be confused for a commoner."

Hannibal eyed his stoic face, quite sure that Hawkes had given him a means with which to grant Will his place here while rescuing his own pride.

"I will consider it," he said, turning back to his breakfast, and was surprised by his own sincerity. He read the paper, finished his breakfast, and meandered out into the pleasant mid-morning air to walk the half mile or so the estate manager's office, where he opened the door without knocking.

He found Will there, as Hawkes had said he would be. His dark, curly-haired head was bent to his books and a pair of wire-framed spectacles were perched on his nose, giving him a scholarly air quite at home on him.

"I'm busy," he said by way of greeting, only then looking up at the man before him, "Hannibal."

"I've come to check the books," Hannibal informed him, feeling strangely like an intruder, which only irritated him. If Will was surprised to see him, he did an excellent job of concealing it.

"Yes, I imagine you have, considering," Will said, straightening. That one hung in the air, a defiance of Hannibal's opinion that Omegas lacked both the brains and motivation to do anything more than lie on their backs. It quite surprised Hannibal to hear him say such a thing. It was completely at odds with the boy who had collapsed into a heap of disgrace at very little provocation.

It was very much in keeping, however, with the young man who had slung a fish at his face in frustration.

"Hawkes assures me you've been very meticulous," Hannibal said, unsure how to rescue himself from that one. He could catch no scent from Will, no trace of his Omegan self even this close. There was no trembling, no subservience, no sign that he saw an Alpha before him and that unsettled Hannibal. *Will*, he decided, unsettled him entirely, in fact. He was too calm and collected now, as if entirely unaffected by six years of separation. He'd made it clear that he was no longer frightened of him and had no intentions of deferring to him. He was absolutely out of character for an Omega and it was absolutely uncalled for.

Hannibal took a step further into the room, hands clasped behind his back, looking it over as if searching for any sign of lack on Will's part, but actually finding a convenient excuse not to look overlong at Will's large blue eyes and poised face.

"So much has changed in the last six years," he remarked, attempting to engage him in conversation and offer an apology of sorts for his unintended insult regarding their talk of the estate last night. Too, he knew, if he had any hope of getting the child his grandfather had contracted for, he would need Will's consent. He was coming rapidly to the conclusion it would take more than a few sparkly, distracting baubles to divert Will Grant. Perhaps an allowance to make those purchases on his own and pretend independence?

In response to his meager attempt, Will only said, "Yes."

"I find the house much more pleasant now," Hannibal went on, glancing over his shoulder to see if Will would be flattered by that, at least. Appealing to an Omega's vanity was a certain way to gain their favor.

Will didn't appear to be flattered in the least. He was looking at his balances again. Instead of fawning delight at his accomplishments being noticed, he merely said, "It needed updating. I didn't want your grandfather living in unseemly conditions."

"Ah."

"We used the estate's surplus, of course," Will said, lifting his gaze again with something like fire in his eyes to add, "In case you were worried I was spending your inheritance."

Hannibal frowned.

Will smiled slightly, a flitting ghost of a thing, and idly tapped the quill of his pen against the desk, waiting with polite impatience for Hannibal to do whatever it was he wanted to do and get out of his hair.

Hannibal had never been made to feel like a pest before and he didn't like it one bit.

"I'm thinking of bringing my daughter here now that the house is so well-kept," he said, watching Will carefully for signs of distress, wishing now to get a reaction out of him, some sign that he could be provoked as he'd been yesterday when he'd been barefoot, unkempt, and entirely furious.

Will tilted his head and he said with an elegant shrug, "I assumed you would want her near you if you decide to stay."

Annoyed, Hannibal said, "I'm thinking of bringing her mother as well."

"I never imagined you would separate a child from their mother," Will said, tickling the tip of his own nose with the quill now, bored with their conversation.

Bored.

Hannibal found himself incredulous, to say the least.

"Let me know when she is to arrive and I'll pack," Will said, standing up and straightening his papers.

"Pack?" Hannibal asked, a faint tone of condescension coloring his voice. Had he found something that bothered his spouse at last? Was the prospect of living here with Hannibal's mistress and child finally enough to send him into a typical Omegan temper tantrum?

"I would imagine she'll be needing the adjoining suite," Will briskly said, setting his desk to rights and straightening to meet Hannibal's gaze without reserve. "It would seem strange, after all, if the spouse you despise has more status in the house than the woman you've chosen to have children with."

It was so damnably practical that Hannibal scowled at him, unable to find the smallest trace of the boy he'd been married to in the young man before him.

"And where, pray tell, would you go?"

Will shrugged again as if he hadn't thought about it before, saying, "The Capital, perhaps. It's been six years, I could visit my sisters, or take over another one of your estates and make it productive... *well*, as productive as I can manage with my feeble intellect and inconstant nature. It's no business of yours what I do."

Hannibal bit back his retort at the mocking way Will sent his own words back at him, unwilling to open that particular door. Before he could sufficiently recover, Will moved the opposite way around the desk, avoiding him, and headed out the door, calling, "Everything should be in order. If not, feel free to blame my empty-headed vanity for claiming so."

Thinking things had not gone at all as he had planned, Hannibal settled at the desk and opened the account books with a heaving sigh of bored resignation, the faint trace of Will's warmth evaporating quickly with his absence.

⌘⌘⌘

Will took the long way back up, cutting back across the hedgerow to meander through the garden. He knew every square foot of Hartford House inside and out —the gardens, the vast forests where game slid sly-eyed and fearless, the echoing halls with their disapproving portraits, the labyrinthine passages that ran between the walls connecting the rooms in a maze of escape routes, the cellars with their bellowing furnaces spilling heat up waiting pipes. He knew it all as intimately as he knew himself, but that did not make it his. Neither familiarity nor a Duke's decree would give him a right to stay here. Not now. Not anymore.

He kept hearing Hannibal telling him that he would bring his mistress and daughter here.

He kept hearing his own calm reply, said with a detachment that had surprised even himself.

Because he didn't feel detached. He felt insulted and, above all, angry to the depths of his soul that all he had worked so hard for would be lost all over again, as it had been in his father's house, and it would not matter if Hartford House was his. He could not imagine dislodging Hannibal Ledford from his ancestral home if he decided to stay. Will would be forced to leave, or else spend the rest of his days living alongside his spouse's real and desired family, once more the object of pity and ridicule.

It took a long time of walking to work off the worst of it and remind himself that he had no say in things. Hannibal was his husband and, by law, could do as he pleased. Will, as his Omegan spouse, had no other choice but to accept it.

But that didn't mean he had to accept it gladly *or* easily.

"Mr. Grant, His Grace would like to see you," Will was told the moment he made his way up to the House proper, Mr. Hawkes appropriately blank-faced. Will was, however, well acquainted with the many types of blank faces the aging butler could give and knew he was excited about something.

"Thank you, Mr. Hawkes," he said, striding through towards the Duke's suite, ignoring the flurry of servants around him but wondering why they were so energetic.

He knocked softly and let himself in, calling ahead, "Grandfather? It's Will."

"Ah! Will! Come, come here!" Grandfather said, sounding more lively and aware than Will had heard him in months.

He found the elderly Duke up and dressed and already in his wheelchair, looking such a picture of health that Will wondered at it.

"Come here, my dear," His Grace said again, gesturing him closer to the desk where he was seated.

"Has something happened?" Will asked, crossing the room to lay a fond hand on the man's shoulder, the only affection he ever allowed himself. "You seem very hale this afternoon."

"I am feeling much relieved to have this business with Hannibal settled," Grandfather said, pouring over something before him.

"*Is* it settled then?" Will asked, unable to bring himself to ask what would become of him.

"Yes, all neat and tidy," the Duke said, scrawling names down. "Nothing to worry yourself over, my dear! I'm hosting a small dinner party to celebrate Hannibal's return and your marriage, as we never had a formal reception. There will be another, no doubt, when you remove to the Capital for the Season, but this one is for family and close friends."

"Grandfather, I don't think holding any sort of celebration of my being here is all that Hannibal could ask for," Will said, voice tightening with worry as he gazed at the length of the list. "I have already quite ruined one homecoming for him. It wouldn't do to ruin another."

"Nonsense!" Grandfather said, chuffing his displeasure. "I have been absent of company some six years now for the sake of his temper! The least he can do is indulge me in this."

"I have no desire to burden you, Grandfather," Will said, his thoughts still tangled up in Hannibal's statement, "but I need a wiser, clearer head than mine right now."

"Well I'm certainly older, my darling child," the Duke said, amiable with him. "What is it? Why are you so pensive, Will?"

"I think it would be appropriate if I leave Hartford House," Will said, concern pinching his voice small, a distant echo of the frightened, uncertain Omega he'd hoped to leave behind him. "Perhaps after the dinner party."

"Certainly not!" His Grace said, indignant. "Hartford House is your home!"

"No, Hartford House is *Hannibal's* home. *He* is a Ledford," Will said, feeling the pain of that statement deeply. "He should be able to live here comfortably and he cannot do so while I remain. Perhaps if I am gone he will grow bored of life in the countryside on his own and return to the life he enjoys. Will you not reconsider your decision to give the estate to me?"

The Duke's keen brown eyes searched him, knowing he was withholding more than he was sharing but willing to let him keep his secrets if he chose.

"I am increasingly less comfortable here," Will admitted, his voice barely more than a whisper. "In truth, I do not belong here and I never have."

"You *do* belong here and I will not allow you to dash off at the first snarl from my grandson! Now, don't fret, Will," Grandfather said, patting his free hand but briefly, knowing very well Will disliked being touched by anyone anymore. "I will see that you are well cared for, hm? And being well cared for means having a proper introduction to polite Society. You are a noble, Will Grant, in your own right, your status from my family aside. You have no reason to hide your face here at Hartford House and Hannibal can help undo some of the damage he has done."

"It is the damage *I* have done that he fears," Will mused, still thinking of their meeting in his office, "as he is even now reviewing the ledgers for some clue of my treachery."

The Duke snorted and laughed shortly, saying, "He'll be lucky to find a stray penny."

He handed Will the list he'd been working on and said, "Run along and give that to Hawkes, my darling boy. I expect he and Mrs. Henderson will organize as they always do."

"Yes, Grandfather," Will said, wondering what on earth the old Alpha had bartered to settle his argument with Hannibal. He could not imagine what Grandfather's intentions were regarding his place here concerning his grandson and heir when the disposal of Hartford House was such a large wedge between them.

Troubled and thoughtful, he sought out Mr. Hawkes and handed over the list, asking, "Is this what has the staff so excited?"

"Yes, Mr. Grant," Mr. Hawkes said, fair beaming with delight. "At long last this house will be as it was. Mind you, most of the younger staff will be quite silly, but I am pleased with the announcement all the same."

"I confess I am not," Will said, distracted and uneasy. When Mr. Hawkes arched a brow in polite inquiry, he said, "His Grace wishes to make this a celebration of Hannibal's marriage."

"You mean *your* marriage, Mr. Grant?" Mr. Hawkes inquired, his tone delicate. "I should think some celebration is in order. You have been six years out of Society, Mr. Grant. If Lord Clarges intends to stay, as he has said, then I expect Society will be rather more present."

Will frowned, quailing at the thought.

"His Grace is starting small, which is some comfort, Mr. Grant, is it not?"

"Not nearly as much as banishment, Mr. Hawkes," Will said, giving him a weak smile. "Which I should prefer to Lord Clarges taking the opportunity to denounce me in public."

Mr. Hawkes sighed heartily. "I am very fond of you, Mr. Grant."

"As I am of you, Mr. Hawkes," Will said, his smile genuine but worn with too much thought.

"I would like to reassure you that Lord Clarges is too much a gentleman to take such action," Mr. Hawkes told him, solid in his faith.

"I wish I could share your certainty," Will said, exhaling on a sigh, his stomach tight with dread at the eventuality of Ledford relatives and Hannibal's life without him descending on him in due time. He very much wished to tell Jimmy to pack for him and remove himself to another estate altogether, but no matter what happened, Hartford House belonged to him and he had a responsibility to care for it properly, if only for Hannibal's own children.

"Have my mare saddled, Mr. Hawkes," Will said, deciding to stick to his schedule. "I'm late for my rounds."

"Yes, Mr. Grant, of course."

⌘⌘⌘

Hannibal found nothing untoward in the books. Indeed, the more he delved into Will's work, the more admiration he began to feel. For all intents and purposes, his Omegan spouse had dragged Hartford House up by the bootstraps and forced it into screaming compliance, if the early years of his efforts were to be believed. His deft business sense had allowed for profits that stacked with each year, building on investments made the year prior. He had to hand it to him, Will Grant knew how to plan long-term and was not one to indulge in quick schemes.

Tenancy was up to full capacity, and Will had, with Grandfather's permission, even purchased and annexed packets of land from the impoverished, nearly extinct family of nobles who had once neighbored them. Hannibal was left wondering what on earth he planned to do with it.

He was well and truly astounded and, truth be told, rather ashamed of himself regarding the assumptions he'd made about Will's intelligence. In Hannibal's six-year absence, Will had managed to make headway no estate manager had been able to in decades. It was no big secret that great Houses like theirs were falling to decay and bad business all around them. Seeing his ancestral home thriving where others failed brought a quiet sense of pride to him. Pride in Will's actions. Pride in Will's keen foresight and admirable mind.

He was no simple, childlike dimwit idling away in a drawing room wasting space, air, and money. He'd seen a problem, found the cause, effected a solution, and did the job better than the man who'd come before him.

It was far better a job than Hannibal himself might have managed, he knew. He wondered if there was any way in which Will Grant betrayed his Omegan nature, as he had yet to see it.

With nothing to pick on and deprived of Will's presence, Hannibal quietly left the tidy little office and took the path back up to the house proper, aware in a vague sort of way that there was unusual activity among the domestics. They were very much like a disturbed bees' nest, buzzing and milling in agitation.

A footman spied him coming up and hopped to get the door, even if it was unorthodox for a Marquess to use the servant's entrance. Several of the other house staff stared at him in consternation, caught in the middle of their cigarettes and letters, unsure how to react.

Hannibal ignored them and entered the house, moving with swift, easy grace down the hall and turning up the servants' stairs to emerge on the main floor near the front door in time to hear Will request his horse.

"Saddle my stallion as well, Mr. Hawkes," he called, gloating somewhat when Will was startled into looking at him, his annoyance apparent on his lovely face. It was quickly replaced with blank indifference and his face just as quickly averted, which left Hannibal scowling as he reached him.

Mr. Hawkes wisely escaped out of earshot to give instructions to a footman, leaving Will alone with Hannibal in the foyer.

Hannibal smoothed his waistcoat, aware he was grooming again but unable to prevent it, not that his mild peacocking made a bit of difference to his composed spouse.

"Back so soon, Lord Clarges? I had thought you would take rather more time to thoroughly investigate my wrongdoings," Will said, turning away to present Hannibal with his profile and the slender sweep of his shoulders.

"Yes, well," Hannibal said, shifting slightly as if he'd done something wrong, which only irritated him. "Naturally, I could not take the time to look through all of it. I will have the accountants come in for that, though I do admit to being curious as to why you are amassing land like a general."

"Who knows," Will said, cocking his head to angle an irate look Hannibal's way. He wasn't wearing his spectacles and his eyes were large and gleaming, the sparkling color shifting from blue to green and stormy gray depending on how the light struck.

Hannibal found it vastly unsettling to see. Proper people's eyes did *not* change colors or cause a gentleman's gaze to linger overlong where it should not. He could not fathom how Will could be so uncommon in every respect he was capable and thought it must be from sheer spite. "Though I am sure you have your sound theories."

"Considering what I know of your capacity for violence, I shall keep my opinions to myself," Hannibal said, too proud to admit he was brimming with curiosity to know what Will had planned, as he was far too intelligent to have made the purchases impulsively.

"If you wish to ensure your safety from my violence," Will said, "then you have my delighted permission to avoid me."

"Nonsense, I will accompany you," Hannibal said, picking a bit of lint from his jacket and dropping it with a wrinkle of his noble nose. "It is Grandfather's wish that we spend time together."

"That was your grandfather's wish six years ago," Will said.

Before Hannibal could scold him for being so abrupt and surly, Mr. Hawkes returned to open the door for them to meet their saddled horses on the drive.

"Thank you, Mr. Hawkes," Will said, striding swiftly away to mount his horse with feline grace, settling into the saddle and gathering up the reins in his slender, deft hands.

"Thank you, Hawkes," Hannibal echoed, rather shamed into it as Will was so persistently polite to the staff. *Entirely* uncalled for, in Hannibal's book. He settled into the saddle and turned to tell Will as much when he realized his mate was already riding away.

As if he simply couldn't wait to get away from him.

From *him*.

Offended, Hannibal urged his stallion after Will's sturdy little mare and overtook him on the lane heading opposite Hartford Town. The dirt trail Hannibal knew from his childhood here which led on to the next town, worn flat over the years by the merchants moving back and forth over the land, had been replaced as well with cobblestone. The entirety of the area had, in his absence, been connected up to the greater roadwork. It was quite the undertaking, he realized. A road to connect Hartford House and Hartford Town to the main roads was one thing, but finding it extended past those bounds was even more impressive.

"These roads are quite an improvement," he said, hoping to coax Will out of his silence. "It is a wonder we never had one in before now, really. It must make everything much easier for everyone."

"It does," Will said, a soft smile curving his full lips. Hannibal caught a bare glimpse of it before Will turned away, ahead of him enough that it blocked Hannibal's view of his face.

"Long overdue," Hannibal decided, straightening in his saddle and moving abreast of him. "Very clever, though, whoever brought it to fruition. No doubt the City Council."

"No doubt," Will said, chuckling, turning his head away again when Hannibal glanced over at him to catch a bare glimpse of his lovely profile. It brought an uncomfortable reminder to both of them of that day six years ago when Hannibal had reacted so violently to little more than Will simply looking away.

Hannibal found himself thinking of that day and frowning at his memory of Will, slight and far too young, staring up at him with tear-filled, terrified, bewildered blue eyes. It gave him a pang of guilt that refused to be quashed when its source was so enticingly present and entirely changed.

"I assumed you had better ways in which to spend your time, Lord Clarges," Will said, riding with purpose but not precisely haste, "than waste it on me."

"I had arranged a gap in my calendar to come deal with Grandfather," Hannibal said, realizing Will's destination was Gold Meadow Farm, the first of the estate's farms let out to rent. "I will have to make further arrangements, of course, considering I intend to stay. For now, I will ensure Hartford House is not suffering from your handling."

The halfhearted remark got the intended reaction. Will cut a sideways look at him that was quite menacing. Hannibal feigned not to have noticed, though he was pleased that his needling, at least, got a response.

"And what is our business here?" he asked instead, seeing the farmer and his older son turned out in the front yard, clearly expecting his visit.

"Every first Tuesday of the month I get reports from the dairies," Will said, lifting a hand in greeting. "Production, headcount, the status of their needful items, any concerns they might have."

"Goodness, how clever," Hannibal said, brows rising, unwilling to admit to Will himself just how intelligent he found him. Unable to resist needling him, he asked, "Who told you that you should do such a thing?"

Will ignored him, choosing instead to call a greeting ahead and urge his mare faster. He drew to a stop, swung down with supple grace, and was shaking hands with the farmer before Hannibal arrived.

"Ah! Lord Clarges! I'd heard you was back, m'Lord! Riding the rounds this morning? Seeing how the old homestead is coming along, m'Lord?"

The pink-cheeked, rather round fellow beamed at him while a strapping huge lad strode off with Will towards the sheds, already in deep conversation.

It was fairly irritating to see.

"Forgive me," Hannibal said, easing from his stallion's back. "When I was a child, this was the Osgood family farm."

"Ah, well, we're the Pattons," the man said, beaming at him. "The Osgoods moved to a bigger farm, bless 'em. Mr. Grant found them a tenancy that suited them and their hogs better and had us in, since we got the best heifers in the area!"

Hannibal looked around with critical eyes, noting the tidy state of the place, the signs of a happy and thriving home. He could see the cattle in the distance, ranging unpenned but for the bull, who was safely enclosed. The lane passed by with a neat cobblestone path from the dairy branching out to meet it.

"And does your situation here suit you?" Hannibal asked, lacking any sort of good conversation material. He very much doubted Farmer Patton was either interested in or aware of the latest opera in the Capital. "The Osgoods had a devilish time getting their meat to market, if I recall correctly."

"Oh, aye, m'Lord, they did," Patton told him, unmindful of a pig-tailed little girl who ran up and started swinging from his burly arm. Hannibal saw a whole passel of round and bright-eyed children slowly emerging from the house, enticed by the presence of an unfamiliar face. "But the lane here is a blessing, indeed! Halves the time to get to town, and makes it easy to reach the road to the Capital. Why, once the rail comes, we'll be fair set on, won't we?"

"Indeed," Hannibal murmured, trying to parse out where on earth the rail would run through this area since all of their available land was being used.

Except the land his clever little spouse had begun parceling up in his absence.

"Not to step out of line, Lord Clarges, but I wanted to say how glad we all are that His Grace hired in Mr. Grant," Patton said, dragging Hannibal back to their conversation so abruptly it must have shown on his face, because the man promptly added, "It's just that he's done so much for us, your Lordship, investing in our businesses, having all the roads built—which put a fair number of men into honest work—even setting up buyers in the Capital. We all hope once you return you'll keep him on for all the good he's done here."

"This road?" Hannibal echoed, dumbfounded. "This road right here?"

"Er... yes, m'Lord," Patton said. "It was one of the first things he did when he took over. Built the roads up, and didn't even up the share for Hartford House, said it would pay for itself, and it has."

"Wait, Patton," Hannibal said, his surprise about the paved road giving way to genuine bewilderment. "Did you say you hope I'll *keep him on*? I wouldn't exactly word it as *hiring him in*, sir."

There was a long, cautious silence. Hannibal could see Will returning with the farmer's older son at a sedate walk with less urgent conversation now.

"Begging your pardon, m'Lord," Patton said, unsure where he'd gone wrong. "But as your land agent—"

"*That*," Hannibal said, pointing at Will, "is my *spouse!*"

Patton stared at him, flummoxed into silence.

"Why do you have that look on your face as if you're confused?" Hannibal demanded, scowling to see Will look up at that boy, tipping his face to meet the smile of the much taller man.

"Er... 'cause I'm confused, my Lord," Patton offered. "Not to speak out of turn, but most times a noble don't marry their land agent—"

"*He is not my land agent*," Hannibal said, frustrated. "He is my spouse! He was my spouse six years ago when he first came here, whatever he allowed people to believe afterward! Why do you still look confused?"

Patton's eyes slid to Will. With no other recourse to soothe an addled and powerful Alpha, he said, "It's just... Well, he's a man, ain't he? It isn't every day a Duke's heir marries a m—"

"He is *Omegan*!" Hannibal said, pointing at Will so that there was no mistake. "*Omegan*! How is this a mystery? Why has no one come to this conclusion? He is Omegan and—he is smiling." Hannibal squinted at Will to confirm it, then scowled and looked at Patton. "Why is he smiling?"

"I wouldn't dare say, m'Lord," Patton told him, looking at Will with a fresh perspective. His voice was thoughtful and vague when he added, "Omegan? That explains why he's so pretty."

"*Pretty*?" Hannibal echoed, rounding on him, shocked that someone might make such an observation about his spouse. "I beg your pardon?"

"Beautiful, m'Lord," Patton hastily corrected, no doubt thinking he had offended his future Duke with such a summation. "He's very beautiful, m'Lord."

"Yes, he *is*," Hannibal said, surprised into agreeing, unexpected as it was. "And he is currently *smiling* at your son. He never smiles at me. Not in any kind of nice way."

"I'm sure it's just his temperament, Lord Clarges," Patton said, thoroughly exhausted by their conversation. "He's a solemn little fellow, truth be told. Stern as a vicar most times, but very good at his job."

Patton flushed brick red, embarrassed to have brought up Will's questionable status as the Hartford estate manager.

"Mr. Patton," Will called as he reached them, irritated when Hannibal moved to insert himself between the Patton lad and his spouse. Shrugging it off as more of his nonsense, Will said, "Everything seems to be going well. Have you any particular concern for me?"

"No, my Lord," Patton stammered, flushing harder and looking away.

"My *Lord*?" Will whispered, looking from Patton's round face to Hannibal. "I see. Well, I did mean to let you know that there will be someone replacing me very soon."

"Well, we understand, yer Lordship, don't we?" Patton said, eager to make it up to Will. "A-and I apologize for how I've treated you in the past."

"How have you treated me that you believe you need to apologize for it, Mr. Patton?" Will asked, grim and increasingly unhappy.

"Well, I mean... We didn't know, your Lordship," Patton said, fumbling over the words. "I mean, we never would have said some things in front of you or spoken so easy with you had we known you was a noble and an Omega."

Will flinched, but managed to nod softly. "Yes, well, I am certain my replacement will suit everyone much better. Thank you, Mr. Patton, for your kindness in indulging me so long."

Will quickly mounted his mare, ignoring Hannibal's sharp call after him. Hannibal excused himself without further ado and went after him, catching up to Will in the midst of pasturage where he turned off onto a dirt trail.

"I suppose you're very pleased with yourself," Will said, refusing to look back at him, stiff with offense.

"Is there some reason I should be ashamed of myself?" Hannibal asked. "Why on earth did they believe you're the land agent?"

"Because I *am*!" Will snapped, guiding the horse along the trail.

"Well, in a manner of speaking," Hannibal said, conceding the point. "You have substituted in the role admirably. But they do not seem to be aware you are also my spouse. I assumed Hawkes was exaggerating when he said no one knows who you are. The townsfolk I can understand, but certainly the tenants must know! That is not a secret that would keep in such close company!"

Will said nothing, which only served to rankle Hannibal.

"Why did you never correct them?"

"To what end, Lord Clarges?" Will asked, ducking low to clear a tree branch which Hannibal nearly rode straight into, he was so intent on his mate.

"Well..." His reasoning failed him. His assumptions, he knew, would not sound the same coming from his mouth as they did in his head. "Because you could."

"Not everyone does things because they *can*," Will reminded him, letting the mare pick up her pace once they were clear of the small hedgerow. "Not everyone is like *you*, Lord Clarges."

"What is that supposed to mean?" Hannibal asked, annoyed.

"I am not lowering myself to a discussion with you on this subject," Will said, aware of Hannibal's darkening scowl. "Suffice it to say, I had no more desire to be associated with you then, Lord Clarges, than I do now."

"Do you seek to offend with every word? You are my spouse," Hannibal said, huffing with indignation. "Your *desire to be associated with me* notwithstanding."

Will pointedly ignored him.

It was entirely unsettling.

Hannibal glowered at his back, annoyed. He could not fathom why Will had kept his status a secret. He would have imagined Will would have soundly corrected anyone who misidentified him, Hawkes' assertions notwithstanding. His father's concubine would have flown into a spitting rage to be mistaken for a land agent. She no doubt would have died of self-immolation to have actually performed the duties of one.

She certainly would not have done so with anywhere near the success Will Grant had.

Frowning, Hannibal cleared his throat and loudly scolded, "You should have told me the road was your idea."

"It is infrastructure, Lord Clarges, not scientific advancement," Will said, refusing to look back at him. "It hardly matters whose idea it was. What matters is that it is there and it does its duty."

"Well," Hannibal said, pride thoroughly pricked, and expertly so. "How interesting to expect the road to do its duty when you will not."

Will did look at him then, a flash of angry, narrowed blue eyes filled with far too much consideration for Hannibal's comfort.

He was very glad there were no trout at hand.

"Pray tell me, Lord Clarges, what duty I have failed," Will said, gazing steadily at him. "As I recall, it was not I who left Hartford House in a snit!"

Hannibal had the good manners to flush, Will was pleased to see.

"This is the land you asked about," Will said, back to doing brisk business. He drew his mare to a stop at the start of a flat meadow and looked out across the rolling waves of grass with the fond pride of a mother beholding their brood.

Hannibal's eyes flicked over him and he shifted, discomfited by Will's lovely profile. He recalled his irate exchange with Patton and bristled, thinking of Will smiling at that hulking great boy and himself defending Will's beauty with such instant and automatic affront.

But he was beautiful. To say otherwise was a blatant lie, and the proof was present before him.

Will glanced his way, his dark brows slamming down over his bright blue eyes when he caught Hannibal inspecting him.

"If my appearance offends you, Lord Clarges," he said, his low voice dangerously soft. "It would behoove you not to stare at me."

"I thought you had a twig in your hair," Hannibal said, looking at the meadow with a perfunctory air.

So much for honesty.

"And what am I to make of this?" he asked, irritably aware that he sat straighter in his saddle with his shoulders squared, spurred to present an appealing image in the face of Will's frank disapproval. "Or might this have something to do with the rail line Mr. Patton spoke of?"

"The rail line is cutting north from Chesterton," Will said, oblivious to his jibes and not the least bit surprised that Hannibal had gleaned his intentions. He pointed his slender finger in the direction of the town he'd mentioned. "I've spoken with the surveyors and seen the plans; they intend to bring the rail straight through here and on to North Larkstow."

"So you purchased the land before they did," Hannibal mused. "They have the law of the land."

"I have offered them the use of the land without argument if they would place a station at the south end of Hartford Town," Will said, soothing his mare when she shifted beneath him.

Hannibal's brows rose with surprise. He was impressed all over again with Will's forethought, and was forced to admit that his spouse was surprisingly insightful and bold on top of being alarmingly clever.

115

"The rail company agreed," Will said, no sign of pride or bragging about him. "It will profoundly benefit your tenants and the townsfolk, and improve the distribution of their goods to their buyers."

Hannibal absorbed that, considering all the facets to such an advantage.

"The rail line will pay for the station, of course," Will said, taking his silence for disapproval. "And I negotiated a lifetime contract for a flat rate for any goods sent under the Hartford stamp."

"You are very determined that our people are well served, aren't you?" Hannibal asked, a smile tugging at his mouth when Will huffed softly, impatient with even the hint of praise.

"It was my place as the estate manager to see that the estate is productive," Will said, turning away to give Hannibal a view of his dark curls and the delicate curve of his ear peeking out at him. "For that, the tenants must be productive. It was all necessary, Hannibal."

"I realize that," Hannibal said, admiring Will's quick, decisive actions to secure the estate's success. "You surprise me, Will."

Will shot another glance at him, his dark glare softening somewhat when he realized that Hannibal wasn't disapproving of him.

"You are truly unusual," Hannibal said.

"I am practical," Will said, blushing slightly and turning his mare to escape Hannibal's handsome smile and his unconscious, charismatic Alpha draw. "I have a duty to ensure that this place does not suffer in your absence. So tell me, Lord Clarges, do you still believe Hartford House is teetering on the brink of ruin?"

"No," Hannibal said, surprising Will when he reined his stallion around in front of him to get an unobstructed view of his face. "I believe you have acted with impressive verve for someone with no practical experience in running an estate. I stand corrected."

Will's eyes widened so much they showed white all around. His expression of stunned shock was so amusing that Hannibal chuckled softly and told him, "Even my stubbornness has its limits, Will."

Will got himself under control and averted his face again, tipping his head down in that effacing way of his, managing to turn his mare at the same time so that he swung away towards the next farm on his rounds.

Something about his reaction made Hannibal's grin widen, warmth blossoming in his chest for no reason he could imagine. He reasoned it was because he'd rendered Will speechless.

But deep down he knew it was because he was finding Will to be far more intriguing than he'd ever imagined.

Chapter 8

They parted ways in Hartford House once more after all the rounds were passed, Will upstairs in a preoccupied rush and Hannibal with plans to see his grandfather.

"Ah! Lord Clarges!" Mr. Hawkes said as he swept open the door, no doubt having watched carefully to time things to the second. Hannibal knew he had no hopes of catching old Hawkes off guard, no matter that he had lingered behind fussing over his stallion before handing him off to the stable hand. "Welcome home."

"Is Grandfather up?" Hannibal asked.

"Yes, my Lord, he is," Hawkes said, accompanying him to his grandfather's suite and rapping smartly on the door for him, announcing, "Your Grace, Lord Clarges is here."

"Honestly," Hannibal said, equally amused and annoyed. He allowed Hawkes to open the door for him and strode inside, drawing up short when he saw his Grandfather at his small desk, head bent to his work. "Well, well, aren't you feeling much improved today, Grandfather. Not so near Death's door, are we?"

"Ha! Not as near as you no doubt wish," his Grandfather said, angling his head to give Hannibal a grin. "I'm busy, boy."

"Busy with what, pray tell?" Hannibal asked, coming closer to see his Grandfather working on a letter of some sort. "Plotting again?"

"Not in regards to you this time. We're throwing a dinner party," Grandfather said, leaning back in his chair to look up at his grandson, who came to lean against the desk with a thoughtful frown on his handsome face. "You look very much like your father, Hannibal. Very much like him, indeed."

"I have rather unsteady memories of him, Grandfather," Hannibal said, thoughts on his encounter with Will. "But I would suppose I do look like him, as I look like you."

"Why are you here?" the Duke asked, pushing him out of his curious imaginings. "Hm? Pestering?"

"I came to check on you, you old goat," Hannibal said, smirking at the unholy gleam in his grandfather's eyes. "Honestly, I would have thought you near expiring by now, yet here you are all dapper and young, almost as if you were having me on."

"Well, nothing's to be done about it now if I were," Roland said, unperturbed. "Have you been lazing about all morning?"

"No, I was with Will today," Hannibal said, then automatically corrected, "Rather, I *accompanied* Will today. I rode out with him on his rounds. Is he always so persistently engaged? I had hoped to have a chance for a quiet moment, but he scurried upstairs the second we returned. He is deadly difficult to pin into place for long. Very fixated on being busy."

"He has his hands full running the household as well as doing the work *you* were to have done!" Grandfather said, scolding him. "And very well, mind you. He isn't the boy you met six years ago, Hannibal. He's grown up and he's grown up well. Gave you the slip, did he?"

"Did you know he's up before the sun?" Hannibal asked, a thoughtful frown on his mouth. He knew his grandfather likely knew everything there was to know about Will by now after six years sequestered with him, but felt compelled to add, "And all that business with the rail line. Wicked clever maneuvering, isn't it?"

"He's a very clever boy," Roland said, leveling a curious glance at him to measure his sincerity. "Have you managed to be friendly with him, at least?"

"Yes, of course... well, not entirely," Hannibal admitted, a little uneasy when he thought of how he'd provoked him earlier in his office. It reminded him of what he'd said about his mistress, Alana, and his plans for the future, which did not include the solemn, quick-tempered Omega he'd spent such an unusual morning with. Flustered, he added, "We did start off on the wrong foot."

"He told me you were going over the ledgers," Roland said, amused, knowing full well he'd found nothing to complain of.

Hannibal flushed, rather annoyed with his grandfather's delight in his discomfit. "I asked about the books, yes. He very politely agreed I should have a look due to his infirmity of the mind."

Roland cackled, well amused. "And what was your summation? Can he tell his decimals from his zeros?"

119

"Please don't start," Hannibal warned, exasperated. "I can say with complete confidence I would never wish to pit myself against Will in the case of numbers. I would much rather give him a trout."

Grandfather's gaze turned quizzical, bewildered by the odd statement.

"I made the mistake yesterday of questioning Will and Anthony on the matter of an afternoon spent fishing," Hannibal admitted, frowning at the memory. "He slapped me with the trout he'd caught."

Grandfather's lips twitched against a smile.

"He then turned around and fed it to me at dinner."

Roland guffawed, clapping his hands once in sharp appreciation, saying through his laughter, "Oh, I very much wish I had seen *that!*"

"He is nothing like I imagined he would be," Hannibal confessed, managing to mostly disguise his own amusement. "One moment he's smiting me with a fish like an angry god and the next he barely pays me any mind at all."

"He has very little patience with nonsense, Hannibal, which you," Grandfather said, patting his hand, "are unfortunately filled with at times. Especially on the subject of Will's gender."

"I find myself goading him to see what he will do, because I can get nothing from him in the least," Hannibal said, confounded by his observations from the day. "There was a moment where we were conversing and I surprised him, but from then on he kept his distance."

"He is respecting your wishes, Hannibal," Grandfather said, his amusement fading to something like sympathy as he looked at his bewildered and upended grandson. "If there is distance between you, it is because you have only ever told him you wish for it."

Frustrated, Hannibal restlessly drummed his fingernails against the desk, mulling that one over. Even during the rest of the rounds Will had remained closed to him, a surface of calm that refused to be breached, as if one slip had steeled him against another like it.

"How am I to close that distance when I cannot know his mind?" he asked, entirely confounded. "He is impossible to read! I do not recall he was so reserved when he first came here. It seemed the least of his thoughts showed on his face."

"Yes, well, he's very different now," he was told. "And no doubt happy to sharpen his claws on you. Make no mistake, Hannibal, that Omega has claws aplenty."

"I told him I wanted to bring my daughter and her mother here and he *shrugged*," Hannibal said, straightening to put his hands on his lean hips, perplexed. He looked down when his grandfather chuckled, annoyed he could find anything humorous in it. "What is so funny?"

"Ah, that explains some things. Hannibal, I keep telling you he isn't the same boy you married," Roland wheezed, finding it quite amusing. "What did you expect, eh? Did you want him to throw a fit? Stomp and toss things and create a row?"

Hannibal frowned, not sure how to answer without sounding foolish, especially given what he now knew about Will's temperament as well as about Will's character.

"You keep trying to force him to act as the Omega you've decided is typical and the truth of the matter is we're all simply human, Hannibal," Grandfather said, shaking his head. "*One* Omega ruined you. *One* Omega imprinted these ideas on you, leading you to these terrible assumptions, and you've been trying to pin them onto Will since the day you met."

"He's an Omega, Grandfather," Hannibal quietly said, falling back on old rejoinders from habit, uncomfortable with the guilt he felt, and the anger even the mention of his father's concubine could stir. Flushing with renewed upset, he said, "When it comes down to it, whatever feats they manage to accomplish, in the end they are what Nature has made them."

"As are we all, yet you don't seem to be ravaging young ladies every time you go into rut," Grandfather scolded.

"We have more self control—"

"Oh, *nonsense*," Grandfather scoffed. "Yes, they are softer by nature, designed to yield with grace and be a source of comfort and beauty for Alphas, but that doesn't make them *less* than us, Hannibal."

Hannibal smirked, saying, "I can hardly picture Will *yielding* or *comforting*, Grandfather."

"No, thanks to you," Roland sourly said, surprising him. "Oh, don't give me that look, Hannibal. You crushed that poor child at a time when he was still forming his own sense of self. You made him look in a mirror and despise what he saw looking back at him. He changed himself purposefully, Hannibal."

Hannibal looked away, brows drawing together in consternation.

"That was not my intention—"

"The hell it wasn't!" Grandfather flared, whacking him on his backside with the same sure sharpness as he had used when Hannibal was a child, shocking him to no end. "You surly brute! You wanted to make him sorry for being what he is and you succeeded. Other Omegas his age already have children, status, a *home* and spouse they can be proud of. Will has this estate. You took the rest from him, made him feel like it was all nonsense, pitiful, laughable nonsense. In the six years since you've left, I have *yet* to see Will deliberately catch his own reflection. You left scars on him Hannibal, on the inside where they don't show but hurt all the same."

"If Will is shy of his own reflection, it's no matter to me," Hannibal said, perhaps more sharply than he intended due to the growing guilt he felt when faced with the consequences of his actions and how deeply they had affected Will. "If anything, at least he isn't vain."

"He *should* be," Grandfather darkly said. "You're the envy of everyone who meets him, Hannibal, and you're too stubborn to see it. Even though he hides himself behind those spectacles and hides his shape in bleak clothing, he can't change the fact that he's an *unmated Omega* and it burns him up from the inside out that he can't change it."

Hannibal drew in a deep breath, unwilling to get into an argument with his grandfather.

"He hates what he is because of *you*," Roland said, smacking him again for good measure and scowling at him. "I'll be damned if you're bringing your mistress and daughter, cute as they no doubt are, here into this house, onto this estate, the last thing Will has that he takes any pride in. I won't let you do that to him, Hannibal. You've done quite enough as it is, walking away for six years and leaving him in pieces behind you. I'm half a mind to sign it all over to him in perpetuity no matter the circumstances, just to make sure you don't do anything more to him once I've died!"

"Grandfather, please, you know as well as I do that I would do nothing of the sort! And you can hardly threaten me with something you've very nearly already done!" Hannibal said, incensed by the mere mention of such folly and reminded all over again of why he'd left in the first place. In an impulsive attempt to push back against his grandfather's scolding, he irritably said, "To be capable of tormenting Will, I'd have to have even a modicum of interest in that creature you all foisted off on me and, believe me, *I don't*."

Grandfather coughed then, stammering out, "Ah! Will! Come in! Come in, my darling boy!"

Hannibal flushed, realizing Will had come in just in time to hear him speak. His patrician, lovely features were schooled to show nothing, however, no outward sign he'd heard Hannibal talk of him in such a way.

More scars on the inside, perhaps.

"Excuse me," Hannibal said, drawing a deep, calming breath. He noted with a frown the wide berth Will gave him as he moved into the room.

"I am sorry, I didn't mean to intrude; here is my report from the farms," Will said, barely sparing Hannibal a glance.

"It's rude to enter a room unannounced," Hannibal said, scowling, annoyed and embarrassed that Will had heard him say something so ungracious after the tentative peace they'd managed on their ride this afternoon.

"I merely follow the example my betters have set for me," Will told him, and Hannibal bristled, preparing to set him straight.

"Now, children!" Roland said, deflecting the tension. "Here, I'll take those, my dear."

"Will you be joining us at supper this evening, Grandfather?" Will asked, handing the documents over as he was bidden and managing to thoroughly and successfully ignore Hannibal in the process.

"I believe I shall, my darling boy!" Grandfather said, effusive in his delight with Will's presence. Hannibal wrinkled his nose, irritated by the display and uncomfortable all around.

"And have you delivered your own report on the books, Lord Clarges?" Will asked, not quite lifting his eyes. There seemed to be something in the middle of Hannibal's chest he found quite interesting and Hannibal brushed his hand over the spot with the odd, alarmed thought that he might have something on him.

"Oh. Yes, indeed," Hannibal said, clearing his throat, deeply aware of his grandfather watching him, ready to glower and scold if he became provoking. "Everything seems to be in order at first glance. You have done an excellent job, as I said."

"Considering I lack what Nature has so graciously provided those who are *not* Omegan, Lord Clarges?" Will asked, and his eyes turned quite vividly blue and furious, fastening to Hannibal's own amber gaze with the relentless tenacity of a bulldog. "Or considering you abandoned Hartford House to an inept estate manager? That you never once offered to help your grandfather? That there was nothing more to be done than allow an Omegan *creature* to muck about in things? We must be in possession of all the facts, mustn't we? Including the fact that your stubbornness does, in fact, lack any limits, Lord Clarges."

Roland's face showed nothing but secretive glee which quickly vanished when Will glanced his way.

"Don't presume to scold me in my own house," Hannibal said, though Will's tone had never been anything other than soft and mildly inquisitive, no more weight to it than there would have been had he been asking after Hannibal's well being. *Polite*, and nothing more.

"I presume nothing when I am in *my* own house, not *yours*, Lord Clarges," Will said, the tightness of his mouth and jaw giving away his sudden ire. "Yet I cannot say confirming the facts can be construed as *scolding*."

Roland wheeled his chair towards the door without a word to either one of them, Hannibal muttering, "traitor," after him for abandoning him on what was surely to become a battlefield.

"Excuse me," Will said, looking quite determined and dangerously agitated as he headed for the door in Grandfather's wake. "I have work to do."

"No, I will not excuse you," Hannibal said, blocking the way before he could reach it, closing the door and turning the key in the lock. Will's eyes tracked the key as he deposited it into his jacket pocket and patted it, thinking it very safe there indeed. "You seem in dire need of venting your spleen, Will Grant. I suggest you do so now before I lose my patience with you."

"Lose *your* patience with *me*?" Will echoed, incredulous, a shocked laugh escaping him. "In what ways have I tried your lauded patience, *Lord Clarges*?"

"I have told you before to call me Hannibal," he reminded, comparing Will's vibrating frustration with the Omegas he had met since his return from the war. He couldn't recall a single one showing even a quarter of Will's unyielding backbone, though he could admit to having truly known very few of them. "Which you repeatedly decline to do. As I am your husba—"

"*Don't!*" Will's sharp, snarled response cut him off, and Hannibal felt renewed wariness, the trout making a sudden, unwelcome appearance in his mind's eye. Will trembled with something very like anger but seemed more akin to pain, his fists clenched at his sides and his eyes showing white all around. "Don't you *dare* claim to be my husband! You spent two days in my presence and left us here to rot! Were it not for your grandfather's illness—which I am becoming suspiciously aware may not have in fact been so serious as he claimed—you would never have come back here but to be rid of me entirely!"

Hannibal's mouth pursed, unable to find a suitable rejoinder when Will was so entirely truthful.

"I have spent six years shaking the dirt off of this place, allowing it to reach its potential," Will said, gesturing around him at the evidence, even here in Grandfather's own suite, "while you were playing the bachelor in the Capital and taking up with every female you could sniff out! And yet *I* am the one your precious Society fellows all laugh at behind their hands, aren't I?"

"Be very careful, Will," Hannibal said, eyes narrowing. "You are in danger of sounding jealous."

"*Jealous?*" Will asked, roses blooming in his pale cheeks. "You mistake me, Lord Clarges, I am *furious*! And now I will face the gauntlet of your family come to snipe at me and pick apart my shortcomings! What *polite company* you will find yourself in, sir! Free to disgrace me at your whim when I, as an Omega, am expected to simper brainlessly and smile and pretend I am nothing more than some pathetic excuse for ornamentation!"

"You have no cause to be furious, you twit, living here in the lap of luxury while—"

"While you ignore your duties to your family along with the gossip that plagues it?!" Will asked. "What *luxury* have I basked in, sir, pray tell? I have lived as a *stranger* in this house, knowing I remain at your *whim* and I know better than to think you wish me any kindness!"

"I doubt I have been dressed down so thoroughly since I was in knickers," Hannibal said, finding the strength of his anger quite impressive, small as he was. "Your list of complaints aside—" Will drew in a shocked, affronted breath "—I am willing to remain here at Hartford House and give you the child my grandfather is so desperate for."

He offered Will a magnanimous smile, waiting for him to melt into a puddle of relief, thinking himself well secured, surely. A child to stamp the official seal on their marriage. A child to legitimize Will as his spouse in the eyes of Society. A means to ensure Will would always have a claim on him which was, Hannibal knew, the one thing any Omega truly desired at heart, even one as frighteningly intelligent as Will.

Hannibal fully expected Will to start the laborious process of making up to him now that he had what he truly wanted in the promise of a child.

Little did he know what he would lose in getting one.

Will stiffly stepped to one side, Hannibal's curious eyes following him, bewildered by his wide-eyed outrage.

"Will?"

He cocked his head when his silent and tense Omegan spouse picked up his grandfather's cut crystal rampant horse, quite a heavy and costly thing.

"Put that down before you drop it," Hannibal said, mystified. "You should know better than to pick up something you haven't the strength to hold."

Will, however, seemed quite suddenly a brawny little thing to Hannibal because he *lifted* that horse quite high and flung it at him with a only small huff of effort.

"*What on earth is the matter with you?*" Hannibal asked, surprised when it hurtled soundly against his chest. He grappled hold of it lest it shatter on the floor, shocked to his toes when Will used his distraction to fish the key out of his pocket, quick and deft as a street urchin.

"Oh, no you don't!" Hannibal said, his voice rising with his own anger, aghast Will could manage such a thing in the first place. He hastily deposited the weighty horse into the nearest armchair and rushed to snag hold of Will's jacket as he wrested the door open. "You mean-tempered little termagant!"

"*Don't you dare touch me!*" Will hissed, wriggling very much like a trout to escape Hannibal's startled grip. "You have *no right to touch me!*"

"Goodness! Your violence is staggering!" Hannibal said, equal parts outraged and impressed to see an Omega—malleable, simpering, flighty, effervescent— once again behave in such a savage, shocking manner. He grunted when Will's booted heel came down hard on his foot and the little minx twisted out of his grip, leaving his jacket behind in Hannibal's fist. He darted off and Hannibal flung the discarded jacket to the floor, mouth pressed into a grim, unhappy line. He tore off after him, a strange anticipation rising up at the sight of Will's slender form fleeing ahead of him.

Mr. Hawkes, drawn by the shouting and the sounds of a struggle, quickly turned to shoo the other servants away, not wishing to be drawn into it.

Will hit the main foyer, desperate to reach the front door, his brain stuck on fleeing because it was his only option where Hannibal was concerned. Distance, safe distance, where he could collect himself and put all this unnecessary excess behind him.

He made it halfway there before the carpet beneath him was rudely jerked hard from behind, sending him sprawling face first into its soft weave.

Hannibal was on him in a heartbeat, wrestling him onto his back and straddling him, too large and too heavy to throw off.

"Good gods, you call yourself a gentleman!" Hannibal said, fighting to take hold of Will's wrists when he got that violent gleam in his furious blue eyes again. "Honestly! I have never seen nor participated in such uncouth behavior in my life, and I survived a war, mind you!"

"*Get off of me!*" Will snarled, baring his sharp white teeth. Sweat sheened his skin and Hannibal could smell him again, sweet-hot and mouth-watering.

"I will not!" Hannibal said, glowering down at him. "You should be ashamed of yourself, tossing valuables about like they mean nothing!"

"*You shouldn't have locked me in!*" Will said, eyes blazing. "Then I wouldn't have *had to!*"

It was quite fascinating, really, the way his cheeks pinked up with effort and his blue eyes glistened with anger. Quite fascinating to think this same writhing, furious hellion had once been flung at him in the guise of a woman, trembling and uncertain and easily crushed.

Hannibal found himself holding Will's wrists in one tight fist and reaching for his neckerchief with his free hand, seeking to unleash more of his scent. Will's eyes rounded in sudden fury and he thrashed, hissing and spitting like an angry cat.

"*You're not my Alpha!*" The words broke from him like gunfire, loud and urgent, pausing Hannibal only momentarily. They burst from his throat in a snarl of denial, as if he could break the bond he'd formed to Hannibal through sheer willpower.

"That's hardly the point," Hannibal said, fingers curving under the fine cloth of the neckerchief to feel Will's heated, fear-dampened skin, sketching over the underdeveloped scent glands below his jaw in a touch that made Will wriggle.

"*Stop this!*" Will said, trying to writhe away from his hand, the light touch of Hannibal's fingers bringing his warm scent floating up at last, though concerningly faint even to Hannibal's keen nose. "You are *not my Alpha!*"

Hannibal realized he was bending over him, searching for his scent, very much intending to bury his nose beneath Will's jaw to seek it out. Will's eyes were wild with shock and fear, the whole of his slender body vibrating with shivers beneath the pinning weight of Hannibal's heavier one. Just a taste of it, he decided, would suit him just fine. Just a taste, to match a flavor to that scent and learn it. There was no harm in such a thing. He'd done more to others during his time in the Capital, then gave them a nip to send them falling to tears and outrage at his rejection. Just a taste would surely not be out of the question considering what else he was entertaining where Will was concerned.

"Goodness, hello! I say, Hannibal, have you agitated Will again?"

Snarling with frustration at the intrusion, Hannibal lifted his gaze to see Anthony before him with the whole of the Diment clan ranged in the open doorway, all of them in varying states of surprised shock to see the future Duke of Westvale pinning his unfortunate and seething spouse to the foyer floor with the ready intensity of an Alpha about to do exactly what would please him most.

All he could offer the situation was a weary, irritated, "*Damnation!*"

⌘⌘⌘

It had not, in retrospect, been one of his more brilliant moments, Hannibal would own.

"Hannibal. What on earth are you doing to that poor child?"

He wrinkled his nose at his cousin, Bedelia, aware Will was no longer struggling beneath him, but lay frozen with instinctive terror as the disparate scents of several Alphas overpowered him all at once, sheltered as he was. They all, in turn, were peering at him, curious about the Omega no one but Anthony had ever seen.

"My business is none of yours," he told her, getting one foot braced and standing to drag Will to his feet. For a moment, he wasn't sure Will would manage, but he did, his wrists still trapped in Hannibal's fist and his wide eyes staring in panic at Hannibal's chest as the strange scents were sorted and defined. "Honestly, bursting in here this way! Is there a fire?"

"Clearly not yet," Anthony said with a lopsided grin, earning a scowl from both Hannibal and Bedelia, the latter of whom fanned herself lazily, delicate nose tasting the air for the faint trace of Will's scent.

"This is entirely Uncommon!" Uncle Robert proclaimed, the emphasis not lost on Hannibal, who had seen the portly Alpha take enormous exception to such. "Lying on the floor with your spouse in the foyer? What will the servants say! *Uncommon*, I tell you!"

"Uncle Robert, thank heavens you are here as well or we would all be in danger of putting this behind us," Hannibal said, scowling at him, his anger at their interruption draining away. It took him a moment to realize the reason why —he was kneading Will's pliant nape with his free hand vigorously enough to warm his palm with pressure. If he wasn't mistaken, by the gradual looseness of Will's body and the lessening of the fear in his eyes, it was soothing him as well.

"Who on earth is that boy?"

"And Aunt Grace, how delightful," Hannibal sighed, resignation setting in as the whole of the Diment family put their two cents in, every added voice and new scent no doubt battering at Will's senses. "Have you brought the Fernhill servants as well? In for a penny, in for a pound, I suppose."

"That is Will, Mother, Hannibal's spouse," Anthony said.

"That certainly doesn't look like any Omega *I've* ever seen!"

"Mother, hush!"

"Hannibal," Will said, so low he almost didn't hear him over the bickering of his Aunt's family. But it certainly got his attention when Will hissed his name again with crackling tension. He glanced away from the thickening mess of family at his doorstep and down at the Omega in his grip.

The Omega who was staring up at him, not with frozen terror but with simmering indignation.

The Omega who was potentially rather *agitated*.

Gods help him.

"If you let them see me like this," Will said, nearly as calm and placid as he had been in his office earlier this morning. *"There won't be a trout one left in that river by the time I'm done with you."*

Hannibal was amused despite himself, wondering how such a small and fey-looking little beauty could manage such a ferocious threat when he was still rather loose-limbed and pliant from Hannibal's roughing of his nape.

He looked further, seeing all manner of dirt on Will's shirt. He had bits of carpet fuzz in his curls, which looked as if they were attempting to escape his head entirely. Not to mention his waistcoat had ripped open thanks to Hannibal's weight atop him, a single button hanging by a thread, another laying on the carpet where he'd fallen.

"You look frightful," he said, and when the sharpness in Will's eyes gave way to outrage, he hastily said, "I was agreeing with you, you fractious creature!"

"Bedelia," Anthony said to his elder sister, smiling their way, "This is Will Grant—"

"This is no time for introductions," Hannibal said, sweeping around behind Will to block their view before they got a very good look and marching Will before him, careful not let go of his wrists lest he take a mind to kick up a fuss. "Will you people please behave as if you have manners and take yourselves to the day room?"

That got a tittering wash of laughter from them, which brought Mr. Hawkes straight away to gather them into a semblance of dignity.

Hannibal could *feel* Will growing more tense with every step and, once they were out of eye shot, he scooped him up around his slim waist, hefted him up off of his feet, and carried him rapidly towards his suite, scolding him, "Are you half a wolf? Good gods, I've hunted boar who were better-tempered than you! *Stop wriggling!*"

"*Put me down!*" Will said, his cheeks flushed red with embarrassment. "I am perfectly capable of walking!"

"Not a chance!" Hannibal told him, managing to get the door wrangled open without letting Will escape him. "We haven't finished our conversation and we shall do so now!"

"That was not a conversation," Will said, skittering away from him when Hannibal dumped him inside of his suite. He rounded on Hannibal, who closed the door behind him and leaned on it, warily watching him. Will, however, calmed dramatically without the threat of being exposed as foolish before unknown Alphas, and said with a slight tip of his chin, "It was an insult, Lord Clarges."

"Considering your penchant for violence, I will not point out who was the victim of having valuables flung at him," Hannibal said, aware of the way Will glared at him. Certainly meek and terribly malleable, was Will Grant. *Entirely* unsettling. "I cannot find an insult anywhere in my offer to give you a child."

"*Hannibal,* you *just* insulted me to your grandfather!" Will said, taking a deep breath and turning away from him, the cinch of his waistcoat emphasizing his slender rib cage, even loosened as it was. "It has been *six years*. Do you honestly believe me so mindless that I would welcome you back with open arms? There is nothing about this situation that has changed since."

"*Everything* about this situation has changed," Hannibal said, sobering when he thought of the deal he'd struck with his grandfather. "Grandfather is aging, *I* am aging. An heir is needed."

"Oh, don't give me that old tale," Will warned, giving him a withering look that lasted only briefly. "Your mistress could very well give you a son this time. There is no reason you can't legitimize him. I've been telling your grandfather that for years."

Hannibal's brows rose in surprise, but Will took no notice of it, not reckoning the cause. He sent a searching glance over one shoulder, thoughtful and angry. "So tell me, Hannibal, what is the basis for your magnanimous acceptance? Wanting a child with someone you haven't *a modicum of interest in*? How absurd! Why would you even consider such nonsense?"

A soft knock at the door made Hannibal leap away from it, barking, "What is it?"

Jimmy opened the door, bearing a tray with a small teapot and two cups. He settled it on the vanity with a soft smile and said, "Sorry. It looked like this called for a spot of tea, Mr. Grant. For fortification. My apologies for barging in, Lord Clarges. Will you need my help dressing, Mr. Grant?"

"No, Jimmy, please don't trouble yourself," Will said, still flushed and breathless.

Hannibal waved his hand at Will's studiously composed valet, irritated by the interruption, and waited peevishly until Jimmy left once more, both of them eyeing one another with wary alertness.

"The *nonsense* I am considering, Will, is the fulfillment of the contract which obligates us both," Hannibal said, retreating into cold distance for the sake of his pride, with no idea how to reach Will or where to even start. "I love my grandfather dearly, Will, and he is smitten with you. It would make him deliriously happy to have our child running around Hartford House."

Will cocked his head, politely appalled. "Running around *this* house? What, alongside your own children when you move your family here?" he asked, and laughed softly, a raspy and sultry sound Hannibal found rather flustering. "This conversation is absurd. You loathe me, I have no interest in you, and this is far too ridiculous a prospect to entertain outside of a cruel joke."

Frowning, Hannibal picked up one of the teacups and settled in the small armchair next to Will's vanity, weighing his options. The cup was light in his hands, thin and precious and crafted to appeal to the senses.

Inspired, Hannibal held it aloft by the base and turned it this way and that to view the fading scene painted on it.

"You, Will, are like this teacup," he said, aware of Will's sudden stillness. "Admittedly beautiful but serving a function."

His amber eyes were steady and weighty when they landed on Will's pale, emotionless face.

"Your function here is to bear an heir to please my grandfather and let us all get back to our lives. Mine at Galley Field, and yours as master of Hartford House," Hannibal said. "I understand our dealings in the past have not been pleasant, but that does not excuse us from our current circums—"

He cut off when Will crossed the room and took the fine little cup away from him. With grave, stony-faced silence, Will lifted it and dropped it to the floor where it shattered into a mess of shards.

"What the devil—"

"Tell it to gather itself up," Will ordered him, and Hannibal subsided, looking from the shattered cup to the Omega he had compared it to. "*Go on*. Tell it to do its duty now, Hannibal, in the state it is in."

Hannibal shifted, uncomfortable now that his comparison was turned against him.

"*Can* it do its duty in such a state?" Will asked, his voice never rising above a taut monotone. "Is it functional as it is? Or has its *circumstances* affected it?"

Hannibal swallowed hard and cleared his throat, forcing himself to meet Will's blazing, angry eyes.

"As I said," he told him. "I understand our dealings have not always been to your benefit—"

"Tell it to be whole again all you like, Lord Clarges," Will said to him, trembling with dangerous anger. "But it will not heed you. Make of *that* what you will."

Hannibal frowned, wishing he had never drawn such a parallel in the first place.

"What I make of it, Will, is that you are a violent and disruptive menace," he said, getting to his feet and straightening his clothing with a dignity that barely covered the fact that he was preening again, driven to self-grooming to allay his mate's ire. "One who will no more hesitate to trample all over well-behaved gentlefolk than you would hesitate to fling a priceless piece of china on the floor."

Will drew in a shocked breath, eyes flying wide with outrage that Hannibal would yet again paint him a villain. He stiffened abruptly, sudden frozen calm falling over him like a mask. His full mouth tightened and his lids fell, half shuttering his eyes, which fixed on Hannibal.

Hannibal was rather more disconcerted by it than he felt he properly should be, and vastly ashamed, all things considered.

"Will—" he said, starting to formulate an intricate speech that would allude to his regret without sounding in the least bit like an apology.

"You shouldn't keep your guests waiting," Will said, maddeningly polite as he overrode his husband. "I will do my best to appear to advantage for your sake, Lord Clarges. If you will excuse me?"

Uncertain what to do with such a clear dismissal other than heed it, Hannibal let himself out, glowering as he closed the door behind him. Unsettling, indeed, and dangerously Uncommon, as his Uncle would put it.

"My Lord?" Berger piped up, spying him there in the hallway loitering at Will's door like a spurned lover. "Is he not well, my Lord?"

"*No*, he is *not well*," Hannibal said, irritated all over again at how Will had retreated into good manners, putting up walls like a fort. "He is provoking and violent and entirely Uncommon!"

"M-my Lord?" Berger asked, uncertain what to do.

"Oh, for gods' sake, Berger," Hannibal sighed, striding past him to reach his own suite and tend his bedraggled appearance. "Start praying, will you? My Aunt's family has arrived and I will no doubt need all the help I can get."

Bewildered but glad to not be in some sort of trouble, Berger said, "Certainly, my Lord. Certainly."

Chapter 9

Thanks to the chaos downstairs and the unexpected arrival of the Diment clan, luncheon was forfeited and Will found he was not at all sorry. He was in no state to be in company, not while he was still trembling in the aftermath of his clash with Hannibal.

Will suppressed a shiver at the memory of Hannibal's warm fingertips pressing along his jaw, seeking the sensitive little scent glands Will had worked so hard to render useless. His fingers had felt like coals on his skin, searingly hot and frightening, but Will's heart had hammered in something like excitement, with a keen kind of terrified pleasure in being pinned down and helpless beneath the weight of his bonded Alpha. Hannibal had been surprisingly rapt in his attention, his amber eyes half-shuttered and his mouth slightly parted as he'd stared down at Will, intent on seeking the source of his scent. He had worried Will even more so in that moment because he'd felt nothing more than an eager, aching desire to allow Hannibal to do anything he wanted, anything at all, as much a product of his father's abuse as it was the response of touch-starved instincts.

Hannibal would be appalled to know it, no doubt, repulsed into turning his noble nose up so he could glare at Will down its length, haughty and secure in his confidence.

"It's too dangerous," Will said, leveling a glare at his reflection. If Hannibal was to find out about the bond Will had to him, then he would use that knowledge, that power he had over Will, to his own advantage. Certainly too dangerous to risk it.

Will resolutely returned to the forlorn tea set and poured himself a cup, his hand still trembling with irritation at Hannibal's high-handed actions. He deeply regretted breaking the other teacup as he had, now that the first flush of emotion was out of him. It was his favorite tea set, long since retired from regular use for missing pieces, but one Jimmy knew he particularly liked for those very reasons.

It was not priceless in the ways Hannibal had claimed, but in ways Will alone understood.

"It's just the two of us, now," he murmured, rubbing his thumb over the lip of the fragile teacup. "I suppose that's just fine."

He honestly never knew who he'd hoped would use that second cup. The staff would never serve anyone else with such a set. The fact that Jimmy had brought it into Hannibal's presence at all was a subtle rebellion on Will's behalf.

Yet some part of him had always found hope in the presence of that empty cup waiting on the tray, as if any moment a friend might arrive and share their time with him. It was a pleasant illusion no more, he knew.

You, Will, are like this teacup... admittedly beautiful but serving a function...'

Hannibal's words had found the crack in his composure and slithered beneath, an outrageous insult said with such silky seriousness Will was still aghast at his husband's capacity to entirely and deliberately miss his point. It had taken an example of extreme proportions to get through to his husband, and the sacrifice of something precious to do so.

"It will never be whole again," he murmured, grim. "Not in a million years."

Angry at Hannibal, angry at himself, Will surged to his feet and put the matter behind him. He viciously scrubbed his neck, jaw, and other scent gland areas with the liquid scent neutralizer Jimmy procured for him on a regular basis, determined that Hannibal should not have any reason to claim it was provoking.

He couldn't fathom how Hannibal had caught his scent in the first place since even Grandfather had assured Will his neutralizer was frighteningly effective. He bleakly considered that it could be a side effect of their bonding, but he lacked the experience to know for certain and refused to borrow trouble.

He donned a fresh shirt and waistcoat, abandoning the abused ones to his vast and nearly empty dressing room for Jimmy to take downstairs. He buttoned up and replaced his neckerchief with another one soaked in the neutralizer and left to dry before being ironed free of stiffness. It was still rather scratchy and uncomfortable but he would much rather bear it than give Hannibal any cause to go running his fingers in where they didn't belong, even if Will's touch-starved body warmed at the suggestion.

"I am more than a bundle of mindless instincts!" Will reminded himself, tugging his cuffs and settling his jacket on, looking nearly passable enough to meet Roland's daughter and her family. He gave his reflection a stern stare, trying to swallow down his frustration. "You are not an Omega, Will Grant. You are not a man, nor a woman. You are only *yourself* and that is all you need be."

It was the only thing he could do in his situation, finish what his father had started and Hannibal had so eagerly continued, pare all of his Omegan nonsense and foolishness out with ruthless force.

In a ritual which always helped him feel more in control, Will made himself review what had happened downstairs as if watching from afar. He analyzed where things had gone wrong, what Hannibal had said to prick his temper into rising, which he seemed to have a talent for. He felt his frustration well up again —Hannibal was insufferable on a good day, most times; it was no surprise he would make such an appalling suggestion about a child with a pleased, clueless smile. It was also no surprise that, having been done in, he would give chase.

If there was one thing Will was beginning to realize about Hannibal, it was that his husband felt compelled to have the last word on a given subject.

"Insufferably arrogant," Will breathed, cheeks growing hot when he recalled how Hannibal had tackled him in the foyer and been distracted with near immediacy by the very Alpha impulses Will's sisters had secretly warned him of. His flush intensified when he imagined what Hannibal's family must think of him. No doubt that he had used his Omegan wiles to seduce Hannibal right there in the doorway, unable to wait for a proper setting for a tryst.

He tugged his jacket again and quickly blotted his forehead and cheeks with the cloth soaked in scent killer, cooling his heated skin.

Hannibal had not, however—and much to Will's surprise—left him to flounder in embarrassment alone. It had been entirely unexpected when his husband had tried soothing him with that firm kneading of his nape, and Will felt goose-flesh rise all over again recalling the touch. It had calmed him and centered him, though no little part of him resented and rebelled against it, knowing it was nothing more than mindless instinct at work. The shock of it could not compare to the surprise of Hannibal swinging around behind him, effectively hiding him from scrutiny when he had a perfect opportunity to expose Will, and he could not blame Hannibal for thinking he might struggle.

Every interaction they *had* was a struggle, it seemed.

His careful recollection of the instance complete, Will took a deep breath, focusing on his accomplishments and everything he had managed to date here at

Hartford House to find his equilibrium again. He was no simpering, silly Omega whose only hope was in a baby. He was a quick mind bent to details who had the misfortune to inhabit a body he had no need of nor desire for. He had spent six years living as a beta male with such success nearly everyone in his limited acquaintance assumed he was one. He was not what Hannibal thought he was. He was intelligent, serious, and calm.

It was a difficult reminder to focus on when he had only just been floundering about on the floor, struggling with his husband on the foyer carpet, both of them behaving appallingly. Will knew if he'd had the time or chance to get hold of something before they'd been interrupted, he would not have hesitated to make Hannibal regret his decision to flatten him on the rug.

Somehow, his calm seemed to flee when confronted with Hannibal's presence. His husband had no good effect on him and Will seemed to bring out the worst in him. Rather, they brought out the worst in *one another*. Adding a child to this nonsense was folly, and they both knew it.

So why on earth would Hannibal even consider it long enough to bring it up?

"A cruel joke," Will said, knowing it was the only reasonable possibility. "A cruel joke and nothing more. I should leave here no matter what His Grace says. Surely he will see for himself that Hannibal and I cannot share even so large a house as this..."

And if they did clash—which was inevitable—and Roland *could* see there was no cause to hope, then perhaps he would consider an annulment after all.

It was the only option he could see working, one he had begged for more than once in the past six years. The Duke, tight-lipped and grim, had steadfastly refused to annul their marriage, telling Will that someday Hannibal would make all of this up to him.

But Will was entirely out of patience and he would not wait any longer, not with Hannibal back and so strangely, reluctantly conciliatory.

Nodding to bolster his renewed confidence, Will tugged once more on his jacket, lifted his chin, and quietly left his suite.

Mr. Hawkes informed him the family was in the day room and that tea and cakes had been served.

"Thank you, Mr. Hawkes," Will said, steeling himself to make a good impression no matter what they might believe of his character. "I apologize for any inconvenience my behavior caused."

"I am afraid I am not aware of any behavior of yours that could cause an inconvenience, Mr. Grant," Mr. Hawkes said, stern in his dignity.

Will blushed floridly. "A teacup has been broken in my room, Mr. Hawkes. Please have the pieces boxed for me and left on my vanity."

"Of course, Mr. Grant," Mr. Hawkes said, ever attentive. "As for now, Lord Clarges has asked after you."

"Unfortunately, Mr. Hawkes, he cannot pretend I do not exist when his relatives descend on us like a murder of crows," Will said, feeling as ungenerous as his summation sounded. "I will endeavor not to give them any reason to dislike me more than gossip and conjecture already have."

Mr. Hawkes opened the door for him and Will stopped short, eyes flicking from one to another in turn and matching them to stories Anthony had told him over the years. The slender blonde woman was Bedelia, Anthony's eldest sister. The spare and frowning older woman was Roland's daughter, Hannibal's Aunt Grace, who had married Lord Robert Diment, the current Earl of Bredon. Anthony he knew, of course, but he was not so certain of Bedelia's grown children, who had spouses and children of their own.

Every one of which was staring at him and almost half of which were Alphas of varying degrees of strength.

Will took a deep breath, calming when his senses sorted Hannibal and Grandfather out among them. He knew he had nothing to fear from these Alphas but their disparagement, but it was threat enough to make him nervously smooth his waistcoat over his trim belly.

"My gracious, look at you!" a young man said, beaming at him, his blue eyes wide and sparkling with appreciation. One of Bedelia's sons, no doubt, by the look of him.

"Such a delicate young man, is he not?" Bedelia said, every nose in the room upturned to catch his scent. Will was deliriously glad he had used such copious amounts of neutralizer to confound them.

"Exquisite, Roland, darling," a matronly woman said, nodding her approval to Roland. "Certainly an overdue boon for the family. He is the very image of Charles, isn't he?"

"He certainly is, Margaret," Grandfather said to her, beaming at Will with pride shining in his amber eyes and a smitten smile on his lips.

Will controlled his trembles with sheer determination, though the slight movement of his dark curls no doubt betrayed him. The married adults were nearly all older than he, interspersed with various children, all of them intensely curious about him.

Hannibal was standing near the windows but his gaze was sharp, offended, and his posture was tense enough to put Will's teeth on edge.

"Wexley's Omegan spouse sings like a songbird," that same, bright-eyed youth called out. "Do you sing, Mr. Grant?"

"Oh, you're like a lovely little jewel, darling, aren't you?" Bedelia purred, descending on him in a perfume of strong Alpha scent and soft silks, her pleasantly pale arm rising to trail her fingers down the side of his throat, a trace of touch beneath his jaw. Will tipped his head despite his best intentions, allowing the touch and submitting to it, which made her lovely face even lovelier with delight. She turned her head fluidly to Roland and said, "Grandfather, it was badly done of you to hand him to Hannibal."

Hannibal crossed the room in three quick strides, his hands clasped behind his back but his amber gaze livid as he said, "It is inadvisable, dear cousin, to test an Omega in such a public setting. You know how easily frightened and scatterbrained they can be."

Will bristled, knowing Hannibal was deliberately baiting him and well aware that he'd pricked his husband right where it hurt him the most—his *pride*.

Annoyingly enough, Hannibal's scent was the strongest in the room, but at least it rendered the others less intimidating and managed to be moderately comforting in that respect, however little Will enjoyed it.

"Bedelia, light of my life," Grandfather said, sounding weary. "I assure you it was not done thoughtlessly."

She turned her attention back to Will, her light blue eyes dancing at Hannibal's scolding. She was a vision of pale beauty, from her light, near-white hair to her icy-bright blue eyes to the delicate shell pink of her smiling mouth.

"Come along, dearest, yes," she crooned, petting him when no one else dared to touch him, as if his gender was contagious somehow. That, or they feared how Hannibal might react. Bedelia, however, was an Alpha much used to dealing with Omegas and soothed him with gentle strokes and murmurs, keeping him tight to her side as she sat with him near her grandfather. "Not well done of Grandfather at all, I must say."

"Now stop gawking, the lot of you!" Roland ordered, annoyed at their interest.

"I can hardly help it!" a young lady declared, a young and innocent version of Bedelia. "I swear, he is precisely like her! I had no idea she had a twin!"

"You were certainly not the only one without that knowledge," Hannibal said, annoyed by how genuinely impressed they were, the traitorous bunch.

"You could change places with no one knowing!" the young man said, grinning so that he looked quite a lot like Anthony.

"Not precisely," Will said, thinking of that awful day over six years ago when Mina had conspired to send him here in her place. "But I am sure Lord Clarges would not complain if we did, considering she is a proper woman."

There was startled silence following his statement. Will looked to Grandfather, who was not bothering to hide his slight smile, then at Hannibal, who looked fit to murder him.

Anthony laughed, saying, "The first time I met Will, he was dressed in Lady Rathmore's clothes!"

"*Anthony*," Hannibal said, warning him. "Keep a civil tongue in your head or excuse yourself."

Anthony said nothing more but his grin proved there was plenty he would like to add.

"Well, now that we are all together," Roland said, wheeling his chair closer to the head of the loose group. "May I introduce Hannibal's spouse, William Ledford, formerly Grant, the Omegan child of the Earl of Reddig."

"Reddig?" Uncle Robert echoed, his round face crumpling in concentration. "Isn't he the one who hunted with you all the time? You were quite close in your youth, if the stories are to be believed."

"I was close with his father, Charles, the former Earl and Will's grandfather," Roland clarified. "The demands of family, unfortunately, conspired to put distance between us as we aged."

Hannibal moved to the empty seat at his Grandfather's side, Will across from him and nestled cozily next to Bedelia, who looked fairly pleased with herself. The rest of the Diment family was strung the length of the room, still curious and watchful, though the younger ones were rapidly becoming bored with adult matters.

Hannibal sighed and sipped the tea he was served, staring at Will's studiously blank expression in mingled irritation and concern, their last conversation replaying with uncomfortable clarity. The tick of the mantle clock was annoyingly loud, rattling his desperate composure.

"Well... I can honestly say six years in Society have *not* improved your social graces, Hannibal," Aunt Grace loudly announced.

He sighed again, knowing with that opening shot there would be no more peace. He carefully settled his cup back into the saucer and gave his Aunt Grace a bland, expectant look.

"The children were *shocked*, brother!" Margaret said to His Grace, fanning herself vigorously. "*Shocked!*"

"I am aware that there were unfortunate circumstances surrounding your arrival," Roland said, angling a repressive look at Hannibal, who turned his own on Will. "I am sure we can all agree such irresponsible and crude behavior will not be repeated in the future."

"Still, what a sight for the children!" Aunt Grace sniffed. "What an example to set!"

"You are profoundly persistent, Aunt Grace," Hannibal remarked, unhappy with her tenacity.

"I am afraid that scene was my own fault," Will said, summoning such a forlorn look Hannibal nearly laughed at him. He then grudgingly recalled that Will was an Omega and such falsehoods were their stock in trade, which only left him feeling vaguely irritated and wronged on top of amused. "I took it into my *scatterbrained* head that I should run, you see."

"But darling, why would you run?" Bedelia asked, making over him.

Grandfather snorted.

Anthony grinned.

Hannibal felt a dread certainty he was not going to come out of this unscathed and cursed Will's surprisingly convoluted and cunning mind for it ahead of time.

"Perhaps you should ask Hannibal," Will said, raising his languid eyes in Hannibal's direction.

"Ha!" Hannibal barked a short, sharp laugh. "You scheming little minx! Don't you dare turn this on me unless you fancy another meeting with a carpet! There is a marvelous Turkish monstrosity in the library you haven't yet—"

"*Hannibal!*" Roland snapped, appalled at him. "What on earth has gotten into you?"

"I beg your pardon, Grandfather," Hannibal said, feeling strangely flushed and upended, which he blamed squarely on the little Omega looking at him with hazy, unfocused eyes which darkened to near brown in color beneath his thick black lashes. "I find I am not myself today."

"What an uncomfortable feeling," Will murmured, his gaze hardening to diamond sharpness. "To not be one's self."

Hannibal clenched his teeth abruptly, subsiding but not liking it one bit.

"Grandfather," Bedelia said, shifting her deceptively soft blue gaze to His Grace, a slight smile on her mouth as she expertly turned the subject. "You should have written that Hannibal had returned. We were already at Fernhill, there would have been no bother to call us here."

"Only to *me*," Hannibal said beneath his breath, cutting his amber eyes at his cousin. "Bedelia, you realize how rude it is to show up unannounced."

"No more rude than speaking when you are not spoken to, Hannibal," she murmured. "I addressed Grandfather, if you recall. That aside, I did send word. Through Anthony."

"Ah!" Anthony said, grinning. "I must have forgotten to deliver it, I suppose! No matter, we are family all together."

"Together at long last!" Aunt Grace said, complaining, "Sixteen *years*, Hannibal! Sixteen years we've been waiting for you to put up or give up your place to our Anthony, and you waste six full years bandying about the Capital with your tarts, refusing to see us, when you should have been here securing the line of inheritance!"

"*Indeed!*" Uncle Robert said, adding his own booming complaint to the growing list of Hannibal's misdeeds. "You are *not* getting any younger, Hannibal! And it is far past time for Anthony to be married! We have our own family matters that cannot be attended to until you settle *yours!*"

"Honestly," Margaret said, leveling A Look at Hannibal that reminded him uncomfortably of his younger years. "Here we had *assumed* you would gracefully hand off to our Anthony that which you *clearly* do not want! And shame on you! *Shame!* He is a lovely Omega, quite lovely, indeed!"

"Yes, Hannibal," Anthony said, gleeful with all the hounding going on. "I am more than happy to relieve you of your burdens. Merely say the word."

Hannibal's mouth tightened. He was certain Will was repressing a smile, and it was oddly irritating to see Bedelia petting him like an oversized cat, mainly because he allowed it without even a hint of violence. He *should*, by all rights, be flinging teacups about and snarling at people. *That* would certainly be an interesting distraction.

"Your opinion was neither sought nor required, Anthony," Hannibal bit out, glowering at how smug his cousin was. "And to settle the question—you will *not* be taking even a one of my *burdens* from me, thank you very much. So you are quite free to get yourself married as hastily as possible, preferably to someone who doesn't suit you one whit."

Will flinched and Hannibal subsided, shifting with discomfort.

"Well, he *has* turned up!" Uncle Robert said, breaking the uncomfortable silence with his overly-loud approval on that count. "Uncommon though he has been, he has finally turned up!"

"Like a bit of good luck, hm?" Anthony put in, relishing Hannibal's discomfit.

"More along the lines of a bad penny," Will said, his voice mild and bland, his sparkling gaze lifting to Hannibal's and showing nothing but mute fire.

There was no limpid grace here, no, as Hannibal well knew. He could look for a thousand years and find no sign of wilting or widening eyes or Omegan frailty, just a smoldering, awe-inspiring fury that refused to die down.

"Stop needling me, you perverse creature," Hannibal said, wrinkling his nose at him in a soft snarl to cover how he had been staring. To Aunt Grace and Uncle Robert, he said, "I am here, ready and resigned to doing my duty at last, have no fear on that count."

"Are you *sure* you're Omegan, dear?" Aunt Grace asked again, peering at Will through a pair of thick spectacles.

"Grace, don't be tiresome," Roland warned. "Will is an Omega, and kindly cease being so rude!"

"It is nothing, Grandfather," Will said, straightening where he sat, his spine stiff with dignity. "I realize I am not in the least what you all hoped for in a spouse for your heir and I am certainly not what Hannibal himself hoped for. I apologize for my lack of feminine charm and comfort; my upbringing was unusual for an Omega."

"You seem perfectly marvelous to me," the young man said, his grin wolfish. Anthony cuffed him soundly and Bedelia made a sharp gesture for him to take himself off to the back of the room, which he quickly did under their censure.

"Considering we had no chance to see you, Hannibal, last time you visited Hartford House," Bedelia said, "you can understand how eager we were to visit."

"Eager to get glimpse of the Omega your cad of a brother married me off to," Hannibal said, his voice gruff, a frown pulling his mouth down when Will's shoulders slumped slightly. They were back up in a heartbeat, straighter than before, but it bothered him to see it all the same.

"I had only mentioned I was coming over to see Grandfather," Bedelia said, all cunning innocence. "I'm afraid once word got 'round the whole family wished to come."

"Such touching concern for Grandfather's health!" Hannibal scoffed, glaring at no one in particular. "When not once in six years have any of you set foot inside Hartford House!"

"How would we dare when you forbid it?" Margaret asked, tapping her cane on the floor. "Hm? You brat! I had half a mind to take you over my knee and paddle you when I heard! And then we return to find you making sport of that poor child on the foyer floor, no less! Shocking conduct, Hannibal! Terribly *Uncommon!*"

"I have never banned you from this house, Aunt Margaret!" Hannibal flared, feeling put upon. "Where did you get such an idea?"

Will ducked his head again and Hannibal frowned, making a note to take it up with him later. "And I was not making sport of him, your *poor child*! Poor! Ha! He is a violent-tempered little harpy!"

"Yes," Bedelia said, her mild amusement only fanning the flames of his temper. "He seems a perfect fright, Hannibal."

Hannibal bit back his reply and settled for glowering at her, which she responded to by tucking Will closer to her side. It was a wonder they didn't meld together right there in front of him. He half expected Will to purr from pure spite.

"I hope you will show more self-restraint Sunday, Hannibal!" Uncle Robert said, blundering his way into an otherwise dangerous conversation. "I won't have you manhandling anyone and distracting the other guests!"

"What?" Hannibal asked, drawing a blank, his brows rising over his amber eyes. "Sunday?"

"Our garden party, of course," Bedelia said, tilting her lovely head. "I'm afraid I sent your invitation to the Capital. I assume by now it has gone on to your other estates in search of you, though in all honesty, after six years of ignoring my correspondence and avoiding your family as if your life depended on it, I did not dream you would actually *attend*."

"Ah, the lauded annual Fernhill Garden Party," Hannibal sighed, rubbing his forehead. "I can hardly wait. As I am here, I cannot possibly refuse."

"No you *cannot* refuse," His Grace said, disapproving. "There is nasty gossip that has come to my attention and it needs to be dealt with!"

"I have no concern for gossip, Grandfather," Hannibal said. "It is the currency in which fools trade."

"And in which you carry a very high stock," Grandfather snapped. "You have damaged Will's reputation. Let us hope it is not irreparable damage. Your cousin has very kindly extended her invitation despite your churlish behavior and you *will accept*."

Bedelia smiled, pleased, looking rather like a cat herself.

Hannibal wrinkled his nose at her again, a slight snarl she was well acquainted with from their childhood years.

"Then you will, naturally, be bringing Will," Bedelia said, cocking her lovely head.

"Unfortunately, no," Will said before Hannibal could answer, every eye in the room landing on him. Calm and serene, he said, "I will be leaving tomorrow for Marsham Heath. There is a good deal of work that remains undone there and the estate requires attention."

There was such an air of collective consternation around him Will almost smiled at it, amused.

"Ah, yes, I'd forgotten," Hannibal said, seizing on the excuse with fervor. "Marsham Heath is in quite a state. We'll be leaving come morning, I'm afraid."

Will's eyes widened with his own consternation, then narrowed when Hannibal dropped a smug wink at him. He could hardly argue about it now but he ached with wanting to and clenched his jaw to prevent it.

"Neither one of you is doing anything of the sort!" Roland announced, his voice flat and solid. "We will go to the Fernhill garden party, all of us! We will put this ugly gossip to rest and, by the *gods*, we shall enjoy ourselves immensely!"

Will glowered at Hannibal, who glowered right back, each blaming the other for closing that particular escape route.

"Perhaps later, once things have quieted down, it would be more conducive to your situation to take a holiday together, perhaps to the Capital," Grandfather said, and Will's cheeks bloomed with rosy color when he realized his heat was coming due before too much longer. No one else seemed to notice, though Hannibal was thoroughly amused by his maidenly blushes.

Will absolutely *refused* to be anywhere near Hannibal when his heat came. Even being near him for so short a time, he could feel his attachment to his Alpha strengthening. His uncanny imagination instantly supplied him with every reasonable scenario of himself in such a state, and given his experience of his heats these last six years—each one increasingly more desperate—he was not about to risk any one of them. He simply wouldn't give Hannibal the satisfaction of having his horrid opinions validated on that count.

No, he absolutely refused to be at Hartford House when his heat came; that would simply be too much ammunition for Hannibal's arsenal and Will well knew it. Just the thought of it broke him out in a cold sweat. There was only so much coshing a gentleman could do, after all.

"For now," Roland said, his assessing gaze not missing Will's sudden absorption with his thoughts. "We are all decided we will attend the garden party and have a lovely time."

There was a moment of silence that followed his gruff command, one broken by Anthony, who said, "Will, would you play for us?"

He was on his feet before the request was complete, glad to have an excuse to sit alone away from so many distracting people. He ignored the burning weight of Hannibal's amber eyes on him and settled at the harpsichord, setting up sheet music and playing softly as the family caught up behind him.

It was soothing and chased his tension away, his fingers skimming lightly over the keys, a small smile curving his mouth. A shadow fell over him and he looked up in time to see Anthony arrive. Without asking, the young Alpha sat down on the bench next to him and turned the pages in companionable ease, offering only, "They are dreadfully boring."

Will laughed under his breath, knowing Anthony would much rather be riding or hunting or on his way to the Capital to gamble at one of his clubs.

"They are currently discussing my marriage prospects," Anthony said, looking over his shoulder at his family. "*Dreadfully* boring."

"You should have more interest," Will suggested, smiling at him. "Whoever she is, she'll be with you for life."

"And I her, though men are allowed more options than women," Anthony mused. "Don't fret over it, Will. I have someone who suits me very well."

Will skated a glance his way, laughing again when Anthony said, "And if *you* won't marry me, why, then, I have someone already picked out, provided your blasted husband agrees."

"Honestly, it's no wonder people thought I was your lover," Will said, shaking his head, his fingers skimming the keys in automatic response to the notes. Even half-attentive, he still managed to make the harpsichord sing with vibrant melody. "The way you go on. You're a terrible flirt, Anthony. I do hope once you marry that you'll show her more respect than to make eyes at everything with a pulse that comes near you."

"Or them," Anthony said, waggling his eyebrows at Will when he glanced over at him again. "A few Omegas are on offer for me, remember? I've no interest in swaying them one way or another—pants or skirts, it's all the same to me. It's what's under the clothing that counts."

"Your grandfather would whip you for such talk," Will scolded, moving his hands to his lap when he finished the song. He gave Anthony a repressive look, adding, "You are a gentleman, Lord du Millau, pray act like one."

"Then I shall, in a very gentlemanly manner, leave this room and go have a cigarette," Anthony whispered, grinning. "Care to join me?"

Will smiled and, without a backwards glance, gladly joined Anthony in leaving a room which he had no place or purpose in.

⌘⌘⌘

Hannibal listened to his family discussing Anthony's potential mates with only half an ear, frowning at the sight of Anthony and Will sharing the harpsichord bench. Will found his cousin amusing, that much was obvious, by the way he smiled and spoke. He played very well, the harpsichord making the somber piece rather more merry than was intended.

"Hannibal? What is your opinion?" Bedelia asked.

"That you should marry Anthony to the ugliest heiress you can suss out," he shot back, annoyed at the interruption. He bristled at the way his cousin's shoulder brushed Will's, and added with sharp irritation, "As quickly as propriety allows for!"

"You cannot possibly still be angry at your cousin for doing as he was told," Aunt Margaret said, disapproving. To His Grace, she said, "My dearest brother, I had hoped you would speak in Anthony's defense!"

"Maggie, now is not the time," Roland said, quelling that particular discussion. "We must concentrate on Anthony's pending engagement."

"Hannibal—"

He stood, ignoring Bedelia's second attempt to gain his opinion, and moved towards the harpsichord with every intention to sit between them if needs be, blaming his pride rather than his instincts for wishing to separate them.

He got no closer than a few paces before Anthony stood and, with Will right behind him, quit the room without a word, every foolish Diment under the age of thirty running off after them and glad of their sudden, fortuitous escape from the boring matters that plagued their elders.

Incredibly annoyed by their behavior, Hannibal reluctantly rejoined the family, wondering what on earth the two of them were up to and why on earth he gave a damn.

⌘⌘⌘

Amidst a small flurry of young Diments, Will and Anthony managed to make their way to the garden, idly watching the youngsters take up an unruly and confounding game of pall-mall with no discernible rules, teams, or points system. They played for the fun of it, enjoying the afternoon sun and their youth.

Even though he was barely older than some of them, Will felt removed from their carefree enjoyment, aged by his heavy thoughts and circumstances.

"You're frowning," Anthony said, standing with Will in the shade of an arbor placed for spectators.

Will softened his expression with a smile, saying, "I was thinking. I find my thoughts distasteful recently, now that Lord Clarges has returned."

"*Lord Clarges*," Anthony snorted, amused. "He *is* your husband, Will; you can call him by name."

"He has told me to, but he does not see us as equals," Will murmured. "It would only rankle his nerves were I to call him by name."

"Then rankle them," Anthony suggested, grinning at him. "Gods know he's caused you enough grief. There's no harm giving some in return."

"I have no wish to cause him grief," Will said, smiling when the smallest of the children stepped on the hem of her dress and sprawled onto the lawn, only to sit up laughing. "I have caused this family too much grief already."

"You *should*, by all rights," Anthony said, his humor slowly draining to irritation with his cousin. "After all he's done."

"He's been well *within* his rights," Will said, mouth pursing. "I should not resent him."

Anthony regarded him in silence. When he spoke again, it was a low, urgent whisper so the children wouldn't hear.

"Will, regarding what I said inside just now... I'm going to make a decision tomorrow," he said, the seriousness of his tone making Will look over at him. "If you have any inkling to escape what Grandfather and Hannibal have done to you, tell me now."

"Anthony—"

"I mean it, Will. I'm being absolutely serious, not flirting in the least," he said, leaning close to grasp his shoulders. "I'll not be Grandfather's heir, I know that, so there's no fear on that count. We could leave, now even. Just go and let them do whatever it is they need to do to untangle you from Hannibal."

"Anthony, I appreciate that you're trying to save me," Will said, touched. "But there's no point in sacrificing your standing with your family for something like me—"

"*Someone*," Anthony said, giving him a soft shake and uttering a huff of disbelieving laughter. "*Gods*, listen to how he has you talking! You're a person with feelings, Will. Feelings Hannibal has dismissed without a moment of regret. I know we regard one another as nothing more than friends, but given time I am certain we could love one another. You're amazing and funny and delightful and I wouldn't regret a thing if you'd marry me."

Will's eyes misted with tears and he pressed his hand to his heart where it ached, wounded and wretched, his vast affection for his dearest friend tightening his chest.

"You *would* regret it, Anthony," he said, managing to meet his gaze. "Because I'm bonded to Hannibal."

Confusion and understanding flooded Anthony's blue eyes. Brow furrowing, he asked, "When did you—"

"We didn't," Will hastily said, flushing. "We *haven't*. If I have my way, we never will. It happened the day after you brought me here. There was an awful moment between us and it just... happened."

"Well," Anthony said, giving his shoulders a squeeze. "That explains so much about you. I'd thought a time or two that perhaps the two of you had bonded—"

"Not the two of us," Will corrected, wincing. "Just me. Please don't tell Hannibal, Anthony. If he knew—"

"Gods, if he knew, he'd break you all over again," Anthony said, his tender expression turning grim.

Will nodded, drawing a deep breath to calm himself comforted by Anthony's warmth and nearness and wishing things could have gone very differently.

Anthony squeezed his shoulders again, gaining his attention once more. He smiled at Will and asked, "Partners in crime, then?"

Will nodded vigorously, grinning when Anthony laughed and hugging him back without restraint when Anthony embraced him.

"Well then," Anthony said, setting Will back only enough to make room to roll a cigarette. "If that's your final decision, then let me tell you about a lovely certain someone who *won't* reject my ardent and smitten proposal."

Will laughed and said with vast affection, "By all means, Anthony. By all means."

Chapter 10

The Diments did not stay for supper with the exception of Anthony, but Hannibal suffered through it all the same.

Mrs. Pimms, ready to either kill someone or drop into a dead faint from all the disruptions to her service, delivered them a delightful supper Grandfather made much over in order to keep the atmosphere light. Will, despite Anthony's insistent chatter and determination to engage him, remained silent and thoughtful in his place across from Hannibal, only leveling the occasional, dangerous glare at his husband when Hannibal chanced to remark on Anthony's persistent attention.

Hannibal was glad to see his cousin go back to Fernhill, damn him, and was oddly disappointed when Will excused himself from a nightcap in the White Drawing Room with Hannibal and Grandfather.

"Does he often do that?" Hannibal asked, frowning at the empty doorway where Will had softly bidden them both a good night.

"Leave rooms?" Roland asked, smirking. "Yes, quite as often as we all do, I'm afraid. He's rather limited by his circumstances in that respect, bless him."

"You're certainly in good form," Hannibal observed. "No, I mean does he often excuse himself from company?"

"He is not often *in* company," Grandfather said. "These past six years he has been as a stranger to me, no matter my attempts to engage him, though he has never refused my requests for his company. He has his quiet hobbies, his fishing, his work here. He is as content as he can manage, but he keeps very much to himself unless I ask after him particularly. Half of the time even the servants have no idea where he's off to."

"That is rather cunning of him," Hannibal said, annoyed by how guilty that made him feel. Will's time here had not gone at all as he'd imagined.

"Only you would see it as such, Hannibal," Roland sighed. "He is a gentle, intelligent, and quiet young Omega and would suit you quite well if you would but allow it."

Hannibal frowned, peering into his glass as if it might offer some insight.

"Why is this the first I'm hearing of your interest in Will's family?" he asked, swirling the liquor around before taking a swallow, cutting a sly look towards his grandfather.

"It was all long before you arrived here at Hartford House," Roland said, a somber, poignant sadness draining the weight of his years from his lined and weary face. "The last time Charles and I had any exchange of depth was shortly after your birth, in fact. It was then that we drew up the contract between our families."

Hannibal arched a brow. "My, my, aren't we feeling rather vague on details."

"We may be as vague as we like," Grandfather reminded him. "As we are old and lament the loss of our youth."

"Which this *Charles* was a large part of, I take it? Perhaps I should ask Aunt Margaret?" Hannibal asked, willing to risk his grandfather's scowl. "She seems to know a bit more than you're willing to tell me. It is strange to be so close to someone and never speak of them."

"There are things in the world we love that are too precious, too dear to us to parse down into words, Hannibal," Roland said, the weighty sadness in his voice surprising his grandson. "Suffice it to say, age descended on him much sooner and much more viciously than it has on me. My only regret is that I was not with him when he passed."

It made Hannibal curious about this man he'd never heard of, this man who had been so dear to his grandfather. He wanted to ask more, but it obviously distressed him and Grandfather seemed so fragile in that moment that Hannibal didn't dare.

"And on that note," Roland said, putting his unfinished drink down with a hand that trembled slightly. "I am going to bed. We have a party to attend soon and we all need our rest."

Hannibal bid him goodnight and finished his drink. Feeling restless and at loose ends, he abandoned the drawing room for the library, glad to see a few lamps were lit and casting a cozy-warm glow over the plush surroundings.

Will saw his husband come in and close the door behind him and wished he'd taken his book upstairs. He was moving just as Hannibal swung back towards him and both of them froze, momentarily startled into stillness when they came face to face.

152

"I apologize, Lord Clarges," Will said, taking note of his page and closing his book carefully. "I had not considered you might come."

"Why should you? You have your own habits, after all," Hannibal said, recovering quickly. He squared his shoulders and moved to take the chair opposite Will, lifting his hand in a staying gesture when Will made as if to leave. "Please, stay where you are."

Will subsided into the comfortable chair, his book in his lap, his thumb running over the spine as Hannibal settled before him. Will looked to one side, ignoring the easy way Hannibal sat with his booted ankle crossed atop his opposite knee and his arms loose on the armrests in the spread-open habit of an Alpha used to taking up space. Will felt much smaller by comparison, sitting as he did with his legs crossed at his ankles and his arms in his lap, making himself a smaller target from force of habit.

Hannibal considered Will's delicate profile, the nub of his nose and the fullness of his mouth above the soft curve of his chin. He was not so small as his delicacy had first rendered him; he was trim and spare in his movements with a tendency to hold his posture in tight, stiff control, which created the illusion of being smaller than he was. His ear peeked from the thick locks of his curls, a flash of pale skin against hair so dark brown it was nearly black in the faint light. He was quite a beautiful person, as Hannibal was forced once more to admit. Comely enough to argue the point with a stranger, no less.

"You were very quiet at dinner this evening," Hannibal said, his frown fearsome when he recalled how Anthony had pandered to Will at the table, grinning and easy with him in ways which Hannibal could not manage.

"I had nothing of interest to share," Will said, wishing him away.

Hannibal's mouth quirked in a smile and he said, "I doubt that very much."

Will was startled into looking at him, a furtive flash of blue eyes wide with surprise that died quickly under the weight of suspicion.

"Has my grandfather ever discussed with you the nature of his connection to your family?" Hannibal asked, his amber eyes tracing the curve of Will's jaw when he turned his head away again. There was a stubborn set to his chin that suited him, feeding up into his full lower lip the way it did. When Will's mouth parted for him to speak, Hannibal started a little, made aware he had been staring.

"I have never heard of a connection between our families until today," Will said, feeling Hannibal's gaze almost like a physical touch. "I had no idea our grandfathers ever kept company, nor did my father, not that he ever admitted to. Mr. Stammets' arrival with that contract was quite a shock for him."

"I admit to being unreasonably curious at any given time," Hannibal said, his scrutiny falling to Will's hands and long fingers, which had played the harpsichord with sensitivity and grace. Almost as an afterthought, he added, "But Grandfather is being cagey."

"It is his own business," Will said, curling his fingers around the book in his lap to avoid Hannibal's gaze. "If he does not wish to share it, then he has no obligation to."

"Aren't you the least bit intrigued by it?" Hannibal pressed. "The fact that our grandfathers were close? I had imagined there was some type of monetary or land alliance they sought in producing that damned contract, but it would appear to be something else entirely."

"There are many things in life that are quite different than they appear to be, Lord Clarges," Will reminded him. An unexpected smile curved his generous mouth when he said, "And your grandfather can be very determined in some things."

"You needn't tell me that," Hannibal said, irritably thinking of the stubborn old Alpha who had maneuvered him with the effortless talent of long expertise.

Will's glance lingered into a look, assessing. His voice was soft and almost vague when he said, "He has twisted you into an untenable position and set you at odds with yourself. How terribly frustrating that must be, Lord Clarges."

Hannibal shifted with his sudden scrutiny, surprised to hear him speak so. "You show surprising insight, Will. It's unusual to find it in one so young."

"I am merely what my nature dictates, Lord Clarges," Will said, his nerves putting a bite in his words as his father's rebuke came to mind. *Nonsense*, he'd always called it. Something to be dampened down lest it offend those around him.

Recognizing Will was on the offensive, Hannibal gruffly reminded him, "Do try to call me by my name."

"We are not well enough acquainted for that, I think," Will said, shaking off the momentary haze of his perception. He realized Hannibal was looking back at him and directed his attention back to the Turkish carpet Hannibal had threatened him with earlier.

"I am your—" Hannibal broke off before he could finish, remembering how well his declaration had gone in Grandfather's suite this afternoon. "There are documents which say otherwise."

"Documents do not make people acquainted with nor contented with one another," Will said, tightening his grip on his book with every intention to get up and leave. "Please, excuse me. I have no wish to do battle with you again today."

"Sit down," Hannibal said, aggravated by the way Will continuously attempted to quit whatever room he happened to find the two of them sharing. It put an unexpected Alpha bark in the words and his spouse stiffened with offense.

Will stood from sheer stubborn defiance, shoulders tight and straight. "I will *not* and you had best not test me, Lord Clarges. I have no intentions of becoming any more familiar with the carpets of Hartford House than I am just now!"

Hannibal almost smiled at his bravado, thinking him rather foolishly brave in attempting to pit himself against a stronger and altogether bigger man. The smile was mitigated, however, by the reminder that Will, despite his smaller frame, had very nearly thrown him off in the foyer and had done a damned good job of retaliating when cornered.

"Have you a trout hidden on your person?" he asked, chuckling at how irritated his little mate was. "Or, perhaps, a teacup? It is unwise to talk bravely when you are unarmed."

"I have my mind, Lord Clarges," Will said, the sharpness of his voice shredding Hannibal's momentary belief that he could be predictable in the least. "I am never *unarmed*."

Hannibal had to concede the point.

"Yes, you are a frighteningly intelligent little thing," he said, watching the minute play of expressions on his spouse's expressive face

"Little *thing*?" Will bristled, tilting his head to one side, amazed at him. "Can you actually hear yourself speak or is the sound drowned out by the noise of self-admiration?"

It was Hannibal's turn to gain his feet, admiring the fact that Will didn't budge an inch. He was certainly a determined and angry bit of fluffy curls when he was properly riled, and shockingly easy to move to defensive violence.

155

"Have you any other nasty observations to make of my character? Hm?" Hannibal asked, just to see what he would do, knowing very well he was risking having the book in Will's hand flung at his head. "Considering you know me so well?"

"I needn't know you *well* to know how well you think of *yourself*," Will said, meeting his stare with a steely one of his own. "You do as you please, Lord Clarges, and your actions speak to your character!"

Hannibal laughed, the situation having shifted to hostility so quickly he couldn't quite pinpoint where he'd gone wrong. "We are speaking of actions, now, Will? Because I have *many* questions on that count."

Will said nothing, only wrapped his arms around himself in a dismal, unconscious act of self-soothing, the book wedged tightly to his chest.

"Ever since my return I've been piecing together a very strange picture of your time here," Hannibal said, advancing on him. "Your pathetic excuse for a monk's wardrobe, your absence from proper company, your taking on the land agent's work, your insistence on being called by your birth name—it makes me wonder what you hoped to accomplish."

Will paled at his tone, as if Hannibal found it all a staggering bunch of allegations that summed up into vicious intent.

"Did you have some goal in mind, Will, that I might someday yet return?" Hannibal asked, feeling entirely ungenerous with him after the events of the day. "Were you hoping your pious acts would compel me to overlook a marriage I neither wanted nor asked for? An undesired and repellent marriage I was forced into without so much as a warning?"

For a triumphant moment he thought Will might fight back, might show that amazing temper of his.

Instead, Will quietly asked, "What did you expect I would do when you made a public mockery of me by packing your bags and leaving your ancestral home rather than spend one more moment in my presence?"

A faint tremor of pain coursed through him when Will thought of that awful day and what had followed with such devastating rapidity. Sweat broke out over his brow and upper lip, a flush of pink in his cheeks telling to the spike in his temperature. "You are *public property*, Lord Clarges. When you so much as sneeze, it makes the papers. You stamped me with your disapproval for all to see, like a heifer with a brand. I was not welcome anywhere, by anyone. Did you think

I was here in your absence throwing parties? Purchasing a new wardrobe every Season? Making calls and entertaining myself on your coin?"

Hannibal frowned, unwilling to admit he had imagined just that—his brainless and encumbering spouse frittering away a fortune in gleeful ignorance of what happened in the world around him.

"No one would attend any event I held; they wouldn't dare risk your ire in doing so," Will said, closing his eyes against an unsettling roil of nausea, suddenly far too warm. "No one would see the state of my clothing because no one would step foot in this house to be tainted by your distaste. No one would accept a call from me, Lord Clarges, and share my ostracism from Society. Was that not precisely what you hoped for? To isolate me into repentance for my sins?"

The tremor spread to his voice, a wavering he could not even now control, and cursed himself for.

"Well, I repented, Hannibal," he said, his arms dropping as he abandoned any attempt to soothe himself, hardening to the task at hand as he had throughout the entirety of his life. "I have made myself as absent from this house as I could under the circumstances, given that your grandfather would not allow me to go back to my father, and you have the audacity to *scold me for it*?"

He lifted his head, blue eyes sheened with tears but blazing, finally blazing with his powerful, awe-inspiring temper.

"I had no *choice* but to use my own name! As if I could ever be persuaded to take *yours!*" he said, fingers clenching so hard on his book that his knuckles burned white. "I had no choice but to take the position of estate manager and make amends to your grandfather somehow, to be *useful*. The people here *accepted* me, Lord Clarges. They invited me into their homes. They shared their worries and triumphs with me and in the course of a single day you took all of that away from me."

He took a deep breath, the sudden silence ringing in his ears. Hannibal's amber eyes stayed steadily on him, unflinching and unmoved. The same eyes that had looked at him with loathing the day Will had bonded to him. The same eyes that had stared impassively at his vulnerable, nearly-naked body before he'd ordered Will out of his presence.

"But I suppose that is little enough compared to what I stole from you," Will said, his anger leeching away to leave him numb, the warmth dissipating from his skin. "I am a *thief*, Hannibal, as you have so pointedly said in the past. I have no right to live in this house or claim your name. Indeed, I have no desire to burden myself with the name of a man who has so little respect for me or others like me!"

Hannibal could see him trembling, but it wasn't from fear, not anymore.

"But that doesn't change the fact that Hartford House belongs to *me*," Will reminded him. "Dragging it from the brink of ruin and making it prosper? *That* is what I hoped to accomplish."

Hannibal frowned slightly, his conscience twinging in a way that was becoming increasingly and concerningly more frequent now that he had come home. His thoughts over the past six years in regards to the Omega he'd left behind him—when he could be bothered to think of Will at all—had been anything but kind. The consequences of his actions would in no way make this easier on either himself or on Will, he knew.

After a long, pregnant silence, Hannibal softly said, "Well. It seems you have an uncanny ability to render me speechless, Will."

Will turned his back to Hannibal, ashamed to have lost control. He felt ill somehow, too warm and sickened, easily driven to violence or upset by his husband. He longed for the numbness that had engulfed him six years ago and kept him insulated from this awful excess of emotion.

Retreating into icy reserve, he said, "You removed yourself once from an undesirable and repellent marriage to an undesirable and repellent Omega, Hannibal. I expect you to do so again, as we should all exercise those actions at which we *excel*."

He did not slam the door when he left, much to Hannibal's surprise. He could not, even in that, be counted on to be usual, it would seem.

Hannibal exhaled deeply, frustrated, wondering why his usual easy charm always abandoned him to bad temper when he was near Will Grant.

⌘⌘⌘

It took Will a very long time to shake off Hannibal's influence after their clash in the library. His irritation was like a furnace inside of him, newly discovered at Hannibal's arrival and slowly heating him from the inside out. He was overwarm and irritable, confounded and hurt and angry all at once, in such a flux of emotion it was little wonder his skin felt too tight and hot to suit him. When he eventually did sleep, it was plagued with nightmares of his father, deep dread, and the phantom of that cliff.

He woke up still irritated, an unusual enough occurrence for him that Jimmy remarked on it, arching a blond brow in that way he had which invariably coaxed a smile from his young Lord.

"I see your run-ins with Lord Clarges are bearing fruit," he said, flinging his way into Will's dressing room to pick through his clothing. After three years of insisting Jimmy not rise so early to assist him, Will had given in to his pleasant, dedicated valet's insistence on doing just that. "Though not the fruit he might have an eye for."

"There is little chance for *that* particular fruit," Will said, shoving away the comfort of sleep and standing in the chill air simply because he didn't want to. Even so small a concession could breed catastrophic consequences, he knew, and hurtle him down the road to becoming precisely as Hannibal imagined he was. So he shivered and clenched his jaw and indulged in a little well-earned spite. "I am sure he will realize we suit no better now than we did six years ago and rush back to his real family."

"Mr. Grant, I have a *plethora* of opinions on that subject if you'd like to hear," Jimmy offered, his voice echoing from the empty depths of his dressing room.

"No, Jimmy, thank you, I've had quite enough of opinions lately," Will told him, stifling a yawn. "I should go to the office."

"His Grace would prefer you didn't," Jimmy said, poking his head out to give him a steady look. "Work can wait, he said. You've a party to attend soon, Mr. Grant, remember?"

Will sighed, pacing slightly, toes curling against the cold nap of the hand-woven rug.

"I do wish you'd let me have the girls lay a fire—"

"No, Jimmy, it's far too early to bother them and I don't need coddling," Will said, but he didn't resist when Jimmy draped his dressing gown over his shoulders before returning to Will's closet. "What are you doing in there, anyway?"

"*Inventory*," Jimmy said.

"Grandfather wants an inventory of my clothing?" Will asked, surprised.

"No, *I* do."

Will jumped when Hannibal spoke from behind him and spun around to find him standing in the open doorway to their shared washroom, still in his own nightclothes and robe. His hair was tousled, which peeled a few years off of him, reminding Will quite painfully that Hannibal was not so old as all that, in fact.

"I beg your pardon, Lord Clarges, but once more you have wandered into places where you do not belong," Will said, resisting the urge to pat his own wild curls flat. There was simply no taming them without a good deal of water and a heavy comb, however, and well he knew it. "Shall I have Jimmy label the doors for you? I will insist he use very large print so you may read it."

"Ah, yes, please do," Hannibal said, smirking and rather pleased he was so sassy so early in the morning when most people didn't have their wits about them. "As I am clearly suffering from infirmity of age."

"Believe me, my Lord, we are *all* suffering from your infirmity of age," Will said, annoyed and aware he was *en déshabillé*, though he knew well enough how little impact that would make on Hannibal, considering what had happened during his ill-conceived seduction.

"Is there any hour of the day in which you are pleasant?" Hannibal asked, making no move to quit the room or venture further in.

"Whatever hour of the day I am not in your presence, I fear."

Hannibal closed his eyes and slowly took a deep breath, reminding himself that Omegas were delicate, frail creatures without the ability or motivation to save themselves and Will Grant was certainly none of those things, and he should no more want to throttle his mate than he should want to choke a child.

But gods was it tempting sometimes, even if Will would quite reasonably react with violence.

"*Behave,*" he warned, pleased when Will chose to glower at him. "I am in no mood to spar with you this morning, Will Grant. You there, Jimmy, what is the result?"

Jimmy promptly emerged and handed Hannibal the list he'd made, which was dreadfully short and appalling.

"I see," Hannibal said, reading it by the light of the taper Jimmy politely held for him. "And have you some aversion to clothing I am not aware of, Will? You have astonishingly little, considering."

Will bristled. "Considering *what*, Lord Clarges?"

"Oh, no you don't," Hannibal said, pinning him with a firm look. "Contain that tongue of yours, Will, or I'll find better uses for it."

Will's brow furrowed with confusion quickly followed by a blush, which Hannibal took gleeful note of, even if it was more angry than embarrassed.

"So, there's a way to curb your surliness after all," he observed, returning to the list. "This is all of it, even from storage?"

"Every bit, my Lord," Jimmy said.

"And it's all funeral garb?"

"Er... Mr. Grant is not particularly fond of color," Jimmy said, hedging his answer.

"I have no use for such frivolous nonsense," Will said, irritated, "and you have no cause to be inquiring into the state of my wardrobe!"

"I have, I do, and I will," Hannibal said, arrogant and short with him. "We are attending an event at Fernhill, in case you have forgotten, and Grandfather hopes to allay some of the gossip that apparently abounds in regards to us. Your dressing like an undertaker will not further our cause."

"I have no wish for your charity, Lord Clarges," Will said, clutching his robe up around his throat, aware of the weight of Hannibal's eyes when they landed there, searching and attentive. "And no need of your interest. My wardrobe will suffice—"

"Unless you are being buried, Will, it will *not*," Hannibal said. "You will dress and meet me downstairs. We are going into the village. I am sure Mister Avery can accommodate you."

"Would it not be more true to form, Lord Clarges," Will said, his voice sweet enough that Hannibal was immediately on guard, "if I *wheedle* you?"

"You have my permission to revel in the flow of my generosity," Hannibal said, disapproving of his beliefs being tossed in his face with such painful accuracy.

"How delightful that my plan to access a fortune I have had no hand in amassing is coming together so easily!" Will said, glowering and equally annoyed.

Hannibal leveled a glare at him and Will stretched a bit taller, refusing to bend. "Perhaps I should stop at the tack shop while we are there and purchase you a muzzle?"

Will pointed at the door and said, "*Out.* Don't think I can't lift that table and don't think I *won't.*"

Hannibal smirked, knowing it for an empty threat, but left all the same, wondering why Will's prickly nature was so amusing. He certainly was an abrupt and surprising young man. Hannibal looked forward to seeing Will in polite Society and wondered just how his odd little spouse would handle all those irritating people who had snubbed him for six years.

⌘⌘⌘

Will was dressed and downstairs before Hannibal, standing stiff and straight, staring off into space as if occupied by his thoughts. He cut a striking figure there in the early morning light, slender and composed and silent.

Hannibal strained to recall how Will had looked on the day he'd first arrived to Hartford House. Smallish, he thought. Rather, *very* small, young and not yet into his full growth. He'd seemed childlike to Hannibal then, a reed-thin but softly rounded bundle of nervous responses keyed too tightly to Hannibal's Alpha draw. He'd been too young, then, yet Hannibal had not treated him with the kindness and understanding his extreme youth had required.

And before him stood the result, a solemn and reserved Omega who avoided looking him in the face at all costs when *not* exploding into impressive and delightfully uninhibited violence.

"Agonizing over a day's work left unfinished, are we, land agent Grant?" Hannibal remarked, noting how Will started, taken by surprise by his arrival.

"Hartford House requires the full of my attention," Will said, managing to slide out of his reach as Hannibal gained the entryway and headed for the door.

"You were eager enough to leave it for Marsham Heath," he said, nodding to Mr. Hawkes, who swept open the door for them.

"You said you are here to stay," Will said, striding out into the wan morning light. "I assumed you would take over running the estate or else hire someone in."

"I do intend to hire someone," Hannibal informed him. "I also intend for you to have your hands full quite soon."

He glanced back at Will, who looked troubled and thoughtful. Smug, Hannibal descended the stairs to where Peter, their groom, waited with their horses. He mounted, settling into the saddle to watch Will, who pulled up with easy, athletic grace to sit erect in the saddle, his shoulders straight and squared.

"Walk on," Hannibal urged, clucking to his stallion, Will's own mount falling into pace next to him.

The morning sun grew stronger, chasing away the clouds. Hannibal tipped his nose to the soft breeze, enjoying the tang of country air flooding his senses with so many differing and wonderful scents.

"This truly isn't necessary," Will said, breaking the long silence between them.

"Of course it is," Hannibal told him. "You have had no proper exposure to Hartford Town as a member of the Ledford family and it is important for them to understand your true position here."

"Don't be ridiculous, this isn't about my *position* here," Will said, exhaling on a weary sigh. "Mitigating the damage starts now, doesn't it? Your intentions are transparent, Lord Clarges. How better to begin mending the holes you have poked in my reputation than to be seen indulging me in town?"

Hannibal glanced over at him, amused by the serious scowl on Will's lovely face. "You are amazingly perceptive at times."

"Not really," Will said, eyes flicking up to his. "As I said, your intentions are transparent; a child would know what you're about."

"Don't sound so grateful."

"I have no reason to be," Will said, looking away again, swaying with the movement of his mare's gait. "It is merely an excuse to rub my nose in it at any provocation."

"Were you less provocative, it might not be a problem," Hannibal said, urging his horse into a canter.

Will's mare broke into a trot to match, keeping pace.

"*You—*" Will cut off sharply, scrabbling at the reins as his saddle slid sideways and broke free, tumbling him to the paved road where he landed with a sickening thud that stole his breath. Stunned, he lay there trying to sort out if he'd been hurt or not.

Hannibal reined up short, cursing, and turned his mount around to see Will sitting up in the road, dazed and bewildered. A sudden throb of panic blossomed in his belly at the sight of his spouse there in the lane, wincing with pain in the tangle of his saddle.

"Will!" he drew his horse to a stop before him and hastily dismounted, concerned Will might have been badly hurt in his fall. He was uncertain what had happened to send him toppling from the horse. He was an excellent horseman, Hannibal knew, and was not prone to clumsiness.

"I'm fine, I just got the wind knocked out of me," Will said, the mare tugging at the rein he still clutched in one tight fist. "She must have blown out her belly. She sometimes does. I should have saddled her myself."

Hannibal caught his scent, the faint sweetness tinged with acrid pain and traces of something he could not name. "Have you any sharp pains, Will?"

Will shook his head hesitantly, his leg and hip aching where he had fallen. He hadn't been able to free his foot from his stirrup before he'd hit the ground and lay in a heap with the saddle tangling him up.

Hannibal bent and helped sort him free, frowning because Will was in pain and he could tell, even if the little twit wouldn't admit it.

"Here," Hannibal said, focusing on checking his limbs. Will flushed and batted at him with one hand, appalled to have Hannibal's hands roaming all over him, gently squeezing to feel the bones beneath as he checked for breaks. "Will you stop flailing about? I'm a doctor, Will, if I need remind you."

"I told you, I'm fine!" Will said, unsure what to make of his concern. "I'm *fine!*"

Will blushed to the tips of his ears when his assurances made no dent in Hannibal's examination. Indeed, he seemed so focused on what he was doing that Will just watched him, seeing the man who had tended the wounded in a war far from their own shores. It made him wonder how many had died despite Hannibal's best efforts, how many lives he felt responsible for in his near-decade overseas. He could see the grim intensity on Hannibal's handsome face and wondered if he, too, was thinking of those soldiers he had tended and lost.

"It is not the lives you saved that you remember, is it?" Will breathed, and Hannibal's startled amber eyes met his.

Will immediately dropped his gaze to one side, tamping down his Gift, his father's warning still fresh all these years later. It seemed to bubble up helplessly in Hannibal's presence, more troubling to him in the past few days than it had been in six years.

Hannibal's gaze skated over Will's stubborn profile but his little mate gave him nothing more than that sharply perceptive observation.

"No," he said, his professional reserve fading along with the grim memory of those he had failed in the war. "It is those who are lost which I remember most clearly."

It escaped him how Will would have any knowledge whatsoever about his experiences, nor did it make sense to him how Will could have hit on his thoughts so effortlessly, as if he'd been granted a peek into Hannibal's mind. It was not the first time Will had surprised him with such an observation, but it was the first time Hannibal felt curious about it. It was not coincidental, he knew. Once was a lucky guess, twice was intriguing enough to make him want to know more.

Yet, Will looked so terribly uneasy he decided against remarking on it. He was, after all, entirely Uncommon and there would no doubt be another opportunity for his sharp insight to make itself known again.

"Nothing is broken," Hannibal decided, and slid his fingers through Will's tousled curls, gently searching the fragile dome of his skull, his fingers curving of their own accord around the contours of Will's little ears. "Did you strike your head?"

"No, we weren't moving all that fast," Will said, blushing as Hannibal's long fingers brushed down his ears, stroked back through his hair once more, and then withdrew, the tingle of his touch remaining behind. He cringed when Hannibal pulled him to his feet, the leg he'd fallen on mightily sore. It was overshadowed, however, by the kernel of sympathy he felt for his haughty and proud husband. War changed people, Will knew, and the battles Hannibal had fought were etched into his memories forever, a wound that would not heal no matter how much time passed.

It was a wound that begged Will's Omegan nature to soothe it and he struggled to fight down the urge, to fight his bond, to be the Omega Hannibal desired, the Omega his father had molded him to be.

Absent.

"Gods forbid we had been," Hannibal said, aware of Will's solemn, thoughtful silence. He dragged the mess of saddle up and flung it to the side of the lane with the same suddenness he dragged Will from his somber thoughts. "You might have broken your neck."

"Neither of us is so lucky today, Lord Clarges," Will said, reminded again what Hannibal stood to gain from his loss.

Hannibal dropped an uneasy, assessing look at him and pulled his stallion around. The panic he'd felt seeing Will so helpless there in the road had abated somewhat knowing he was not greatly harmed, but it was not gone entirely. Indeed, each time he pictured Will in such a state, it returned with no little

165

insistence. Softly, thoughtfully, he said, "That's a dismal thing to say, even for so surly a fellow as you."

Will shrugged, his smile tight and unhappy, turning to discomfort when Hannibal's hands slid around his waist. Before he could protest, he was hefted up into the stallion's saddle sideways.

"You're going to walk to town?" Will asked, scoffing. "I didn't expect such chivalry from you, especially towards an Omega."

"Good, because I'm not being chivalrous," Hannibal said, taking the mare's reins and tying her to the stallion's saddle. He briefly crowded Will, grabbing hold of the pommel near his thigh and looming into his space as he mounted up behind him. "I'm not walking anywhere."

Will huffed with indignant irritation when he was hefted, tugged, and settled comfortably before him, legs slung to one side over Hannibal's thigh, his wide eyes staring with outrage at the hand that rested on his own thigh to steady him. Hannibal clucked and the horse rolled into an easy walk, jostling Will enough that he reflexively put his arm around Hannibal's side to grip the back of the saddle.

"This is entirely uncalled for," Will said, wishing he wasn't so warm and Hannibal's Alpha scent wasn't so deliciously compelling. It made him feel overheated and lethargic, a curious malady, indeed. He tried his best to sit erect but it was nearly impossible and he wound up leaning into Hannibal's chest, grumpy and sore. It galled him how even this affected him, rendering him nothing more than a touch-starved Omega, the very victim of instinct Hannibal was so repulsed by.

"You're more sensible than most, Will."

"Most *Omegas*, you mean?" Will asked, bristling.

"Most *people*. You realize there are very few options at hand just now," Hannibal said, sputtering a little when the wind tickled his nose with a handful of Will's silky curls. Grinning, he asked, "Unless your head is full of the same fluff that tops it?"

"Ah, finally."

Hannibal's brows rose, wondering at his soft chuckle.

"Insult to injury," Will said, tipping his head forward, taking those soft curls and sweet fragrance with him.

"But you aren't injured, remember?" Hannibal said, unable to resist needling him. He was surprisingly heavier than he looked, solid and firm with young muscle that sat tensely in Hannibal's lap. "Goodness, you are very warm."

"I run hot, and stop squeezing me," Will warned him, tossing a dangerous glare up at him.

Hannibal hadn't realized his hand had slipped from Will's leg to fold around his narrow waist. Feeling a little caught out, he said, "We can't have you falling again, can we?"

"I didn't fall!" Will snapped, angry. "I put great store in my riding, thank you very much. I no more fell from her back than you did!"

"You do have an enviable seat, to be sure. You could handle a much more powerful mount," he mused. "She's a fine little mare, but she's a bit drab."

"I am not interested in how she *looks*," Will said, affronted his horse would be so insulted. "She has a soft mouth and a gentle gait and she is very sturdy! I take her on rounds and she never fusses, which is something you cannot say of your stallion!"

Hannibal chuckled, impressed by his passionate defense of his mare, and conceded the point. "No, he's a handful. We hardly got any bit of business done for minding him. But you are a Marquess, Will. You should have a horse which suits you."

"She suits me perfectly well," Will said, casting an affectionate glance back at her and smiling softly when her ears flicked. "She has been stalwart these past six years. She has never shied, even that morning when you—"

He cut off, flushing to have so thoughtlessly brought up the morning he had bonded to his husband.

Hannibal's amusement fled at the mention of that ride and how things had gone. He had not realized Will had formed such an attachment to his mare, but it made a certain poetic sense to him. When Will had been rejected and terrorized, she had carried him safely home without trouble and had continued to do so since that day.

"I'm of a mind to have all your gear checked," Hannibal said, gruffly not acknowledging Will's slip when he was so obviously distressed by it. "You might have sustained a terrible injury, Will. Even such a capable and loyal animal couldn't manage to unbuckle her own straps. There must be something wrong with the saddle."

"Yes," Will said, uneasy, the sudden spike in his tension making Hannibal's frown deepen.

"I'll get you something for the pain at the druggist's."

"Please, don't do that," Will said, refusing, forced harder into Hannibal's chest as they hit the slight hill preceding Hartford Town. "It is nothing."

"I won't have you limping around Bedelia's garden party," Hannibal said. "Else they'll wonder what other carpets I've been tumbling you on."

Will didn't justify that with a response other than to blush in mortification, doing his best to ignore the way his heart knocked in his chest, surely loud enough Hannibal could hear it.

"You're coiled like a spring," Hannibal complained, shifting Will slightly closer, enjoying the press of his warm, solid body enough that he needed to analyze it for a bit and figure it out. He was not prone to attraction to men, whatever their delicacy, so it couldn't be that, he knew. Fascination, maybe, with the unpredictable nature of such an intriguing and taciturn young man.

"I *cannot breathe!*" Will said. Hannibal noted he had breath enough to complain, "I'm capable of holding on!"

"You'd rather fall face first into a dung pile than hold on to me, Will," Hannibal chuckled, allowing the horse his head. It picked up the pace, ears perked, and trotted down the hill towards town. "I doubt it would improve your disposition."

"To the contrary," Will said. "A dung pile is preferable to being *squeezed in a press.*"

Hannibal eased his grip, chastened by the way Will's complaint ended on a breathless growl.

They passed the last stretch in silence and Hannibal paused at the end of town, watching the village begin its day.

"Mr. Woodward said you like to watch the town wake up," Hannibal mused, idly spreading his fingers over Will's thigh. "Is this what you do?"

"Yes, I find it very calming," Will said, momentarily lost in his own comfortable habits. "There's something very relaxing about seeing the village rise. And it's nice to take some exercise after being in the office for those first few hours."

Hannibal considered that, thinking of his own mornings spent waking next to someone, enjoying the indulgence of servants waiting on them hand and foot while Will was here alone, watching the busy activity of a town he did not feel a part of, separated by a rank he never claimed.

An outsider looking in, making a place for himself through earnest work Hannibal had never dreamed an Omega could manage, let alone as successfully and impressively as Will had.

Will's fingers moved against his back, a light pressure which distracted him from his thoughts. Nudging the horse on down the main road, Hannibal broke his contemplative silence by asking, "You truly do enjoy your work at Hartford House, Will?"

"Yes," Will said. "It's important to be useful and do something worthwhile with one's time. It is consuming and rewarding work."

"Will... I do appreciate what you've managed here at Hartford House," Hannibal said, earning a startled, furtive look from his spouse. "You've managed to make improvements I never expected or would have thought of. I may not have made myself clear on that count towards you, Will, but I am impressed by what you've accomplished."

Will absorbed that, unexpected as it was, but he could feel no lie through his bond to Hannibal and he felt a blush stain his cheeks, the familiar impatience with praise rising in him thanks to his father's lessons.

"I did not intend for you to see me as uprooting your place here, Will," Hannibal said, turning his horse towards the town livery. "The truth of the matter is, a child will require the full of our attention and I know you would not wish the estate business to fall behind in the meantime. The best solution is to hire an estate manager fairly soon so you can instruct them on how things should be properly done. There is nothing to prevent you from taking over again once our son is old enough for school."

Will stayed silent. The rational, business part of him understood Hannibal's position, but he couldn't help feeling stripped of his purpose. Being the Hartford estate manager was all he knew; he had never been educated about children. His father had never dreamed it would be an issue and had taught him to be useful, with good reason.

'Useless things,' his father had said, 'are only fit for burning.'

"You there, boy," Hannibal called, getting the attention of a grubby little stable hand as they rode up. "A half mile up the road is a broken saddle. Fetch it and have your master fix it. And tend this mare for now."

"Yes, m'Lord," the boy said, darting to take her when Hannibal untied the reins. His shrewd little eyes flicked over Will and, at a loss, he said, "Morning, Mr. Grant."

"Good morning, John," Will said, wearily aware Hannibal was determined to be seen with him. Not that it mattered anymore, if he was to hire an estate manager anyway. That aside, after their visit to Gold Meadow Farm and their other tenant farmers, news of his place had, no doubt, already made the rounds of Hartford Town.

"Wondered where you was this morning."

"*Greatly* inconvenienced," Will said with no little heat. "Please see that my saddle is fixed and my horse is ready for my return trip."

"We can ride double if she isn't," Hannibal said, smirking when Will promptly said, "I am sure the weather will be nice enough for me to enjoy the walk, Lord Clarges."

Chuckling, Hannibal turned the horse back towards the main road and drew to a halt at the dressers, where he swiftly slid down and fixed the horse to a nearby post within reach of a water trough.

"Ah, such a shame," Will said, relieved. "They aren't open."

"They will be," Hannibal said, seeing movement behind the glass. He reached up and caught Will by his slender waist to heft him down, asking, "Does it hurt much?"

"No, I'm fine," Will said. "And I tire of telling you so. Let's finish whatever mischief you're up to and be gone, shall we?"

The mischief, much to Will's exasperation, was engaging Mr. Avery, the tailor, to flesh out his meager wardrobe and Hannibal took great pleasure in the way the staff all fawned over him, eager to please.

It made Will snort with disdain from his seat, his untouched tea beside him and his arms folded over his chest, his opinions unasked after Hannibal declared him tetchy and viperish and entirely out of sorts.

"I will expect you to send off to your sister store in the Capital for the quality I require," Hannibal said, rubbing his chin as he looked from one waistcoat to another, trying to decide which would suit Will best as his mate had gruffly claimed to have no interest in any of it. The pale green with soft shell patterning would make his eyes seem all the lighter, but he was rather more partial to the rich blue, which he knew would both compliment Will's coloring and make his eyes deeper in color.

"This is ridiculously difficult," he said, frowning between the two. "What do you think?"

"The midnight blue is quite lovely," Mr. Avery commented, glancing at Will. "But Mint is all the rage this year."

"The midnight blue, then," Hannibal said, gesturing Will to stand. "I will not have any member of the Ledford family being *trite*."

"Perish the thought," Will breathed, reluctantly standing to be fitted for quick adjustments while Hannibal set about choosing his jacket and ordering a new pair of boots for him. "Honestly, Mr. Avery, is this entirely necessary? I have not changed all that much since last spring, surely?"

"Last *spring*?" Hannibal echoed, pausing in his perusal to fix Will with an incredulous look, sparing Mr. Avery an answer.

"I required a new riding coat," Will said, a touch defensive from his tone. "Nothing more. Mr. Avery, however, is very thorough and takes measurements in their entirety, no matter one's haste."

"As well he should!" Hannibal said, bringing a flush of pleasure to Mr. Avery's wan cheeks. "And he will be seeing a great deal more of you, you can be sure! This appalling lack of wardrobe simply will not do! We must visit the Row in the Capital before the Season starts and see you properly outfitted."

"You are so generous, Lord Clarges!" he was told by the tailor's assistant, and nodded graciously, pleased they had noticed. "Your son is so *very* lucky to have a father like you!"

Will's eyes rounded and he swallowed his laughter, almost undone by the horrified, bewildered expression on Hannibal's handsome face.

"Are you new here?" Hannibal asked, cocking his head.

"Yes, m'Lord, only just in from—"

"*This* is Will Grant," Hannibal said, pointing at Will.

"Yes, Mr. Grant."

"My *spouse*!" Hannibal clarified.

"Oh..." the tailor's assistant went pasty pale and trembled while Mr. Avery merely stifled a smirk, knowing well enough who he was and having been paid handsomely to keep his silence on the subject these many years.

"Good gods, man, how on earth would I have a child his age when I am not even forty?" Hannibal asked, thoroughly annoyed. "Why does everyone think he is something he is not?"

"*You* do," Will said, earning himself a startled look which immediately fell into a dark scowl.

"He... he looks so young," the assistant said, a meek and diffident offering.

"And I so old?" Hannibal inquired, a dangerous glint in his eye.

"Of course not, Hannibal, don't be petty," Will said, deciding to stop things before the poor man fainted dead away from embarrassment. He reached out without thinking, giving Hannibal's forearm a squeeze. "Considering this is the first time anyone in the village has seen you in six years, you can hardly complain that some did not know you were married to me."

Hannibal gave the assistant a dark look, but the hand on his forearm distracted him from his anger, even brief as the touch was. Without thinking, he corrected, "*Am* married."

When he looked down at where Will's slender fingers lay on his arm, Will immediately dropped his hand and stepped away, embarrassed by his impulsive reaction.

Flustered, Hannibal reluctantly returned his attention to ordering things Will neither wanted nor needed, forgetting it was all for the sake of public opinion when he imagined how pleasant it would be to see his spouse in something other than funeral black.

To Will, it was an impressive waste of time, honestly, and he felt the first hour pass into a second with keen anxiety, wanting only to return to his little office and have some peace and quiet. Once word got around Lord Clarges was in the dresser's buying the place up for his spouse, the little shop got an unusual amount of activity until it became quite crowded and Will did his best to remain unobserved in his seat. Those in town who knew him by sight knew him only as Mr. Grand, the estate manager. Even those who knew him well enough to pass conversation with him had no idea he was the spouse Hannibal had abandoned Hartford House to escape.

Hannibal, however, made quite a show of charming the townsfolk, many of whom had never really made his acquaintance. The population had swelled significantly since Hannibal had left for the military and the newcomers had only heard stories about their Duke's heir, only knew what they read about in the Society column of the Capital newspapers.

Will watched him, envying the effortless way he spoke even to strangers, a teasing amusement that left them feeling flattered and singled out. He could be very charming when it suited him, though Will had never chanced to feel Hannibal's charm turned on him with much effect.

"M'Lord?"

He turned to find a goodly portion of the female customers crowding the store were watching him, equal parts shy and excited.

"I do apologize, m'Lord, for not recognizing you before," he was told by Mrs. Kirkland, whose husband leased their most profitable grain fields. "I was sure my husband were having me on when he said you was a proper Marquess!"

Will laughed softly, relieved she and her bevy of plump farm wives seemed more pleased than aghast at his duplicity. "Mrs. Kirkland, I assure you my own father would hardly recognize me as a Marquess. I'm afraid I was intent on deceiving you. I humbly beg your forgiveness."

They tittered and exchanged glances like a group of school girls, which coaxed a smile from him.

"You've always done right by us!" he was told. "We do hope things won't change much now he's come back."

"Only in that I will no longer serve as estate manager, Mrs. Pembroke," Will said, and hastily added, "For a time, at least. There are family matters which need tending."

"I've had my fill of them *family matters*, I own," Mrs. Kirkland confided, blushing at her own boldness. "But I reckon it will be no chore, handsome as your Marquess is!"

"I will admit my husband's faults cannot be found in his looks, ladies," Will said, smiling at the assembled group. "He certainly will make some lucky woman very happy someday."

There was a round of scandalized, amused gasps and laughter, good-natured and inclusive, as if finding out Will was Omegan granted him not only a place with their husbands' businesses, but also a place in their feminine circle. It was surprisingly pleasant to feel such camaraderie, even if their sense of propriety caused them to excuse themselves from too much socializing. Despite everything, Will was a Marquess thanks to his husband's status, and everyone knew that set him apart. He contented himself with simply staying out of the attention Hannibal drew and amused himself watching how Hannibal controlled the room like a delighted puppet-master.

"Mr. Grant! I will have the breeches, waistcoat, and jacket all delivered before the end of the day," Mr. Avery said, awash now in good spirits at the sudden bustle of business in his little shop.

"Have them given to Jimmy, as usual," Will said, standing gingerly, glad when his weight did not overly bother his leg. "He will tend to it."

That earned him a trilling little laugh and the tailor immediately turned his attention back to Hannibal, who kept casting meaningful looks his direction to beckon him closer.

Will, however, had nearly had his fill of the crowded store, and headed towards Hannibal to tell him so when the door clanged noisily and the buxom, dark-eyed Widow Reynolds breezed in, scanning the room to find Hannibal.

"*Lord Clarges*!" she called, pushing through the polite press to reach him, her eyes alight with excitement and her formidable bosom heaving beneath her rather garishly-colored red dress. "It's been *too long*!"

Will came to an abrupt halt at the sight of her snagging Hannibal by the arm and cozying up to him, rendered mute with shock at her gall and embarrassment at her lack of discretion.

"Beatrix Danvers?" Hannibal asked, placing her face at last. He tried to shake her off but she clung like a damned barnacle, much to his consternation. "What on earth are you doing here?"

"It's Reynolds, now. I heard you'd come home," she said, fluttering her lashes at him in a way she no doubt thought was becoming. "I came as soon as I could to offer you my condolences."

"Condolences?" Hannibal echoed, frowning down at the samples he was attempting to choose from and wishing Will would come join him. "And who has died?"

She uttered a shrill little laugh and squeezed his arm, breathing, "*You know*."

Hannibal glanced at her, ready to tell her that he bloody well did *not* know, but he spied Will staring at him and got distracted by the strange, assessing look on his face. It was concerning enough that he began to step towards him but Beatrix held fast, whispering to him, "Your *marriage*, Lord Clarges! I know you are away from your mistress for some time here at Hartford House and I have come to remind you that I am a widow for many years and *very much* available to offer you comfort when you need it."

"How odd," Hannibal remarked, tipping his face close to her ear to keep his words private. "As I find myself more discomfited now than I was before your arrival."

He smirked, pleased, and looked up to see Will's blue eyes on the pair of them, half-lidded and glittering, his full mouth tight with disapproval. It made Hannibal aware that everyone in the dresser's was staring at him with varying shades of frank disapproval, for all the world seeing him standing with an old lover on his arm and trading whispered banter with her right in front of his silent, still spouse.

He could almost *see* the gossip starting, destroying everything he'd hoped to accomplish. Annoyed, he removed Beatrix from his arm and shortly ordered, "Will, please join me, I am in need of your opinion."

Very calmly, his voice never rising above a soft, sultry purr, Will said, "My opinion is that red is a color which suits you immensely, Lord Clarges. You wear it with the ease of long familiarity. If you will excuse me, I am much too busy to indulge your whims at the moment."

Hannibal gaped at him, as did the rest of the shop, including Beatrix.

With that shocking statement made, Hannibal's Uncommon mate turned on his heel and marched out of the shop with the same stiff-backed dignity of a soldier off to war, leaving Hannibal staring after him.

"Goodness gracious, Lord Clarges, is *that* your spouse?" Beatrix asked, an overdue flush of embarrassment lighting her cheeks.

"Yes," Hannibal said, watching Will leave the shop with a soft, admiring smile on his face. "He *absolutely* is."

Chapter 11

Quietly fuming, Will stalked out onto the street into the cool late morning air. He took a settling breath, then another, annoyed when he recalled the pitying, knowing looks directed at him when that woman had engaged his husband, as if he had any interest at all in whom Hannibal bedded.

But it *was* too much to be borne, no matter that he was expected to be complacent and mindless on the subject of Hannibal's affairs. Entirely finished with such an extravagant waste of his time, Will decided to walk down to the livery to check on the state of his saddle, determined to head back to Hartford House.

John spied him coming and ran up to him, eyes bright with curiosity.

"Your mare's enjoyin' herself," he offered, making conversation the only way he knew how.

"And my saddle?" Will asked, absently rubbing his aching hip, still absorbed in his thoughts. Of all the debacles that could have taken place, of *course* it had to center around Hannibal's blatant infidelities, the sheer number of which had reached Will, even sequestered as he was. It was no stretch of the imagination that he would, being bereft of his most recent favorite, locate an obliging body here in Hartford Town.

He urged himself not to care, to consider it for the best because at least now Hannibal would not be demanding his rightful access to Will's bed, no matter his bizarre reversal on the subject of a child.

It was no use, however, and the longer he thought about it, the more offended and put out he became. It wasn't enough for Hannibal to shame him from afar. He had to make it locally known he had so little respect for Will, that he considered Will so utterly insignificant, that such flagrant dalliances could be conducted in his presence.

Whatever respect the people of Hartford Town may have harbored for Will would certainly not survive long after today.

"Dunno if it's enjoyin' itself, but Matthew's fixin' it," John said, kicking a stone down the paved walk, his high voice dragging Will out of his dark thoughts. "He said it was a strange thing."

"Yes, I imagine so," Will said, giving him a few pennies as he was wont to do, feeling churlish for wishing him away but not wanting company just now.

"He your husband? That fancy fellow you come in with?" John asked, bursting with curiosity, skipping alongside Will, who nodded here and there at various people going about their business, trying to pretend as if nothing had changed.

"The paperwork would lead me to believe so," Will answered him, sour.

"He nice to you?"

"We don't know one another well enough to be nice," Will told him. "We are polite, as you are polite with strangers."

"Hm. He staying?"

"Unfortunately, it would seem he is," Will said, sighing heavily. "Run along, now, John, and give those pennies to your mother."

"*All* of them?"

He looked so woeful that Will handed him a larger coin and said, "Go buy treats with this—enough for everyone, mind you—then take it all to your mother."

"Yes, sir, Mr. Grant!"

Will watched him dash off, envying his energy, and turned back to continue limping towards the livery, hoping to reach home before his irritation overcame him.

⌘⌘⌘

It took Hannibal longer than he liked to settle with the tailor, confirm his order, and extract himself from Beatrix, who refused to take his hints or even his outright rebuffal. The gathering of town gentlefolk who'd come to introduce themselves and better themselves through acquaintance had gotten a show, he knew, and no single part of it would help Will's besmirched reputation.

If anything, Will was worse off now in public opinion than he had been, and Hannibal was vastly annoyed as he was not a man who took failure easily or gracefully.

Especially when it was his own fault.

It was a full half an hour almost before he found himself outside of the shop once more with nary a spouse in sight and by then he was fuming as much at his own culpability in things as at Beatrix's behavior. At least *she*, ignorant opportunist that she was, had a good reason to cause a scene! Gossip would cast her in the imaginary role of his lover, which would garner her deference in Hartford Town. He, on the other hand, should have known better than to entertain her attention for more time than it took to politely disengage. That he hadn't, that he'd given the entire town a spectacle when they clearly favored Will, just irritated him all the more.

'*Red is a color which suits you immensely...*'

Will's flaying, parting comment—so quickly conjured and so delightfully astonishing—had left Hannibal undeniably and thoroughly impressed with him, no matter how shocked the rest of the shop had been. He did feel it had not been entirely called for since he had never had any carnal relations with the Widow Reynolds and had no intentions of seeing her again if he could help it, but he was not surprised Will had deliberately upended that particular apple-cart. The remark stung some when he thought of how easily he'd been imagining Will in the new clothing he'd ordered for him. It was the first time he'd actually *not* been actively attempting to get under Will's skin, but still managed to embroil himself in his mate's stern disapproval. Not to mention how oddly ashamed he felt to be called, in essence, a scarlet woman by his mate when he'd come here with such good intentions.

"Honestly, it's almost worse if I attempt to please him!" he breathed, looking up and down the street for his wayward spouse.

It didn't take much to work out where Will would have gone—for his saddle, his mare, and his way home.

Hannibal untethered his horse and mounted, heading towards the livery at a light canter, wondering what on earth it was going to take to get Will into a receptive frame of mind and rescue *both* their reputations in their community.

⌘⌘⌘

Will waited in the stall with his mare until Matthew could talk with him, spending his time in the relative peace of the horses and allowing his irritation to burn itself out. His mare munched quietly on oats, a treat Will was generous with, and the soft blow of her breath and small sounds of her eating relaxed him enough that he leaned his head on her shoulder.

"Mr. Grant?" Matthew said to get his attention, and waited for Will to come to him, his green eyes strangely hooded. "The saddle is repaired, sir."

"Mr. Dunn," Will said, smiling at the Alpha who had always been so thoughtful of him. "Was there some terrible difficulty with my saddle? I have never had such a thing happen before."

Matthew's voice was strained with upset when he lowly told him, "Mr. Grant, that girth strap had no weak points, not even where it buckled." He pulled the strap from his work apron and held it out for Will's inspection, showing him where the break had occurred. "It looks like it's been—"

"Cut," Will breathed, paling at the implications.

"Mr. Grant, I know I'm no one to advise you," Matthew said, worried. "But you should tell His Grace—"

"No, that's not necessary," Will said, shaking his head. "And I would prefer you keep this information to yourself."

"But, Mr. Grant—"

"Matthew, I appreciate your concern," Will said, resisting the frightened tremble threatening to emerge. "But I have no intentions of remaining here for much longer."

Matthew's worry faded to uneasy understanding, and his voice was soft when he said, "John told me about you riding in... and Patton was in the pub last night."

Will took a deep breath and said, "I did not purposefully deceive you. I have, in all honesty, truly been the land agent for Hartford House. The fact that Lord Clarges was required by contract to wed me is so inconsequential as to be dismissed."

"But he's back now. For an heir at last?"

"He is," Will said. Reluctantly, he said, "I'm sorry, Matthew, I've been passing myself off as a beta m—"

"Mr. Grant, I've always known you're Omegan," Matthew interrupted, unperturbed on that count. "But you had everyone else fooled... at least until Patton got a few in him."

"Yes, apparently word travels fast. Now everyone knows my place here is not what they first believed, that *I* am not what they first believed," Will whispered, embarrassed to be so exposed, "and there is no way now to explain myself."

Matthew frowned, his green eyes flicking to the street outlet for signs of intrusion. "If you're his spouse, Mr. Grant, then your saddle being rigged makes a lot more sense."

Will's stomach clenched. Barely able to force words past the constriction in his throat, he asked, "What on earth do you mean?"

"I mean he's got a history, Mr. Grant," Matthew said, "and you wouldn't be the first one to get in his way and be buried for it."

Will's shocked silence went on for so long that Matthew whispered, "You need to tell someone you trust. In case the worst happens."

Will paled, increasingly queasy to think of who stood to gain the most from his death, who Matthew was so quietly telling him might have been responsible for creating an accident that could have resulted in a broken neck with no one the wiser.

Hannibal.

The same man who had once threatened to arrange just such an accident six years ago, and Will had no reason to think he had changed his mind. Freed of his marriage and his obligation to their respective grandfathers' contract, Hannibal would have no reason to stay absent from the largest estate of his inheritance and could claim his place without impediment.

It was little wonder he'd returned so willing to do his "duty".

Thoroughly unnerved, Will wet his lower lip and breathed, "How much do I owe you, Matthew?"

"He may charge it to Hartford House," Hannibal said, striding into the stable from the end that lay open to the lane.

Matthew tensed in a way was sensed more than seen but still made Will's nerves tighten nonetheless.

He swallowed hard to see his husband coming towards them, tall and powerfully-built and capable of unknown violence. The heat of Hannibal's temper was like the rasp of a file on his skin and he flinched, bristling in response, unwilling to allow it to affect him.

"You, there, please have someone saddle Will's mare for him—"

"No, Matthew, I am capable of saddling her myself," Will said, responding to his order with tight anger.

Hannibal pinned him with a look and said, "*Matthew* will have someone *saddle her for you*. His trade is just this; I am sure he can manage to saddle her correctly."

Will subsided, not willing to risk a row in front of witnesses over something so trifling, though he doubted very much it could do further damage.

Irritated to be ordered about by another Alpha, Matthew vanished to fetch Will's repaired saddle, leaving the two of them somewhat alone.

Hannibal reached for Will, cocking his head when he pulled out of reach on a twitch of instinct.

"Will Grant, what on earth has gotten into you?" Hannibal asked, reaching again and grasping his elbow with warm fingers to propel him back outside. "You should not have left the shop in such a fashion."

"I have no *sense* of fashion, as you have pointed out," Will said, deliberately missing the point. "Nor have I any desire to watch you engage *services* of such a select type!"

"The only *services* I engaged were those of Mr. Avery and his insufferable assistant!" Hannibal said, his own temper rising to meet Will's. "Whatever feats of imagination your impressive mind has managed, Will, I was *not* pandering for a mistress! That would be bad form, even for me, to do such a thing with you present."

"*With me* present?" Will echoed, horrified into laughter. "*You* are entirely unbelievable, Lord Clarges!"

"As are *you*! I have just spent a small fortune on clothing you," Hannibal said, turning him to stare down into his face. "Your gratitude is more than lacking!"

"I did not ask you to," Will reminded him. "And why should I be grateful for that theater you attempted to put on? My presence was not required, Lord Clarges. You could just have easily gone without me and achieved the same aim *without* making a public fool of me once again!"

"My *aim* was to see you properly outfitted for the Garden Party," Hannibal said. "My *aim* was to bolster your reputation in this village by publicly accepting you!"

Will's eyes widened with offense. "But instead you destroy what little was left of my lauded reputation by accepting the attentions of a widow with notorious appetites! You had no thought for me at all, Lord Clarges! Perhaps you should bolster your *own* reputation, sir! After all, *you* are the one who will have to live with them!"

For a surprising moment Hannibal thought Will had found out about the agreement he'd made with Grandfather and he gaped at him, wondering how on earth he had managed to do so.

"Or have you changed your mind about bringing your family to Hartford House?" Will asked, sensing he was at a loss and wondering at the cause.

Hannibal got hold of himself and said, "You are not going anywhere, Will. You will stay here at Hartford House and bear the child my grandfather has asked for."

"Lord Clarges, your humor has crossed a line," Will said, pulling out of his grip. "While it may seem a good joke to you, I assure you that I am not amused."

"You are not amused because I am *not joking*," Hannibal said, the stern tone of his voice making Will look up sharply at him. Taking a deep breath, Hannibal said, "Will, I am deadly serious when I say there will be a child between us."

"That would require my consent," Will said after a surprised silence.

He was entirely unprepared when Hannibal said, "Not *necessarily*."

Will flinched, knowing Hannibal referred to his heats. There were ways to prevent them, he knew, ways used by Omegas who fought in the military and could not afford to be found out. They sacrificed their fertility in the same way they sacrificed their lives, but Will had found himself possessed of a tiny thread of hope that had kept him from using such methods. He never dreamed he would bear a child for Hannibal, but perhaps for someone, someday, after the dissolution of their farce of a marriage.

"That is disgraceful, even for you," Will whispered, looking away so that Hannibal was left staring at the line of his jaw and his fine profile. "I doubt even a heat fever could blind you to an undesirable and repellent Omega."

Hannibal exhaled softly, recalling what he had said last night in the library.

"I should not have said such things to you," he admitted, uncomfortably aware he was in the wrong. "And despite what you may feel you know of me, I should hope you know I would not stoop to taking advantage of you in such a terrible and unforgivable way."

Will's skeptical, raised eyebrow spoke volumes about what he imagined Hannibal was capable of, prompting his husband to say with unusual sincerity, "I am trying to gain your favor, Will. You do like gifts, do you not?"

"That was not a gift," Will told him, crossing his arms over his chest. "That was a public mockery."

"I have complimented your fine work at Hartford House," Hannibal pointed out.

"You have shown great shock that an Omega could muster the intelligence to manage such a thing," Will said. "It was not a compliment to my accomplishments, Lord Clarges, but a rebuke against my gender."

Hannibal frowned, brows pulling down as he reassessed.

"The Omegas I have known are all simple creatures with simple pleasures," he said, completely upended. "Why are you so difficult to please?"

Will laughed scornfully and shook his head. "It is very easy to please me, Lord Clarges."

"Tell me, then," Hannibal said, relieved. "And I will do it."

Will's blue eyes met his for a heartbeat, just long enough for him to say, "Have our marriage dissolved and let me forget you."

⌘⌘⌘

It was a strained and silent return ride to Hartford House made with a telling gap between their horses, both in contemplative silence, though for vastly different reasons. The moment he handed his mare off to waiting staff, Will retreated to his suite and settled nervously at his small writing desk. Goaded by Matthew Dunn's strained warning, Will dipped his quill, wiped at the slight sheen of sweat on his brow with his free hand, and wrote.

My Dearest Sister,

I am writing to confide in you that a matter of some concern has occurred. As you may have read in the papers, my husband has only just returned to Hartford House and I find I have reason to believe I am no longer safe. This very morning while riding there was an accident with my saddle—an accident I have no doubt would have been fatal had I been riding at any great speed at all. Upon inspection it was found that the saddle had been tampered with, the girth strap sliced to pull free under pressure.

I believe that my life may be in danger and I wished for you, my twin, the only one whom I can trust, to know my suspicions. No one else knows of this occurrence and I would prefer to keep it that way. I trust you will keep this to yourself for now.

Please do not trouble yourself with a reply, dearest Mina. I merely write against a fate I fear I cannot escape.

Ever your loving twin,

Will

He sealed it quickly and prepared it for the post, swiping at his forehead yet again. There was no sign of his husband as he made his way downstairs to deliver the letter into Jimmy's hands, knowing its existence would be held in strictest confidence.

That accomplished, he headed towards the stable and spied Peter still rubbing down Hannibal's stallion, murmuring gently to the large horse, who was behaving rather better than it usually did.

"Peter," he softly called, and smiled in response at the way the gentle beta man's face lit up.

"Mr. Grant!" he called, delighted. "I-it's good to see you!"

"It's good to see you, too, Peter," Will said, coming closer to lay his hand on the stallion's nose, unspoken permission for Peter to continue his task if he wished. "Peter, I... I have a question. About my saddle."

"You got the strap redone," Peter said, a slight frown flitting across his face. "I-I saw it, Mr. Grant. I saw it was new. Matthew, he did a good job."

"Peter, did you see anyone near my saddle before I rode out? Anyone who should not be here?"

Peter shook his head faintly, then with more force. "No, Mr. Grant. No one comes here."

"Someone meddled with my saddle, Peter," Will confided, lowering his voice to a bare whisper. "I tell you this in strict confidence, trusting you will tell no one. The girth strap was cut—"

"Mr. Grant, I-I check them, I swear—" Peter stammered, furiously shaking his head.

"No, I trust you did, Peter, you always do excellent work," Will said, hastening to assure him, relieved when it calmed his fear. "No, Peter, it was cut high up, no place you would think to check for weakness. Can you think of anyone who might have had access to do such a thing?"

Peter shook his head again, saying softly, "No, Mr. Grant. The t-tack room is locked."

"Does anyone have access to your keys?" Will pressed, anxiety bubbling up within him. He tugged at his neckerchief, uncomfortably warm.

"My keys are where they always are, Mr. Grant," Peter said, his forlorn glance at Will conveying his worry. "On the nail next t-to my desk."

Will subsided, realizing that anyone who knew which saddle belonged to him would know well enough where Peter kept his keys.

"Thank you, Peter, you've been very helpful," Will murmured, doing his best to tamp down his nerves. "I appreciate your assistance."

"T-Thank you, Mr. Grant," Peter said, diffident and endearingly earnest when he added, "If I remember something, I-I will tell you."

"Thank you, Peter," Will said again, summoning a smile that quickly faded as he made his way back up to the House.

⌘⌘⌘

It was something of a talent of his, Hannibal found, Will avoiding him like a plague. He barely saw more than a dark curl or the gleam of a blue eye the rest of the week since that morning in Hartford Town. Will even took meals in his room, when he ever ate at all. Hannibal knew full well he could walk down to the estate manager's office and find him there, hard at work against Grandfather's wishes, but he could not bring himself to intrude on the one place Will seemed genuinely at home.

After what he'd said, Hannibal was reluctant to force his company on Will at all.

'*Have our marriage dissolved and let me forget you...*'

It was troubling, to say the least. It weighed on Hannibal for days after they'd ridden home in stiff and hostile silence. He simply could not fathom that his spouse would ask so bluntly to be released from their marriage. It was entirely outside of his experience, limited though it was, for an Omega to turn their nose up at a gift and ask to be *parted* from great fortune rather than thrown headfirst into it.

"You're brooding, boy, when you should be courting your spouse," Grandfather said, finding Hannibal in the library. When Hannibal looked up at him, he chuckled softly and asked, "Have you been dancing around Will again?"

"I cannot find him even for that, Grandfather. He is confoundingly Uncommon," Hannibal said, recalling the sadness in Will's large blue eyes. "He's avoided me as if I'm a leper ever since I took him to the village. I bought a fortune in clothing for him, you know, and I've seen neither hide nor hair of him since. If I spent even half so much on one of my mistresses, they'd have been delighted for days! Yet he has made me feel in the wrong for it."

"You *are* wrong for it, if you did it for the reasons I imagine you did," Grandfather said, wheeling over to the shelves and beginning to put the stack of books in his lap back in place, which would no doubt send the House librarian into palpitations when he realized it and was probably Grandfather's intention. "Will has never been interested in *things*, Hannibal. He isn't one of your easily-sated women in the Capital and he isn't *cheap*. He would much rather spend a day fishing from his dock than being plied with gifts. The way to his good graces is much more complicated and rewarding than the sum of your women together."

"Is there something very wrong with him? Is he ill, you think?" Hannibal asked, frowning at the fire as it had the sheer audacity to be rather merry and comforting just now.

Grandfather snorted, cradling a book in both hands. "There is nothing wrong with him and Will is never *ill*, Hannibal."

"He was ill the evening before I left," Hannibal reminded him, clearly recalling how Will had been absent from the table that evening, taken with some malady that Hannibal had figured for childish retribution.

And how nervously determined he'd been after, coming into Hannibal's room in his nightclothes. Young, frightened, and trembling with resolve.

His stomach clenched with shame thinking of what he'd done to him then.

Roland's brows lowered and he said, "Yes, he was upset a good few weeks after you abandoned him, but not ill a day since. He makes it a point not to be a burden on anyone here. It was all I could do to convince him to keep Mr. Prince."

"Prince? You mean his valet, Jimmy?" Hannibal asked, not overly familiar with the man who had been hired during his absence at war. "Yes, well, he has certainly not been burdensome. I had imagined all sorts of horrors awaited me here, especially when I learned of old Mr. Vorgert being dismissed."

"Will has thrown himself into running this estate," Grandfather remarked, putting away the last book and sighing. "He cares for it like he might a child."

"Don't start," Hannibal warned, glowering at him. "How am I to get a child out of that prickly Omega when we cannot share a room, let alone a bed?"

"You could try speaking to him as an equal and making friends with him," Roland suggested. "Will is very receptive to kindness, Hannibal, and it may lead to other things in the long run."

"He would brain me with a vase if I look sideways at him, the violent little thing," Hannibal cursed, annoyed.

"Goodness, how you do go on," Grandfather chuckled, amused. "Shame on you, Hannibal, saying such things about Will when he is the very picture of gentility and calm!"

Hannibal angled a dark look at his grandfather and got nothing more than a slight, satisfied smile in return.

He sighed heavily, considering things from his spouse's perspective and how he would feel in his place.

"As Will himself so keenly pointed out, it *is* rather offensive to show up after six years and demand access to his bed after the way I have treated him. Any Omega worth their salt would want some wooing after that, I suppose."

"If Will *requires* wooing it is not because he is maneuvering for your attention, Hannibal," Roland said. "It is because your expectation of him is his absence and that is all he knows. Just as you require persuasion to believe that Omegas are not all like your father's concubine, which is counter to your expectation."

"Please don't mention that monster to me," Hannibal said, his glower becoming a scowl and his mood instantly plummeting.

"She was an Omega," Grandfather said, bewildering Hannibal until he said, "Miska, your sister. She was an Omega."

"The *hell* she was—"

"Hannibal," Roland said, his sad resignation reaching his grandson when reason could not. His voice was gentle, cautious, but firm when he whispered, "She was an Omega."

Hannibal stared at him, struggling to make that truth align with his memories of the child he'd been so deeply loving of. His darling baby sister, precious and dear to him even if she had been borne of that frightful abomination.

"Miska—" He paused and cleared his throat, buying himself time, his thoughts churning in a mire of memories he had not given acknowledgment to in far too long. "I find it hard to believe that, Grandfather."

"It's rather hard to mistake them when they're still in nappies, Hannibal," Roland said, careful with him. "There are Omegas all around you and you never realize it, not even with that keen nose of yours, and I have my suspicions as to why that is. You spent ten years away at war thinking you were in company bereft of Omegas but I can tell you with certainty that you have treated a great many who would have died on the battlefield for their country the same as the Alphas and betas who did so."

"*That* is a ridiculous notion," Hannibal breathed, unwilling to consider it and finding a safe retreat from the information he simply wasn't prepared to deal with yet. "There are many valid and sound reasons why they are not allowed to enlist, one of them being that an Omega would immediately be betrayed by its scent and heats."

"Not with suppressants and scent blockers," Grandfather said. "Science is a remarkable thing, Hannibal. Omegas have always been taught how to mask themselves when needed. You have wandered a world in which those whom you have met stand only to gain by playing to your perceptions, to the stereotypes your experience has cultivated. It has, unfortunately, only made you even more certain you are right in your assumptions when in fact you have seen the whole of their gender through a very narrowly-defined lens reflecting back what you expect to see."

Hannibal restlessly tapped his fingers on the mantle, his mind whirling with too much clarity, too much new information, reluctant to think his grandfather could be right in this.

"You are intelligent, fair, and committed to being just," Roland reminded him. "I know you can take a second look at what has plagued you since childhood and see it for what it truly is—a cobbled-together prejudice based on anger instead of fact."

Grandfather gave him a fond smile and wheeled his chair silently out of the room, leaving Hannibal alone before the fireplace, riddled with uncomfortable thoughts.

Miska, his little sister, born when he was young enough that he didn't clearly remember the world before her, and gone so long from him that it was difficult to remember his life with her in it. She was a blur of color and sound, a memory of sweetly-scented hair and abandoned, gleeful laughter, the sum of everything good he had ever felt in his father's house for the few short years before tragedy had taken her from him.

His Miska, his little Queen, the apple of her mother's eye, the light of his world.

A light snuffed out too soon and for such pointless reasons, whose first gurgling coo had captured his heart in a way not even death could remove.

He imagined his judgments applying to her, his darling little sister, and it made him cringe. It was almost too much to believe as the truth, but he knew Grandfather would never tell such an outright, ghastly lie, and it left him troubled, trying to reconcile the fact that Miska was Omegan, just like her wretched mother.

"My Lord," Berger called to him from the doorway, startling him out of his thoughts. "I've your things all prepared, if you've still a mind to go."

"Yes, Berger, thank you."

Confused, thoughtful, and wanting a soothing soak, Hannibal headed upstairs, still trying to wrap his mind around the things he'd just been told. He was so preoccupied with his thoughts that he barged into the bathroom still stripping off his clothes and drew up short, his brain scrambling at the sight of Will making a hasty exit from the tub at his intrusion, a flurry of white limbs and wild blue eyes in a billow of steam.

"What on earth—"

Will snatched his sheet around him, almost falling in his haste to escape the bath he'd only just entered.

"Do you *never knock* when you enter a room?" Will flared, struggling to cover himself from throat to ankles and failing miserably, his shapely calves and long feet exposed below the hem of his sheet. He was so much more slender than his clothing gave the illusion of him being, supple muscle under dewy skin with a high, round bottom and just the barest peek of a slightly round hip flashing from the folds of his damp bathing sheet.

It was profoundly disconcerting, such delicacy topped with damp dark curls and ill-concealed panic spiced with no little anger, a hint of true fear, and some tantalizing *something* elusively teasing at him. Hannibal caught his breath at the sight, his mouth going dry.

He recovered enough to become terribly aware he himself was barely better than naked, something Will had taken clear note of if the way his blue eyes fixed on the ceiling was any indication.

Feeling graceless and silly for having walked in on him, Hannibal stiffly said, "This is *my washroom.*"

"Not for the past *six years,*" Will snapped, angered enough that those big eyes of his actually met and held Hannibal's own.

Hannibal felt a shocking and utterly unexpected curl of attraction bloom under the heat of Will's gaze, confronted as he was with the after-image of Will's lithe and supple body and the promise of his formidable temper. He had never in his life met someone as entirely unexpected as Will Grant, and he was intrigued by his own growing interest in the feisty, easily-irritated, and rather surly Omega who was his spouse.

Glowering, showing altogether too much of his pearly white hide and the dark mottling of a bruise down one delightfully-muscled thigh from his fall, Will drew his sheet around him with all the affronted grace of a snubbed goddess and hissed, "*Enjoy it while the water is hot.*"

Hannibal stared at the bounce of his perky backside peeking from below the lip of his sheet as he strode away, shocked into silence when Will had the audacity to enter his suite and close the door behind him before Hannibal had finished properly almost formulating an apology to him.

"*Bloody hell!*" he shouted, damned if he would both offend Will then chase him from his bath in less than an minute's time. He was *not,* by *the gods,* a *monster.*

Hannibal crossed the washroom in three quick strides and jerked the door to Will's suite open, surprising him all over again. Standing imperiously in the doorway, he pointed back at the bathtub and stiffly said, "*Get back in that tub immediately!*"

Will's chin went up, blue eyes sparking, hands clenching into fists on his sheet, which was doing a poor job of hiding his body at this point, enough to be more than moderately distracting now that a large pink areola was partially exposed, a delicate blush color that complimented Will's pale skin.

"*No,*" Will said, the word short and clipped. "As you so graciously pointed out, it's *your washroom,* and of the two of us, Lord Clarges, *you need it more.*"

"You cheeky little twit," Hannibal swore, pointing more vigorously, incensed to be disobeyed when he was actually conceding to his unconventional spouse. The sheer gall of his mate was absolutely staggering! "*Back*, or I will *put you back.*"

Will's eyes widened dangerously and Hannibal braced himself, alert to any potential weapons in the room. He very much doubted Will could lift the hassock near his bed but he wasn't about to risk being coshed into unconsciousness by his meek and retiring mate. His pride would never survive it.

He wasn't entirely sure *he* would survive Will Grant.

"Go back to your suite," Will said, and when Hannibal began to retort, he loudly added, "*Then* I will get back into the tub."

Fuming, Hannibal dropped his arm and took a deep breath, reminding himself that he was a calm and rational man of even temper and lauded reserve. He certainly was not a man strongly fighting the urge to turn his unclaimed mate over his knee and paddle the sass out of him. *Certainly not!*

"Do as you please, you confounding creature!" he said, turning on his heel to slam back the way he'd come, banging the door to the washroom closed behind him only to be immediately confronted by his valet stammering apologies.

"Your spouse is in the washroom, my Lord—"

"I am *aware*," Hannibal snapped, irritably going for a brandy. He poured an unmeasured amount and flopped into a chair.

"He usually isn't long," Berger said, heading for his dressing room with Hannibal's freshly-polished boots. "I'll get your clothing ready, m'Lord."

"Leave it, I'll do it myself," Hannibal murmured. When he wasn't instantly obeyed, he slit his eyes open to glare at the man still hovering before him and was rewarded with compliance at last.

Once Berger was gone and he was alone, Hannibal closed his eyes again and took a sour swallow of his brandy, the soft sounds of water moving in the next room prickling at his nerves. His traitorous mind unhelpfully conjured images of Will slipping out the bath like a supple little water nymph, startled and fey and delicate as a roe deer flushed from hiding.

The thought of his mate's undeniably lovely form made him think about the child he'd promised his grandfather, which led his thoughts on to Will's heats. He was certainly grown enough to be having regular heats by now, though no one would discuss something so appallingly private with anyone other than a lover.

He wondered what means Will had settled on to deal with them, unmated and unbound as he was. He probably sent every Alpha in the vicinity into rut when it happened. It was a wonder no one had been hurt.

It left him scowling at his empty brandy glass as if it had somehow betrayed him, thinking that if he hadn't been so blasted dead-set on rejecting Will, he might even now be the one Will turned to during such a time.

'Let me forget you...'

Will's blue eyes stared at him from his memories, the fire of the washroom replaced with the sick despair of understanding that last day six years ago when Hannibal had spoken so harshly to him, had rejected him and everything he had so innocently offered.

'Alpha...' Will had whimpered then, appealing to a good nature Hannibal had been in no mood to indulge. He'd been little better than a child and Hannibal had treated him like a worldly courtesan. Worse, he'd accused Will of deliberately wielding his charms like a weapon and had ruthlessly cut him down in a savage attempt to disarm him.

The water sloshed again, a faint pattering of drips that brought the image of Will stepping from the tub, water running down his limbs in silvery trails, dripping from his skin to meet the surface of the water.

Feeling absurdly envious of the bathtub was *not* something gentlemen of good breeding should succumb to. Frustrated, Hannibal flung the brandy glass down and finished undressing, doing his best not to think of Will naked in the washroom just a short distance away. The knowledge that he was shockingly desirable was just another fact to be mused over and considered.

It seemed he was destined for a wearying day of revelations, and Hannibal knew it was only just beginning.

Chapter 12

The ride to Fernhill was longer by coach than by horseback, Will realized, watching the terrain roll past as Roland spoke to Hannibal of Anthony's prospective fiancee. As Will had been told of Anthony's intended in confidence, he excluded himself from the conversation and neither man took notice of it, though Hannibal was unusually somber and preoccupied in his responses. It made Will wonder if something had gotten into his husband, he was so strangely not his routine, overbearing self. He'd certainly behaved oddly after crashing in on Will's bath this afternoon, demanding he finish as if personally offended by the idea of Will conceding his place.

Very strange, indeed, considering his usual behavior.

Determined not to think of unpleasant things for the day, Will nervously straightened his jacket, appreciating its fine cloth and color despite himself. Quality was a pleasure he partook of so little that he was helpless against it and was surprised Hannibal had not baited him on the subject by now, no doubt having seen him surreptitiously fingering the hem of his waistcoat where it peeked from beneath the front of his unbuttoned jacket.

The grand namesake of Fernhill itself came into view around the bend, a massive and sprawling structure Will had only glimpsed from the uppermost turrets of Hartford House. It had seemed so distant there on the horizon, a tiny speck of stone set against the blue sky. Now, traveling past its foundations, it seemed a monster on par with Hartford House itself, aged and noble and secure in its sheltering of generations of Diments.

"What on earth are you gaping at?" Hannibal asked, sounding more himself. "I can't imagine Anthony hasn't had you over when the family is out, yet you act as if you've never been here before!"

"I haven't," Will said, shrugging, tipping his head to see more of it.

Hannibal leaned over him, an easy thing to manage as Will was slender and a bit shorter than he, and looked with him.

"Damn that cousin of mine anyway, never inviting you over," he muttered, trying to see Fernhill through Will's eyes and finding it very grand indeed. The press of Will's slender back against his chest distracted him as much as the tickling fluff of his sweetly-scented curls. He recalled how he'd looked fleeing his bath this afternoon, pink and pale and lovely in all, and his pulse pick up.

Entirely uncalled for...

Very nearly.

Clearing his throat and pushing the thought away, Hannibal asked, "It's impressive, isn't it?"

"Though not so impressive as Hartford House," Will said, his cheeks pinking at the pressure of Hannibal's body against his back and shoulders, the man's warm breath stirring his curls. "Is it just as lovely within?"

"Even more so," Grandfather said, the pleased expression on his lined face causing both of them to nervously retreat in opposite directions. "I'll have Anthony give you a tour."

"Please, do," Will said, delighted at the prospect.

"How your face lights up at the mention of that bounder," Hannibal observed, smirking when Will's cheeks reddened further. "I'm surprised he didn't marry you for himself."

"According to you, he *did*. Such unfortunate luck for us both that the law says he didn't, as he finds me pleasing enough," Will said, feeling as if a complaint lay lodged in Hannibal's words, as there so often was. "I think I should have been happy as Anthony's spouse."

The wistful lilt to his voice made Hannibal feel uncomfortably guilty and irritated. Guilty for how he had behaved that Will would wish for such a thing, and irritated he had maneuvered himself so quickly out of Will's regard so many years ago. He had no one to blame but himself, but that did little to aid him. *Regret* would not, he knew, pull a teacup together, no matter how one might wish otherwise.

Once, he'd deemed his actions justifiable. Now, comparing the poised young Omega at his side to the youth he'd walked away from, he questioned his own decisions, and what he found did not settle him nor give him peace of mind.

"Will, there is no cause for that type of thing," Grandfather scolded, glowering at both of them. "You are married to Hannibal and that is that."

"Yes, that is that," Hannibal echoed, watching Will drop his head in contrition. "We will have to make the best of things as they are."

The coach pulled to a halt and footmen rushed to get the doors, gesturing them out onto the expanse of the back garden where the sun cast a merry glow on all sorts of revelers.

Will stared, anxiety pinching his features as he looked out over the vast acres of green lawn and carefully-tended flower beds, lanes of trees and copses leading onto thicker wood all framing an enormous lake. He was used to the sprawling embrace of the Hartford estate but this was the first time he'd seen so much land covered by so many people.

"Hannibal! I wasn't sure you'd come," Bedelia said, drifting over their way as the footmen got Roland settled into his chair. She looked fresh and comfortable in the cool air, the colors of her day gown light and complimenting her pale coloring. She held out her hand to Will and stroked his cheek, smiling when his eyes dilated.

"Is there something on his face?" Hannibal asked, bristling. "You spend an inordinate amount of time fondling him."

Will sighed, already tired, and stepped away from the slight comfort of Bedelia's gentle touch.

"Just because you have no idea how a civilized Alpha communicates with an Omega, Hannibal, does not mean I am at fault," she said, the slow cadence of her voice never rising above a soft purr. "I am happy to instruct you, should you ever decide to forsake your barbaric ways."

"*You—*"

"Bedelia, light of my life!" Roland said, wheeling rudely past Hannibal to greet his granddaughter. "Let's be pleasant, shall we? Show me to those children! I insist on holding all the new little ones!"

Bedelia gave Hannibal a lingering, amused look and settled her hand on Roland's shoulder, saying, "Of course, Grandfather. Oh, and Will? Anthony has been waiting impatiently for you to arrive. Do go put him at ease with your presence?"

Will drew a deep breath as she moved off with Grandfather, fussing with the tail of his coat, nervous of his appearance.

"Will?" Hannibal said, busy tugging at his own cuffs, preening when Will glanced at him. "You're very pale. Is something the matter?"

Will didn't respond; he looked out at the groups of neighbors and Society members with trepidation before saying, "I have never seen so many people in one place before."

Hannibal frowned and followed his line of sight, ignoring the other newcomers who milled around them to find their respective ways into the garden.

"I had thought it a rather smallish party, actually, compared to most," he said, considering it. "Parties I've thrown at Galley Field make this one seem quaint."

"I'm sure," Will said, casting another look around. "Yet to me this seems a veritable ocean of humanity, Hannibal. I am not used to it."

"No, I don't imagine you are," Hannibal said, mouth pursing with concern. "It is very good luck we have time before the Season starts to acclimatize you to such gatherings."

"I am sure you will be far too busy attending parties in the Capital and filling Grandfather's Parliament seat to throw very many parties all the way out here," Will remarked.

"Quite right, but considering you will be with me at those very same parties," Hannibal said, amused by the light scowl that crossed his little mate's face, "we should strive to numb you to them while we have a chance to do so. Ah! There is Anthony!"

Will looked around to where Grandfather had drawn a large gathering of family to him, all delighted to see him out at long last.

"Will," Hannibal said, catching him by his elbow and guiding him towards the gathered group. "Please don't forget the purpose of attending today."

"How could I?" Will asked, gracing him with a dour glare. "You wish to show the world how you have returned as a hero, graciously excusing me my existence and nobly looking past my deficiencies to do as your grandfather bids you. What a long-suffering martyr you are, Saint Hannibal."

"Well thank all the gods *you're* in good form today," Hannibal said, chuckling at his venom. "I should hate to suffer through this provincial horror without your surly peevishness. No one would ever believe me a saint otherwise."

"Don't worry yourself on that count, Lord Clarges," Will said, wishing the mere presence of this man didn't give him such conflicting signals of safety and danger. "Your reputation precedes you, however—sainthood will be difficult to obtain."

"You've remarked on my reputation more than once, Will, but I have no idea how on earth you'd have heard very much," Hannibal said, amused by the way Will glowered up at him. "Stuck out here in the country for six years like a monk in a monastery. I doubt anyone could carry much gossip that far."

"They can and do," Will said, relieved to hit the shade of towering old trees which kept the worst of the sun off. "The servants chatter among themselves and I hear it, in part."

"Why on earth are you mingling with the servants?" Hannibal asked, bewildered. "Honestly, first passing yourself off to the county as an estate manager and now hobnobbing with servants! Your upbringing has been particularly peculiar!"

"Yes, you could say so," Will said, relaxing enough to start looking at those around him, admiring the many lovely colors of dresses and fashionable jackets that abounded.

"Did your father not instruct you?" Hannibal asked, curious. "I imagine he must miss you very much. Has he been banned from the premises as well?"

"My father is a busy man and has no reason to see me," Will said, his throat constricting painfully with his words. "His instruction was vigorous and weighty and I bear the fruit of it all these years later. His wisdom in raising me has served me well, I can never say otherwise."

"And your sisters, have none of them contacted you?"

"Not so much as a card," Will admitted, blushing when a woman caught his eye and winked at him for staring overly long at the pattern on her dress. "They are grown women with households to run and families to rear, all happily paired with men who suit them. It would be rude to press on their happiness."

Hannibal wrinkled his nose. "A very strange family, it seems. My family certainly has no qualms *pressing upon* my happiness. I am sure I have met one or another of your sisters over the years. They should have asked after you."

"Lord Clarges, they would never," Will said, laughing at his indignant huff. "Speak to a man of standing of his detested spouse—their own brother—while in *public*? He may have bewailed his rearing of me, Lord Clarges, but my father raised his daughters to be better than *that*! Heavens, they'd have died of apoplexy if you'd even breathed my name to them. I'm very glad you never recognized them. I shouldn't want that on my conscience, thank you."

"I would assume once word gets 'round about our reconciliation, they will be clamoring at the doors?" Hannibal said, smirking.

"Only at your invitation," Will said, and looked down at his feet as they walked, his eyes tracing the pattern of pebbles beneath his boots and the fine silt of dust gathering on the polished leather. "And I would not call this *reconciliation*, Hannibal. I am not entirely certain how to interpret your intentions considering what I know of your opinions."

"Do they require interpreting? I have told you, Will, I desire that child from you for my grandfather's sake, and you must surely have given thought to a little one now and then," Hannibal said, distracted by the idea of Will with a baby. "As we are both adults with functioning senses, we should be able to manage without undue fuss and nonsense."

They drew near enough that Anthony caught sight of them and he strode their way with a happy grin, proudly escorting a lovely young woman on his arm.

"Anth—Lord du Millau!" Will said, vastly relieved to see him with his intended. Anthony had told him of her, a feisty and humorous Omega who suited him entirely. He shot a sharp look at Hannibal, willing him not to be rude, and gave her an honest smile she returned with open friendliness.

"Hannibal, you made it!" Anthony said, unable to resist needling him just a little with, "Has anyone been coshed yet?"

"Give it time," Will said, ignoring Hannibal's sour look.

"Anthony, you're being rude to your friend," Hannibal said, and took her hand to grace it with a soft kiss, saying, "Young lady, you are a vision of loveliness. Allow me to advise you *not* to continue on with this dandy as you are far too fetching to settle for the likes of him."

Will blushed, uncomfortable with his effusiveness but not surprised. Even Hannibal could get over his dislike of Omegas for the sake of spiting Anthony.

"Lord Clarges, you are too kind," she said, her perfectly modulated and sweet tones speaking of someone with musical inclination. "Anthony warned me you might be dangerous. He clearly fears your charm."

"As well he should, as he has none for himself," Hannibal said, finding the scent of her skin quite strangely absent. Most beta women used some type of perfume, and usually the ones courting Alphas used scents designed to attract attention, not subvert it.

"Don't encourage him, Fredricka. He has far too good an opinion of himself as it stands," Anthony said, and extracted her hand from Hannibal's grip to hold it in his own, saying to Will, "May I introduce Miss Fredricka Loucks?"

"Will Grant," he said, unused to anything else, and he kissed her hand as he knew he should. "Anthony has told me so much about you."

"You are the very image of your sister," she said, delighted with him and, no doubt, knowing he was an Omega the same as she. "It is truly uncanny."

"So I am told," Will said, dropping her hand as well as his gaze.

"Do you not find them strikingly similar, Lord Clarges?" she asked, amazed.

"I have never set eyes on Will's sister, nor any one of his kin," Hannibal said, wondering at Will's strange behavior with her. "And, as you know, this one right here married him for me, so I have never had the pleasure of meeting Will's family."

"No, Lord Clarges?" she asked, amusement shining in her light blue eyes. "I was not given to understand you have been terribly busy these past six years."

"Yes, well, it has lovely meeting you," Hannibal said, summoning a smile. "Would you care to join Grandfather, Will?"

"Not so fast," Anthony said, grasping Will by his elbow and guiding Fredricka into place. "You're my cousin and no one has let slip yet but I wanted to tell Will first—it's been decided. Freddie and I are going to be married!"

"Oh! Anthony, that's wonderful!" Will said, delighted for them both. "Congratulations to both of you! I'm sure you'll be perfectly happy together! The family must be very excited!"

"Yes, they are," Anthony said, grinning from ear to ear. "Or, rather, they *will* be once Hannibal's opinion is settled on the matter."

"Why should my opinion carry a feather's worth of weight?" Hannibal asked, unspeakably relieved by Will's obvious delight for their union. "I am sure your parents would not allow you to choose a young woman who was unsuitable for you."

"Not that exactly," Anthony said, exchanging a long glance with Fredricka, who tipped her head in silent agreement and laced her hand through Hannibal's elbow, saying, "Walk me around the lake, Lord Clarges, so we can get to know one another better."

"I would be delighted," Hannibal said, eager to be seen as accommodating by those present and perhaps show his more chivalrous side to his reserved spouse.

Will watched them stroll off together and looked at Anthony, who seemed fairly satisfied and amused.

"He hasn't realized," Will said, swallowing nervously, anxious on her behalf. "Anthony..."

"Don't worry so much," he urged, draping his arm over Will's shoulder to draw him into a stroll some ways behind them. "Freddie can handle my cousin, Will, and it's all the more amusing he can't figure out she's Omegan. That keen nose of his is so blind in such oddly specific ways. It truly is uncanny."

"I'm not sure if his nose is blind or if her products are stronger than mine," Will said, lamenting the efficacy of his own regimen. "He still manages to catch my scent."

"Well," Anthony said, and gave Will a soft, lopsided smile when he added, "You *have* bonded, Will, haven't you, even if he doesn't know it?"

Will sighed heavily, frowning at the idea of it. "It only goes one way, Anthony. I doubt that could be it. Perhaps it's just his keen nose, after all."

"Well he does seem to be more interested," Anthony said, smiling and nodding at those they passed on their way. "Or at least more attentive. I guess he was serious after all about reclaiming his place."

"Yes," Will said, his thoughts returning to his saddle and what Matthew had said. Taking advantage of the moment, he asked, "Anthony, what would Hannibal do to keep his place as heir?"

Anthony's brows rose and curiosity filled his eyes. "I would have had a different answer for you a week ago, Will. Now? I can honestly say I'm not sure."

"Accept an Omega, perhaps?" Will suggested. "Would he go so far as to do violence?"

"Violence?" Anthony echoed, immediately more attentive. "Will, why would you ask me that?"

Will swallowed hard, reminded in an instant that, for all their differences, Anthony and Hannibal were cousins. When it came down to it, blood would always pool together, and it was dangerous to ask Hannibal's family such questions.

Unnerved, Will wet his lips and told him, "Please forgive me, Anthony. I spoke without thinking."

"He was a soldier, Will," Anthony said, his uncertainty about Will's purpose making his words cautious and careful. "He left the war behind, but he will always be a soldier. Violence is a part of him, now, but if there is something specific you have heard, gossip, perhaps—"

"No, Anthony," Will said, controlling his nerves with difficulty, knowing Anthony knew something was amiss. "Please... things have been very stressful for me recently. I have no idea why I asked such a thing. Think nothing of it."

Anthony stared at him for a long, assessing moment, but gamely nodded in honor of Will's wishes.

Will remained silent at his side, grateful he hadn't betrayed his fears to the man who had always been his friend. A man who would feel compelled to defend Hannibal, or perhaps warn him of Will's suspicions.

"Whatever you may hear of Hannibal today, Will," Anthony said, his fond gaze on his intended where she strolled arm in arm with Hannibal. "Please take it with a grain of salt. There is nothing people love more than to tear down something they think is above them."

Will smiled, tight and unhappy smile that it was, and tried his hardest to put the saddle and its implications to the back of his mind.

⌘⌘⌘

"Anthony often speaks about you," Fredricka said, floating at Hannibal's side with the grace and weightlessness of dandelion fluff on the wind. She was rather smaller than Will, and had an abundance of riotous red curls that refused to be tamed into submission. "Always in terms of Will Grant, though."

"Ah, yes. Will," Hannibal said, annoyed to be reminded of his cousin's close relationship with his spouse. "We, however, have not had the pleasure of hearing about you in turn."

"Not surprising," she said, laughing softly. "He was nervous for your approval. He does set an enormous store in your good opinion. Not to mention he has, until very recently, always imagined he would eventually marry Will."

Hannibal stiffened, irritated to hear it put in so many words.

"And that doesn't bother you? The fact that he wanted to marry my mate?"

"No," she said, a merry twinkle in her blue eyes at his choice in words. "Will is perfectly lovely, all the more so for not believing himself to be anything such. There is a melancholy in him that seems to lure Alphas, especially ones as good at heart as Anthony. In truth, Lord Clarges, knowing Anthony would choose me when Will Grant might still be his only tells me how much Anthony truly loves me."

"In that you are mistaken, Miss Loucks," Hannibal said, frowning at her summation. "There was never a possibility Anthony would marry Will. I would never stand for it."

"You certainly gave everyone a vastly different impression," she said, her blue eyes full of mischief when she looked up at him to gauge his response.

"I cannot control what assumptions people make from my prior actions, but I assure you, I am back to take my place and ensure Will takes his own," Hannibal said, smiling to think of Will getting his proper due. "Relationships are not always what they seem. You will understand once you are wed."

"On that subject, I must be sure you approve," she said, turning quite serious. "Anthony is adamant, as am I."

"I have no grounds to disapprove," Hannibal told her, wondering at their persistence. "You are moneyed, I assume, young enough to bear him heirs, deep enough in his esteem that he is caught in public with you, intelligent enough to recognize his faults and wise enough to understand they are few."

"*Am* I?" she asked, smiling. "Intelligent, that is?"

"You are not holding his relationship with Will against him, knowing it is nothing like he may have once wished," Hannibal said. "You do not feel threatened by my spouse but you do admire him."

"Even though he is Omegan?" she innocently inquired, and Hannibal had the good grace to flush, winning a mischievous smile out of her. "Lord Clarges, you might want to tug your waistcoat down a bit, your prejudice is showing."

Hannibal scowled at her. "My opinions are based on facts, young lady. Facts speak for themselves."

"Do they? And what do your facts tell you of Omegas?" she asked, squeezing his arm to her modest bosom. "I am curious, now."

"In my experience, omegas are flighty, flirty little butterflies," Hannibal said, reciting his hard-learned lessons like dogma and doing his best to keep his opinions safe for feminine ears. "They like nothing more than to idle about spending money that is not theirs on things that catch their fleeting attention. They are children, most of them, easily distracted by something sparkling and pretty but prone to throwing fits and acting out if not indulged. I find them tiresome, annoying, mindless baggage..."

He trailed off, his memories of the Omegan courtesans who had plagued his childhood giving way to thoughts of Miska and Will, a jarring juxtaposition, indeed.

Freddie absorbed his lecture in silence, her red brows drawn together in a slight frown.

"*Will* is not at all as you described," she finally said.

"No, he defies explanation," Hannibal said, focusing on the image of his poker-faced Omega. "He is argumentative, hot-tempered, violent, and altogether Uncommon."

"Goodness, Tony must not know him half so well as you do," she said, laughing softly. "Which is passing strange as he has spent a good deal more time with your spouse than you have."

"Why must I find myself surrounded by provoking creatures?" Hannibal asked, angling an exasperated, amused glance down at her. "Do you fish, madam?"

"Fish?"

"Never mind," he said, looking away to view the lovely scenery. "I will spare you the explanation. Be warned, however, never to agitate Will or you'll go the worse for it."

"I have no intentions of agitating him in the least and can't imagine why anyone ever would! He is such a friendly and thoughtful young man," Fredricka said. "It is my hope we can be fast friends. Ah! *Cards*! Shall we play, Lord Clarges?"

Hannibal looked around to find several tables had been set up beneath a billowing canopy, attracting those seeking shelter from the sun into gaming. A table was emptying as they drew abreast and Hannibal nearly declined for lack of more players, but Fredricka called behind her, "Hurry up, Tony! You'll partner me, won't you?"

Anthony, ambling along some distance behind them with Will at his side, hurried his step and came to sweep out a chair for her, settling her with an indulgent, smitten grin.

"Well," Hannibal said, sparing a glance for Will, whose somber expression did nothing to detract from his undeniable beauty, even if he seemed excessively troubled. "Will you partner me?"

Will took his seat next to Freddie without responding, still far too distracted by his worries and the people around them to feel at ease.

"I do hope, Mr. Grant," Freddie said, a teasing gleam in her eyes, "that you can overcome your Omegan nature well enough to count?"

It startled Will into a soft huff of laughter and he skated a glance at Hannibal to find him scowling, indignant and offended.

Clearing his throat, Will said, "Yes, Miss Loucks, I do well enough."

"Well enough?" Hannibal echoed, and snorted. He sat down across from Freddie and began gathering the cards up in his long fingers to shuffle them. "Miss Loucks, do not be deceived by his modesty. Will is deadly sharp with numbers, as the Hartford House accounts can attest. I dare say he will do you in before this game is done."

Will's brows rose in his surprise but Hannibal seemed hardly aware of the compliment he'd paid, which made it feel keenly precious to Will, and his cheeks pinkened with a faint blush.

"Despite his being an Omega?" she inquired, her tone playful, and Anthony nudged Will beneath the table, grinning.

"He is Uncommon," Hannibal reminded her, and his amber gaze landed on Will with weighty assessment. "There are many surprising facets of him I have found so far and, no doubt, several more of which I have not yet become acquainted with."

"Provided those facets don't involve you agitating him," Anthony said, sweeping his cards into a pile as Hannibal dealt. "Then you should be safe enough."

"Oh, I'm not so sure agitation should be avoided as such," Hannibal said, smirking. "It can create many an interesting situation for those with the spirit to act on them."

Will bristled and gathered up his cards, telling Hannibal, "As I have said previously, Lord Clarges, I refuse to become any more intimately acquainted with the carpets of Hartford House than I am just now."

Anthony laughed and Freddie's red mouth curved into an appreciative smile, no doubt having heard the entire story from Anthony.

Will put all such thoughts and aggravations out of his head to focus on the game. As Hannibal had predicted, he was dangerously adept at counting and played with aggressive determination Anthony couldn't quite counter. Freddie, for her part, matched Hannibal play for play but was trumped by Will's formidable imagination and before long they had attracted a small group of observers.

They won the first round and began a second, all idle conversation set aside for the sharp, rapid slap of cards on the table.

Will justified his praise by taking the trick twice in quick succession and they won by a wide lead, leaving Hannibal grinning and delighted in the reserved, embarrassed young man across from him. Will hesitantly returned the smiles and congratulations of their small crowd, slowly relaxing, Hannibal was pleased to see.

Freddie, utterly charming and looking strangely pleased, excused herself in the changeover to stroll the lake on Anthony's arm, leaving Hannibal with Will and a growing, admiring crowd.

Hannibal stood, smoothing his jacket as he did so and warmly accepting the compliments given on his game.

"I have to admit, the bulk of the win falls to Will," he said, moving to Will's side as he, too, stood to make way for new players. He still seemed uneasy to be in the middle of such a large crowd, though he cut a fine figure. His new wardrobe suited him, a sleek and fitted tailoring that made the most of his athletic physique and subtle curves. Hannibal was pleased to see he'd drawn quite a few admiring gazes, and not entirely for his prowess with numbers.

"... *employee!* I have no idea why on earth he would be *here* of all places..."

The whispered speculation reached Hannibal's keen ears, carrying over the conversation rising around him. He'd been expecting such comments, but he hadn't expected how angry they would truly make him.

Will heard it as well and tipped his chin up, searching out the scandalized couple eyeing him through the crowd. He straightened his shoulders and stretched a bit taller, unwilling to summon the least bit of regret for his actions at Hartford House.

"I'm afraid that is a misunderstanding, Mrs. Wilkes," Hannibal said, his voice carrying over to them, bringing immediate, alarmed stillness. He graced them with an easy smile, taking advantage of this opportunity to quash some of the gossip. He settled his hand at the base of Will's spine and stepped closer to him, aware of Will stiffening in response. "Lord Clarges, as you've seen for yourself, has enviable intelligence. He has indeed spent his time at Hartford House

205

running the estate, but always in the capacity of my spouse and in the Ledford name."

There was consternation from no few, though the rest continued to mill about, anxious to renew their acquaintance with both Hannibal and Will.

Will cautiously tested his bond to Hannibal at that unexpected defense, surprised to find only sincerity and a low, burbling undertone of anger that was not directed at him, but rather *for* him. He looked up at Hannibal to weigh his expression, but his husband was already conversing with other guests, an easy smile on his face as everyone tried to engage them both at once, excited and eager.

Will tried to smile at them in return, but the darkest part of him that spoke in his father's voice fed him doubt about their sincerity. He was unused to so many people, unused to so much positive attention directed at him. He found it all rather overwhelming, but his tension subsided some with the steadying pressure of Hannibal's hand against his back. The touch was warm and firm, pressed right to the base of his spine where the slight, exaggerated Omegan curve swept down into his pelvis.

Yet he couldn't shake the shadow of his father's voice that whispered of a broken saddle, a cut girth strap, and a fall that could have killed him. Will tried to tamp it down as best he could, knowing he lacked vital information regarding his accident and that dwelling on it was only making him more nervous.

"What do you think, Lord Clarges?"

Will realized the silence had stretched a beat longer than it should have and glanced up to see Hannibal, three gentlemen, and several lovely ladies looking at him expectantly.

"Excuse me, I was wool gathering," he said, blushing to seem so inattentive. "I'm afraid I didn't hear you. Please forgive me."

"My fault entirely, I should be more specific which Clarges I'm speaking to, what with there being two of you now," Will was told, and everyone chuckled politely as if it had been clever.

"If you'd care to come for a visit at Hartford House, Mr. Katze," Hannibal smoothly cut in, "we could have more time and more comfortable surroundings for estate talk. We would dearly love to have you and your lovely daughter for dinner."

"As long as we aren't the main course."

Will looked at the young woman before him, surprised by her tart response, a smile curving his mouth at the open amusement on her lovely face.

"Beverly," her father said, his repressive tone holding a note of pleading that spoke of years' worth of losing on that particular front.

"Miss Katze, lovely as you are," Hannibal said, an appreciative grin baring the tips of his sharp teeth, "I value your company far too much to make a meal of you. My spouse sets an elegant table, I am sure you will not be disappointed, especially if he can procure another trout."

Will felt oddly relieved to find Hannibal gazing down at him with fond amusement. He didn't resist when Hannibal rubbed his back, but certainly felt warmer than he had. The earthy-rich Alpha scent of Hannibal's skin seemed to cling to him from his touch, a subtle marking that he was protected. It gave him a feeling of safety at complete odds with the lingering worry over his accident.

"You fish, Lord Clarges?" Mr. Katze inquired, fevered interest lighting his face.

"No you don't," Beverly warned, and reached out to take Will's arm. "Come on, let me save you. I have something of a talent for it."

"Excuse me, gentlemen," Will said, having no choice but to go with her or else be dragged off.

Hannibal merely watched, a slight smile still on his face to see his little spouse in the hands of the capable and deliriously social Miss Katze. No doubt by the time Hannibal reclaimed him, the entirety of the country would know Will Grant better than he did.

"That child will be the death of me!" Mr. Katze lamented with a smitten smile. "But what can one do? Daughters are a gift our spouses give to us, and she is the very likeness of her dear mother."

"She is a delightful young lady," Hannibal said, recalling many times over the past six years when Miss Katze had crossed his path. "And Will needs more companions who are closer to him in age."

"She knows no stranger, Lord Clarges," Mr. Katze reminded him. "You may never get him back."

They laughed together and spoke of upcoming business in Parliament which Hannibal, as a Peer and his grandfather's proxy, would have direct influence with. They were soon joined by others, conversation drifting along acceptable lines of polite inquiry rather than heated debate.

Hannibal, however, kept an eye on Will, whom Miss Katze had installed into a gaggle of young ladies. He was too distant for Hannibal to see clearly, but he didn't seem distressed.

"... with Lord Clarges, no less! It is the very same boy, I swear it! Oh, he and Lord du Millau were *certainly* having us on, claiming he was married to the Marquess of Clarges!"

The comment reached him from a passing group so intent on looking behind them at Will that they didn't see Hannibal next to them.

"... asked him to leave without even setting eyes on him! And it turns out he was nothing more than an *estate manager*, for the gods' blessings! Can you *imagine*?! How on earth he hasn't been fired by now is beyond me!"

Hannibal's glower deepened as the snippets of their gossip reached him, conversations behind hands, whispered conjecture, all of which boiled down to one glaring summation—Will was too far beneath them to be Hannibal's mate.

It made him that much more determined to define Will's place in this world.

The fact that his place collided rather soundly with that of Hannibal's mistress was not one he could be bothered with at present, not when he was so busy trying to find away across the distance of wrongdoings that separated him from his little mate.

"Excuse me, please," Hannibal said, stepping away from the gathered group.

"Off to find better company, Lord Clarges?"

It was playful ribbing Hannibal was well used to, and promptly responded to with, "And prettier, as well. Or have you not yet met my spouse?"

He strode away to a roll of delighted laughter and moved down the lakeside towards his mate.

Will, who so often seemed lost in his thoughts or far removed from himself, had been drawn into conversation by Miss Katze's friendly social circle, though she herself was nowhere to be found. Yet he seemed engaged enough, smiling and chatting. To the flighty, young, and curious ladies who surrounded him, Will Grant was nothing other than a handsome, distracting young beta male with whom they could flirt and befriend. They had no knowledge of who he was and Will, by his ease with them, had made no move to inform them.

Hannibal drew to a stop on the path and leaned against the trunk of a towering tree, watching Will for a time, enjoying the bright sparkle in his eyes and the animation in his face that lit him up like warm sunlight.

It made Hannibal wonder how he would look when he was truly happy.

"Such a fuss everyone is making over that boy."

Hannibal only spared a small sliver of his attention for the woman who drifted up next to him, a voluptuous beauty greatly testing the seams of her dress with her handsome figure.

"Is he truly your estate manager?" she asked, tipping her head Will's direction. "Lady Darnell insists he tried to pass himself off as married to *you*, Lord Clarges, when the papers first published your announcement. I am sure you had no idea he had done such a thing. Are you not terribly shocked he has come here?"

Hannibal angled a tight, polite smile at her, amused by the naked envy in her gaze as she looked at Will. "No, I am not terribly shocked, in truth. He does precisely as he pleases, which is an admirable quality in my eyes."

"Imagine, a man in your employ attending a function such as this," she sighed, fluttering her lashes up at him. "We are inundated with such unpolished company these days."

"I have indeed noted a surprising lack of well-mannered gentlefolk, but I doubt very much my cousin would invite a working class man to her gathering," Hannibal said, smiling slightly when Will smiled, finding the curve of his generous mouth suited him much better than the tight press of his lips that kept him perpetually frowning.

"I met him in Hartford village on chance some time ago, your Mr. Grant. I find him rather plain and common," she said, fanning herself. "Don't you simply despise the plain and common, Lord Clarges?"

"*Indeed*," Hannibal answered, his eyes fastened on Will. He was laughing, delighted, blue eyes sparkling with good humor. He had been pressed to sit on a blanket spread on the lawn and his small entourage of young admirers fluttered around him like colorful, chirping birds, tittering with empty-headed amusement at his sharp and surprising humor.

Hannibal pushed away from the tree and straightened his jacket, prompting the young woman to ask, "Are you off, my Lord?"

"Yes," he said, angling a look down his nose at her. "I am afraid you have the right of it, madam. I *do* despise both the plain and the common. As such, I am removing myself from their presence to find relief in the company of my lovely spouse. Good day."

Had he looked back, he would have seen her gaping and furiously embarrassed behind him.

But Hannibal only had eyes for Will.

⌘⌘⌘

It was uncanny the change that fell over Will when he spied Hannibal heading his way. His dark brows drew down over his narrowed blue eyes, his full mouth pressed tight, and a mutinous expression overcame his lovely features, transforming him from a merry, careless youth into a surly, glowering one.

"Ah! Lord Clarges! Have you come to scold us?"

There was a round of laughter, silly and meaningless.

"No, young lady, I have not," Hannibal assured her, not for the first time painfully aware of the twelve-year age difference between himself and Will. His ferocious little Omega was young enough to enjoy a place here among a bevy of youthful beauties while Hannibal was old enough to be their father, most of them. It was unsettling, to say the least. "I have come to have a word with Will."

"Are you friends?" one of the younger ladies asked, her green eyes empty in a way Hannibal detested.

"I would not say we are friends," Will told her, a wry smile curling one corner of his mouth and his sly blue eyes sliding up to read Hannibal's expression, "or that we are even friendly."

"I would not say we are *not*," Hannibal bantered. "Or have you not told your admirers that we are married?"

Will bristled and stood, annoyed, Hannibal was pleased to see. He was also pleased to see the keen disappointment on their faces at both the news and Will's absence.

Stiff with offense, Will strode towards the shade of the nearby trees and gave Hannibal his back when he arrived.

"What is so terribly important and world-ending that you must pester me?" Will asked, arms crossed over his chest.

"I merely needed to escape the attentions of a rather dull and unimaginative woman," Hannibal said, not about to admit his satisfaction of parting Will from his admirers.

"So you sought out the company of a dull and unimaginative Omega?" Will asked, huffing a short, irritated laugh. "Lord Clarges, your reason is excessively disturbed."

"I have a large measure of opinions, Will, but your being dull or unimaginative does not number among them. Trust me, anyone possessed of wits enough to oust Mr. Vorgert and use a trout with deadly force certainly does not lack for imagination," Hannibal said, taking his elbow to walk him towards the hedge maze. "Where is your savior?"

"I may have offered a convenient excuse for Bev to escape her father's vigilant doting," Will admitted, his smile wry.

"*Bev*?" Hannibal echoed, and chuckled. "If she insists you call her that, Will, you merely provided an opportunity, not an intention. Miss Katze is well known for her steadfast friendliness. She would not purposefully use you."

"No, I don't think she would," Will said. He smiled then, adding, "She is very personable. I would so enjoy if they did come to Hartford House, but I am not used to entertaining."

"You've certainly never bored me," Hannibal teased him, delighted by the way Will's cheeks reddened. "The air is fresh and the clouds are out. Walk with me awhile, Will."

Will did so, amicably for a period of time until the hedges rose up around them. He then pulled his elbow free, unsettled by the warmth and strength in Hannibal's touch, and promptly tucked his hands into his jacket pockets.

"There are a great many people still who do not realize we are married," Hannibal remarked, head tipped down slightly to see Will's thoughtful profile. "You sequestered yourself at Hartford House all these years, just as you said. Yet you have your chance now, Will, to take some satisfaction in their discomfort. Why would you not do just that?"

"I have my own future to think of, Lord Clarges. I still have to carry on once you finish whatever mischief you're up to at Hartford House, and being exposed to the world as your spouse will only inconvenience me," Will said, aware of his attention and turning his face away. He risked Hannibal's ire, he knew, but it was far too ingrained in him that his looks were unpleasant to his Alpha. "You made it very clear when I came to Hartford House that you did not want me. You have spent six years pretending I do not exist and Society believes your spouse to be dead, either by illness or pining. I am, in essence, a ghost, I believe. I would prefer to remain that way."

"I had no idea the extent of the speculation surrounding our marriage as I pay no mind to such drivel," Hannibal said, taking a deep breath of the cool air, checking his comfortable, long-legged stride to accommodate Will's slightly shorter legs. "Today has been revealing for me. I hear there was an incident in which you attempted to visit with the neighbors?"

Will laughed again, a throaty, raspy sound that played over Hannibal's senses like velvet-covered fingers. "I attended the Darnells' soiree with Anthony at his insistence about a month after you left. I was summarily called an impostor, refused entrance, and asked to leave as my supposed husband was in the Capital with his mistress and never spoke of having *married a man.*"

Hannibal frowned, mouth pursed, and clasped his hands behind his back, thoughts turning.

"It was... eye-opening," Will said, sighing heavily. "Before very much time had passed it was about that I was simply Anthony's lover and we were playing a joke, as the whole of Society knew Hannibal Ledford had married a proper woman and I was certainly not *that.* I told you before, Lord Clarges, how I was perceived in the wake of your disapproval."

"So, you hid yourself in Hartford House and put about to my family that I had forbidden them to visit?" Hannibal asked.

Will released another weighty sigh and told him, "I did not want them to know me, Hannibal. As you had not mentioned me, I hoped to mitigate what damage I could and keep them from attempting to mend a situation that did not bear mending."

"They would have had you out into Society in a heartbeat, Will," Hannibal said, shaking his head at the young man's stubborn nature. "A slap in the faces of those who had shamed you."

"Yes, and you would have been exposed as having married someone you considered patently unsuitable and embarrassing," Will said, his words sharp and clipped. "Which is precisely what you did *not* want, Lord Clarges. And as I did *not* want to be further ridiculed publicly by your many exploits and inattention, it seemed the best course of action I could take. Little did I realize it would follow you back to Hartford House with such immediacy!"

"I will say it only once more, Will—that woman is not and *will not be* my lover," Hannibal said, glowering when he thought of the Widow Reynolds and her grasping hands. "I barely knew her in my childhood and wish I hadn't then, either! Honestly, it escapes me why so many people take such an unseemly interest in my personal life."

Will, thinking he meant himself, tightly said, "I do not consider my interest unseemly, Lord Clarges, as it only extends far enough to spare me further damage. Beyond that, I only hope your boredom will send you back to your proper family and away from Hartford House before people begin to believe there is anything of substance between us."

"And who are you trying to spare with that, Will?" Hannibal asked. "Me or yourself?"

"Can it not be both?" Will asked, stopping to give Hannibal a steady, unflinching stare. "You have no reason to stay here, Hannibal, and every reason to leave. If your grandfather comes to his senses and grants us a separation, then I may yet find someone who truly enjoys my company. Our marriage would only be in the way. I stand to gain nothing by being named as your spouse."

"*I* do," Hannibal said, swinging to face him and meet his moiling eyes. They were sparked with green against the frame of the hedge behind him, flecks of amber peeking up through them. Such changeable, unusual eyes, melancholy lurking beneath growing ire and bewilderment. "Some of them believe I have killed this imaginary woman they assume I've married. Some of them believe she is trapped up in Hartford House. Others believe she is a fiction altogether, as no one has ever heard of or seen Willia *M* Grant."

"Such *drivel*," Will softly said, one brow quirking over his eye as he smiled, darkly amused. "What wondrous luck you pay no mind to it."

"Ah, but I have been forced to pay mind to it today," Hannibal said, and took a step towards him, enjoying the slight widening of Will's eyes and the reflexive way he tilted his chin up, as much stubborn defiance as it was baring his covered throat. Hannibal caught the faintest trace of his scent and that strange, strengthening undertone sharpened with his sudden nerves and leaned closer to seek more of it.

"I suggest you ignore it, Lord Clarges," Will said, taking a step backwards and snagging the heel of his boot on the pedestal of the statue behind him. He caught himself and stepped up on it, gaining a precious few inches to bring him level with Hannibal's own height, rebellion shining in his sharp blue gaze. "As there is no easy or satisfying solution otherwise."

Hannibal turned his head in the direction of soft laughter that drifted from behind them, aware that a sizable group was blundering through the maze in their direction. He turned back to Will, who bristled at the scheming he could clearly read on his face, and swiftly slid his hand around Will's waist to press his palm to the base of his slender spine.

Will tipped forward in a clutch for balance, one hand lifting to brace on Hannibal's shoulder, alarmed by how close they were, so close he could feel the heated puff of Hannibal's breath on his mouth and was engulfed in his Alpha scent. It was heady stuff, and Will shivered, the fine hairs on his arms and nape lifting in response, his body betraying him with warmth that flooded color into his lips and cheeks and widened his pupils despite the strong sunlight.

"Hannibal, what are you doing?" he hissed, alarmed by his own responses, pushing away only to have Hannibal's other arm slide up beneath his, pulling him flush to his chest. "*Stop this!*"

"It is too late, I think," Hannibal murmured, smirking and amused, his nose brushing Will's as the younger man struggled. Will's soft scent teased his nose, a warmth that slid down his throat with a burn like fine liquor and left him thirsty for more. "As we now have an audience, pray don't make a fuss."

Will's breath came sharp and fast, flooding his lungs with the scent that so affected him. His eyes flicked to the group of young ladies and their beaus who stumbled into the small clearing with them, startled and curious at their position, for all the world a pair of lovers caught stealing a kiss in the privacy of the maze.

"What are you about?" he breathed, confused and furious. His traitorous heart picked up its pace, his bond to Hannibal tugging him like a line to an anchor, overwhelming him with the desire to abandon himself to Hannibal's careless, thoughtless keeping.

"*Behave,*" Hannibal warned him, shifting closer. "I am being found besotted by my spouse. It wouldn't do to ruin the show now, would it?"

Will tightened with anger but summoned a sweet smile for the young people staring openly at them, now, agog at what they were witnessing. It was an act of sheer willpower, but he forced himself to ignore the demands of his bond to this man. He was not an Omega. He was neither a man nor a woman. He was simply himself, and that self refused to give Hannibal the satisfaction of thinking him cowed.

"Well, I suppose if one is to be a bear," he said, because two could play this game as well as one and if Hannibal was determined to light a fire, they may as well burn together, "one should be a grizzly."

He cupped Hannibal's face in his hands and tipped his head, for all the world begging a kiss.

Hannibal leaned in, pulse quickening in surprised anticipation, oddly delighted that Will was so suddenly and completely receptive. He moved close enough that Will lips teased against his own when the young Omega whispered, "That should be close enough to fool them, don't you think?"

Hannibal froze, keenly disappointed that Will had stopped just short of kissing him, the little minx, and only by virtue of his own deadly pride did he manage not to close the distance. It was almost more intimate than a kiss would be, eyes locked together, lashes mingling with every flutter of lids, breath pulsing against lips and hearts pounding. It would almost be a relief to just go ahead and kiss him, to force Will's angry blue eyes to close, to see him undone just a bit, jostled out of his sadness and quick temper by the touch he surely craved after six years of solitude.

"Excuse us, Lord Clarges," one of the young gentlemen said, mustering up the bravery to intrude. "We did not mean to interrupt your..."

Hannibal smiled and Will smirked, sharing a moment of amusement at someone else's expense for a change. Will's fingers fell to curl against his shoulders, firm and strong. The subtle shift of muscle down Will's side as he moved was warm and silky against Hannibal's hand. It was with great reluctance that he tugged Will down from the statue's pedestal and let him catch his feet, but he did not relinquish his hold as he looked back at their audience.

"Please, excuse *me*," he purred, unaware of pulling Will tight against him but enjoying the light pressure of his touch on his chest and side. "I am sometimes rather overcome with affection for my spouse."

"Your *spouse*?"

There was such an air of unabashed consternation about them that Will's shoulders shook with silent laughter, though he kept his head turned away to hide it.

215

"Yes," Hannibal said, clearing his throat to keep the amusement from his voice. "Why do you all look so surprised?"

"I... we..." They exchanged glances among themselves, at a complete loss.

"Yes, well, excuse us," Hannibal said, deftly swinging Will around to settle his arm around his waist, feeling possessive under so many watchful eyes. "We will move along then. Shall we, Will?"

He cut straight through the middle of them, propelling Will along with him and not stopping until they were well clear.

"And just what on earth was that, Lord Clarges?" Will asked, too flustered and amused to be angry.

"I told you what that was," Hannibal said, still affected by the lingering feel of Will's warm body against his. He was beginning to reconsider his initial thought that he was not given to attraction to men, because the recollection of his eagerness for that almost-kiss made him tighten with unexpected anticipation.

He glanced down at Will, at the gleam of light brown highlights in his curls picked out by the sun, at the rim of his ear exposed by the wind, at the arch of his thick brows over his sparkling eyes, and knew his attraction to his Omegan spouse depended not at all on the beauty before him, but the ferocious intelligence he wielded like a weapon against the world.

Tearing his gaze away from his delightfully formed, undeniably beautiful, and entirely distracting little mate, Hannibal briskly said, "We have to give the appearance of being satisfied with one another."

"What an impossible task you've set yourself, Lord Clarges," Will said, sidling away to gain just a bit more distance. "Pretending domesticity with an Omega."

"Should I rather jump on hot coals and call it a waltz?" Hannibal asked, quirking his brow at Will, who gave him a menacing-sweet smile and said, "If it would not trouble you to do so."

"Ah, your tongue is excessively sharp, Will," Hannibal said, delighted.

"I am happily everything of which you disapprove," Will said, attempting to make his point.

"I did not say I disapprove," Hannibal said, surprising him. "I merely made an observation on your nature."

"Shall I make an observation regarding your own?" Will inquired, curious. Their pace slowed somewhat, aided by the cool air blowing beneath the lane of trees casting shade over them.

"That depends," Hannibal said, amused by the way Will looked at him, forgetting his stiff reserve in favor of his burning curiosity.

"On whether they are *nasty observations*?" Will asked.

"No," Hannibal said, determined not to make reference to their unfortunate clash in the library. "It depends on whether your observations involve violence."

"Give me a moment," Will said, a reluctant smile curving his full mouth. "I am rather resourceful."

"Trotting out your finer qualities on my behalf, Will?" Hannibal asked, his own half-smile failing when Will checked, his straight shoulders squaring and familiar blank calm falling over his face.

"I have no need for your approval, Lord Clarges," Will said, remembering what a precarious situation he was in where Hannibal was concerned. "Only your absence."

"I am sorry to disappoint you."

"You have never been sorry before," Will said, hands clasped behind his back.

That got Hannibal's attention. "Disappointment implies expectation, Will. Did you have expectations of me?"

Will frowned, recalling how hopeful he'd been in his father's house with Mina whispering how happy he could be. *Happy.* And he had been so foolish and hopeful and stupidly young.

"Once, maybe," he said, knowing it required an answer or else Hannibal would badger one out of him. "But only for a short time."

"Until I left you?"

"Until I *met* you, Lord Clarges," Will corrected him, tipping his face into the breeze.

Hannibal fell silent, chastened.

The lake spread out before them, but they were mostly alone. Hannibal chanced a look at Will and cleared his throat, venturing, "I never asked you, Will, what you expected to find at Hartford House when you first arrived."

"It never occurred to me you would be interested," Will said, gazing out at the lake, forgetting to keep his face turned away.

"I had imagined you a spoiled thing," Hannibal mused. "Cosseted and indulged, deeply enamored of your own looks and well aware of your own worth, expecting to coil me about your little finger."

He watched the wind ruffle Will's curls, exposing the curve of his ear again in a peek of pale skin. He had the oddest impulse to push Will's hair back to see his ear in full.

"I never gave myself a chance to know you. I never gave you a chance to show me who you really are," Hannibal said. "I never let you know me in return."

Will turned those blue eyes on him, weighing his sincerity against a cut girth strap and an accident that could have killed him.

"I know you, Hannibal," he said, his voice soft and low as he loosened his hold on his perception. "You are the last Alpha male in a direct line stretching back through history to our country's royal family. Pride and importance are bred into your soul, a fort of blood and bone housing a pedigree few can rival. You are offended to the core of yourself by that which is less than you."

Hannibal stared down at him, absorbing his words, those vague, brilliantly blue eyes fixed rigidly on his own.

"Unfortunately for the world, we are *all* less than you," Will murmured, his lids lowering as he averted his face. "Though perhaps, in the end, it is more unfortunate for yourself, Lord Clarges. It must be very lonely, being one of a kind."

"I am no more alone than you are, Will," he said, and impulsively reached out to tuck Will's hair behind his ear, satisfied to see it was just as lovely as he had imagined. "You are certainly one of a kind."

Will didn't pull away from the touch, only murmured, "Then we are alone together, I suppose, but alone nonetheless."

"We don't have to be," Hannibal said, his gaze skipping over the beautiful scenery without really seeing it, his focus entirely on his thoughts.

Will stared at him, feeling once again he was missing something which would explain all of Hannibal's behavior, something above and beyond—or perhaps akin to—the accident that had occurred.

Hannibal clasped his hands behind his back, thoughtful and silent when Will did not respond. They walked further down to the lakeside and stopped in the shade of an awning put up for the party-goers. There were several large groups about the lake and many small boats launched. Will heard music drifting over the water, a pleasant, lively tune meant to invoke good spirits.

"Will, the contract our grandfathers signed hinged on one outcome," Hannibal said, "that of an heir."

Will took a deep breath, steeling himself for unpleasantness.

"Grandfather is insistent, Will," he went on. "And your place as my spouse depends on you providing that child. Grandfather has been patient with us both, but he will not wait forever. He hasn't the time."

"That *child*?" Will asked, wondering at the change. An heir could only be a Ledford male, preferably an Alpha.

Hannibal cursed softly under his breath at his quick mind and hastily said, "Well, an heir is a child; either way I believe you can grasp the basis of how such a thing must come about."

"Goodness, be careful with your compliments of my deductive capabilities, Lord Clarges, lest I faint," Will said, sharp and quick.

Hannibal snorted and wrinkled his nose, "Then we would both be indisposed because I would faint alongside you from pure surprise."

Will laughed, a short, raspy bark of sound that quickly tapered.

"Honestly, your humor is perverse and you are spiteful," Hannibal said, unable to repress his own chuckle.

"It must be disturbing for you to find common ground with an Omega," Will said, looking up at Hannibal, his eyes a lovely, cool blue beneath his black lashes, changing to suit the sky above them.

Hannibal smiled then, admitting, "No, it is not."

Surprise flashed over Will's face, a furtive glance laced with heavy skepticism.

"Hannibal," he said, using his given name to ensure his full attention. "Over six years ago, I offered to give you an heir and you refused me."

Refused.

Hannibal flinched, the scent memory of that encounter returning with sudden, profound clarity—warm sweetness, desperation, fear, and the salt of Will's tears.

"You made yourself pointedly clear," Will said, his voice never rising above a soft purr. "Not just that even the idea of it sickens you, but that there is nothing you want less than a child with me."

Hannibal frowned, a dark flush rising in his cheeks, his own recollection of that night as crisp and clear as Will's seemed to be.

"Now here we are, six years later," Will said, squaring his shoulders. "The offer no longer stands, Lord Clarges."

Hannibal tipped his head up the slight breeze, hoping it would cool his burning shame.

"I don't want a child from you," Will told him, a pointed echo of his own words. "There is nothing I want less, in fact, than something which will bind me to you for the rest of our lives."

"I suppose I deserved that," he admitted on a chuckle, darkly amused.

"Yes," Will said, cutting a look at him from beneath his heavy lashes. "You did, and there is plenty more where that came from."

"Well, I *am* glad to see you are not suffering overmuch from the gossips, my darling."

Will's eyes widened to painful proportions as he turned to find behind him none other than his dear twin sister.

Chapter 13

For a disorienting moment, Hannibal saw two Wills—one in a gentleman's proper gear, the other in a beautiful, expensive day gown with a parasol shielding her from the sun, her glossy dark curls piled atop her head and a smirk on her full mouth.

It was the smirk that startled him, full of a viciousness that Hannibal hadn't expected, and it immediately put him off. He stepped closer to Will on instinct, tensing in response to an unspoken threat.

"Mina," Will breathed, every bit of love he'd ever felt for her welling to the surface. She was effortlessly beautiful, a petal blush on her creamy skin, her blue eyes sparkling with good health, her long lashes as curled and perfect as her dark hair.

"My sad little mirror," she teased, reaching up with a gloved hand to cup his cheek as she always had. "We're less alike now than we were."

Her blue eyes flicked to Hannibal and she said, "Good afternoon, Lord Clarges."

"Lady Rathmore," Hannibal said, focusing on where her hand lay on Will's cheek and how bespelled he seemed. "I've been anticipating meeting you for... what? Some six years, now?"

She cocked her head and laughed, a floating and contrived sound, but at least she dropped her hand.

"You must have Will in a panic with that infamous tongue of yours," she said, smiling at them both.

"Sadly, he has not yet had the benefit of my tongue," Hannibal said, pleased when Will blushed and Mina's blue eyes widened in startlement. "Since I've returned there has been nothing but throwing of valuables, arguing, and an astonishing amount of violence."

A thread of nervousness shaded the furtive flick of Mina's eyes from Hannibal to Will, as if seeking proof of abuse on his pale skin.

With a smirk of pure relish, Hannibal added, "I have no idea how anyone survives him, frightening as he is."

"Frightening as *he* is, Lord Clarges?" she asked, her voice small.

Will angled a look up at him, torn between laughter and outrage, but it was enough to nudge him out of his surprise. He smiled despite himself when Hannibal looked down at him and said, "Just look at him, ferocious and prickly. Yes, there is an unbearable plethora of sharpness given on a daily basis, I'm afraid."

"Shame on you, Will, for abusing him so," Mina said, following it with a sultry laugh that sounded quite practiced to Hannibal's discerning ear. "The gossip is backwards on that count."

"It can be dangerous to listen to gossip," Hannibal warned her. "I'm very glad I did not listen to those rumors you were having an affair with an actor. How terribly mortifying that would be for you, if people listened to such things."

Will sighed and Mina just looked furious, a faint crease in her brow smoothing quickly when she realized it.

"Will you excuse us, Lord Clarges?" she asked, looping her hand through Will's arm. "I would like to catch up with my brother."

Hannibal was reluctant to do so, but said with a strained smile, "Will doesn't require my permission in anything, Lady Rathmore."

His gaze lingered on Will's troubled face and he felt the strangest inclination to accompany him. Instead, he watched them begin on the stone path around the lake, so alike in so many respects it was uncanny.

"Lord *Clarges*! *There* you are! I have been *dying* to speak to you!"

"If only I were so lucky," Hannibal breathed, and pasted on a smile that surely must look every bit as false as if felt.

⌘⌘⌘

"Mina, what are you doing here?" Will asked, his initial surprise at seeing his sister fading to curiosity.

"Darling, after that frightening letter you wrote me, what did you expect I would do?" she asked, tipping her head to him. "Tell me, has that terrible husband of yours given you any suspicion with his actions since your accident?"

"No, Mina, nothing," Will said, his anxiety rising with her words. "I am not even sure it was by his hand, in all honesty. I acted in haste, in thoughtless haste.

I would never say he is behaving as he should, but he is making an effort to be polite to me—"

"To get close enough to harm you, you mean!" Mina said, not buying it. "Men like that never change, dearest, believe me."

"Honestly, Mina, I should never have written my unfounded fears to you, I was just—"

"Frightened," she said, hugging his arm in hers. Will found the soft brush of her skirts against his leg, the familiar scent of her perfume, the nearness of her and pressure of her arm on his were all things he had missed and adored, things that soothed his growing worry. "Will, *someone* has tried to kill you. Considering your husband's reputation, it takes little imagination to lay it at his feet."

"I was... *informed* there has been another in his past who has thwarted him and, perhaps, paid with their life," Will reluctantly told her, concern furrowing his brow when he thought of Matthew's warning. "I had no idea to whom he referred or under what circumstances, but it gives me pause."

"As well it *should*! There *is* terrible gossip about your husband, Will, and I believe it is just what this person was hinting at," Mina said, halting when Will stopped in his tracks. "I don't normally pay attention to such things, but considering he is here now, back in his ancestral home with you, I cannot be silent! I feel I should tell you, Will, as you have suffered one *accident* already, that it might not be the last."

"Mina," Will said, his rapid retreat forcing her to grasp his face again, staring into his mirroring blue eyes.

"Will, listen to me and listen well," she said in an urgent whisper. "Lord Clarges was married once before, for a short time only, right before he took on his commission. Indeed, he fled to the military to escape possible charges for her death, his late Lady Clarges."

Will stilled in her grasp, a deep and terrible fear rising up inside of him that he didn't want to acknowledge, didn't want to be true.

"They were married less than a *month*, Will, and she died under such mysterious circumstances no one properly knows what happened," Mina said, leaning close to hiss the words against his ear. "His grandfather made discreet compensation to her family and cleared the way for his return home. Will, I would never dare repeat such unfounded misery, but I fear for your safety."

"I have been six years at Hartford House—" Will began, unwilling to believe it could be true, his thoughts snaring on the fact that Hannibal had been married once before, unbeknownst to himself.

"And he has been six years away," she cut in, overriding him. "Will, listen to me. If he is back now, it is only to be rid of you, and this episode you described only confirms it! He has murdered a wife once already, by all designs one of his choosing who happened to displease him somehow. How much more danger are you in, Omega that you are, when he could easily be rid of you?"

Will pulled away from her grip, rejecting it, but the seed was already planted. His eyes traveled back to Hannibal, a lion among sheep, standing tall next to the graceful and delicate form of a woman who was tittering and fawning on him, the picture of every feminine excess he desired.

"I am frightened for you, Will," Mina purred into his ear. "Look at him. Even now he could be searching for your replacement. It is why they throw themselves at him, Will. They know you are unsuitable and he will soon find a way to be rid of you."

Hannibal's amber eyes caught Will's and he dropped his gaze, turning away in time with Mina to give him their backs.

"Don't fret, darling," she cooed, tugging him to walk with her. "You are clever and resourceful, Will. If you are alert and know what he is about, then he might not get the best of you."

"He wants an heir," Will said. "At least, I think he does. His sincerity is suspect and his humor is ghastly, so it is difficult to tell."

"Then you must not give him one," Mina quickly said, and tugged on him to chide him, "Come, now, Will, use your Gift! You have seen enough of him to see yourself through his eyes!"

"Rather more than that, Mina, I'm afraid," Will admitted, shivering. "I have bonded to him."

She stopped again. She was breathless with dread when she said, "Will, you never!"

"I couldn't control it," he said, a poor defense. "Mina, I... my Gift—my *curse*—was bearing on me and he was rightfully displeased with me and it just... happened."

"He terrified you into it, is that what you mean?" she asked, and lay her hand along his cheek to pet him. "My darling, what a terrible reward for your love of me you've been given. A one-way bond to a man who detests you is a pitiable and terrible thing. No wonder you are so wan! No color in your cheeks, no life in your eyes. My poor dear."

Will flinched from her assessment, but accepted it as he had always accepted her.

"Mina... is that why you were so frightened when Mr. Stammets came with the contract?" Will asked, his voice a pained, soft whisper. "Because you were afraid he would do the same to you as he had to the former Lady Clarges?"

There was sorrow in her blue eyes as she gazed at him, but no contrition, only the sharp determination of self-preservation Will had suffered for more than once in their childhood.

"You understand, Will, don't you?" she asked, softly and gently as if imparting the sweetest of life's secrets. "Why I would wish to avoid him? You understand your place with him, as well? How fragile it is? How he sees you?"

"Yes, Mina, I know it very well," he said, breathing the truth she wanted to hear.

"So you understand how I worry for you?" she pressed.

"Yes," he agreed.

"I beg you to have a care, Will," she said, satisfied she had delivered her warning. "I do not wish to lose my twin."

"I will be as careful as I can, Mina," Will said, offering a tense, nervous laugh, his thoughts turning once more to his riding accident. "All things considered."

"To that end, darling, I am sending someone to keep an eye on things," she informed him. "I spoke with father and he, too, is *very* concerned about the situation you have found yourself in."

"*Father—*"

"No, don't be so surprised, dearest, you are his child in the end," she reminded him. "No matter his disappointment in you, he has no wish to see you buried before your time, and neither do I."

Will felt he could argue that point, but held his tongue as Mina said, "Do you recall Francis, darling?"

"Vaguely," Will said, frowning. "We were very young when he left."

"Yes, we were," Mina said, pulling him back into motion on the path. "But I found him some time ago and gave him employment in my Household. He is invaluable to me, dedicated and loyal as he is, and he remembers you fondly."

"I cannot imagine why he would," Will admitted. "I hardly recall him."

"It's little matter," she said, waving his doubt away. "I have dispatched him to Hartford House with instructions to keep you safe, and that is precisely what he will do."

"*Mina!*" Will said, appalled. "You cannot possibly send another *Alpha* to Hartford House! His Grace would never stand for it! *Hannibal* would never stand for it! Even if he is a servant, he is still—"

"Tell them he is coming ahead of me, then," she said, smiling and amused by his worries. "Inform them I have decided to retire to the country to spend time with my darling brother."

Will hesitated, questioning her motives when she had not once attempted to contact him in all this time.

"Will, are you terribly cross with me?" she asked, able, as always, to sense his disquiet and guessing the cause.

"Why would I be cross with you, Mina?" Will asked, hardly aware of the soft deference in his voice, it was so ingrained in him to cater to her.

"For pushing you into his bed in my place," Mina said, smiling when he blushed. "For abandoning you to his nastiness and not speaking to you in six years?"

"You have had a life to live, Mina, the same as I," Will said, letting his strange distrust fade to the back of his awareness. "I imagined you were happy and enjoying yourself; that is all I hoped for."

"Ah, well, yes," she said, leaning into him. "Life as Lady Rathmore was an enjoyable enough distraction, I suppose. Timothy and I do not suit so well as I imagined as a child, but that's neither here nor there."

After a pensive, troubled silence, Will asked, "Would you truly come stay with me at Hartford House, Mina?"

"Darling, of course!" she said, hugging his arm yet again, her touch a comfort he had missed for too long. "I often thought of you over the years, shuttered away at that awful old house with only an old man for company. How lonely you must have been, my poor darling. I would be delighted to come relieve your tedium! What fun we shall have together again, Will!"

She gave him another squeeze and pulled him back along the path, glowing with accomplishment.

Hannibal was extremely unsettled by the way Will and his sister had been staring at him when he'd chanced to look up. It was eerie to see two such similar people so dissimilarly dressed, watching him with the same blue eyes but with one set narrowed and the other sorrowful.

He was immediately suspicious what that woman—because a sister would have at least attempted a visit in the last six years and none of Will's relatives had even tried—was filling Will's head with.

Luckily for him, Will was too intelligent by far to be easily diverted from the facts, but Hannibal knew there were plenty of damning facts to conjure Will's melancholy to the fore. In a matter of seconds, he could think of dozens and that prompted him to say to the woman clinging to his arm, "Should you like to meet my spouse and in-law, Miss Green?"

"*Your* spouse?" she echoed, too thoughtless to keep the surprise out of her voice. "Lord Clarges, I had no idea she was here! I am simply *dying* to meet her!"

"Yes, just here," Hannibal said, dragging her towards Will and his sister, who had slowed to a stop again. He could swear when Will noticed them approaching there was sudden fear in his gaze and Hannibal wondered at the cause. He had not seen such a thing from his spouse since his return, and had done nothing to his knowledge to provoke actual fear. By the time he reached them, poor Miss Green quite out of breath from his pace, Hannibal was sure he had been mistaken.

"Lord Clarges," Will said, taking a step back in tandem with Mina, both of them rather alarmed by his sudden, urgent appearance. "My sister was just confirming her plans to take an extended stay in the countryside. Her guard will be arriving tomorrow ahead of her."

"How lovely," Hannibal said, forcing a smile. "I have no means to protest, considering. Ah, excuse me, introductions are in order. May I present Miss Green? Miss Green, this is my spouse—"

"So delighted to make your acquaintance, Lady Clarges," Miss Green simpered, directing it at Mina, whose smirk returned full force.

"*Gods* no, not that one," Hannibal corrected, turning her by her shoulders to face Will. "I realize they are twins, but they are not so similar as all that. No, *Will* is my spouse."

"*Lord* Clarges?" she asked, confusion stealing her smile when she beheld Will's stony, blank expression. "But, Lord Clarges, how on earth do you expect an heir?"

Oh, dear," Mina said, chuckling softly in a way that set Hannibal's teeth on edge. "I believe I see an acquaintance enjoying the music. If you will all excuse me?"

Will's face tightened imperceptibly as his twin hastened away and his mouth pressed into an alarmingly taut line. Hannibal was quite wise enough to his moods to read Will's agitation when he saw it and frowned at the woman who was in serious danger of earning herself a trouting.

Before he could point out the obvious, Miss Green cried with utter simple-minded realization, "Why, you're *Omegan!*"

"Yes," Will said, his voice calm and steady despite the slight blush that graced his cheeks. Hannibal couldn't tell if he was embarrassed or about to plunge the unfortunately-dim young lady into the nearby lake.

"But I had heard Lord Clarges wouldn't go *near* an Omega!" she tittered, looking to Hannibal for approval.

"I never said there weren't advantages," Will said, a slight quirk gracing his lips.

A spasm of confusion marred her brow and Hannibal cleared his throat to keep from laughing at her puzzlement.

"My darling girl," Hannibal said, wishing he could set her down but unable to hold her own stupidity against her. "I am sure you have simply misunderstood."

"Have I?" she asked, and tittered nervously. "I would simply *die* should I give offense!"

"And yet here you stand," Will said, ever so mild. "*Miraculous.*"

"Shall we?" Hannibal asked, sweeping Will past her.

"Are we late for something, Lord Clarges?" Will asked, irritated by the jolt of nerves he felt when Hannibal took hold of him.

"I felt compelled to remove you before you drew blood from that ignorant, spoiled creature," Hannibal said. "Do try, Will, not to sharpen your claws on such a simpleton. She is no match for you in any regard and is a dreadful gossip *simply dying* about everything. She will carry news of your status far and wide."

"Interesting, Lord Clarges, how you defend that *ignorant, spoiled creature* for the very qualities which you revile in Omegas," Will observed, his stride quickening in time with his temper.

"I *revile* stupidity in any package, Will," Hannibal said. "Not exclusively in Omegas. There are numerous important reasons why I do not associate closely with such people as Miss Green."

"I was made to understand—and thoroughly—that your revilement *is* exclusively for Omegas," Will said, unwilling to stop now that he had a chance to get some answers. "It makes me wonder, Lord Clarges, what you must have suffered to make such associations."

"My suffering is none of your business!" Hannibal informed him, escorting him back towards the manor house with every intention to set out for home no matter the early hour.

"It is when it affects me," Will said, keeping pace with him despite their height difference. "I think, considering I bear the brunt of the result, I should know the source of your opinions!"

"I will not speak on this subject one second longer," Hannibal said, his voice sharp and clipped. Will flinched again, but it was gone in a heartbeat. Still, there was no mistaking his tension and it prickled Hannibal's instinct to protect him from what had made him so nervous.

Such a quandary when he himself seemed to be the cause.

"Why do you flinch from me?" he asked, alarmed when Will met his gaze with a challenge in his eyes, again bracing as if expecting violence. "Will Grant, what on earth has come over you? Why are you acting as if you fear me?"

Will tipped his head up and said, "*I* will not speak on *this* subject one second longer, Lord Clarges."

Hannibal drew up and opened his mouth to question him further, but was forestalled by Aunt Margaret waving them down from the upper garden where Grandfather was greeting and visiting with acquaintances. Her beckoning interrupted them, luckily, before any more harsh words were exchanged, but it came far too late to prevent the damage that had already been done.

⌘⌘⌘

The two of them stiffly took their places at Grandfather's side where Will put his hand on the old Alpha's shoulder, seeking to steady his nerves after what

Mina had told him and his small, heated clash with Hannibal. There was little time to dwell on it, however; they were converged on by friends and family all eager to meet Will as well as speak with their long-absent future Duke.

"And have you had the pleasure of meeting Miss Loucks?" Aunt Margaret inquired, her innocent tone putting Hannibal on his guard.

"Yes, Aunt Margaret, we have. She is a very beautiful young lady and suits Anthony very well," Will said, calming when Hannibal's scent lost the smoky undertone of threat that seemed to coil around his senses. He felt less exposed here, with the stone wall to his back and Roland to one side, and he tried not to be nervous of the people around him, many of whom had snubbed him six years ago.

"*Lovely* girl," Aunt Grace said, fanning herself. "We are *very lucky* she accepted our Anthony's proposal!"

"Miss Loucks will do quite nicely, provided she doesn't amuse herself by insulting Will again. I refuse to stand for it and she should have better manners," Hannibal said to her.

"No, you simply cannot withhold your approval now, Hannibal!" Aunt Grace said, rousing her temper in the wake of his statement. "Such a rare opportunity to find a young lady of her persuasion unattached! Your cousin is a very lucky boy, Hannibal, and *I* won't stand for *you* obstructing him!"

"I have no other reason with that aside, Aunt Grace, and no intentions of ruining Anthony's chances for happiness," Hannibal said, risking a look at Will's tense, uncomfortable face. "Ruining one life is quite enough, I've learned."

"*Two*," Will softly corrected. "It has not been as exciting as your own, Lord Clarges, but I believe mine still counts as a life?"

"It was yours I was referring to," Hannibal said, noting how his eyes widened in a split second of surprise, a glimpse of the true Will beneath his reserve.

"Children," Roland said, reminding them they were not in private. "Some conversations are best left to the bedchamber, don't you think?"

Will blushed to the roots of his hair and Hannibal sighed, wondering if he was half as provoking as his grandfather could sometimes be.

Will gradually relaxed, able to fade into the background of conversation as the afternoon crept on. He kept an anxious eye out for his sister, but she never approached. Most of those gathered in Roland's vicinity were family of one ilk or another to the Diments and knew Hannibal well, though they were mostly strangers to Will. It must have shown in his expression, as Hannibal leaned closer to ask, "Are you putting faces to names so far, Will?"

"Yes," Will said, realizing Grandfather had shifted his chair away, leaving Will in Hannibal's company, caught in a small bubble of privacy within the press of people. "There are a great many of them. More than Anthony has mentioned."

"More than he is probably aware of," Hannibal said, his smile wry. "Anthony has no great interest in the extended family. Something I suppose he will need to develop when he becomes Master of Fernhill in Uncle Robert's—"

"You're looking well, Lord Clarges. And is this the mysterious spouse we've all been hearing of?"

Will braced when his hand was swept up and delivered to a whiskered face for a wet and entirely inappropriate kiss. He looked down at his trapped hand, then transferred his bland gaze to the person holding it. Under his disapproving, offended stare, the man hastily dropped his hand with an uncomfortable chuckle.

"Darnell," Hannibal said, doing his best not to bristle, though the sight of that bounder taking liberties with Will's person mortally tested his self-control.

The gleeful, predatory look on Darnell's face was only matched by the cunning expression his wife wore. "Have a care with my spouse, if you please. Will dislikes being inexpertly handled," Hannibal said, knowing well enough if Will wasn't in the mood to tolerate it, he certainly would make his displeasure known.

"Warning me off of your pretty mate, my boy?" Darnell asked, chuckling.

"As a matter of fact, I am," Hannibal said, ever so cordial. "And it's *Lord Clarges*, in case it escaped you."

Will bristled next to him, but held his tongue out of respect for Roland. He had no desire to embarrass or shame the man who had sheltered him these many years if he could help it, but he chafed to remind Hannibal he didn't need his dubious protection. Not anymore.

"You needn't worry so for him, *Lord Clarges*," Darnell said, openly leering. "I don't bite."

"Oh, I have no worries for Will, Darnell," Hannibal said, his smile entirely indulgent, though beginning to strain at the edges with temper. "He is more than capable of dealing with any man whose hands might seek to wander where they are most certainly not welcome. I only hope you won't test him in that regard; you will certainly come out the worst for it. Agitating my husband is extremely dangerous, I've learned."

Much to Will's surprise, Hannibal was serious, and was *smirking* at Mr. Darnell's consternation.

"Speaking of not welcome," Hannibal said, maneuvering the conversation to his advantage. "I believe you are acquainted with my spouse, Mrs. Darnell?"

Her sharp, unhappy face nearly caught fire with the blush that filled her cheeks.

"Will?" Hannibal asked, looking down at him so that Will was unexpectedly the focus of their attention.

"Yes," Will said, tipping his chin a bit higher, his shoulders straight and stiff with his pride. "We met at your soiree."

"I'm afraid I don't recall," she said, her smile so forced and false Hannibal was amazed it did not crack around the edges and fall right off her face.

"I accompanied Lord du Millau when I was newly married," Will said, considering her closely, knowing she knew him and knew precisely how she had treated him. He could see the brittle fear in her face, vacuous terror of stepping wrong in a Society that could break her like an aged, dried twig. Terror of mistakes exposed, gossip turned back to bite, shamed and shunned for misguided attempts to fit in.

He felt pity for her, selfish and self-important woman that she was, married to a lecher with a roving eye and no standards, trapped in a marriage as empty and meaningless as the good opinions she worked so hard to engender. An empty life spent half in fear and half in vicious enjoyment of the suffering of others. So long as she was not the target, never the target, and that was why they always looked, all of them. Searching restlessly to find fault in others to paper the cracks in their own character...

"I imagine you would not remember it," Will said, seeing relief fill her eyes. He waited a heartbeat and added, "I had nearly forgotten all about it. One soiree is very much like another, I fear."

"Yes," she said, her pride offended, but she didn't dare give it away. "I do hope you will attend future events, with my warm welcome, of course! We would be so delighted to have you!"

"I have very little doubt of that," Hannibal said, immensely enjoying the frank irritation on Mr. Darnell's face as he realized what was happening.

"Thank you, that is very kind," Will said. "However, my time is precious and I prefer to spend it on things which are important enough to warrant the loss."

Hannibal's brows rose and he grinned, saying with pleased indulgence, "Will has been running Hartford House for Grandfather for the past six years. I am afraid he has very little time for provincial gatherings as his presence will be in such high demand when the Season commences, now that the estate is in such good working order."

"I-is that the Baileys?" Mrs. Darnell asked, peering intently anywhere but at Will for anything that might offer polite escape from the line of fire.

"Yes, I believe it is!" Mr. Darnell said, quick to throw in his support. "If you will excuse us, Lords Clarges?"

They departed with near immediacy. Hannibal smiled at them as they eased away, his hand falling to the small of Will's back without his permission or awareness.

Will stiffened slightly, an unintentional response to his own nerves. He wasn't entirely sure how much store to set in what his sister said, but he couldn't discount it out of hand, either. His cut girth strap had been no accident. He could not in good conscience condemn Hannibal without proof, but there was no convincing his tightly-strung nerves of that.

Hannibal didn't retreat, not while the Darnells were still casting uncertain, assessing looks their way as they merged back into the crowd. The moment they were out of eye shot, however, Hannibal dropped his hand. Will's continued nervousness did not escape him, nor did his relief when Hannibal put some space between them.

Hannibal's mate *was* frightened of him, just as he'd suspected. He was hiding it well, but he was frightened nonetheless and Hannibal hadn't the first idea how to address it.

"Mrs. Darnell will certainly think twice before crossing you in the future," Hannibal said, noting Will seemed somewhat overwhelmed on top of the bubbling nervousness that kept him looking restlessly at the crowd. Tension strained the corners of his full mouth and tightened his slender body, his subtle agitation not lost on Hannibal.

Despite not wishing to upset his spouse again, Hannibal decided to take Will somewhere quiet with the vague idea he might be able to get to the heart of whatever had scared him. He wasn't entirely sure how to approach the subject, but if anything he would at least see that Will got a much-needed break from the festivities.

Gods knew Hannibal could use one.

He lightly touched Will's elbow to get his attention and waited for Will's troubled gaze to lift to his own.

"Don't object, please, just come quietly," he said, steering Will behind a row of potted shrubs, past the alert servants, and in through an unmanned door.

Once inside, he took Will directly to the Fernhill library, which was blessedly empty. He let go of Will's arm the moment he was able, hoping to prevent another swell in Will's sudden, strange fear of him.

No one had marked their absence, Hannibal noted with relief. He closed the door quietly, and when he turned he saw Will was already a good measure less tense just being away from the crowd. "You need to tell me when things become too much, Will. You aren't used to these events, after all, and I do not relish my relations to such an extent I cannot bear to be out of their company."

"It would not seem terribly intelligent of me to bring more of my faults to your attention, Lord Clarges," Will said, his voice quiet but his tone as feisty as ever.

"If growing weary of my pushy sea of scolding relatives is a fault, Will, then it is one we share," Hannibal said, moving closer and frowning when Will moved further away. Wondering just what on earth Lady Rathmore had whispered into Will's ear and hoping to get the truth of it, Hannibal remarked, "You are skittish as a fawn, Will Grant."

"But not as harmless as one," Will warned, shooting a sharp look over one shoulder. He moved to the bookcase and looked over the selections, landing on a volume with a soft exclamation of surprise. He pulled it free, saying, "I was reading this very book at Hartford House! If you have no qualms, Lord Clarges, then I will spend some time quietly here."

"My only qualm is that you expect me to leave," Hannibal said, and bluntly added, "I refuse to go back out there. I am thoroughly exhausted of them all."

That won a brief, small smile from Will. "They have not had a chance to visit with you, Hannibal, for so long, considering you were gone at war for nearly ten years, then put them off six more—"

He was interrupted by a trilling voice calling, "*Hannibal?! Will* dear?! Where *are* you?!"

Hannibal glanced about in half a panic, judged the settee too small to hide them both, and promptly went to the window.

"What are you doing?" Will hissed, skating a wild-eyed glance at the door as footsteps and Aunt Grace's unmistakable voice neared.

Hannibal forced the pane open and slung his leg out. Pausing there with one foot to freedom, he held out his hand to Will and asked, "Are you coming?"

Will hesitated, too surprised to respond. The great Lord Clarges, Marquess and future Duke, slipping out of a window like a thief to escape his Aunt. Will stifled his laugh but couldn't hide his slight, amused smile. Hannibal certainly didn't seem like a man plotting murder, just a man who had experienced quite enough familial chastisement to suit him for one day.

It was a split-second decision on Will's part. He blamed it on the compulsion of his bond rather than a slip in his own judgment, even knowing he most certainly should not be alone with Hannibal Ledford. Clutching his book to his chest, he took Hannibal's steadying hand and followed him out onto the lawn.

"The trick," Hannibal whispered, easing the window closed, "is to go somewhere they wouldn't think to look."

"I think parting from the other guests is a good start," Will remarked, flattening against the cool manor wall when the library door was flung open for a searching glance. After a tense, frozen silence, Hannibal laced Will's fingers in his own and pulled him down the closest path, hoping not to be seen. "Everyone is gathering on the lawn, we should join them. It was rude of me to wish otherwise."

"There is nothing rude about needing a bit of space, Will," Hannibal said, his hand warm and sure around Will's fingers. "No, we will find a quiet place out of the sun for a bit."

His amber eyes slid to the lake and lit on the small armada of party boats servicing the otherwise-occupied guests of Fernhill. They were fine rowing vessels meant for two, each with a billowing canopy to block the sun and, luckily enough for him, all empty just now.

"Though I doubt it was under these circumstances," he said, hurrying towards them with Will at his side. "I believe we can use one of those."

"One of *these*?" Will asked, surprised by the small boat Hannibal directed him towards. It was a delicate and lovely vessel with padded seats and plump pillows, for all the world a place for lovers to lounge alone.

His cheeks flamed with brilliant heat. He was aghast at even the idea of it, the surprise overcoming the tug of his bond so that the potential danger of his situation returned in a startling rush.

It didn't do so in time for him to avoid Hannibal's hands, however. He was caught around the waist and deposited into the boat like he was nothing more than a sack of potatoes.

"*Lord Clarges—*"

Hannibal moved in after him, forcing Will to retreat to the stern, skittering back over the rowing bench to land in a pile of pillows on his backside. "*Honestly!*"

"You may lodge a complaint with me momentarily," Hannibal said, unmooring the boat and pushing away from the small tie-on. He slid onto the rowing bench, planting his boots on either side of Will's spread legs, and promptly set about turning them. "Your nerves are frayed. You need quiet."

"*This is not helping,*" Will said, eyes blazing as he struggled to sit up, finally gaining a semblance of dignity by working the pillows into a seat of sorts, though he was scrunched into the stern.

Hannibal, focused on getting the boat turned and away from land on all sides, spared him a look and said with a smirk, "You look like an angry kitten."

"If you have brought me here to insult me—"

"Ah, hush," Hannibal said, chuckling. "When you get furious, it does *not* help your cause. Just relax and read your book."

Will glowered at him, weighing his intentions. He didn't feel anything particularly murderous from Hannibal, no prickle of anticipation from him, no building determination to do him in. He seemed relaxed, focused on rowing the boat without paying particular attention to Will at all.

Will tried hard to reason that Hannibal, should he wish to do so, would never dare try to drown him here at his family's annual Garden Party.

He very much doubted it would be worth the cost of the scandal that would follow.

Relaxing somewhat, Will settled back and opened the book with a prim air that made Hannibal chuckle all over again.

"Your family will be furious," Will said after a long silence, his blue eyes lifting from his book to sneak a look at his husband again.

"They are gentlefolk," Hannibal said, resting from his rowing to let the boat drift lazily towards the center of the lake. "They will be furious quietly, within the bounds of common decency, and in the privacy of their own thoughts."

Will huffed a soft laugh, wriggling into a more comfortable position and stretching his legs. He made a soft sound of surprise when Hannibal let go of the oar to grab his ankle, but he just propped Will's booted foot up on the bench next to his hip and patted it.

Knowing he was tempting Hannibal to do the same to the other foot if he did not act, Will obligingly propped his other heel up next to it, finding the position quite comfortable for reading. The breeze was cool and the canopy kept off the sun, and with everyone on the lawn for games, they were alone on the water. The frogs sang their buzzing song in the shallows and an occasional dragonfly inspected them, but they were otherwise undisturbed. It was, in all, a peaceful quiet Will desperately needed.

He peered at Hannibal from the screen of his lashes, taking in his profile as Hannibal looked off towards the bank, his mouth pursed in thought and his sharp eyes flicking. It really wasn't fair for him to be so compelling. It was easy for Will to *want* to forget the truths between them when he looked at Hannibal, when those amber eyes observed him and that perfect mouth of his parted on a wolfish grin.

He felt that tug within him, a strong pull to just push forward and wrap his arms around Hannibal's waist and enjoy it, and cursed his bond to Hannibal for pressing on him yet again, an irresistible call towards the crumbling bluff.

"You're smiling," Hannibal said, catching his gaze, equal parts suspicious and amused. "What on earth are you thinking about that your cheeks are so pink?"

"It's the heat," Will said, diverting his attention to his book, his face coloring even more.

"You do seem exceptionally flushed," Hannibal noticed. "Are you overwarm?"

"I'm very well, thank you," Will said, finding it difficult to focus on his book when Hannibal decided to focus on him. Desperate to distract him, he asked, "Shall I read to you, Lord Clarges?"

"Goodness, how thoughtful," Hannibal said, cocking an eyebrow at him. "I find myself amazed you have not yet bashed me about the skull with that thing." Will scowled and Hannibal grinned, saying, "Please, do. You have a very pleasant voice, in all. It will be some little balm for the cacophony of my Aunt's guests."

Will cleared his throat, immediately regretting his decision due to the awkward placement of where he had left off. He shuffled the pages, annoyed when Hannibal said, "Pick up where you left off, if you please, Will. Perhaps *that* will explain your flush better than the paltry excuse of the heat."

Glowering at him, Will defiantly skimmed down to where he'd last been reading at Hartford and began.

"Let one never forget, however, that vanity is the snake which bites the foot of the unwary man and renders him insufferable to his friends; indeed, the mark of a true gentleman is in his deportment, his character shewn in what he does not say in place of what he could. Silence, dear friend, is the blessing of such a man, who holds his accomplishments dear and speaks not of himself. Do not fall prey to self-credit, to excesses of feeling or passions that might move others. Neglect that piece of yourself for your own betterment. Stand fast in your understanding that there is no greater weakness, no greater mark against a gentleman's character than to abandon himself to base desires and cling to what is outside of his own power and control. Limit thyself in such interactions and be ever wary of promises that have no grounding in truth and reason."

"Even your reading material is bleak," Hannibal said, wrinkling his nose.

"Did you expect a romance novel?" Will asked, relieved that Hannibal had not been paying too close attention. "Or something a child might read? Simplistic and rhyming?"

"*Behave*," Hannibal warned, amused by Will's dour look. It gave him some little hope he had been wrong, and the fear he'd thought he'd seen was merely the result of too many demands on Will in an unfamiliar environment. It was hope enough that he did not break their temporary truce with questions that would upset his spouse. "That is not an instruction for gentlemen, Will, *that* is an instruction for monkhood!"

"Abstinence from excessive feeling has its merits, Lord Clarges," Will said, irritated by his summation. "This book was much present in my childhood, your opinions notwithstanding! My father found it an excellent example for me."

"Your father sounds delightful," Hannibal said. "Was he buried at the time?"

Will's glare sharpened. "That is *not* funny."

"Gods forbid we find levity, Chaplain Grant," Hannibal said, prodding him until he saw the familiar gleam in Will's eyes that usually preceded a coshing by mere seconds. "Lucky for me, I have both the oars and you value that book too much to slap me with it."

"I am weighing the satisfaction of doing so against my host's attachment to it," Will warned him.

Hannibal smirked, well amused by his steady stare. "Be very careful, Will. You are nearly falling prey to '*excesses of feeling or passion*'."

Will's glare deepened but he refused to rise to the bait, much to Hannibal's disappointment.

"Being wary of promises that have no grounding in truth and reason is an excellent method to avoid harm," Hannibal said, frowning as he turned the words over in his mind, recalling each word merely from the remembered inflections of Will's voice as he had spoken them. He examined them against his own experiences and said, "It is, however, the most dismal approach to love I have ever been exposed to."

"For those of us who have not *been* exposed to love," Will said, irritated that Hannibal had been paying closer attention than he'd first assumed, "it is a dire warning well heeded. Had I been silly enough to encourage feelings for you before we met, how much worse would it have gone for me once we did cross paths? The foolishness of my youth was tempered by such thoughtful and experienced warnings as those in this book."

"And what of the foolishness of your adulthood?" Hannibal asked, unwilling to risk Will's further ire by questioning him on how he had felt as a newly-married bride. He was no mage, able to reverse time and change what had already passed. No, it was the youth before him he was interested in; perhaps through him, Hannibal could make amends to the boy he'd been.

"Adulthood has proven that I was right to be so cautious," Will said, closing the book with a snap. "As I have seen those around me greatly reduced in their circumstances for the folly of such notions as love. Lives have been ruined and altered beyond repair—not just those of the lovers, but of their children and families. It is a ridiculous notion that gives rise to ridiculous behavior."

"So it is unseemly to love?" Hannibal asked, intrigued.

"Of course it is," Will said, remembering himself and turning his face away to look out at the water. "Familial affection is ingrained in us, but to step beyond that is to encourage destruction."

"Or retribution?" Hannibal fished, watching him closely. "Do you believe, Will, that there is some power outside of yourself which seeks to destroy any happiness or relief you may find?"

Will's sharp glance confirmed his suspicions, and Hannibal softly said, "That is a very sad thing, indeed."

"I do not require your pity, Lord Clarges, nor your observations," Will said, his voice stiff, embarrassed to have given away one of his deepest-held beliefs. "The circumstances of my life have taught me well enough what I may expect in my future. Not everyone gets a happy ending."

Hannibal held his gaze, wondering at the sudden challenge he saw in Will's fierce blue eyes, almost as if he expected an unpleasant reaction in return. Wishing to allay him, Hannibal said, "Well, certainly not with that attitude."

Will blinked, startled. He had expected Hannibal to respond to his statement, to realize Will knew about the saddle, about his intentions. He did not expect such a droll reply and it baffled him. It made him wonder if, just perhaps, Hannibal had *not* been the one to cut his girth strap after all.

But if not his husband, then who?

"Had I any notion such a power existed," Hannibal said, leaning slightly closer, "I would thumb my nose at it. I would chase love to the ends of the earth, drown myself in happiness, and dare it to attempt to strip it from me."

Mystified, Will read his belief in his expression; indeed, he could see it was just how Hannibal truly *did* live his life—spitting in the eyes of the gods and doing as he pleased, secure in his own power.

"They wouldn't dare take anything from you," he whispered, seeing the pattern through the course of Hannibal's life, defiance after defiance. Not in marriage, nor station, nor study would he be anything other than precisely what he wished. "You have elevated yourself to their level and they are *afraid*."

"But you aren't," Hannibal murmured, unabashedly pleased.

Will started, shaking his head to cast off his Gift, a potential of understanding that never quite bore fruit. He clutched his book to his chest and murmured, "I would not say I am not, Lord Clarges. But my fear is tempered by my understanding of how little you fear in return."

His blue eyes shifted, mournful and beautiful and sparkling like jewels behind his thick lashes. "A man who fears nothing is capable of anything."

"Indeed," Hannibal said, his gaze dropping to Will's soft mouth, to the stubborn tuck of his lower lip, as if Nature herself had known what he would become and had armed him accordingly. He thought of their faux kiss in the

240

hedge maze, how warm Will had been and how calmly he'd played along, and his heart picked up in answer.

He leaned closer, his strange intensity affecting Will, who pushed back into the stern, folding his legs up to frame a wall between them.

"What are you doing?" Will asked, brandishing the book at him. "Why are you Alphas always *sniffing people?*"

"I'm not sniffing you, I'm examining you," Hannibal said, congratulating himself on his inspired quick thinking. "You're flushed. You might be overheated, in which case all this—" he gestured at Will's neckerchief and jacket, "—would need to come off."

"I will do *nothing of the sort!*" Will said, appalled, and lurched sideways to find a more dignified and proper position.

The boat bobbed hard with his movement and shifted. Hannibal swayed forward on the bench to catch his balance, not expecting the sudden motion, and Will reacted instinctively.

Without thinking of the consequences, he shoved back against the man tipping towards him and sent Hannibal tumbling over the side of the boat into the green-tinged water with a huge splash.

"Oh my goodness!" Will gasped in shocked horror, eyes wide. He dropped his book and grasped the side of the rocking boat, leaning over to look down at the frothing water. "Hannibal! *Hannibal!*"

Hannibal surfaced, sputtering and treading water, just as surprised as Will was.

It was not, however, until he glared at Will that Will felt the first stirrings of amusement and clapped his hands over his mouth in a vain effort to hold it in.

"Will Grant," Hannibal said, blowing water out of his face, his wet hair hanging around his forehead. "If you laugh, I swear to *all the gods—*"

Will's laughter escaped him, then, undone by the stern warning from a man trying to be dignified while treading water. He hitched with laughter, squeezing his sides, his slender shoulders shaking and tears welling in his blue eyes.

"You violent little harpy!" Hannibal cursed, but felt a smile curve his lips in response to Will's laughter. He'd never seen him so undone and his laughter was infectious, carefree and raspy, without the edge of sardonic bite that always seemed to tinge his throaty voice.

He grasped the side of the boat to steady it and looked up at his spouse, asking with a grin, "Are you enjoying yourself?"

Will laughed helplessly, wiping his cheeks with his hands and trying to get himself under control. Once the worst of it had passed, he tentatively moved to the side of the boat where Hannibal was clinging and offered his hand, saying with burbling laughter, "I am so sorry, Lord Clarges. Let me help you out."

Hannibal looked up at him, at his open face which looked his age for a change, no shadow clinging to his eyes, no tension around his mouth. He looked so damnably innocent it pained Hannibal to think of how much he had done to tear that from him. His aloof and easily-riled mate who believed happiness was a tool the gods used to punish those who dared reach for it and lived a thin, measly thread of a life bereft of any comforts when he should be drowning in them.

Seized with an impulse he couldn't ignore, Hannibal reached up for him, his wet, warm fingers sliding into Will's curls to curve behind his ear.

Startled, Will found himself not pulling away, his heart hammering in his ears and his eyes glued to Hannibal's. The strange, intense look on his husband's face held him captive and the soft, unexpected touch vibrated through his skin. He shivered and blamed it on the slight breeze, but knew the true reason was the gentle brush of fingers against his face, the touch six years overdue and all the more affecting for it.

"What are you doing?" he asked, his laughter fading so that the words were barely better than an exhale.

"I didn't steal a kiss in the maze," Hannibal said, a slight smile on his lips. "I should very much like to rectify that. May I rectify that?"

"There are no witnesses here, Lord Clarges. No crowd to impress or deceive," Will reminded him.

"Then we are all the better for being alone," Hannibal said.

Will's pulse sped, even as his common sense urged him to pull back, to grab the oars and row away because Hannibal likely wanted him dead and this would be such a perfect chance.

But even the cliff threatening him deep inside of his soul could not still the soft shiver that coursed through him when Hannibal pulled up against the side of the boat with every clear intention to kiss him.

Hannibal's fingers curved around the back of his skull and tugged him closer, lips parting. Will's eyes flew wide and he uttered a stifled, enticing little yelp that made Hannibal's blood rise to boiling point in an instant.

Hannibal's tug shifted Will's center of balance and he found the the small craft pushing away from him. Having taken all the abuse it could handle, it promptly tipped, dumping Will gracelessly out on top of his husband before righting itself to drift off in a bobbling wave.

Hannibal barely managed to keep them both from going under and hitched Will up, cursing the damned boat for interrupting a moment so ripe with potential.

"Well *hell!*" Will spat, his hands gripping Hannibal's shoulders and his slender legs churning the water. He was entirely too close, smashed to Hannibal's chest as he was. He could feel the warm muscle of Hannibal's forearm against the small of his back steadying him, somehow worked beneath his jacket, which floated up behind him.

Hannibal grinned, one outflung arm balancing him, finding it easy enough to stay afloat with Will's little legs paddling as furiously as they were. He was also delightfully disgruntled and temptingly close, doing his damnedest not to look at Hannibal even though they were nose to nose.

"Ah, there goes an oar," Hannibal remarked, watching it slide from its open oarlock and drift off on ripples from the boat's movement, "and the other as well."

Will fought to turn, for any excuse not to be face to face after that strange and startling encounter, but Hannibal's grip on his waist was unrelenting. More distracting was that Will could feel the length of him from chest to belly. He was desperately relieved their bodies were not pressed any closer below the waist because he was certain he would not survive the embarrassment of it.

He was so aggrieved that Hannibal chuckled, amused.

"I'm glad you find this situation laughable!" Will complained, making the mistake of tipping his face to Hannibal's. When he saw Hannibal's sharp-toothed grin, he couldn't help but return it with a lopsided one of his own, realizing the absurdity of their situation.

"Tell me, Chaplain Grant, what about this situation is *not* laughable?" Hannibal asked, and when he laughed, Will chuckled in response. "Hold tight."

Will held fast to his shoulders, his smile fading as his thoughts raced. He stared at his own white fingers clenched on Hannibal's dark coat as his husband bore him through the green, murky water of the lake to reach the boat. His skin tingled where Hannibal touched him and he fought the urge to touch those same places, to see if some change would be felt in the texture of his skin, to discover if his own touch would wake a similar response or if it was something uniquely conditioned to his husband.

It preoccupied him so much as he was hefted onto the side of the boat that Hannibal's hand on his backside came as a shocking surprise, so stunning Will had no time to protest before he was levered up by that touch to tumble back within.

He scrambled to his sodden knees, flailed while cursing the plump pillows that seemed everywhere, and managed to turn around to scowl at Hannibal.

"If I attempt to crawl back in as you have," Hannibal said, using his grip on the side of the boat to guide himself to the stern. "I will capsize this unfortunately top-heavy creation."

Will fell on his backside and gripped the boat's sides as it began to turn. Cautiously, he made his way back to the stern where Hannibal was pushing, and just watched him as his efforts guided the light craft towards the shore.

"Why did you do that?" he asked.

Despite his panting, Hannibal managed to tell him, "Because it was the fastest way to get you back into the boat?"

"No, I—" Will flushed and broke off, wondering why he was prodding.

"You're my spouse, Will," Hannibal said, realizing what he was getting at. "There will be a bit more than an unfinished kiss between us before it's said and done."

Will's eyes widened but he got that stubborn look on his face Hannibal had so quickly come to relish. Grinning, he added, "I understand it might make you nervous, considering you've never been kissed before."

Will's chin tipped up and he retreated from view. When he heard Hannibal's satisfied, delighted laughter, however, he flung himself back to the stern and leaned over it with a nonchalance he did not quite feel to say, "It so happens, Lord Clarges, that I have no interest in kisses, unfinished or otherwise. I find the whole idea of it terribly dull."

"Terribly dull?" Hannibal echoed, amused.

"Yes," Will said, prim as a schoolmarm despite the telling pink in his cheeks. "I doubt the inconvenience required to create a child could even distract me from my book."

He cracked said book open again, having retrieved it a little worse for wear from its trip but still usable, and felt for a change he had managed to render Hannibal speechless, which left him rather satisfied.

"Is that a challenge?" Hannibal asked, panting hard as he worked to bring the boat to shore. It didn't stop him from grinning, however, well pleased with his little mate. "Or shall we set a bet?"

Wary, Will angled a look down at him and softly asked, "What?"

"A bet," Hannibal said, the soft slurry beneath his feet solidifying to gravel and packed earth as the lake shallowed. "On whether or not I can distract you from your book."

Will slammed the book closed again, heart racing and mouth tingling at even the *suggestion* of such a thing.

But it could work to his advantage, he knew. When he considered the bare facts, there was no danger in such a silly bet. Hannibal would not win.The likelihood of them ever sharing a bed was less than zero, and even should they do so, Hannibal would surely be unable to overcome his revulsion to perform any such act, let alone successfully. On the off chance he *did* manage to somehow win, his own deeply-ingrained distaste would keep Hannibal from anything more than puffing up like a gamecock and crowing of his victory.

"If I win, you will stop pestering me with such tenacious constancy," he stated, deciding it was worth the risk.

Hannibal's brows rose, impressed. "If I win, you have to let me kiss you whenever I like."

"Whenever you like?" Will echoed, thinking that didn't sound like a prize at all. "Are you sure you are not confused? Perhaps, if you win—"

"Whenever I like," Hannibal firmly repeated, getting his feet solidly under him and standing to shove the boat towards the mooring.

"Very well," Will said, holding the book carefully away from him and sliding to the rowing bench as Hannibal brought them to shore. "You have yourself a bet, Lord Clarges."

Hannibal's grin was so triumphant and woke such a clamor in Will's nerves he immediately wished he could take it back.

Little as he liked to admit it, if there was any one person on this earth who could rattle Will Grant, it was certainly his eccentric and overbearing husband.

Chapter 14

Dripping wet and entirely disheveled, Hannibal and Will made their way back up to Fernhill Manor. Luckily for them, the majority of party-goers were still enjoying their games on the lawn, though people were beginning to drift back towards the other, smaller activities so thoughtfully provided by the Diments.

"Well," Hannibal said, seeing Will shiver in his layers of wet clothing, the book held carefully away from him so as not to ruin it. "I don't suppose that did much for your nerves?"

Will laughed softly, flicking a glance up at him, and admitted, "I was too worried we would drown to worry about the crowd, Lord Clarges. It was an unorthodox therapy, but not entirely unsuccessful."

Hannibal smiled and took Will around the side of the manor, managing to catch a passing servant's eye. When they were approached, he said, "Please inform my cousin that my spouse and I are in a predicament and need to speak with her."

The man nodded and made as if to leave, but stopped when Will abruptly thrust the book out and said, "Please return this to the library as well. I will replace it if there has been any damage."

"If that is the title I am thinking of, a fire would not be damage enough," Bedelia said, drawn from the crowd by the oddity of a servant darting out of view. She looked at them both from head to toe, taking in their wet clothing and cautious expressions. "Explanations can wait, I believe."

She took the book and sent the servant on his way, murmuring, "Come with me, please, both of you."

Cheeks rosy with embarrassment, Will quietly followed Bedelia at Hannibal's side, hoping she wouldn't think too badly of him. He hadn't pushed Hannibal with the intention to dunk him, but he was responsible nonetheless for Hannibal's state.

Just as Hannibal was responsible for *his* state with that entirely uncalled-for advance.

"Both of you, please leave your wet things in the washroom," she said, opening a door onto a lovely tiled room well lit by the afternoon sun. "Will, that door leads to the Violet room. Your clothing is in the wardrobe. I'll see if father's valet can assist you."

"My clothing?" Will asked, bewildered as she urged him into the washroom. "Have I missed something?"

"Am I to assume I have clothing here as well? Or will I be wearing your purple silk?" Hannibal asked, cocking an eyebrow at his cousin as she closed Will into the washroom to clean up despite his obvious consternation. "Though I do imagine it will be a bit loose in the shoulders."

Bedelia gave him a repressive look, not amused.

"You are incorrigible," she said, her tone smooth despite her annoyance. "And I have no idea what you were up to with Will Grant—" she held up a staying hand when he looked as if he would like to interrupt her, "—but if you intend to get closer to your spouse, Hannibal, you might wish to start with something less... troublesome."

Hannibal wrinkled his nose at her because he knew she disliked it, and pressed, "Well? Has Grandfather been meddling again?"

"That is something you should discuss with *him*," Bedelia said, a faint, fleeting smile curving her mouth. "But yes, your clothes are in the wardrobe just there. Please give your husband time to tend to himself before you intrude on him, hm?"

She moved back the way they'd come and Hannibal let himself into the suite she'd indicated. Ignoring her warning, he immediately made his way to the washroom door where he knocked once, sharply.

"Yes?" Will called, approaching but making no move to open up.

"It's only me," Hannibal said. "I wanted to warn you I was here. These rooms share the washroom but, alas, no locks yet again."

The door cracked and Will peeked out at him, just the barest glimpse of one large blue eye and arched eyebrow. "Have you any idea what's going on? Why is our clothing here?"

"I have my suspicions," Hannibal said. "Suffice it to say, I am relieved we'll not have to travel home early due to our *incident*."

The door closed in his face without comment from Will, followed by the soft squeak of the taps which brought an unspoken but thorough stop to any mention of what had just happened.

Hannibal grinned, feeling pleased, all things considered, and not entirely annoyed to think his grandfather was playing matchmaker again.

In a short time, Will was done and enclosed in his room to dress, and Hannibal made short work of washing up. Luckily, the lake water was not terribly foul and was easily overpowered by his Aunt's taste for strong lye soap.

He was still dressing when he heard a soft knock at the washroom door and called entry.

Will slipped in, vastly uncomfortable but his chin at its usual stubborn angle. He was fairly well put together and dry, if not presentable.

What was more immediately noticeable, however, was the sweet-hot scent of him, thicker for his plunge into the lake and the strong lye soap. Hannibal ducked his head to mask his notice, but it played immediate havoc with his senses, a scent he could taste on his tongue when he drew in a deep breath, as if he could trap it and hold the memory of it in his lungs.

"I'm afraid I have ruined your hopes for that waistcoat. I doubt it will ever be the same again," Will said, skirting the room to linger near the hallway door. "And my old boots seem rather shabby now, but I will have to do."

"The clothing can easily be replaced and you look perfectly lovely," Hannibal told him, testing the air again. "Have no fear on that count. Your new wardrobe suits you."

Will ducked his head at the offhand compliment, but smoothed his hand down his trim belly, unable to resist touching the fine cloth. "I am glad the second set was delivered so quickly, though I do admit I am still curious how it has ended up here."

"I suggest we ask Grandfather," Hannibal said, tugging on his jacket. He crossed to Will in a few quick, long-legged strides and took up his hand.

"Hannibal, what—"

Hannibal moved to refasten Will's cuffs, telling him, "It is easier when one has help."

Will swallowed hard, but nodded. He waited until Hannibal was finished, then gingerly offered, "May I?"

Hannibal held out his hands, watching Will carefully refasten his cuffs, his movements spare and his touch gentle. His brow furrowed ever-so-slightly with concentration, as if some dire outcome weighed on the perfection of Hannibal's cuffs.

It made Hannibal smile for some reason, seeing Will so deeply intent on something so mundane. He wondered what it would take to distract Will from his book sometime in the hopefully-near future and win that bet. Just imagining what might occur and how Will would react was enough to win a soft chuckle out of him.

Will's blue eyes rose only briefly, long enough for him to notice Hannibal's soft expression and ask, "Am I amusing you, Hannibal?"

"No," he said, turning his wrist just so to allow Will a better angle. "I was merely thinking of our situation."

Will's brows rose in inquiry as he got to work on the other cuff.

"I have been trying for days to think of a way to have time alone with you, Will," Hannibal said. "Had I only realized it required a boat, I would have reassessed my resources."

"Ah, yes, the unfortunate boating option," Will said, chuckling. "Dunking one another in a lake is an unusual way to spend time together, even by my book, but I suppose it's a viable alternative when all else fails."

Hannibal laughed with him, pleased his mate's strange fear of him had subsided as mysteriously as it had risen. It was a pleasure to see Will without his usual guarded tension and heartening to think he could be coaxed out of his serious, somber rigidity.

"There," Will said, finishing his adjustments and dropping his hands to his side, remembering to compose himself. The events on the lake had affected him perhaps more than he realized, and it was all too easy to imagine Hannibal could always be the teasing, charming man he seemed.

The truth, however, would not sustain even so fleeting a fantasy. As his book had warned him, it was folly to believe in promises that had no grounding in truth or reason, no matter how he might wish otherwise.

"Hannibal..." he said, hesitating as he gathered his thoughts. "You really needn't trouble yourself to seek my company. I appreciate the lengths you are willing to go to in order to please your grandfather, but really all we must do is wait."

"Wait?" Hannibal asked, somewhat flattened to recall Will so easily telling him, '*I have no interest in you...*'

"Yes," Will said, clearing his throat. "I realize it is not spoken of in polite company, but the truth of the matter is Miss Blume is advancing in her pregnancy. Should she give you a boy, your grandfather will hardly complain."

Hannibal blinked, watching the way Will held himself with such still, practiced composure. His defense, Hannibal knew. The studied retreat of someone who had learned to expect unpleasantness in response to his very presence.

"You behave as if the outcome doesn't affect you," Hannibal murmured, seeing the minute twitch of Will's eyebrows as he fought a frown. "Is it preferable to you, Will, that Alana gives me an heir rather than provide one yourself?"

Will gazed up at him, his blue eyes hard but thoughtful.

"When you offered to give me a child, I humiliated you, deliberately and cruelly," Hannibal said, and Will almost flinched. "I have no right to ask your forgiveness—"

"You wouldn't get it," Will said, abruptly overriding him, his back stiffening. He looked away, his profile all soft curves but for the stubborn tightness of his mouth. "It's meaningless, Hannibal. We are nothing to one another but an inconvenience. I have done a great deal to keep your grandfather happy these past years, but I will not do that."

He fixed Hannibal with his half-lidded, weighty blue gaze before he added, "I have nothing to offer you, nor you to offer me."

"I disagree," Hannibal, as serious now as Will was.

Will's slight scowl dropped to surprise, taken aback as he always was when Hannibal managed to avoid his expectations.

"I think you have quite a lot to offer me, Will," he said. "And I have far more to offer you than irritation and cruelty. I am determined to know you."

"You're wasting your time."

"Then I will waste it," Hannibal shot back, pleased by the way Will's eyes narrowed with calculation, summing his intent against known variables. "I have never minded spending time or money on something when it is worth it."

Will shifted, brow furrowing, and turned away from him towards the door, troubled and thoughtful.

"I hope Grandfather will not be too annoyed with us," Hannibal said, deliberately changing the subject. He opened the door and waited for Will to pass through before joining him in the hallway. "Though I highly doubt he could be annoyed with *you*, considering you are the grandson of his dear and precious friend."

Will cut a look up at him, still mulling over what Hannibal had said.

"If you are really so determined to find out about them, couldn't you ask while we're here?" He inquired, willing to let the matter drop. "Perhaps Aunt Margaret might be amenable to divulging what she knows. Uncle Robert seemed privy to a great deal."

"I may just yet," Hannibal told him, striding swiftly towards the stairs at Will's side. "If you chance to speak with Uncle Robert—"

They were interrupted by Bedelia, her voice raised to reach them on the landing, "Hannibal, Grandfather wishes to see you."

"Lecture me, more like," Hannibal said, he and Will descending the stairs in tandem. "You always have had a predilection for euphemism, Bedelia."

"And you a predilection for chaos," she said, reaching out to take Will's arm as he reached the foot of the stairs. "Would you walk with me, Will? Please don't keep Grandfather waiting, Hannibal."

Hannibal lingered, hesitating, but then reluctantly left his spouse in the care of his cousin to answer his grandfather's summons.

⌘⌘⌘

Grandfather was still in the thick of things when Hannibal finally located him and promptly wheeled his chair towards Hannibal, frank disapproval on his face.

"Bedelia has informed me the two of you got into a situation," he said without preamble, wheeling past Hannibal so that he was forced to turn and follow his grandfather back inside Fernhill, footmen anxiously jumping to clear a path and open doors for them.

"Still a tale-bearer at her age! Honestly! Will was growing nervous," Hannibal said. "I thought some time on the quiet of the lake would soothe him."

"You just conveniently forgot the boat, did you?" Grandfather asked, one brow arching. "What on earth do you think people would say had they seen the two of you? Hm?"

"I didn't *conveniently forget* anything," Hannibal said, scowling at him. "Nor did you, it would seem! Or was it simply by happenstance our clothing found its way here to Fernhill?"

Roland frowned but owned it all the same, telling him, "If I must take extreme measures to bring the two of you together, I will do so! Leaving you stranded at Fernhill overnight is not precisely dastardly. Half of the party is spending the evening and your Aunt very graciously agreed to extend her hospitality to you. I thought it would be a good opportunity for Will to take time away from Hartford House!"

"Grandfather," Hannibal sighed, rubbing his forehead. "You needn't exert yourself. Will and I are... managing."

"*Managing*," Grandfather echoed, and huffed softly. "I highly doubt that! I have been watching you both very carefully today, not always personally, but by whatever method I could. From what I could tell, the only thing making Will nervous was *you*, Hannibal."

"*Me?*" Hannibal asked, Will's strange fear of him coming to mind.

"Yes, *you!*"

Hannibal was glad they were alone where he wasn't forced to be so terribly formal. He crossed his arms over his chest and braced for a show of his grandfather's rare, true temper.

"You affect him with your moods because you're his Alpha," Roland said, a disapproving frown on his mouth. He turned his chair around to face Hannibal and stopped there, staring up at him with unwavering amber eyes.

Hannibal snorted a bit and said, "Not in the traditional sense, Grandfather."

"So. You will deny it, then," Roland said, his gaze fierce enough to put Hannibal on the defensive. "Hannibal, I am going to warn you only once, that Addendum *will* be filled. I *will* have that child. I will *not*, however, allow you to leave Will in pieces behind you yet again. Do whatever you must in the bounds of his consent to fill your end of our little bargain, but do not charm him into loving you unless you intend to remain at Hartford House with us and be the man I so hoped you would be."

Hannibal stayed silent, two distinctly separate futures before him, all hinging on the hopes of the Omega he had used so badly six years before.

"Will deserves some little happiness," Roland said, his stare stark and grim. "If not with you, then with someone of his choosing. Do not ruin him for someone else, Hannibal. He is so much better than what you would make of him."

"I have no intentions of charming Will into loving me, Grandfather," Hannibal said, the words wooden and uncomfortable, some small window inside of him shuttering itself at the reminder of what he was asking from Will. A child, all for the sake of getting Hartford House back into his control and out of Will's. "It's a sentiment neither one of us is much acquainted with. I will try my hardest to leave Will better off this time than I did before."

"So, you *will* leave then?" Roland asked, a faint tremor moving through him. Pain, perhaps. Disappointment, most definitely. "Your talk of taking him to the Capital during the Season, your sudden fascination with him, all of these plans of yours I've been hearing of?"

Hannibal looked aside, uneasy and caught out. He summoned a smile but it was tight and didn't fit well, tied as it was to the memory of Will's laughter and soft, gentle touch.

"I got carried away," he said, wishing he meant it, thoroughly chastened to be reminded of the Addendum and how easily he'd put it from his mind. "Will would never wish to leave Hartford House in my company. Why should he? What could he possibly expect?"

Another teacup shattered? Another scar on the inside?

One more scar, perhaps, than a soul could reasonably be expected to take.

Grandfather said nothing. He turned his chair slightly and moved around Hannibal, who could do nothing more than watch him go, all the while a deep and searing regret moving through him.

Regret which had a somber frown and sparkling blue eyes that slowly turned away from him.

⌘⌘⌘

Bedelia pulled Will at a sedate pace deeper into Fernhill's sprawling ground floor level.

A servant jumped to open the door for them, admitting them into the rear portion of the conservatory. The lush scent of green growth filled Will's lungs with humid air. The dappled screen of fading sunlight filtered through the verdant growth, teasing along the shimmering water of the ornamental pond within.

After a long, comfortable silence, Bedelia said with weighty consideration, "You confound my cousin, Will."

The soft Alpha scent of her skin teased around him, a soothing balm that put him at ease and numbed some of his concern about her perception of him.

"I do not do so deliberately," Will said, and added with a wry smile, "Though if I knew how, I would."

She chuckled, strolling with him along the path between the carefully-tended plants. She did not press him for conversation, but Will could feel her attention focused on him, reading the subtle cues of his posture and tension in ways only an Alpha could.

"It is so beautiful here," he said, smiling at a pair of swallows that had found their way into the vast paradise of Fernhill's conservatory.

"I thought perhaps you might like it," Bedelia said, her smile slight but genuine. "But I wanted to show you something else you might be interested in."

Will nodded, willing to let her take the lead. They moved through the conservatory and back into the house proper to the opposite wing. He took his opportunity to look around Fernhill as they walked. He found it quite lovely and suitably grand, if not as updated as Hartford House itself.

He was so busy trying to take everything in he almost did not notice when she pulled him into a gallery. It only took him a heartbeat, however, to realize they were strolling among a collection of family portraits.

She did not stop until they reached a tall portrait that seemed strangely large compared the rest. Will searched it, finding a man who looked very much like Hannibal gazing out at the world with amber eyes full of mirth and a slight smirk beneath his heavy mustache.

"This portrait used to hang in Hartford House," Bedelia said, dropping his arm to lay her hand on the frame. "Perhaps you recognize the place it once held?"

"Yes," Will said, a strange, sinking feeling in his stomach as he reckoned the cause. "It sits empty, conspicuously so."

"Hannibal is not the only Ledford to be possessed of a temper, Will," Bedelia said, her even tone softening her words. "I remember the day it was brought here to Fernhill. I could not understand then the explanation given to me, but as I grew up, I began to."

Will searched her face, seeing the slight vagueness in her blue eyes, sensing the melancholy in her voice despite her unwavering cadence.

"Shortly after Hannibal was born, my Aunt passed away. My Uncle Cyrus, Hannibal's father, delivered my cousin into my mother's keeping while he removed to the Continent," she sighed, transferring her gaze to Will's own. He could feel the sorrow pooling there, and reached out without thinking to take her hand in his, relieved when she smiled. "Mother said it was the grief that drove him to do it, but when Grandfather called him home, he did not return alone."

She cut another look up at the portrait, assessing and full of rebuke. "He and Grandfather fought like beasts, year in and year out over the woman he brought home with him. *Unsuitable. Disreputable. Notorious.*" She smiled again, wry and weary, and added, "You see, Uncle Cyrus returned with a famous opera singer, a woman of powerful opinions and vast beauty who was, Grandfather feared, more in love with the Ledford titles and fortune than with his son. He forbid them from marrying, so... they merely lived together to spite him."

Will blanched, the scene playing out in his imagination, a vicious row that must have frightened everyone for miles. It called to mind the argument that had followed his arrival at Hartford House, his only experience to reference remotely like the fight she spoke of.

"The Ledford men are also possessed of a rather grand impression of their own opinions," Bedelia said, chuckling softly, a purring sound filled with bitterness and sorrow. "So when Uncle Cyrus announced his attachment, Grandfather announced *Hannibal* was to be his heir, cutting Cyrus out entirely."

Will pondered it, considering the familiar face in the portrait that seemed to hold such mischievous good humor, yet did not quite cover the turmoil within.

"Rather than discuss it, they clashed like rams, battering their heads against one another in a vain attempt to force sense where passion ruled," he murmured, saddened. "What terrible hurt it must have caused to sway Grandfather to take such actions, sending this portrait here in disgrace."

"It *was* terrible hurt and terrible anger," Bedelia agreed. "It took years to mend the damage, but the breach was never fully filled. Cyrus was never reinstated to be heir, and all our hopes rested on Hannibal, who never spent a moment of his youth without feeling that weight like a stone around his neck."

Will somberly met her gaze and nodded, offering, "I understand he has a heavy burden to bear, Bedelia. I have no desire to add to his troubles."

"It is not the burden you might add that I wish to convey to you, Will, should you even manage to add an ounce," she said, her voice as firm and direct as her gaze.

"Insight," he said. "He is his father's son."

"Yes," she said, satisfied. "I see fire in you, Will."

Heat stained his cheeks but he did not drop his gaze.

"It has been tamped down and smothered in ash, but it is there nonetheless," she said, pleased with him. "He will needle and prod and provoke you to find it, because he knows it is there. These Ledford men," she cast another glance up at Hannibal's father, "they are passionate men, men who are righteous in the stands they take and roused to fury when they are challenged, but one thing they cannot resist, one thing they are weak for above all other things, is something which *does not yield.*"

Will looked away, overly warm of a sudden, understanding her purpose in all this.

"You confound my cousin," she said again, and brushed his curls back behind his ear, giving one a playful, slight tug to get his attention. "I would say, regardless of your intentions, you have managed to secure his interest. Whatever you do with it is entirely up to you."

"And do you think I am up to the task of managing a Ledford Alpha?" Will asked, steadying his voice in a way his nerves refused to concede to.

Bedelia's smile was wide and true when she said, "I have never believed anything more in my life, Will Grant."

Will blushed, flustered but strangely flattered. He did not fool himself into believing he could sway Hannibal one way or another, but perhaps, just perhaps, like Scheherazade he might be able to keep himself alive.

He took another look at Cyrus Ledford, stubborn and proud but somehow still vulnerable, his grief a wound that would not heal and drove him to desperation.

"He lost so much," Will said, feeling a strange kinship with this man who would have been his father through Hannibal. "His wife, his inheritance, his father's good regard. It must have been difficult for him. It must have been difficult for Hannibal to lose him."

"No one has ever told you of that night, have they?" Bedelia asked, her somber thoughtfulness returning. "Grandfather has kept you insulated from what ugliness he could manage, a beautiful bird in the cage he constructed of Hartford House."

Will was startled into looking at her again, questions in his eyes.

"There was a terrible accident," Bedelia murmured, clasping Will's hand in both of hers, her fingers strong but chilled. "Grandfather and Uncle argued. It was spring, and the storms were unrelenting. The river had risen even to the bridge, but for reasons I to this day do not know, Cyrus attempted to leave. Their carriage overturned into the river in the darkness. Cyrus, his concubine, and their daughter, Miska, all died. Hannibal was the only one to survive."

Will winced, trembling, his vivid imagination painting a terrifying portrait of what had happened to them. The roar of water was loud in his ears, so real he could feel it eddying around him, trapping him in suffocating darkness while the horses screamed in terror.

"He walked for miles through the woods in a raging storm to reach Fernhill," Bedelia said, so soft and faint Will could barely hear her over his Gift. "I will never forget that night as long as I live. Hannibal was never the same after losing them... after losing little Miska."

Will blinked hard, fending off the pain that reached him when his imagination showed him Hannibal as a child, fighting his way the through storm-ravaged forest for help that would always be too late.

"He was never the same," she breathed again, turning her glittering eyes to Will. "To this day, my father will not speak of what he saw when they pulled them from the river. I was not entirely sure Grandfather would survive it."

Will shuddered, grimacing against the onslaught of so much pain and terror for one family to deal with all at once. For *one child* to deal with all at once.

"There is a certain kind of fortitude that comes from enduring terrible trauma. It leaves the survivor... unpredictable," Bedelia whispered, and Will flinched, turning away, too vulnerable in that moment with his empathy unbound, unable to defend against her.

"*You* are unpredictable, Will Grant," she said, and lay her hand against his cheek to calm him. "You have that in common with Hannibal."

"Bedelia," Will said, taking a breath that ached in his lungs, as if water poured out with every pulse of his words. "Hannibal's stepmother, was she—"

"*Here* you both are! Come along, come along, darlings!" Aunt Margaret called down the gallery at them, tapping her cane with imperious impatience.

Will started, the remnants of his perception shredded by the interruption. He closed his eyes, grateful for Bedelia's cool hand against his flushed cheek.

"Both of you, now!" Aunt Margaret urged. "Cousin Atticus has arrived and wishes to meet Will! It won't do to keep him waiting, you know. He's traveled all the way from the Continent!"

"Yes, Aunt Margaret," Bedelia said, looping her arm through Will's again with a small, conspiratorial smile. "We wouldn't dream of inconveniencing Cousin Atticus, would we, Will?"

Will swallowed his question down, but it lingered in the back of his mind, gone yet certainly not forgotten.

⌘⌘⌘

Hannibal watched from the garden proper as the sun began to set and Fernhill servants moved about lighting paper lanterns all throughout the pathways and lake shore. He was reluctant to rejoin the party with so many heavy thoughts weighing on him and used the growing darkness to his advantage on that count. His grandfather's pointed questions regarding his intentions towards Will still occupied his thoughts and left him reflective.

He'd lost sight of his goal. Rather, he'd lost sight of the ugly method he'd agreed to in order to get Hartford House back. The plans Grandfather had spoken of had been made with no thought to that Addendum and had been, he knew, entirely selfish on his part.

But he'd signed his name. He'd agreed, and that said more about his character than he honestly wanted to face.

It was easy for him to imagine a life at Hartford House, settling into domesticity with Will, fathering his children and keeping him company until time stole everything from both of them. He could ask Grandfather to destroy the Addendum, pretend it had never existed, and have that life yet.

But he had no right no ask that of Will, not now. He'd forfeited his right when he'd walked away six years ago and left his husband behind him without a backwards glance. There was no future to be had, only filling the Addendum and finding some way to give back to Will what he'd unknowingly taken from him.

"It's rather unusual to find you alone at a party, Hannibal," Bedelia said, the gentle waft of her feminine scent reaching his nose before the soft purr of her voice disturbed his unhappy thoughts. She came to settle against the balustrade next to him, her blue eyes taking in the beauty of Fernhill's gardens by gentle lamplight. "Did grandfather scold you?"

"No, he settled for being disappointed," Hannibal said, smiling when she smirked. "Which we both know is so much worse."

"Indeed," she said, taking a dainty sip of her drink. "Will Grant is an interesting Omega, Hannibal."

Hannibal looked over at her, searching her profile for some clue to her thoughts.

"I had not expected to find a bond," she said, tipping her head to look back at him. "I suspected... something when I first met him, but not that."

"Bonding? Nonsense," Hannibal said, knowing there was nothing like. "Grandfather mentioned such a thing and I have no idea why. *Entirely* nonsense. Bedelia, you know how degrading I find the subject of *bonding*."

"If you are so dismissive of it then why did you form one with Will in the first place?" she asked, genuinely curious.

Hannibal glared at her, certain he'd misheard.

"You *did* bond with Will," she pressed, surprise erasing her unearthly calm for only a moment. When she spoke again, her voice was measured and cautious but full of deadly curiosity. "Hannibal, Will Grant is a bonded Omega. If it isn't with you, then with *whom*?"

Hannibal felt a flush of terrible anger and jealousy bubble up through him with such force that Bedelia tensed in response. He looked back to where Grandfather was situated and saw Will at his side once more.

Bonded.

It didn't make any bit of sense, not after Will's flustered response to him on the lake. He'd been flushed and alarmed, as open and innocent as any virginal maiden Hannibal had ever met in his day.

Or perhaps it had simply been the embarrassed denials of an Omega already spoken for. An Omega whose relationship was forced into secrecy for the sake of appearances. Perhaps Will's assurance he found the idea of sharing a bed with him *boring* was simply the only way he could think of to put off an Alpha who would know in a heartbeat he was already bonded and taken.

"Hannibal?"

He strained to recall the sight of Will's throat when he'd burst in on him in the bath, but he'd been too entranced by the overall picture to notice such details and felt foolish for having been taken in so easily.

Ashamed and feeling strangely hurt, he said, "You can't possibly know that—"

"I *can*, actually," Bedelia murmured, calming and taking another slow, calculated sip of her drink. "There are certain... *instincts* triggered in unbonded Alphas by an unbonded Omega his age, Hannibal. You can't have gone so long in the world without realizing."

"I feel no such things towards any Omegas," Hannibal said, turning his nose up at even the idea of it. "*Instincts* are merely convenient excuses to indulge one's carnality."

Bedelia's pale brows rose over her blue eyes. "I see."

"Do you?" Hannibal demanded. "Because here you stand, trying to tell me Will has gone and bound himself to some unknown Alpha on the basis of a tingle in your pinky finger!"

"It's rather more complicated than all that," she said, amused by his bluster. "I do find it interesting, however, that you have not noticed or responded to the unbonded Omegas you have met since you've been married to Will Grant."

"That is not interesting in the least," Hannibal said, glaring Will's direction.

There was a tentative smile on his full mouth, shy and diffident as Grandfather introduced him to more party guests eager to meet him. Will tipped his head up and his smile widened to a grin, slightly crooked and endearing. The thought that some unknown Alpha had seen this same smile, had succeeded where Hannibal had failed, was almost too much for him. He wanted nothing more than to walk over to Will, to demand a confession out of him and find out who had *dared* to—

"Hannibal, *stop*," Bedelia said, almost a sigh but with such pressure on her syllables he turned his attention back to her. She blinked once, languidly, and said, "If you continue to scowl at him, everything Grandfather has worked for today will be lost."

He chafed to do just what he imagined but his better sense won out, though he subsided with prickling irritation.

"Honestly," Bedelia said, the word weary with resignation. "You are no better than a child at times."

She put her cup down, daintily brushing her fingers down her dress to make it fall just *so*. Without giving him the benefit of eye contact, she said, "When you are sensible and reasonable enough to realize you need help, Hannibal, please come and see me."

"That will be a long wait, Bedelia," he said, catching sight of Grandfather's slight gesture he was to join them.

"Actually, I don't think it will," she said, offering him a smile that held a world's worth of secretive satisfaction.

Once Bedelia swept off from his sight, Hannibal managed to calm significantly. He wondered if Will, hearing of his exploits in the Capital, hearing news of his daughter's birth, had felt even a fraction of the dismayed disappointment Hannibal felt in this moment. He honestly hoped not, because he didn't like this feeling one little bit and wished to be free of it immediately.

He had no high ground—moral or otherwise—from which to judge Will. As Will had pointed out, six years ago he had been willing to try to make their marriage work, despite how hateful Hannibal had been to him. Like a sacrificial lamb, he'd offered himself on the altar of Hannibal's understanding and been soundly rejected, brutally so. Having abandoned him to silence and isolation in the country for six years, Hannibal could understand what would have driven Will to seek the comfort of a bond, but that didn't make him any happier about it. A short time ago it had seemed a viable option to be rid of him, but now it left Hannibal with a belly full of burning anger and the irony of it stung.

He could not, however, put it entirely past his cousin to be having him on just to rile him and see what he would do. Hannibal refused to give her the satisfaction, were that the case, and knew Will deserved an opportunity to speak of it in private.

Determined to handle things gracefully, Hannibal returned to Will's side. He was relieved to see his spouse was much more at ease now, though deep in thought.

"Did you enjoy your tour of Fernhill?" he asked in the brief lull they had before everyone realized he had returned.

"I did, thank you," Will said, Hannibal's unusual calm soothing him. He was still somewhat adrift after the story Bedelia had told him, aching for the child Hannibal had once been. Hoping to make conversation that would ground him somewhat, he said, "It's very beautiful here, though I admit I find Hartford House more comfortable and lovely."

"You have worked extremely hard to make Hartford House what it is," Hannibal said, trying to find a gentle way to broach the subject without stepping wrong again. "Your years of diligent service show."

Will frowned and angled a glance his way in the relative darkness.

"The lights are beautiful, aren't they?" Hannibal asked. "Would you care to walk around the lake again? Things seen by the light of day change in darkness, revealing themselves for what they truly are."

"Why are you suddenly so agreeable?"

"I am always agreeable," Hannibal countered, fairly caught out.

"Liar."

Hannibal's rebuke died on his lips when he faced his spouse and found him smiling slightly, a genuine smile half unseen in the deepening dusk. Before he could recover sufficiently to continue their conversation, Uncle Robert included Will in a booming recitation of his favorite poetry by taking his hand up to deliver some of the more florid lines in Will's honor. Hannibal wasn't entirely certain Uncle Robert hadn't been at the port unnoticed.

Luckily for them all, the dinner gong rang out. Organized chaos ensued as people found their dinner dates and made their way to the huge spread laid out for them.

"I am sorry to interrupt you, Uncle Robert, but we're being herded to dinner," Hannibal said by way of excuse, smiling to see him take a bewildered glance at his surroundings.

"Ah! I must nab your Aunt Grace before she takes some young man in my place!" Uncle Robert said, and reclaimed the hand Hannibal had just freed to grace it with a quick kiss. "*You* are a delight! Just a sheer delight! Remind me after dinner to show you my collection of *maps*, Will!"

"Yes, yes, Uncle Robert, he is all atwitter at the idea," Hannibal said, shaking his head as his uncle barreled off in search of his aunt. "Goodness, he's exhausting."

"He is clever and well spoken," Will said, smiling after him. "And quite passionate in his speaking."

"Ah, I believe the word you are talking around is *loud*," Hannibal told him. "He is rather hard of hearing."

He fully intended to escort Will to an empty corner and speak privately with him about his bonded status which, as Will's mate, was his gods-given and lawful right. He could not ignore it; neither one of them could. If Will was bonded, then that Alpha had a claim on him which superseded their mutual grandfathers' contract and *that* was a family issue.

"Will," he said, steering him away towards a likely-looking space as everyone sorted themselves to go in. "There is something I wish to speak to you of—"

"*Hannibal! There* you are! I've been looking all over for you!"

Hannibal felt Will freeze next to him just as he did, both of them bracing for an oncoming storm.

"Thomas," Hannibal said, flummoxed to find his mistress's closest friend and supporter bearing down on him with a flushed grin and a glass of watered wine in one hand. "When did you arrive?"

"*Hours* ago! Bedelia just informed me you were here! I can't believe you actually came!" he said, not even glancing at Will. "Alana said you were back. She's *very* excited to finally see the old homestead, simply wouldn't stop talking about the move! How soon will you be fetching them to Hartford House, eh?"

"That was a private discussion," Hannibal said, hoping to hush him, and looked anxiously at Will.

He had hoped and prayed to escape the Garden Party unscathed, but Hannibal Ledford, war veteran, doctor, and future Duke, was nearly laid waste by one look from his composed, newly-reclaimed spouse.

Will's blue eyes had darkened to near brown beneath his shuttered lashes, his face expressionless, retreating into reserved stillness at Hannibal's side as if he imagined himself invisible. It was profoundly disturbing to see him so... *absent*.

"Oh, no, old boy, don't try fooling me," Thomas said, laughing loudly enough to make Hannibal wince. "She's told me all about it! She can't wait for you to send for her and little Marissa! Galley Field is so far away from everything, isn't it? She's bereft of good company! Why, I just saw her last week and she was telling me about your *situation*."

"That was not very well done of her," Hannibal said, searching for a way to disengage from Will and drag Thomas off someplace to set him straight. "As I have said, no plans have been *settled*."

"What's left to settle? Once that *awful* person is out of Hartford House, you're free to bring your family home where they belong, isn't that right?" he gave

Hannibal an expectant look and, when Hannibal merely stared at him in awe of his idiocy, he dared to turn that look on Will and ask, "That *does* sound fairly settled, does it not?"

Hannibal wanted desperately to pick Will up as he had before, just snatch him up and walk away no matter what anyone said about it. Anything, *anything*, really, to make up for this awful, unexpected shock.

"Yes, it does," Will said, his slight smile resigned but still a million miles away, seeking safety in a place far from such unhappy and upsetting circumstances. "Allow me to assure you, sir, that I have no intentions of sharing Hartford House with Miss Blume or any one of Hannibal's mistresses."

Those blue eyes lifted to Hannibal's, hard and bright and deadly.

"And considering the unique circumstances regarding Hartford House, I suppose the outcome is not quite as settled as my husband would hope," he purred. "If you will excuse me, gentlemen."

"Will—" Hannibal attempted to catch hold of him but Will deftly eluded him, cutting through the loose crowd with grim determination. "Damn you, sir, are you completely out of your mind?"

Thomas looked as if he'd swallowed a lemon, peel and all.

"Oh, my! I am so sorry," he managed, reaching out to lay his hand on Hannibal's arm as he strained to see over the hats, hairstyles, and heads of other guests to find which way Will had gone. "I had no idea he was here! You should have warned me!"

"My expression alone should have warned you!" Hannibal scolded, shooing his hand off of him. "Honestly, Thomas, prattling on about private matters!"

"Hannibal, you have never made a secret of your affection for Alana," Thomas protested, an irritated wrinkle appearing between his eyes. "Nor have you made any secret of your contempt for your spouse, though now that I've seen him I can't imagine why you'd complain."

"Oh, *shut up*, will you?" Hannibal asked, completely out of patience. "And stop going on about my affairs, thank you very much! If Alana has spoken of moving to Hartford House, then I know damned good and well she *also* spoke of it not having been settled yet! Now excuse me while I attempt to put a tourniquet to the hemorrhage you've caused!"

Flummoxed, Thomas said nothing and became quite speechless with embarrassment, which gave Hannibal the time he needed to brush past him with an annoyed huff and go in search of his little spouse.

He spied Bedelia and crossed the darkening lawn to reach her, asking, "Has Will passed this way?"

"I believe he is attempting to catch Grandfather's coach," Bedelia told him, concern pinching her fine features. "Honestly, what have you managed to do now? He was extremely disturbed."

"It was merely a misunderstanding," Hannibal said, casting around. He wrinkled his nose at her and added, "A misunderstanding that would not have occurred had you not invited a ridiculous person like Thomas Marlo to your gathering!"

"Thomas Marlo is Anthony's friend as well as yours," Bedelia said, unruffled by his turning on her. "He has come every year since he was a child, Hannibal. You cannot possibly have forgotten that."

"And what of Will's sister, Lady Rathmore?" Hannibal asked, wondering where *she* had gone off to. "Hm? Did you think it might be uncomfortable for him to see her? She upset him, you know, filling his head with ugly gossip, no doubt."

Bedelia made no move to contain her amusement at how flustered and unhappy he was. She took a languid sip of her drink and murmured, "I have never invited Lady Rathmore anyplace, Hannibal. Now, if you'll excuse me."

"Oh, no you don't!" Hannibal warned. "You said Grandfather is leaving?"

"Grandfather has *left*," she corrected, smirking when he cursed. "He had hoped the two of you would pass the night here, but I believe your spouse is, as we speak, attempting to catch up to him. You should have more care, Hannibal, for those with whom you play. Not every doll is as bereft of a heart as it pretends to be."

He glowered after her but she ignored him, making a big show of casting her attention onto her current paramour.

Hannibal turned onto the path that led back towards the drive, threading his way through the party-goers heading in to dinner. He reached the front of Fernhill and asked the nearest servant, "Have you seen a rather slender young man with curly brown hair?"

"He went after His Grace's coach, m'Lord."

"Have one of the Diment coaches readied," Hannibal ordered. "No, wait, bother that. Saddle a horse for me."

"M'Lord, I—"

"Just do it, for the gods' sake!" Hannibal snapped. "Or do you not recognize the family resemblance?"

The man rushed off to carry out his orders and in a short time a rather sleepy-looking horse was brought around, clearly not one of the Diment prizes, by any means. Hannibal mounted and waited impatiently for his stirrups to be adjusted, nudging the horse into a canter and hoping to overtake Will on the way.

⌘⌘⌘

"You are very quiet," Roland said, a faceless and formless voice in the darkness of the coach, but his concern was touching. He had not remarked on how Will had chased the coach down, nor asked him to explain his insistence to return home while the party was still in full swing, and for that Will was profoundly grateful.

"I am tired," Will softly said, glad the darkness could hide so much. He knew Grandfather could sense his distress but he was thoughtful enough not to call attention to it. He looked out at the shadowy treeline passing beyond the windows, his thoughts tangled and taut. Pride urged him to go back with his chin up but he was unable to do so. How could he go back there, where Hannibal's close acquaintances were in attendance, waiting to unwittingly insult him? He could hardly blame them; they knew only what Hannibal had mentioned to them.

'Once that awful person is out of Hartford House, you're free to bring them home where they belong, isn't that right?'

Will shuddered, almost as angry as he was hurt, but he wasn't surprised. It was not a shock to him that Hannibal had spoken badly of him when he'd had the occasion to speak of him at all. Rather, it was mortifying to imagine he'd been the subject of ugly conversation, not only between Hannibal and his mistress but with his friends as well.

It wasn't fair, but—as he firmly reminded himself—*fair* was a child's word and he was no child.

"Will," Roland said, somber and thoughtful. "I have watched you grow increasingly more unsettled here at Hartford House. If you truly wish to do so, then you have my permission to go to Marsham Heath *after* the small gathering I've arranged, but only for a fortnight."

"A fortnight will hardly be long enough to suit Hannibal or me," Will said, sinking back into his seat to hide the sheen of angry tears in his eyes, Hannibal's teasing grin flashing in his mind's eye with the whispered promise of that *ridiculous* bet. "A permanent move—"

"You are as much my grandchild as he is and I want you near me, especially now," Grandfather said, his tone firming. "A fortnight and no more. Jimmy must be at your side at all times, I insist on it for safety. Perhaps after such a time there will be peace enough between you to manage an heir."

"Then it is settled," Will said, closing his eyes and leaning his head back, unutterably weary and strangely hurt to think Mina had been right after all.

If Hannibal was trying to get close to him it was only to do him harm, and Will's only sure defense was to give Hannibal what he most wanted—his absence.

He would leave Hartford House the moment Grandfather's party was over and that was that.

Chapter 15

Hannibal wound up riding the reluctant Diment nag all the way back to Hartford House, having long ago left behind the possibility Will had missed catching the ducal coach and been left stranded. Indeed, upon his arrival, Mr. Hawkes informed him Will had already gone upstairs to bed.

Hannibal grimly strode up the stairs and down the hallway to Will's suite, rapping sharply on the door only once before twisting the knob and letting himself in.

Will's blue eyes flashed with annoyance as he slid from his bed and turned his back, still attempting to pull on a robe to cover his nightclothes, his book tumbling from his lap to the floor.

"Is there some emergency, Lord Clarges?" he asked, head dipping as he belted his robe, giving Hannibal a decidedly pleasant view of his narrow waist and straight shoulders. "Or are you mistaking rooms once more?"

"You worried me, taking off in such a manner," Hannibal told him, standing in the doorway, momentarily forgetting why he was here and wondering if he was, in fact, getting soft in the head. The memory of Will's slender body pressed to his returned with frightening clarity, enough so to temporarily distract him from his purpose.

"It was not my intention to worry you," Will said, turning to face him with his arms crossed over his chest and his chin tipped up in defiance.

"Merely to escape me?" Hannibal queried, his eyes falling to Will's slender throat, searching for signs of a mark.

Will nervously reached up and pinched the top of his robe closed in his fist, hoping to cover himself enough to lose Hannibal's sudden and unwelcome interest.

"Merely to relieve you," Will corrected. "And while we are on the subject, my plans are settled to leave Hartford House after your grandfather's party."

"You will do nothing of the sort!" Hannibal announced, shocked into blurting out the first thing he could think of to put a stop to it. "I forbid it!"

"You forbid it?" Will echoed, and laughed. "And how do you propose to stop me, Lord Clarges?"

"It would be entirely foolish to tell you," Hannibal hedged, having no idea. Usually, the threat of his authority was enough to force obedience but he wasn't surprised his authority carried no weight with his increasingly angry little spouse. Will had no use for, or patience with, such nonsense and Hannibal well knew it.

Will smiled at his attempt to cow him, cocking his head slightly to one side, knowing he hadn't the faintest clue.

"Stop being so smug, damn you!" Hannibal said, annoyed. "You are my spouse, Will, and Hartford House is your home! You will remain here where you belong!"

"No," Will said, the single word heavy with anger despite how softly he spoke it. "*I will not.* I do not require your permission for anything, if you will recall."

Hannibal stared at him in consternation, rankled that Will could so easily dismiss him. After a long, silent moment, he managed to ask, "And where will you go? To Marsham Heath, is it?"

"That is none of your business," Will said, glowering at him.

"To the contrary, it is *entirely my business,*" Hannibal said, wondering with suspicion if he had plans instead to flee to the Alpha he was bound to. Surely, *surely* they were furious, whoever they were, to have their Omega sharing space with another Alpha. Hannibal would certainly never stand for it. "Or is there something you have neglected to tell me about, hm?"

Surprised, Will asked, "What on earth are you talking about, Hannibal?"

"I'm talking about the fact that I know you are bonded," Hannibal said, deciding to play Bedelia's card.

Will drew in a shocked breath, blanking at his announcement. Pure, unadulterated fear gripped him then, because if Hannibal knew, if he even *suspected* Will had formed a bond to him, then he would have absolute control and Will was far too smart to dream he would be careful with him when there was every possibility Hannibal wanted him dead.

Hannibal felt his anxiety like a throbbing punch in his gut and he snarled softly, demanding, "*Who is it?*"

Will's relief was so keen he almost laughed, but Hannibal's anger was palpable, frightening in its intensity, and it quickly chased away everything but dread that rapidly escalated to pure fury when Hannibal asked, "*Anthony,* perhaps?"

"How *dare* you!" Will snarled, forgetting to hold tight to his robe, forgetting he had a secret to protect, forgetting this man had in all likelihood attempted to kill him once already. All of it was flung onto the fire of his anger with the Alpha before him. "Casting aspersions on others and keeping none for yourself! How *dare you say that to me!*"

Hannibal pushed away from the door and took a step towards him only to immediately chastise himself for forgetting Will's penchant for violence. He was prevented from taking another step by his furious little mate proving he was, in fact, quite capable of brandishing a rather heavy marquetry table before him in dire warning for Hannibal to keep his distance.

"*There is no one bound to me,*" Will hissed, and quite honestly so, because his bond only went one way, chaining him to the man before him while leaving Hannibal quite free.

"Why should I believe you?" Hannibal asked, his tone nasty, all of his ugly beliefs about Omegas rising up against his reason, ready and eager to believe the worst of his mate.

But by all the gods he was lovely when he was riled, Hannibal had to admit that. He looked half wild and ready to do battle, heedless of his robe gaping open over his pale skin, unknowing of the picture he made with his blue eyes shooting sparks and his red mouth parted in a snarl, a vengeful god roused to righteous retribution.

Hannibal was so distracted he almost didn't react in time to bat the table away when Will flung it at him.

His anger died abruptly when Will sharply said to him, "You have been unfaithful to me in every *imaginable* capacity, Lord Clarges, but I have *never once* been unfaithful to *you.*"

Hannibal subsided, grimacing at how deep that barb went, chastened by the sight of Will standing before him in the tatters of his pride, panting with the force of his rightful fury.

"And should you ever imagine accusing me of such vile and shameful behavior," Will said, his volume softening but not his anger, "then I *assure* you, Lord Clarges, I will cosh you with the heaviest piece of furniture I can lift and step over you on my way to find a lover, for I will not be charged guilty of a crime without committing it."

It took Hannibal a long, reflective moment to finally manage, "You are profoundly unsettling, William Grant."

"And you are remarkably self-righteous for a man with the morals and deportment of an alley cat," Will said, trying to regain control of himself now that Hannibal's anger had died such a quick and surprising death. "One must be careful casting stones, Hannibal, when one is king of a glass castle."

Hannibal frowned, disliking the chastisement but accepting it. There was every chance Bedelia was wrong, or baiting him somehow, and Hannibal had no way of knowing. All he knew for certain was that Will had been honest in every exchange they'd had since the moment they met, no matter if his opinions irritated Hannibal or exposed a flaw he was ashamed to have bared.

"If you say there has been no one, then I believe you," he said, surprising himself as much as Will with his honesty.

Will was startled into looking over at him, his blue eyes widening with shock, knowing it must have peeled an entire layer off of Hannibal's pride to say such a thing. He felt the tug of his bond to Hannibal luring him closer, enticing him to soothe away the flustered, irritated, and vulnerable look on his husband's handsome face.

And beneath that face lay the echo of a child fleeing the violent deaths of his family through rain-soaked, blackened woods, orphaned and bereft.

It softened Will without his intending it to, that image. That child would always be there trapped in memories of brutal horror, rushing water and loss and guilt for surviving when those he loved had not. That they had loved him in return only made it all the harder for Will to ignore it. He knew how dearly he would have suffered in Hannibal's place, losing a family who cared about him.

Will couldn't tell what provoked him to act. He didn't dare try to analyze his own motives. Was it the child he hoped to soothe, or the man? Was it his Gift or Omegan weakness? It didn't seem to matter, all that mattered was the outcome.

Will moved closer to him and reached out to take his hand.

Hannibal snatched Will's slender fingers in his on impulse and asked, "What are you doing?"

It came out sharper than he intended with his surprise and Will retreated, attempting to free his hand from Hannibal's fingers. He tightened his grip and tugged, asking with less force, "Is something wrong?"

"No, I just—I'm sorry, I shouldn't have touched you like that," Will said, flushed with growing mortification. No doubt the last thing in the world Hannibal wanted touching him was the repellent and ugly Omega he'd been forced into marriage with. "That was thoughtless of me, not to mention incredibly rude."

"Will," Hannibal said, somewhat exasperated that they were essentially in a tug of war over Will's hand. He gave him another tug that half dragged Will against him and said, "Just tell me what you're about."

At a loss, Will lifted his trapped hand and pressed the back of Hannibal's fingers beneath his jaw. His voice quavered with nerves when he told him, "See for yourself."

"See what?" Hannibal asked, releasing Will's hand to turn his fingertips to his throat. It was the first time in six years he had seen it completely bare and he lost track of his thoughts again while searching the soft, smooth skin of Will's neck. It was more slender than he'd expected, almost delicate, and clearly unmarked, much to his relief.

Clearing his throat to chase down the tightness that threatened, he spread his hand along the side of Will's neck and paused, forced into stillness by the thrumming beat of Will's pulse beneath his palm. He tested his scent, the lush fragrance of fertile youth even stronger than it had been at Fernhill, but he could taste no fear, just something fragile and delicate as spun glass even the softest of touches could destroy.

"See?" Will said, forcing a lightness into his voice that sounded strained and anxious even to his own ears. "No bite marks."

Reluctant to give up the warm contentment he felt touching Will even so little, Hannibal brought his other hand up to cup Will's neck and keep him from retreating, saying, "I told you I believe you."

Will flushed, feeling awkward standing as he was in his robe and nightclothes with his throat trapped in Hannibal's large, warm hands while those sensitive fingers spread over his skin.

"Sometimes seeing is believing," Will murmured, the pressure of Hannibal's fingers changing softly as he spoke. The warm, earthy scent of his skin filled Will's lungs with every breath, prickling his senses as surely as the callused fingertips trailing over his throat. The touch brought goosebumps rippling over him, and the mocking echo of his father's voice whispered this touch was what he'd been after in the first place—a deeply desperate bid for attention after the revelations of the evening. It scalded him to think he was so weak after all, just another Omega driven by heats and instinct, pathetic in Hannibal's eyes.

The sour despondence of his thoughts should have ruined it for him. The fact that Hannibal's touch only comforted him made it all the worse. He nearly shuddered to feel the sure quest of fingers down the length of his throat, testing every inch of his supple skin even into the loose collar of his robe, impulse urging him to allow Hannibal to do more, to do anything he desired.

It was terribly dangerous, this closeness. He could feel his bond to Hannibal strengthening, more threads weaving into the fabric which anchored him to his Alpha, a relentless pull dragging him closer and closer to inevitable destruction, broken on sharp stones and scattered to rough seas.

When Hannibal slid his hand beneath the fabric of his nightclothes to seek the soft skin of his shoulder, his amber eyes hazy as if caught in a dream, sudden panic drowned out everything else. The cliff of his nightmares loomed up in Will's imagination, the promise of what awaited him should he freely indulge his impulses or should Hannibal ever discover the twisted nature of Will's bond to him. It shocked Will enough that he pulled back sharply, gasping, "What are you doing?"

"Seeing if you were bitten on your shoulder," Hannibal said, clenching his empty hands into fists to trap the warmth and scent of Will's flesh on his fingers, sweet and compelling.

"I was doing you a courtesy, Lord Clarges," Will said, righting his clothing with sharp tugs, surprised Hannibal had dared to do such a thing. Then again, considering his opinions on Will's capacity to seduce, it was likely Will could strip naked in front of him and garner no more than a raised eyebrow at his gall. "No one has bitten me anywhere, for gods' sake! That was the point!"

"You didn't have to go to such extremes, Will," Hannibal said, dropping his hands to his sides, head tipping to chase the sweet elusive scent that eddied about him. "I have no cause or right to criticize you, considering my past behavior... though I am not complaining of your insistence."

Will managed a scandalized and dangerous little growl that almost made him smile.

"Have I agitated you?" he asked. "Thank goodness there is nothing too deadly at hand with that table out of reach."

"Would it content you to know that I am, in fact, beating you quite soundly with a trout in my imagination?" Will asked, doing a poor job of covering his throat with the lapels of his robe, his hands trembling. He retreated, an impulsive bid for safety which Hannibal, thankfully, did not deny him.

"What would content me, Will, is knowing you will not beat a hasty retreat from Hartford House without provocation," Hannibal said, circling back around to distract himself from thinking of Will's fragile throat.

"You feel I haven't been provoked?" Will questioned.

"Will," Hannibal said, uncomfortable and feeling in the wrong. "What was said tonight—"

"You owe me nothing, Lord Clarges," Will said, mortified all over again by the memory of what had been said, of the events that had taken place at the tailor's shop, of *everything* that had occurred since Hannibal's return home. He took a deep breath and forced it all down as best he could. "Least of all an explanation. However you choose to speak of me to those who know you best is your own affair, though I expected better from you as a gentleman than to gossip openly of our marriage."

A spasm of regret passed through Hannibal. Softly, he said, "It was wrong of me to speak of you to anyone in such a way, Will. You have done nothing to earn my disparaging words."

"Nonsense," Will told him, hugging himself for comfort as he said the words he knew were expected, hammered into him from his earliest awareness. "I *exist*, Lord Clarges. That is offensive enough on its own. I tricked your family into a marriage under false pretenses, forced you from your home and then stole it from you. But allow me to make one thing clear, Hannibal—were it not for His Grace forbidding it, I would have gone from Hartford House six years ago."

Hannibal flinched, his amber eyes flicking over Will's slender body, noting the way he held himself, a pitiful comfort from painful truths. Distress etched every line of his face, bowing his full mouth down into a frown. Frustration and anger were there, too, simmering beneath the surface, a justified, unacknowledged response to what life had heaped on his head.

"Please don't look so surprised," Will said, his voice strained, his eyes deliberately fixed to one side, his face averted. "Did you honestly believe I wished to stay here when they told me you had gone? I was mortified by what had happened, Hannibal, and tried everything in my power to change it. You aren't the only one who begged Grandfather for an annulment. Since the day I met you —" The hitch in his voice thinned Hannibal's mouth and his fingers clenched without realizing it, a twitch of response to somehow negate the still-raw pain in his mate's soft voice. "*Since the day I met you,* all I've wanted is to go away."

Will's large, glittering blue eyes lifted to his, his usual reserve abandoned to show the true pain within. His voice was a silky-soft whisper of regret when he said, "I'm as trapped in this debacle as you are."

Hannibal swallowed hard, fighting the urge to haul Will up into his arms and soothe such ugliness from him. The thought of Hartford House and an heir were far from his mind, rendered down to petty trivialities in the face of what he had cost Will these six long years.

"Please... do not leave Hartford House," he said, the idea of Will's absence just wrong somehow, a shadow that would remain to haunt the halls with his presence.

"I can only say, Lord Clarges," Will said, desperate for him to go away, "that I will at least inform you before I go, but I *will* be leaving."

Hannibal sighed, rubbing his forehead with resignation, and nodded slightly at him.

"That is more courtesy than I have ever shown you," he admitted, and showed himself out, leaving Will flushed and disturbed and quietly trembling behind him.

⌘⌘⌘

Hannibal returned to his own suite, somber and thoughtful in the wake of his clash with Will.

Berger bustled about the room, busy turning down the covers and lowering the lamps. He did a double take when Hannibal walked in, and said with a soft chuckle, "You look like you been put through the ringer, m'Lord."

"I certainly feel as though I have," Hannibal sighed, flopping down into the nearest chair with a heavy sigh. "My spouse would have made a formidable General."

"That so, m'Lord?" Berger inquired, politely interested. "He seems a pleasant and quiet little fellow to me."

276

"It's the quiet ones you must be wary of, Berger," Hannibal warned him. "They are far too intelligent to give themselves away with words."

He frowned slightly, absently tapping his fingers on the chair's arm, trying to order his thoughts. His own exasperated, proud observation of Will brought back his grandfather's words on Omegas. It seemed weeks since their conversation in the library when Grandfather had so casually surmised there were Omegas in the military. Seeing Will in a high and righteous fury, knowing what he now knew, it did not seem so unbelievable a thought and he asked, "Did you know of any Omegas in the military, Berger?"

His valet's hands stuttered and he flinched, answer enough in Hannibal's book.

"Er... yes, m'Lord," Berger admitted, coming to him when Hannibal got up and began to undress. "Quite a few as a matter of fact. Took all manner of meds to keep from being outed, they did. Some even cut their scent glands out. Blessed risky, in my opinion."

"And how, pray tell, did you find out they were Omegas if they were so cleverly hidden?" Hannibal asked, both irritated his grandfather might have been right and annoyed he had somehow not realized.

"When they needed treatment they came to me first," Berger said, cringing through the words as he helped Hannibal undress. "They was scared of you, m'Lord."

"*Scared* of me?" Hannibal echoed, aghast. "*Me*? A *doctor*? Oftentimes the *only* doctor? What on earth were they scared of?"

"That you'd have them thrown into prison for being Omegas," Berger said, not meeting his glare. "That you'd expose them and turn them out in a strange land, some of them. Some of them changed their minds in the end."

"About me?" Hannibal asked, offended by their opinion of him.

"About being treated, m'Lord," Berger said, ashamed. "They decided they was better off healing up as they could without risking it."

Hannibal was speechless with horror, trying to summon to mind a world where someone would refuse treatment from pure fear of the source.

"No," he said, the word faint and baffled. "That cannot be true. Omegas have no business fighting in a war! I've seen grown Alphas packed off screaming from the battlefront; there is no possible way an Omega could manage such pressure —"

He broke off abruptly. A month ago he would have said no Omega could bear up for six years after a harsh rejection and bring an estate from the teetering brink of ruin to fruitful productivity or threaten an Alpha with nothing more than their mind as their weapon.

Unsettling, *indeed*.

"M'Lord, all manner of Omegas was in the last unit," Berger said, intruding on his reflective thoughts. "That's why they was so skittish of you."

Hannibal frowned, recalling Captain Rogers' unit. He'd thought them all too young for duty and had mentioned it to Rogers, had asked him if the draft age had been lowered. He recalled clearly how Rogers had laughed and had shaken his head, greatly amused by something Hannibal found entirely bereft of humor.

"*That* simply cannot be the case!" he said, sure Berger was having him on. "The Alphas would have known! *I* would have known!"

"Captain Rogers had mostly beta males and Omegas, not so many Alphas besides himself," Berger said with a shrug. "He swore by all his men, whatever they hid up between their legs. It never made a difference to him... and honestly, you never was good at recognizing an Omega, m'Lord."

Hannibal was entirely confused. "But Berger, they were a forward unit! I distinctly recall they had an unusual number of sharpshooters!"

"Oh, aye, m'Lord, vicious clever with their guns, they were," Berger agreed, settling Hannibal's coat on a hanger with reverence. "I certainly wouldn't want to run up against an Omega in a war. They got the most to lose of anybody, ain't they?"

"What on earth do you even mean?" Hannibal asked, thumbing through his memories of Captain Rogers' unit for clues he must have glossed over and finding none. They had hidden themselves and done so well enough to fool a doctor of his standing.

"I *mean*, they got a man's own need to protect his interests and a mother's need to protect their young," Berger said, as if it made perfect sense. "Nothing more determined to win than that, is there?"

Hannibal mulled that over, unable to find fault with the reasoning and unable to find chaos in the unit he'd left behind. There *should* have been chaos by all rights, but it had been no less disciplined or effective than any other unit he'd been assigned to.

"Berger," he said, a thoughtful frown on his full mouth. "Those Omegas who did not come to me for treatment... did they survive?"

"A few," Berger said, buttoning him up into his nightshirt and missing the spasm of pain that crossed Hannibal's face. "The others made sure Captain Rogers would settle their pension on their families. A soldier who dies in the field is worth more than an Omega court-marshaled out of the military, isn't he?"

Hannibal impatiently took over, needing to move, to do something. Breathlessly, he said, "They should have come to me."

"They was scared, m'Lord," Berger said, bending to gather up Hannibal's boots.

"Better scared than *dead!*" Hannibal snapped at him. "I would have treated them!"

"If you'll pardon my saying, m'Lord, your opinions on Omegas was fair clear to all who heard them," Berger said, conversational as if they were discussing the weather. "There's some risks a body won't take when they stand to lose their livelihood. Better to die in a strange land, then, and let the money go home where it can do some good, right?"

Hannibal wrinkled his nose, angry and guilty, wondering how many deaths he was inadvertently responsible for, how many Omegas had chosen the betterment of their families instead of their own health for fear he would see them drummed out and penniless.

In all honesty, he wasn't sure how he would have reacted to finding an Omega on the battlefield and that scalded him, shamed him deeply, because it was just that uncertainty which had cost the lives of brave soldiers.

"M'Lord?" Berger asked, watching him with concern.

"I find myself chastened," Hannibal said, his words soft. "I honestly had no idea..."

"Well, they was careful you didn't," Berger assured him, moving to gather up his other discarded clothing. "They was just soldiers, m'Lord, there to defend their country the same as us."

"Yes," Hannibal said, thinking of all the faces he'd seen in his near decade overseas, wondering how many of them had fought with the added element of being exposed and reviled for their gender. "Yes, I suppose they were."

Reflective and riddled with guilt, Hannibal retreated to his bed, his thoughts of the war becoming terrible dreams that so often plagued him, where blood never ceased flowing, where men never ceased dying, where the boom of canons and the crack of gunfire became the anguished sobs of the soldiers he had failed to save.

⌘⌘⌘

Will's restless sleep was spent in nightmares of cliffs and parties full of people pointing their fingers at him, laughing at him, of his sister whispering over and over he was not safe, of Hannibal waltzing him closer and closer to the crumbling cliff edge while the watching crowd roared with laughter at his ignorance.

It was not at all restful or conducive to good health, but it did leave him waking thoughtful and sheened with sweat, flushed enough that Jimmy inquired if he was coming down ill.

"No, Jimmy, please don't trouble yourself," Will assured him, grateful for the cool, damp cloth his valet provided with wordless, pursed-mouth disbelief. Will wiped his heated skin with it, and washed his face in the basin, relishing the cold water on his cheeks. "Jimmy, when did you arrive here at Hartford House?"

"Oh, let me see," Jimmy said, helping Will get dressed in the near darkness. "It was, what, ten years ago?"

Will frowned softly, musing, "You never knew Hannibal before his return from the war."

"No, Mr. Grant," Jimmy said, buttoning him up in the clothing which made him feel so much safer. "Just curious?"

"My sister mentioned a former Lady Clarges," Will said, and noted the way Jimmy's hands stilled. It was only a split second, but it was enough to prompt him to say, "He *was* married once before."

Jimmy turned to his cuffs, focusing on his task and absently saying, "Zeitler would know more about it than I would, Mr. Grant. He's been here since childhood."

"As he reminds me at every possibility," Will said, thinking of Roland's rather lazy and lackadaisical valet who, most times, was conspicuously *not* assisting His Grace. "I doubt I could get answers out of him."

"*Oh*, if you manage to, Mr. Grant, will you tell me?" Jimmy teased, eyes lighting up with his usual ebullience. "I've been trying since I arrived here to turn *that* particular latch."

Will laughed and stepped away from him, pulling his boots on and tapping his heels to situate them. He glanced back and caught Jimmy gazing at him, assessing him with his head cocked to one side. "What? What is it?"

"It's nothing," Jimmy assured him, his wide smile back in place. "It's just unusual for you to ask questions now, after all this time..."

"Jimmy," Will said, angling a repressive look at him. "Whatever you're thinking, it isn't that."

"No, of course not, I know that," Jimmy said, waving it away with one hand.

"It would be absurd," Will insisted.

Jimmy nodded vehemently, adding, "Of course, Mr. Grant, absolutely out of the question!"

"Entirely baseless supposition," Will said, hoping he could quell that assessing, figuring look in Jimmy's eyes before his valet started attempting to mend fences torn down too long ago to be fixed now.

"Naturally, your curiosity has nothing at all to do with Lord Clarges returning, Mr. Grant," Jimmy agreed, amused by Will's scowl. "Might I suggest asking His Grace? He does adore you. I doubt there's anything he would hesitate to discuss with you."

"I can't agree, Jimmy," Will said. "Hannibal's cousin intimated His Grace has kept me ignorant of any family matters, including the accident that took his son."

Jimmy blinked, but it was only a momentary setback before he said, "I'm sure it's just because he didn't want you to worry about it, Mr. Grant! He does value your peace of mind and happiness. I'm certain he'd be more than happy to enlighten you, if only to give you the truth in place of rumors."

Will chewed his lower lip, thoughts churning furiously.

"I'll consider it, Jimmy, thank you," he said. "You can go, take some time for yourself today."

He did debate just asking Grandfather, but he was reluctant to explain himself, reluctant to bring Mina into things and potentially open Pandora's box in regards to His Grace's own role. He had to consider that if the rest were true, so too was the mention that Grandfather had compensated the young woman's family for her death, possibly to keep them from inquiry. It was unnerving to think he could not trust the man he'd grown so fond of in the past six years, but Will knew he couldn't be sure of anything, not even if Hannibal was responsible for the accident with his saddle.

He kept his own council through his meager breakfast then took the matter to Mr. Hawkes, who seemed surprised at his curious inquiry.

"The family graveyard, Mr. Grant?" he asked, echoing Will's unusual question. "It is tended by the groundskeepers, yes."

"I should like to visit it, Mr. Hawkes," Will said, hoping the aging butler wouldn't ask too many questions. "Strangely, as well as I know Hartford estate, I have no idea where the Ledfords are laid to rest."

"Ah," Mr. Hawkes said, nodding sagely. "That is because the family graveyard is somewhat removed from the estate, Mr. Grant. It lies over the crest of the western ridge, near Duxbury."

Will's eyes widened as he figured how far that was. He had never ventured over the western ridge, lacking any reason to, and couldn't contain his curiosity from asking, "Why is it so far away, Mr. Hawkes?"

"Hartford House was once settled there, Mr. Grant," he was told. "A century ago there came terrible rains that flooded the entire first storey. A former Duke of Westvale, His Grace Pharis Ledford, had Hartford House moved, brick by brick, here to its current location to prevent such a thing from ever happening again."

Will couldn't fathom what such an effort must have cost, how long it must have taken, and he was properly awed.

"Those who had previously departed could not, of course, be disturbed," Mr. Hawkes intoned, his sonorous voice knocking in Will's chest. "After the flood waters receded, the cemetery was repaired and staff have tended it faithfully since."

Will nodded, absorbing what he'd been told.

"It is very good of them to remember their family," he said, thinking wistfully of the unkempt family plot on his father's estate, the names and dates worn away to anonymity for the most part, the stones growing moss-covered and crumbling towards the back.

'Stop fretting over the state of that place! You *will never lie there, William...*'

Will shuddered from the remembered anger in his father's voice and shook his head, saying, "Mr. Hawkes, I will be visiting the cemetery today, as soon as I possibly can. Please have my horse saddled."

"Yes, Mr. Grant," he said. "And might I suggest having Mrs. Pimms make you up a basket lunch?"

Will nodded, saying, "Yes, Mr. Hawkes, that would be perfect. I think a little solitude after yesterday is just what I need."

"It is quite a peaceful and lovely place, Mr. Grant," Mr. Hawkes said, smiling at him. "The perfect place to read quietly and reflect on what is important in one's life."

Will gave him a weak smile and moved to the front door, hoping he could be gone before Hannibal made an appearance. He was desperate for some time to think, to consider what Mina had told him and what Hannibal professed to require of him. He needed to look and see if this previous wife was laid to rest there and make his inferences from that.

He wondered if she had displeased him somehow.

He wondered if, perhaps, she had *not* been capable of providing Hannibal with the heir he required, the heir Hannibal now claimed to want from Will despite his former statements to the contrary.

Will's hand dropped to his belly, spreading to cover the place where a baby might flourish, if Hannibal had his way. He had always been told by Roland that if he gave Hannibal an heir, then he would have nothing more to be concerned about and could raise his child here under the old Alpha's watchful eye while Hannibal would, no doubt, go back to his real family.

Last night, thanks to Hannibal's acquaintance, Will realized Hannibal had not been idly picking at him with his comments about bringing his daughter and mistress to Hartford House. She, surely, would not stand for having Hannibal's child with Will under her care, and he imagined Hannibal would send him off to another estate with their son, perhaps to live undisturbed there.

Will's eyes misted at the thought, his vivid imagination showing him that the family and love he'd craved for so long could still yet be his. He had so much love to give, he could more than make up for the lack their son would surely have from Hannibal.

'And what if you give him an Omega?'

Will bit his lip, anxiety clenching like a vise around him when he recalled what Hannibal had said, that he would feel compelled to drown it rather than force it to live in such a demeaning and debasing way. He would have every right to dispose of their child as he saw fit. It was an Alpha's lawful place to cull their line for strength, though it had not been done in great families for centuries, not once wealth became plentiful and livelihoods were no longer threatened by a potential weak link in the chain.

"He would never," Will murmured, absently rubbing his belly to soothe himself. "Even *he* could not be so cruel..."

Yet he could not shake the memory of Hannibal seizing hold of him with such violence Will had been sure he was facing the worst beating of his life, triggering a bond that had no place to exist between them. Nor could he shake the memory of the cold, careless way Hannibal had ordered him from the house, mortified and broken in just his underthings, spurned and exiled to the dangerous night and whatever fate might have in store for him.

Perhaps there was not room enough in the heart of a man like Hannibal Ledford to show clemency to a baby whose helplessness would only incense him all the more for its gender. It was frightening enough Will could not entertain the idea of a pregnancy, and grew more determined to find better and stronger products that could mask his scent and keep him safe from inciting any accidental interest from his spouse before he could leave Hartford House.

He heard Hannibal's voice, just a throaty, wordless rumble traveling from somewhere above him as he rose to start his day, and Will quickly slipped through the front door to wait in front of the house, hoping Hannibal would not ask after his whereabouts.

Will moved out to meet his mare as she was led up, mounting up some distance from the house and taking up the basket one of the kitchen maids scurried out with. Balancing it on his thighs, he clucked the horse into a brisk trot and took one of the side trails from the estate, relaxing once he was sheltered in the thick wood. It was awkward guiding the mare with one hand and keeping the hamper in place with the other, but he found a happy medium and took the trail to the lane towards Duxbury, hoping at least to tease some truth from the tangle he'd been given.

Chapter 16

It took several hours to reach the village and, once there, Will had no idea where he was going. Duxbury was not as large as the town that had sprung up south of Hartford House, but it was large enough to have a main street with a proper cobbled road and several fine little shops doing brisk business. Deciding not to risk getting lost, Will carefully swung down from his mare's back and looped her reins over a hitching ring at the least busy storefront, which looked to be some kind of dress shop.

Holding his basket half behind him, Will pushed the door open, wincing at the merry jangle of bells which got the attention of a bright-eyed, plump-cheeked blonde woman behind the counter.

"Well, good morning!" she said, her voice pleasantly raspy and warm. She came around the counter with a wide smile, so delighted to see him that Will looked behind him to see if someone else was there. "Can I help you?"

"Ah, yes, sorry," he said, flushing. "I'm... I'm afraid I'm a bit lost."

Her brows rose. "Now, *that* is a surprise," she said, chuckling. "Considering what a large and confusing town we are."

Will smiled, her friendliness putting him at ease.

"Maybe I can help you find your way, Mr...?"

"Grant," Will said, offering his free hand, which she shook with the same sure confidence of a beta male. "Will Grant."

"Pleased to meet you, Mr. Grant," she said. "You can call me Molly. Or Miss Forester if you like, but I prefer Molly. We're not much for formalities around here. So, where are you trying to get that you find yourself stranded in my dress shop?"

"I was told there is a cemetery nearby," Will said, and hastily added, "The Ledford family cemetery, rather."

"*Ah.*" Her full mouth pursed and a troubled look fell over her face. "Any particular reason you're looking for it?"

"I'm trying to confirm something," Will admitted. "Seeing the grave markers would help."

"Well, I'm not sure *how* it could help you," Molly said, moving back behind her counter to grab a flannel shawl. She wrapped it over her shoulders and pinned it with absent precision before grabbing a rather floppy and shapeless hat. "But I'll take you there."

"Oh, no, your business—"

"I know, I know, chasing all these customers away," she said, looking around the empty store with a soft chuckle. "Shame on me. I needed some air anyway and I don't want to find out later you've gotten lost in the fields. Come along, Mr. Grant."

She moved past him and flipped the sign on the window, holding the door wide for Will, who hurried back outside in the face of her insistence. He gathered his mare's reins back up and set out after Molly when she beckoned him, following her down the street.

"Where are you from, Mr. Grant?" she asked, precisely his height and keeping a good pace that ate up the distance.

"Hartford Town," he said, figuring it was close enough. He was reluctant to tell her who he was. He didn't want her to feel pressured by his status when he had none in truth.

"*Really*," she said. "No wonder you're interested in the Ledford plots. Are you a writer?"

"No, nothing so interesting as all that," Will said, laughing and picking his footing carefully as they turned off onto a thready, barely discernible trail that vanished into the thickening wood.

"Then what?" she asked, taking the lead.

"I... Molly, I don't wish to lie to you," he said, ducking a branch and holding it to pull the mare behind him. "I'd really rather not discuss myself."

"Fair enough," she said, her throaty laughter floating back to him. "I'll talk enough for both of us! My mother always tried to tell me I chatter too much, but I never did hear her," she looked over her shoulder at him and winked, adding, "I was always too busy talking! Come on, Mr. Grant, it's just this way."

The wood gradually thinned to high grass where the trail was more clearly worn down, branching off in several directions where it crossed a main footpath. The sun was climbing higher in the cloudless sky and Will wished for his hat to shield his eyes, envying Molly the one she kept clapped to her head against the wind.

"Here we are! Just down here, Mr. Grant," she said, vanishing below the level of the grass.

Alarmed, Will quickened his pace to find himself standing on the rise of a high hill looking down at a widespread cemetery in the wooded valley below. The high grass was neatly cut in a wide swath around the outside of the stacked stone wall and the ground within was well cared for. The paths were even and lined with stone, the mausoleums and headstones sitting tranquil beneath the sheltering spread of massive oak tree branches that shaded them.

"Come on!" Molly called, pausing halfway down the hill to beckon him. "She'll be fine!"

Will descended at a careful angle, his mare plodding along behind him, snorting into his ear. Will led her to the cemetery entrance and fastened her to a low-hanging branch, leaving her to munch the cropped grass in the shade where the dew still lay heavy and wet.

"Well... here we are," Molly said, watching him tether the mare.

"Yes, here we are," Will said, putting the basket down next to the wall. He moved inside with silent appreciation and respect, taking in the change in atmosphere here inside this pleasant, shaded resting place for generations of Ledfords. "I had thought it would be bigger."

"They lost a lot of people overseas; they were either buried there or there wasn't enough left to send home," Molly said, just behind him. She pulled her hat from her head and fanned herself with it, looking around with melancholy that seemed odd for people who were strangers to her. "Only the main family rests here, direct heirs and their spouses, whatever children they had who died young or unmarried. Every whip-stitch, they move the far wall out, but I imagine it'll be years before they have to do that again. For a bunch of Alphas, they don't breed much anymore."

Will nodded idly, moving towards the newer stones, searching the names but mainly after the dates. He was vague on the dates—Hannibal had left the continent to go to war when Will was a mere eight years old—but he was confident he could find the grave of Hannibal's first wife and at least put a name to the mystery.

"So, what're you looking for, Mr. Grant?" Molly asked, moving to a stone at the far end of the cemetery where she crouched to trace the lettering.

"I'm just chasing shadows," Will sighed, and laughed softly. "Honestly, I don't know why I'm here or what I hoped to find..."

He trailed off when he reached the end of the row Molly was in, a group of stones catching his eye. One headstone was topped with the likeness of a cherub draped as if sleeping, wings folded in restful repose. It was clearly a child's stone, and engraved beneath the angel was the name Miska Ledford.

Suffocating darkness and terror, the roar of water, the scream of breaking wood and frightened horses...

"How terrible," Will breathed, shuddering as he recalled Bedelia's sad story of what had occurred. "She was so young."

"Miska? Four years was barely enough time for anything. It's always so sad when it's little ones," Molly said, straightening to come closer. "Are you familiar with the family? There was a terrible accident. Her mother and father died with her, see? All buried on the same day."

Will looked at the stones around little Miska's grave as Molly pointed to them. One read *Cyrus Ledford, Beloved Son.* It was a beautiful stone, but certainly nowhere near as grand as the mausoleums that housed past generations of Ledford heirs. It chilled Will to think that the warm, loving old man he'd come to rely on had been capable of cutting his son so entirely free of his affections that this exiled stone was the only marker of his life.

There was a stone to the left of Cyrus Ledford, much more weathered, in the likeness of a goddess gazing upwards at the sky.

"*Saule Ledford, beloved daughter and precious wife,*" Will read, and thought of the portrait in the gallery at Hartford House, the woman with dark ringlets and a secretive smile. That same picture was placed next to the gaping emptiness which had once housed Cyrus Ledford's portrait.

Saule Ledford, Hannibal's mother, whose date of death was precisely Hannibal's birthday.

Bedelia had certainly failed to mention *that*, though in retrospect he should have realized it by her phrasing. The former Lady Clarges had died from childbirth, either during or from complications, and her bereft husband had promptly deposited Hannibal at Fernhill in his sister's care and fled the country.

"Sad, isn't it?" Molly asked, lingering at his side.

288

"The loss of a life is always cause for sadness," Will murmured, thinking on what Bedelia had told him. "I wonder if there was any fondness in their marriage."

"Some, I'm sure," Molly said. "Though when you're breeding for lineage, I suppose things like affection and fondness don't weigh as heavily as one's pedigree."

"Duty," Will sighed, frowning. "A poor man is free in his choices where a nobleman is not."

"A nobleman can afford to be stripped of some choices," Molly said, smiling to soften her sharp response. "I'm sure there's a poor man or two who would marry anyone he was told to if it meant he had warm, sure meals and a place to rest his head without slaving his life away."

"That is an excellent point," Will conceded. His curiosity about Hannibal's stepmother overcame him, then, and he turned his attention to the other stone situated next to Cyrus Ledford's, positioned in such a way it gave Will the impression of exclusion. It was a begrudging grave on the far side of Miska, closest to the path.

There were markings on it, characters in lettering unfamiliar to Will. Below the letters was an etching of an opera mask, with the dates of her birth and death.

Will had imagined she was young, this woman who had snared Cyrus Ledford's interest. It surprised him to see she had been near her fiftieth birthday when she'd died, almost twenty years her lover's senior. It made logical sense when he considered she had been famous in the opera before meeting him, but for some reason, he had imagined her nearer to his own age.

"I wish I had a means with which to read her name," Will murmured, frustrated that even in this she would remain elusive. "I wish I had a means to know more about her at all..."

"Ryu Minamoto," Molly supplied, surprising him. She laughed at his startled expression and said, "Believe me, Lady Minamoto was famous even in Duxbury!"

"In what way, Molly?" Will asked. "Her being an opera singer?"

"Oh, she wasn't just an opera singer, Mr. Grant. Before she was Cyrus's concubine, she was famous on the Continent. She performed for Kings and Queens, and had love affairs and duels fought over her," Molly said, bending to brush a stray leaf from the stone's flattened top, her voice filled with soft admiration for a life of such excitement. "She was from somewhere so far away, I have no idea how people ever get from there to here. Apparently, she came from some kind of royal line there and left when her family was wiped out. There are so many versions of every story, I could never tell what was real or not, but I loved hearing all of them when I could. I mean, I never knew her, obviously, she was dead a long time before I was born, but the stories circulated for years, mostly because she was—"

"Omegan," Will breathed, conclusions rapidly forming. He knew from Bedelia's story that Cyrus had brought her home at some point after Hannibal's birth, and from the dates on Miska's stone it could not have been too long after.

"Yes," Molly said, frowning. "People can be so... awful about it. "

"She was the one who raised him," he said, swiping at his heated forehead, his suspicions confirmed. "An *Omega* raised Hannibal."

"*Hannibal?*" Molly said, snorting with a disdain that startled Will. "You're *that* familiar with Lord Clarges? Be careful he doesn't damage you, Mr. Grant. That man is a menace."

Her sudden vitriol surprised him into looking at her and Will was dismayed by the unhappy expression on her face.

"Why would you say that, Molly?" he asked, nervous his fears would be given life, that he would find out his husband was indeed capable of arranging an accident for him to remove him entirely.

Molly's sparkling eyes flashed fire when she met his gaze and her words were sharp as glass when she spat, "Because he *killed my sister*."

⌘⌘⌘

Hannibal was reluctant to ask after Will come morning, still reflecting on their exchange last night and the revelations Berger had made. Hannibal worried he might look at Will and his perceptive little spouse would see his long-held, bone-deep prejudices had sunk on their foundations, not so much bedrock as sand, shifting and uncertain, and might somehow think even less of him than he already did.

Since his earliest memories, he'd been raised with an understanding he now found to be baseless. To lose that certainty, to question his own judgment and everything he'd thought was reality... it was startling and alarming.

He had, indeed, walked a world where people had played to his perceptions, content to keep him in willful ignorance. Some had done it, he knew, from deliberate intention to use those beliefs to their advantage, to push their own agendas with him. Others, such as Berger, had done it to avoid rousing Hannibal's temper.

And so many lives had suffered for it. So many lives had been *lost* for it. It had taken Will, with his righteous violence and sharp intelligence, to wrap his slender fingers around those scales and pull them from Hannibal's eyes without hesitation, forcing him to see the truth. He had never once been anyone other than himself, so perfectly honest and without guile that Hannibal had no choice but to acknowledge him.

How much he could have changed had Hannibal met someone like Will when he was younger, before he married Melinda, before he fled to the battlefields to drown his guilt in blood and death...

It left Hannibal thoughtful and contemplative, absorbed enough in his musings that he took a small breakfast alone in the solarium. He didn't enjoy it quite so much as he'd hoped, considering his unpredictable spouse wasn't present to distract him, but Berger made his way in with a packet of letters to tide him over.

It was a bundle of mail sent from Galley Field for him, his usual correspondence from patients and tenants, invitations for events in the Capital, and various journals he subscribed to in order to remain abreast of the latest medical knowledge.

Alana's letter he saved for last, and opened it as the servants came to clear away his breakfast.

Hannibal,

I hope this letter finds you well, and having great success in your efforts at reconciling with your grandfather. I did promise I would write to you on occasion in your absence and especially wanted to do so now as a reminder that we are all managing quite happily here without anything in the world to trouble our thoughts but what actions you might take in haste.

Marissa is doing very well and has begun to dash about everywhere. She is running darling Margot ragged; I was sure I would need to ask you for a tonic to soothe her nerves, our girl has been so vexing! She insists on climbing the stairs the moment one's eyes are averted, and it seems she is instantly in any single place that is dangerous for her. I am not sure who to worry over more, the child or my Margot.

I have had encouraging news from the committee you convened on the subject of the school here. I have sent along their letter to you to read at your leisure. By this time next year we will break ground, and I am sure I have never felt more proud at what we have accomplished! Margot, of course, is attempting to keep my head firmly on my business rather than in the clouds, but I find myself dreaming of the day when the women we enabled with knowledge will stand equally with men in the medical field, and it gives me hope.

The babe is healthy, strong and kicking, much as the one before him. I am sure he will be a boy this time. I dearly hope and pray so. You have kept your promise to me, Hannibal, and I will keep my promise to you—a boy for your grandfather, though I remain somewhat skeptical at your assurances that he will accept him as a viable heir.

On that matter, I must urge you—strongly urge you—to remember us with fondness and care and impart some measure of that feeling on your spouse, however you may view him. He has never once intruded on your decisions nor made a burden of himself in any respect. You have chided me before on my defense of him, Hannibal, but I stand by my words, for I know all too well what it is like to be despised by those who should love us.

I will say in closing, be careful with him, Hannibal. You left him a child behind you and he has become an adult in your absence who must all too well recall how badly you parted. Be gentle with him, as you are with us, and do nothing impulsive.

All of our fondest affections,

Alana, Margot, Marissa

Hannibal sighed and read the letter twice before tucking it into his jacket, reflecting on her entreaty. He didn't write back—on those short occasions when they were not together, he had never written back—but he almost wanted to, if only to warn her of what Thomas would no doubt tell her the moment he visited. It relieved him that he was not at Galley Field, in all honesty. He wasn't entirely prepared to handle Alana's scolding, even soft as it would be.

Instead, he opened his letter from the committee, penned a series of instructions to the family solicitor, Mr. Buddish, on the subject of the school he was sponsoring, then composed an advert for an estate manager out of sheer desperate distraction.

He rang for Hawkes, who arrived with such haste Hannibal was sure he'd been hovering outside the door, and handed off his correspondence, saying, "Send these down to the post and have them mailed immediately."

"Nothing terrible, I do hope, My Lord," Hawkes said, turning to hand it all off to the footman behind him, where it was all whisked into the sure hands of Hartford House's serving staff and would be cared for appropriately.

"Just some instructions for the Capital clerks. I'm posting the position for estate manager," Hannibal said, remarking the way Hawkes' bushy eyebrows drew together in disapproval. Smiling slightly at the wordless reproof, Hannibal said, "Will shall soon have his hands full with tending the next Ledford heir, Mr. Hawkes. He cannot be troubled with the running of Hartford House for some time."

"Are congratulations in order, My Lord?" Hawkes inquired, knowing damned good and well he and Will had shared nothing more than mutual baiting and a few meals, to date.

"There is the matter of convincing Mr. Grant," Hannibal said, catching slight disapproval again at his choice in words. "But I am supremely confident in my ability to do so."

"I have every faith you will require such well-deserved confidence, My Lord," Hawkes said, a sly smile barely touching his lips, "as Mr. Grant is a remarkably stubborn young man when his mind is set."

"Well, then, like all bull-headed creatures, we will clash until one of us yields," Hannibal said, amused.

"I am not entirely certain, my Lord, that you should attempt such a thing," Mr. Hawkes offered, causing Hannibal to laugh.

"He is unusual, isn't he, Mr. Hawkes?" Hannibal asked, getting to his feet to look idly around the room, taking in the small, unobtrusive changes his mate was responsible for. Not a single room of Hartford House missed his deft and subtle touch except for his own suite. It was strange to think of Will avoiding it all these years, a quiet respect for his privacy Hannibal had not expected.

"An Original, I believe is the term, my Lord."

Hannibal smiled, "Oh, I do like that."

"I thought perhaps you would."

Hannibal's smile faded, then. "It seems... rather lonely here."

Mr. Hawkes said nothing but remained attentive.

"Hartford House is meant to host parties and foster large families," Hannibal said, thinking of the House as it had been in his childhood. "It is... sad to see it so bereft."

"It has been quiet here, my Lord," Mr. Hawkes said. "All things considered."

"Grandfather's illness," Hannibal said. "But Will... has he had no one to keep him company at all?"

"Lord du Millau visits when he is in the countryside, my Lord," Mr. Hawkes said.

"But none of Will's family," Hannibal mused. "Has he mentioned his father?"

Mr. Hawkes frowned solemnly. "No, my Lord. Mr. Grant has had no contact with any member of his family since his arrival here and rarely speaks of personal matters."

"No contact whatsoever," Hannibal echoed, fixing Hawkes with a stern look. Though Will himself had admitted even his sisters had not dared to contact him, he felt compelled to ask, "Not even letters?"

"I believe he wrote to the Lord Reddig soon after your departure, my Lord, but the letter was returned unopened."

Hannibal frowned, locking his hands together behind his back and rocking slightly, his irritation escaping him in small tells his butler knew all too well.

"Unopened *indeed*," he murmured. He gave Mr. Hawkes a tight, unhappy smile, adding, "I doubt he will return a letter from my grandfather *unopened*."

"One does very much doubt so, my Lord," Mr. Hawkes said, giving him a slight smile in return. "Might I offer an opinion, my Lord?"

Hannibal's brows rose.

"Perhaps it would be more considerate of Mr. Grant if Lord Reddig was not asked to Hartford House," Mr. Hawkes said, unusually candid with him. "I have no firm understanding given that Mr. Grant never speaks of his family, but it would seem the relationship has suffered since his arrival here. Perhaps a less public setting would better suit a reunion in case he were to become... *unpleasant*."

"Surely you jest, Mr. Hawkes? Even had he such an inclination to be rude, Lord Reddig would have to be brave, indeed, to believe he could get away with such behavior," Hannibal said, and when Hawkes became rather still, he darkly added, "Of course, considering my treatment of Will, he would assume his child has no friends here."

"I did not wish to be indelicate—"

"Mr. Hawkes, I assure you, I would sooner expect the ground to swallow me whole than for you to be indelicate," Hannibal said, and sighed heavily. "Thank you, Hawkes. Your candor is appreciated."

That earned him an incline of Mr. Hawkes' silver-haired head.

"Hawkes, might you know of any place here in Hartford House that is Will's?" Hannibal asked, noting the slight spasm of the old butler's eyebrows. "That he is comfortable in, rather. I find little trace of him here at Hartford House, as if he does not live here at all."

"Yes, my Lord," Hawkes told him, recovering. "There is a small space Mr. Grant has claimed for himself in the attic."

Appalled, Hannibal asked, "Why in the seven hells is he sequestered away in the attic?"

Which only garnered him a bland, hooded look from his butler, who said with sonorous dignity, "I honestly did not feel it my place to question him, my Lord."

It carried a subtle undertone suggesting Hannibal should not question it, either, all things considered.

Embarrassed that he had to be chastised by his help, Hannibal took himself off to the nearest servants' passage and clambered up to where the Hartford domestics made their living quarters. The attic proper was not secured against entry, but none of the servants would risk their livelihood for the sake of curiosity, so Hannibal had no doubt it remained undisturbed except for Will.

He made his way cautiously up the narrow stairs and emerged into dusty sunlight admitted through the attic windows. It was a maze of storage, but a goodly portion of the attic was still unused with more than enough large rooms to house whatever hobbies Will managed in his limited spare time.

It took some searching on his part, but Hannibal finally located it back against the far end of the House away from any of the stairways. The room he had chosen, unsurprisingly, was a small one with its own window and was empty of Will himself, much to Hannibal's disappointment.

But it was not so empty of Will's presence as the rest of Hartford House.

The window was clean and sparkling, the walls, rafters, and floor all diligently kept spotless. A single desk was under the window, the chair pushed in, its surface arranged with a plethora of tools and items Hannibal could not make sense of at first.

Then he noticed the lures dangling from fish-line in orderly rows from pegs, and realized what Will was about.

"You are an artist after all," he mused, pulling the little chair out and settling at Will's desk. He had a lure in progress, and Hannibal amused himself peering at it through the supported magnifying glass. Spools of colored thread, snips, bare hooks, assorted feathers, and bits of small found objects were neatly arranged on the desktop—it was quite a collection and each lure was unique.

"These are your watercolors," Hannibal murmured, looking at each in turn with growing appreciation and pain as he thought about Will up here alone, working in silence on pieces no one would ever see.

It bothered him deeply, even more so when he counted the sheer number of lures Will had made over the past six years.

Hannibal got to his feet and really looked at them, picking his favorites down carefully. He gathered a nice showing before heading back downstairs to seek Hawkes.

"Ah! My Lord, there is a gentleman—"

"Hawkes, I want you to have these mounted and framed," Hannibal said, thrusting the lines at him.

Mr. Hawkes, who had not been rattled when his youthful master had flung a frog at him as a child, did not so much as bat an eyelash to have Will's lures offered to him.

"And is there some particular way you would prefer, my Lord?" he asked, adjusting with admirable ease.

"Surprise me," Hannibal said, earnestly adding, "Several small frames, nothing too ostentatious, and have them set up in the various parlors."

"Yes, my Lord," Mr. Hawkes said, "Where they may be seen by visitors, is that correct, my Lord?"

"Yes, Hawkes," Hannibal said. "I find myself impressed by Will's various talents. I should like others to share my appreciation for his efforts."

"I understand entirely, my Lord," Mr. Hawkes said, giving him a fond smile.

"Thank you, Hawkes," Hannibal said, pleased to have it taken care of. There was a high probability Will would cosh him with something for his thievery, but he hoped not. "And have you any idea where my spouse is?"

"He has gone to Duxbury, My Lord," Hawkes said, the very picture of dignity with the incongruous addition of several dozen fishing lures dangling from one hand. "But there is a gentleman—"

"Duxbury? What the devil for?" Hannibal asked, straightening his clothing, his own mention of his mate prompting the need to groom himself against Will's possible censure.

"I believe he has shown some interest in the family cemetery, My Lord," Hawkes said, stopping him cold. "He did mention his curiosity on that count."

Hannibal's nose wrinkled in a soft snarl and he said, "Have my horse saddled, Hawkes! That sharp mind of his is going to be the end of me!"

"And the gentleman, my Lord?" Hawkes inquired. "He says he is a servant sent from Lady Rathmore."

"He can wait, then," Hannibal said, restless with the desire to be on his way. "I, unfortunately, can*not*."

If Will was at the cemetery, it wasn't from idle curiosity. He was going to confirm something, most likely the rumor that Hannibal had been married once before, and if there was one thing he did not wish to discuss with Will Grant besides the Omega who had raised him, it was the woman he had married before marrying Will.

⌘⌘⌘

Will watched helplessly as Molly trembled before him, her small hands clenched into fists and her blue eyes bright with unshed tears.

"Molly," Will said, distressed by her own distress. "I don't understand. Why would you believe Hannibal killed your sister?"

"Because she *inconvenienced* him," she said, stiff with anger and hurt. She swiped her forearm across her eyes and glanced back at the tombstone she'd been standing in front of. "I don't remember her very well, she was already almost grown when I came along, but the whole town knows what he did to her. And just because he's rich and powerful, he was able to get away with it."

Will shook his head slightly, still confused, and leaned to look around Molly at the stone.

"*Melinda Ledford, May You Find Peace In Death*" was inscribed on its face with a span of dates that summed only sixteen years.

"Melinda Ledford," he murmured, his concern sharpening. "She was your sister?"

Molly nodded and laughed, thick with tears. "Not that you'd know by looking at us, but yes, once upon a time we Foresters were part of the Ledford family."

Will took a deep breath, fear settling in his belly like a weight. "She was Hannibal's first wife."

Molly nodded emphatically, wiping her face with her hands.

"My mother always told me when he first came to live with his grandfather, he met my sister at the fair and they became playmates," she said, casting another long look back at her sister's tomb. "She said they were best friends, then, but when she turned fifteen he cut her completely out of his life. Mother said it devastated her. She took to her bed, sick all the time, sent him letter after letter."

Will reached out and took her hand without thinking, squeezing her fingers in his, her painful recollection like a thorn in his imagination, so sharp his heart ached for her and her lost sister.

"I'm sorry," she said, taking a shaky breath. "This isn't anything you asked to hear."

"Please, tell me," Will urged, anxiously watching her. "I-it's something I should know, Molly."

She looked at him for, silent and assessing, and finally nodded when Will whispered, "Please, Molly. Tell me what happened to your sister."

"I couldn't have been more than three or four when she got sick, so I don't really remember much, just some things here and there and what others have told me... but one day he showed up and carted her off," Molly said. "I *do* remember the coach coming. It was the grandest thing I'd ever seen. I thought Melinda was a princess and he was taking her away to a royal castle."

She laughed sadly, and dabbed at her eyes with her shawl, the worst of her tears over.

"But he didn't, he eloped with her like she was some kind of *embarrassment*," Molly said, drawing a deep, steadying breath. "*Gods* it was such a scandal! We didn't see her for a month, then out of nowhere, Mr. Stammets came and told my parents she'd died. He gave them some kind of a settlement to shut them up about it. His Grace had her in the ground that same day, no wake, no service, just brought the coffin over as soon as the hole was dug and put her in."

Will absorbed her words in silence, a strange stillness falling over him to have his sister's gossip confirmed. Hannibal *had* been married once before. She *had* died within a month of marrying him.

He drew a shuddering breath, pulled in different directions by what he knew and what he wanted to be true.

He desperately didn't want this to be true.

"They didn't tell your parents what she died of?" he asked, letting go of her hand to put his arm over her shoulder, comforting both of them the best he knew how.

Molly shook her head again, her loose hair bouncing around her cheeks. "No, they didn't, not that I know of. His Grace was furious when Lord Clarges brought her home, though. Everyone says Hannibal killed her because he was going to be disinherited. He's got a temper, so it makes a lot of sense. Not to mention he fled the country the moment she died. He didn't even come to the graveside. Even His Grace had the good manners to come to the graveside."

Will patted her again, his thoughts racing. He knew too well how easy it was to rile Hannibal, but he also knew Hannibal was not so easily forced into doing something he did not wish to do. If he'd married Melinda by choice, then the threat of being disowned like his father wouldn't have swayed him.

But something had.

Sixteen year old girls did *not* just die suddenly without warning, and Hannibal had finished medical school by then, so he would have known ways to end her life that the local authorities would not think to check for.

He wasn't entirely sure what to make of it, but one thing was certain— Melinda Forester had gone into Hartford House alive and come out again a month later in a coffin without explanation, accompanied by a large settlement.

It certainly put doubts into Will's mind.

"I'm sorry, I just really needed to get that off my chest, I guess," Molly said, offering him a shaky smile. "I've never really talked to anyone about it before."

"Please, don't apologize," Will said, giving her shoulder a squeeze. "It must have been terribly difficult for you and your family to lose her, especially under such circumstances."

She nodded, her smile firming up under the weight of her usual good cheer. "It just gets me that he never paid for it, not like us normal people would. But it's

299

all in the past and there's nothing I can do for it now. I'm sorry for throwing all of that at you, Mr. Grant."

"Please, don't be sorry," Will said, earnest and sincere. "You've had a painful loss, Ms. Forester."

"And you have a kind face," she said, somewhat flushed with embarrassment once the anger and hurt had drained out of her. Tentatively, she smiled at him and asked, "Do you think what you're looking for is here?"

Will gave her a smile of his own and nodded slightly, willing to change the subject at her insistence. "It is, yes. I think I know enough. Thank you, Molly, for all of your help."

"You want to thank me, then feed me, Mr. Grant," she said, her raspy laughter making a welcome return. "That hamper is your lunch, right? You bring enough for two?"

"Knowing the staff, yes, I did," Will told her, grinning. "I am more than happy to share for taking your time."

"Well, let's not eat in here, we'll make them all jealous," Molly said, gesturing at the gate. "That tree makes some nice shade and we won't have to share with your horse."

Will laughed softly, and the two of them left the somber silence of the cemetery to retrieve his packed lunch.

Chapter 17

The ride to Duxbury left Hannibal with too much time to think about the reasons why he had never been back, not since Melinda had been buried. He was reluctant to go there despite his provoking, pressing need to find Will, as if the ghosts of his neglected family might hold him accountable for his absence.

Now, with no company other than his own thoughts and the surety of seeing her final resting place at last, Hannibal found himself thinking about her. Their childhood friendship was still one of his fondest recollections of his time at Hartford House. She had taken the place of his lost little sister at first, being so close to Miska in age. Hannibal had been besotted the instant they met, taking the role of her protector, much to the amusement of her parents. His middling years had passed in a blur of exploration, climbing trees, being carefree and happy, always with Melinda next to him. His grandfather had tried to discourage their association, but Hannibal had found ways around that, as children often would. Even then he'd known he would have to marry well when he was of age. He'd been told time after time by Grandfather that someone was already picked out for him, that it was settled and contracted, that he would have no choice in the matter.

Those warnings had fallen on deaf ears, slamming up against the wall of youthful surety that he knew what was best for himself. He'd been determined to marry Melinda when they both were old enough, the four years of difference between them seeming to stretch forever, long enough that his feelings for her had altered from brotherly to something else entirely.

And then she'd finally caught up to him and everything had fallen apart...

Hannibal shook off his memories of her, teeth clenching hard with feelings that had not died alongside her. He urged his horse up the lesser-used trail and cut across the fields both to shorten the distance and avoid the town itself. The fields gave way to brush and the thick of the treeline, forcing Hannibal to dismount and lead his horse the rest of the way. He came out at the top of the crest and paused, his amber eyes scanning for any sign of Will.

He saw Will's mare waiting patiently in the shade, then he saw Will sitting on a spread blanket just beyond, talking with animation to a smiling, blonde woman, who was busy packing the remains of their lunch back into a hamper.

It took him aback to see Will there, smiling and relaxed in the company of that woman, and it occurred to Hannibal then that no one had ever asked Will where his preferences lay. Everyone, even his grandfather who was the most thoughtful of Will, had assumed that, as an Omega, Will would want an Alpha male.

Seeing them there, Hannibal felt his gut clench with uncertainty, thinking that perhaps in his six years living as a beta male, Will's desires ran towards women, as Hannibal's own had.

Which begged the question why it made him feel so strangely unhappy to consider such a thing, when he had fully intended to breed Will and abandon him all over again.

'*Because you* don't *intend to...*'

The quiet thought arrived without fanfare, warm and small but growing stronger with every heartbeat.

Of course he didn't intend to. He'd barely given the Addendum a thought since riding out with Will on his rounds. He'd been ensnared in fascination and new options had begun to form.

He wanted to know Will. He wanted Will to know him in return.

And the only way for that to happen was to enact vast and permanent change, not only for himself, but for those he cared for.

Will's laughter reached him, a carefree and easy sound drifting up to Hannibal on the slight breeze, bringing an answering smile to his mouth and a blossom of warmth to chase away the ugly anxiety that had plagued him all the way to Duxbury.

He envied her, this young and animated woman who enticed Will into such easy mirth. He envied her, but he could not begrudge her. Will's laughter was too precious a sound to resent the source, even if some small part of him simmered with envy because of it.

"One day," Hannibal promised, his hands tightening on his stallion's reins. "That sound will not be so rare..."

When his horse nosed his shoulder, nudging him for his inactivity, he quietly admitted, "He has an Uncommon habit of scattering my best laid plans. I find myself needing to reform them once again."

The stallion snorted and Hannibal rubbed his velvety nose, deciding not to intrude on Will just yet for fear he would have to see all his relaxed ease tighten into nervous tension.

⌘⌘⌘

Molly was kind enough to lead Will back to Duxbury and put a few pumps of water into a bucket for his mare to slake her thirst. The day was turning humid in the afternoon sun and Will wearily wished his ride home was shorter.

"You came by the main lane, didn't you?" Molly asked, stroking her fingers through the mare's mane as it slurped from the bucket, looking at Will over the top of the saddle and smiling when he nodded. "Just past the shop as you head back, you'll see a trail on the right that cuts you back towards the cemetery. It turns past the ridge and goes straight across instead of around. It'll save you at least an hour."

"*Thank* you, Molly," Will breathed, glad to have been told.

"Here, wait a second," she said, and vanished into the back of her shop.

Will stroked his mare's neck and crooned at her, enjoying the faint breeze and his blank state of mind. He had a lot of information to consider, and all of it was going to change his perception, he knew. He was putting off facing it, putting off the inevitable moment when he would have to look at everything and see Hannibal through the lens it formed. It disturbed him to think Hannibal might have been responsible for Melinda's death, just as everyone thought. It was as if life was determined he would be attached to those without compassion or compunction—first his father, and now Hannibal.

Perhaps, it was simply all he deserved when it came down to it. Perhaps, as his father had taught him, he lacked the value required to be allowed the happiness he had hoped for so foolishly. Seeing the fresh strap on his mare, so new and obvious on his broken-in saddle, the twinge of unease returned with a vengeance and he was glad when Molly returned to distract him.

"Here we go!" she crowed, waving a hat around over her head. "Just what you need!"

"Molly, no, I can't—"

"Sure you can," she said, leaning over the horse to plunk the hat atop his curls. "It will keep the sun off a little, at least. Oh, don't look so guilty, it's one of my father's old hats. It's rubbish, really, so you're doing me a favor by taking it. Only, promise you'll get rid of it, okay? It's too shabby to wear anyplace."

Will grinned and nodded, flattered she would offer it to him, and pushed it firmly down onto his head. "Thank you, Molly. You're very delightful. I really have enjoyed today."

"Well, what can I say, cemetery tours are my specialty," she teased, grinning. "Look, you know where Duxbury is, so don't be a stranger, Mr. Grant, okay? Maybe next time you ride over we can go someplace less gloomy."

"That would be very nice," Will said, grabbing onto the pommel to swing up into his saddle and get comfortable. "It has truly been a pleasure meeting you, Molly."

"I couldn't agree more, Mister Grant," she said, handing him up his basket and stepping back to give the mare room to turn around. "Have a safe trip, and just follow that trail straight back to Hartford, okay?"

"Yes, thank you," Will said, inclining his head at her and clicking his mount into a sedate walk past the edge of town to the trail, just where Molly had promised it would be.

⌘⌘⌘

It was too late to prevent Will from finding whatever he'd sought, Hannibal knew. He idled in the treeline out of sight, plucking small flowers that had found purchase at the edge of the wood. He waited until Will left with his lady friend before he made his way down to the cemetery.

It was a somber reunion, almost an intrusion after so long absent, and it humbled him to be back after all these years. The spreading trees kept the place in shadows, cool and comfortable as the afternoon sun rode high in the sky, a tranquil peace that soothed him. Hannibal moved down the rows to where his closest kin rested. His father, buried with little fanfare for his disobedience; his little sister, Miska; the wretched creature who had ruined his father and cost Hannibal his family there on her other side, close to the path and far from the proper Ledfords, but there nonetheless. His grandfather's small admiration for her tenacity, perhaps; a stubbornness which matched his own.

He could not look at his mother's grave, not without his stepmother's purring, soft voice reminding him, *"There is no love like a mother's love, but you will never understand that, Hannibal. You killed her before she could love you. But I should thank you for that, Hannibal. If you hadn't, I wouldn't be here..."*

Trembling with the memory, Hannibal took a deep breath to steady his nerves. He had thought of her more and more since returning home, a presence that always shadowed him since she'd come home with his father. Death hadn't changed any facet of that where she was concerned. He lived on with his vision— as Grandfather had said—skewed by what she had shown him. He didn't wish to revisit any part of it, or her.

Perhaps that was why he was so reluctant to return.

He shook off the disquiet that thoughts of her provoked and focused on his little sister's final resting place. Once he had himself under control, he bent and placed the small bunch of meadow flowers on Miska's grave, sighing into the quiet afternoon, "I will bring you a proper bouquet next time, my little one."

He felt guilty for not having come to see her even once in the past years. When he'd been young, he'd come nearly every day when the grief was fresh. Those visits had slowly drawn farther and farther from one another as other things had cracked the shell of his sorrow. By the time he had married Melinda, he'd come only on the anniversary of Miska's birth and death, no longer able to summon the tears that had once flowed so freely.

He trembled as he knelt there among the dead in the peaceful shade, the wind picking at his hair like ghostly fingers, cool and formless. He stared at her stone but it was his last memory of her he saw instead, a split second between life and death and the way the light had drained from her eyes. She'd been so frightened, trembling on her mother's lap and reaching for him in the darkness. None of them had been prepared for what had happened. One second she'd been alive, and the next he'd watched her slip away by the ceaseless flash of lightning cracking overhead.

"Will you forgive me?" he asked her, tracing the lettering of her name and replacing the memory of her slack, bloodied face with her sweet little smile. "I couldn't save you, Miska. Why couldn't I save you?"

'Get away!' The voice of *that woman* cracked like a whip in his memories, rejecting him violently even at the moment of her death. *'Get* away!'

Even then she'd held Miska away from him, pushing him back with her hand, batting him away as the carriage filled with water and the storm raged around them.

Her last words on this earth had been an admonishment, a reminder she did not want him, that he wasn't hers, as Miska was, that even in death she could not abide him.

Hannibal took a breath, the tremble becoming a shudder. He wiped at his face impatiently, pushing the memory away, shuttering it up again behind the walls he'd built to protect himself. He conjured all of his fond moments with his sister instead, those cherished times when her laughter filled the world, long afternoons spent exploring the gardens and catching fireflies in the dusk.

He smiled then despite his sorrow, recalling her dashing about in her mother's discarded gown, bawling at the top of her lungs that she would be Queen one day. "Do you remember what I said to you then, Miska, hm? I said you were already my Queen..."

'*She was an Omega...*'

'*Disappointment implies expectation, Will. Did you have expectations of me?*'

'*Once, maybe, but only for a short time...*'

'*I exist, Lord Clarges. That is offensive enough on its own...*'

Hannibal flinched, imagining what he would have done to any person who had treated Miska as he had treated Will. Had anyone dared insult her, called her repellent, sent her fleeing from her new home in nothing but her underclothes, been even a fraction as nasty and spiteful with her as he'd been with Will Grant.

He would most certainly have killed them.

"I have missed you, my little darling, so very, very much," he whispered, tears forming in his eyes because no matter how long it had been, he would never stop longing to see her again. "*So* much. I only hope, had you lived, you would have made me someone much different than I am now."

She would not, he knew, love him for his treatment of Will, and he could not, he knew, continue along the same path of blind prejudice he had followed since her death. Had he known years ago, perhaps he would have changed, but there was no way to go back and change the things that had already happened, much as one might wish to.

Changing the future, however, was entirely within the realm of possibility.

Wiping his face with his handkerchief, Hannibal took a steadying breath and left Miska's final resting place with a loving, lingering look.

He did not stop at his father's grave, stranger that he had always been, a stern and bewildering taskmaster resenting the place Hannibal held in Grandfather's heart.

He moved instead to stand silently at Melinda's grave for the first time.

He brought no flowers, nothing to appease a spirit which must no doubt rail against an unkind fate. He brought only himself, sixteen years removed from the boy who had looked down into her face as she'd died and refused to grant her forgiveness.

"How bitterly you must hate me now," he breathed, stiff and somber at the foot of her grave. "Gone all these years and your secrets buried with you."

He crouched down, fingers digging into the shorn grass and deeper into the crumbling earth, as if he could reach down and find her sleeping, Snow White waiting for a prince who never came.

"I always imagined I could never forgive you," he told her, reaching for a memory of her, surprised that the details of her face came back so effortlessly. "The moment you died—" He cut off, flinching when the memory was there before him. "I should have said I forgave you, Melinda, even though I hadn't then. I should have said it and let you rest. You were young and foolish and had the misfortune to have only myself to turn to. Sixteen years too late, Melinda, but I forgive you and I hope, wherever you are, that you can forgive me, in turn."

He pushed to his feet, tears misting his eyes but refusing to fall.

"I have forgiveness of my own to earn," he said, taking a deep breath. "I will have to tell your story one day, Melinda, *our story*, and soon. Believe me when I say the one I will tell it to would never judge you. He is a far better man than I am..."

He felt the breeze pick up again, a brush of life against his face, and for an instant he imagined she was smoothing his cheek as she so often had.

"I am so sorry for what you suffered, Melinda," he whispered, and quietly left the cemetery, knowing it was but the first of many apologies he would soon have to make.

⌘⌘⌘

Will arrived back to Hartford House that afternoon to an unusual reception. Namely, a furor.

It was quite unusual to see the staff of Hartford House at a loss, but Will knew as he reached the house that they were, indeed, entirely at just such an unfortunate event.

His curiosity momentarily tamping down his anxious suspicions about Hannibal, Will rode up to the small group of gathered footmen and the tall, rather surprising figure they seemed to be watching.

"May I help?" he offered, reining the mare to a stop with a slight smile on his face.

The scent of an Alpha teased his nose, wood smoke and leather and strangely familiar.

"Lord Clarges," the Alpha said, turning towards him and sweeping off his hat, his voice soft and husky, his posture strangely diffident for so large an Alpha. "I've been sent by your sister, Lady Rathmore. Do you remember me, Lord Clarges?"

He looked up at Will with such earnest hope that his desire to be recognized could almost be tasted.

"Francis," Will breathed, his memories aligning the scent and the sight of him to his childhood. "Francis Doranhouse. Yes, I remember you."

He dismounted, handing his tired mare off to one of the staff so he could ask, "Why have you not gone into the house? Is there some problem?"

Mr. Hawkes, harried and annoyed at being late to greet him, appeared in the doorway to offer, "Mr. Doranhouse has refused to come in. I do apologize for the inconvenience. It is extremely unusual for an Alpha to be in such a position."

Will nodded, recognizing the issue at once. Francis had, for his own reasons, decided to wait without for Will's acceptance and, being an Alpha, the rest of the staff did not feel comfortable forcing the issue. It was bound to cause more problems in the future, he knew, but for now he was relieved to have someone near him who was not connected to Hartford House and had nothing to gain from misleading him.

"Would Lord Clarges not come?" Will asked, wondering why his husband had not made an appearance by now, drawn by the tension and the scent of another Alpha.

"Lord Clarges left some few hours after you, Mr. Grant—"

"*Lord Clarges*," Francis corrected, bristling slightly.

"Please, Francis," Will said, lifting his hand but hesitating to touch him. Though he could match the man before him to the youth he'd known as a child, he was not entirely sure he should be so familiar with him. "The staff all call me Mr. Grant, as should you. And I apologize for your reception. You are very welcome here."

Francis relaxed, the tension running out of his rather alarming frame, which dissipated the strange consternation and worry gripping the servants of Hartford House.

"Mr. Doranhouse will be accompanying me about," Will announced, looking at each of them in turn. "My sister, Lady Rathmore, is planning to join me here at Hartford House and has sent Mr. Doranhouse ahead. As he has come both at her request as well as my own, I hope you will treat him kindly and give him every accommodation Hartford House can offer."

"We have taken the liberty of preparing a place in the men's quarters for Mr. Doranhouse," Mr. Hawkes said, firmly back in control of the situation. "If you would like to go 'round to the back entrance, Mr. Doranhouse, I will have one of the boys familiarize you."

"Thank you," Francis softly said, but hesitated before producing a letter from his jacket and offering it to Will.

"What's this?" Will asked, taking it while Mr. Hawkes stood watching, politely waiting to assist. Frowning, Will turned the envelope over in his hands, finding no markings at all except his name and a plain wax seal hastily and sloppily applied.

"How did you come to be in possession of this?" he asked, searching Francis' face.

"I stopped in town to ask the way," Francis murmured. "A boy from the village brought it to me, Mr. Grant. When I asked him where he got it, he would not say, not even with a promise of candies. He was a wild little boy, Mr. Grant. I was reluctant to accept it."

"I am glad you did, for my sake," Will said, slipping his finger beneath the wax seal and prying it up, ripping the cheap paper somewhat. He unfolded it, his concern growing with every heartbeat.

He did not recognize the writing and there was no signature, he noticed at once. He read it once, then again, his heart pounding hard in his chest, hoping the second time the contents would have changed.

Mr. Grant,

You are in mortal danger. Your husband intends you harm; indeed, he has attempted once already to murder you, just as he did the former Lady Clarges. Please, consider this warning from a place of good intentions and remove yourself at once from Hartford House!

"Mr. Grant?" Mr. Hawkes inquired, concern replacing his usual stoic calm. "Are you quite alright, Mr. Grant?"

Francis watched him with unblinking, unsettling intensity, as if able to taste Will's anxiety.

"Yes," Will said, barely a whisper. He folded the letter and pushed it into his jacket pocket, clearing his throat to say with more conviction, "Yes, I am quite well, thank you."

The girth strap breaking had not been an accident and Will had never told anyone of it outside of Matthew Dunn, who would certainly never send him such a letter. Only someone who had cut the strap or else witnessed it being cut would know his accident was no accident, in truth. It did occur to Will to wonder if the culprit might not be the one sending him the letter, but there was nothing anyone could gain from trying to separate him from his husband when they were little better than strangers to one another. It did seem more reasonable that the warning was genuine and the threat real.

"Mr. Grant," Francis said, pitching his voice low so only Will would hear him. "If there is something I should know... "

"Ah! And here comes Lord Clarges," Mr. Hawkes remarked, sounding vastly relieved. "What wondrous timing he has."

Francis tensed and Will turned, stepping back into the shadow the large Alpha threw.

Hannibal, spying Will lingering out front, urged his horse to gallop the last stretch to Hartford House and drew up short when the acrid, sulfuric scent of another Alpha reached him.

"I've been looking for you," he said, choosing to address his mate first, his eyes sweeping from Will's slender, composed form to the tall, glowering Alpha hovering just behind him.

"I went to Duxbury," Will said, assessing Hannibal as he dismounted, flushed and bright-eyed from his outing. Will shielded his gaze with his lashes, studying Hannibal's reaction when he said, "I wanted to see where your relatives are buried."

"Unfortunately, the most annoying among them have not yet been planted there," Hannibal said, offering Will a wry smirk. He tipped his head towards the Alpha and asked, "And may I ask who your visitor is?"

"Francis Doranhouse," the Alpha said, bristling as if Hannibal offered some threat. Almost as an afterthought he added, "My Lord."

"Francis is the guard I spoke to you of," Will said, unnerved by the tension which rose between the two of them. Mr. Hawkes, never a fool, hastily gestured the waiting footmen back inside in case things escalated.

"Ah, Mr. Doranhouse," Hannibal said, wondering why Francis was staring at him with such intensity, but finding himself returning it, his instincts prickling in response. "Of course, you're here to prepare the place for Lady Rathmore's comfort, I expect? And when is she due to arrive?"

"She comes as she pleases," Francis said. "My Lord."

"Mr. Doranhouse, if you will go 'round to the back, please," Mr. Hawkes said, choosing an opportune moment to intervene. "We will get you settled directly."

The look in his eyes skirted the edge of a challenge, but he obeyed Mr. Hawkes with surprising meekness once Will gave a nod, vanishing around the side of the House with his fire and iron scent lingering to wrinkle Hannibal's nose.

"You failed to mention that Mr. Doranhouse is an Alpha," Hannibal said once he had gone, gesturing Will ahead of him through the door which Mr. Hawkes graciously held wide for them.

"Are you rethinking your stance that I am not bonded?" Will asked, turning over his hat and the basket to the staff. "Perhaps Francis is my Alpha and I have merely brought my lover here to spite you, as you wished to spite me."

"No, I am *not* rethinking my stance," Hannibal said, glowering at him. "You are far too honest to have been lying and far too proper to have concocted such an inelegant situation, but I find it troubling nonetheless."

"It makes little difference," Will said, putting some distance between them as they moved through the dim, cool foyer. "You cannot refuse his presence."

"I have no means or right to refuse his presence, little thought I like the idea of an Alpha dogging the steps of my unbound spouse," Hannibal said, pausing there on the carpet and turning to face Will, whose eyes were even more elusive than usual. "There is a reason Alphas are not admitted into service, Will. They tend to provoke their employers."

"Unless you are less than half the Alpha you believe you are," Will said, his blue eyes fastening on Hannibal's for a split second, firm and fiery, "then you should have little problem establishing your control over the staff of Hartford House, Francis included. But you should not trouble yourself, Lord Clarges. He has come at the insistence of my sister and father and will be attaching himself to me."

Hannibal frowned. "I have myriad issues with that statement, Will."

"None of which involve you or require your attention," Will shot back. "Please, excuse me—"

"Will, wait," Hannibal said, reaching out to lay his hand on Will's arm. There was no force behind his touch but Will stilled all the same, his nostrils flaring and his anxiety spiking. Hannibal dropped his hand immediately, his fingers brushing over the fabric of Will's jacket. "Did you find anything of interest in Duxbury?"

"Yes," Will said, staring up at him with a directness that spoke volumes to his husband. "A great many things, Hannibal."

Those large blue eyes flicked over him, taking in the minute details he drew such unsettling conclusions from. Hannibal was not at all surprised to hear him ask, "Why does it concern you that I should know of your past, Hannibal?"

Hannibal took a deep breath, knowing Will could have gotten little more than a sum of dates laced together with his curious intuition, unless that young lady of his had given him the generally-accepted fate of his former wife.

"There is little happiness in my past, Will," he said, noticing how his mate responded to his honesty with almost imperceptible softening. "And little worth speaking of. I am frightened of the image you will have of me when all is said and done."

Will's mouth curved down in a frown. Thoughtful, he softly ventured, "Please, do not waste a moment of worry on my estimation of you, Hannibal, as I have never wasted a moment of my own regarding your estimation of me."

"Then we are agreed not to trouble one another," Hannibal said, a strange sinking feeling fluttering through his stomach.

312

They scaled the stairs, the silence between them a ghost of what might have been had things not gone so terribly wrong.

Wishing his usual charm would not abandon him in the presence of his young mate, Hannibal said, "I thought considering the prior instance, I should tell you that I intend to have a soak... unless you wish to do so?"

Will cleared his throat and said, "No, thank you. Were there locks on the doors, it would not be an issue."

"I will have that remedied," Hannibal said, lingering in the hall outside of Will's suite, reluctant to leave him. Strange as it felt to admit it freely, he enjoyed Will's prickly company and wanted to find a way to mend the damage he'd done, especially after the soul-searching he had done over Miska's grave.

"Don't trouble yourself," Will said again, turning away, his hand on the door of his suite. "I will be leaving soon and you won't need them."

Hannibal frowned to be reminded of Will's departure, frowned at the way he would not look at him, wondering at his tense posture and frayed nerves. He was a far cry removed from the young man who'd lunched in the shade with a pretty girl from Duxbury.

"Will," he said, noting the faint gleam of worry in his mate's eyes when he stirred as if to come nearer. "I suppose it is too late to ask, but I realize no one has taken your tastes into account in regards to this marriage."

Bewildered, Will skated a glance at him and nervously asked, "Does anyone but a man get that luxury?"

Hannibal sighed. "Not usually, no, but in your case I feel it is rather important. You have lived your life as a beta male. I wonder if your tastes must match."

"Match?" Will asked, feeling increasingly agitated by the direction of this conversation and certain he would not enjoy what it was steering towards.

"Many beta males prefer women," Hannibal said, somewhat taken by Will's vivid flush and awkward retreat, as if striving to put distance between them would somehow lessen the severity of his discomfit.

"I prefer women to be as any other person on this earth," Will said, horrified by what was being so gently prodded at. "If you mean to inquire as to my *other appetites*, it will please you to know I have none!"

Hannibal's brows rose. "None?" he echoed, cocking his head with a soft half-smile eloquent of disbelief. Trying to cajole just a glimpse of Will's sharp humor from him, he added, "Even so moral a person as yourself will have *other appetites*, Chaplain Grant."

"I will not discuss this," Will said, indignant, fully prepared to go into his suite and slam the door in Hannibal's face to escape this awful conversation. "Have you so little respect for me that you would engage me in a conversation so tasteless?"

"*Taste* is precisely what this conversation revolves around," Hannibal said, exasperated. "And I ask because I *do* respect you and *will* respect your answer, Will. Do your preferences lie with women, or do they lie with men?"

"If I said 'women', Lord Clarges, then would you cease your misguided attempts to please your grandfather?" Will asked, hoping it would be so easy that such a small and unimportant lie could change things for the better. He might even escape Hartford House with his life and limbs intact.

"Sadly, no," Hannibal said, disappointed by his answer, his hope of living here with Will suffering a heavy blow. "It is our duty, Will, whatever our preferences, and," he hesitated, thinking of the blonde woman Will had been with, how disappointing their own coupling would no doubt be for his husband, and added, "however distasteful it may be."

Will's brows rose, his flush fading.

"A distasteful discharge of duty," he said, angling a fathomless look Hannibal's way. "How charming. Let's both be grateful my disinterest in you spares us the horror we might otherwise face. Your virtue is perfectly safe with me, Lord Clarges, however little it is worth."

Before Hannibal could say one word to explain, Will opened the door of his suite with forced calm and strode within as quickly as he could before closing it firmly in Hannibal's face.

⌘⌘⌘

Hannibal had not been prepared for Will's reaction, nor his own strange response to it.

'*...however little it is worth...*'

It stung him, that soft barb delivered with such placid calm. It stung him because Will was right, he knew. Though it was expected conduct of gentlemen to seek the pleasure of company where they pleased in lieu of a spouse's favors, he did not at all enjoy feeling... *cheap*.

Hannibal retreated to his suite to wash off the travel dust, casting more than one glance at the washroom door that fed onto Will's room. He had the strangest compulsion to seek him out and admit he had seen Will in Duxbury with a woman, to ask him how he knew her and who she was, to find out the truth of where Will's desires ran.

To be honest and tell him it did not seem a horror, that duty did not have to be onerous.

Sex and love were things Hannibal had little interest in for the most part, outside of the purpose they could serve from those around him, but his interests were leaning towards Will with surprising regularity. He had never been demonstrative that he could ever remember, not since the loss of Miska. Even his companions had been kept at arm's length, given only enough of his attention to keep them from pestering him with complaints, but otherwise serving their purpose for him.

But Will was Uncommon.

When he ran, Hannibal wanted to chase after him.

When he was distressed, Hannibal wanted to soothe him.

When he was angry, Hannibal wanted to witness his temper.

He was perplexing, intelligent, perceptive, and unpredictable.

And Hannibal was hungry for more.

He had to find a way around Will's resistance, he knew. It no longer depended on the Addendum—there must be a child eventually to carry on the Ledford name, yes, but not for the sake of regaining control of Hartford House. Will's child would be heir for both of them, inheriting Hartford House regardless. Nothing had to change about that and Hannibal was determined to keep it that way.

His plans had folded at right-angles from their original intent. The thought of securing Hartford House through Will had lost its appeal. In just a short time of knowing him, the empty shell he had imagined in the place of his spouse had found flesh. He was a young man, badly used through not fault of his own, forced into circumstances he had not asked for by those who never asked his opinions. He had feelings, hopes, and dreams, all of which had been soundly discounted by the person who was supposed to be his partner in life. And Hannibal, ignorant of Omegas, never more than negligently interested in personal relationships, had handled him with all the care of a bull in a china shop.

"Well," he said, dressing after his bath and still thoughtful, but determined to seek a new start. "I do not have to repeat those mistakes."

"M'Lord?" Berger asked, putting the finishing touches on dressing him and curious about his statement.

"Have my horse brought around, Berger," he said, deciding. "And send word to Grandfather that I'm heading to Fernhill."

"Ah, yes, m'Lord," Berger said. Then, after a hesitant pause, he asked, "You're not after Lord du Millau?"

Hannibal chuckled, amused. "No, Berger. If was going to call my cousin out, I'd have done it six years ago. Let us hope Bedelia has not packed off back to the Capital as yet, now that the Garden Party has concluded."

"Of course, m'Lord!" Berger said. He scurried off to do as he was bidden, leaving Hannibal fairly well pleased with himself.

He would see Bedelia and find out just precisely what it would take to appeal to Will's Omegan nature. They could learn together, he and Will, more about each other, more about themselves. They could learn to tolerate one another and, eventually, enjoy one another's company. The rest, surely, would sort just fine from there and they could work something out between them to their mutual satisfaction. Love wasn't necessary to create a connection, after all. Kindness and polite attention, as Grandfather had told him, could serve just as well to begin with. One had to start somewhere, after all.

It wasn't as if either one of them any illusions about love.

So what other way could there possibly be?

⌘⌘⌘

Will did not wait to calm himself once he gained the privacy of his suite. He went directly to his jewelry box and pried up the lining to secrete the letter beneath, hopefully hiding it well enough to keep it from prying eyes.

The contents, however, were not so easy to dismiss.

Hannibal was responsible for his accident.

Will wiped his brow, tugging fretfully at his neckerchief, overwarm and anxious.

He heard movement in the washroom, the slosh of water as his husband bathed. His memory conjured the image of Hannibal the day he'd burst in on his bath, stripped to his waist and still shedding clothes, his inherent Alpha strength slumbering but never entirely absent.

A strength he would turn against Will without compunction.

"I am never unarmed," he breathed, blotting at his damp brow with his sleeve. "I am *never* unarmed."

He calmed by slow degrees, soothed by the mantra he knew to his core was true—he had his wits, he had his knowledge, he had his Gift, and with those things he was far more dangerous an opponent than his husband might expect him to be.

"You are not an Omega, Will Grant," he said, staring sternly at his reflection, bolstering his confidence in his own strength. "You are not a man, nor a woman. You are only yourself and that is all you need be."

He rang downstairs and tended to his appearance in the time it took Jimmy to reach him.

"Jimmy, please have my mare saddled and bring a fresh horse for Mr. Doranhouse," he said, feeling Hannibal's presence just a room away like a physical touch against his nerves. "Mrs. Pimms has taken care of him, has she not?"

"Yes, Mr. Grant, he's fed and had tea and unpacked already," Jimmy said, his smile uncertain. "Rather hasty man, your Mr. Doranhouse."

"In this instance his efficiency serves my purpose," Will said, relieved. "Tell him he is to meet me downstairs. I'll be tending to some estate business this afternoon and he is to accompany me."

"Mr. Grant," Jimmy said, reluctant to do so and disturbed by his plans. "Are you sure you should be alone with a stranger who also happens to be a pretty intimidating Alpha—"

"He is no stranger to me," Will said, though that was not entirely true, as he recalled little about Francis in the least from his childhood.

But Mina had sent him, and Mina, for all of her spoiled behavior, was the one person in the world who had ever tried to shield him, little though she had succeeded.

She was his twin, another half to his to make a whole, and he trusted her now as he always had—fully and without any option to do otherwise.

"Mr. Grant, if I may—"

"Please, Jimmy," Will said, weary and worn. "Please, do as I say."

"Of course, Mr. Grant," Jimmy said, contrite. "He'll be waiting downstairs. And in case it might matter, Mr. Grant, Lord Clarges has asked for his horse to be saddled, so you might take a few moments."

"Thank you, Jimmy," Will breathed, glad to have been warned, and waited in the silent room once Jimmy left, listening for some indication Hannibal had already gone.

It was only once he heard him descend downstairs that Will wondered where he might be going or, worse, who he might have gone to see now that he knew he would find no welcome in Will's own bed.

Chapter 18

The rhythmic, relentless ticking of the clock over the mantle filled the growing silence and Hannibal shifted in the stiff, uncomfortable parlor chair, pinned beneath his cousin's cool, assessing blue gaze.

She blinked, a soft frown pursing her mouth.

"Bedelia," Hannibal said, striving for patience. "Have you anything to say? If you prefer to stare silently at me, I will return to Hartford House—"

"I am... attempting to find something beneficial to say to you," she informed him, an expression of polite horror tightening her smooth features as she settled her teacup delicately on the saucer in her opposite hand. "Considering what you have just told me."

What he had told her was, of course, everything. Everything to do with Will, at least. How he had reacted, the words he had said, the actions he had taken since the moment they had met.

It felt like hours since he had stopped speaking, hours in which Bedelia silently watched him, sipping at a cup that never seemed to empty.

"And yet in all of that I never heard you speak of a bond," she said, and Hannibal shifted in his seat again, fidgety as a child. She cocked her head, watching him as if he was some oddity on display.

"Will is not bonded to anyone," he said. "You were mistaken."

"Mistaken," she softly echoed, an amused smile curving her lips.

"*Yes,*" Hannibal said, summoning a scowl. "He insists no one is bonded to him. I believe him."

"You *choose* to believe him," Bedelia corrected.

"I trust he tells me the truth," Hannibal said, surprising her.

After a long silence, she murmured, "That is, perhaps, the most comforting thing I have heard you say thus far."

"Comforting enough that you will help me to understand what I have neglected up to this point?" Hannibal asked, somber and serious.

Her mouth pursed with the force of her thoughts. She gazed at him, assessing him, and softly said, "One of the first things an Alpha child is taught, Hannibal, is that touch holds a sacred place between us and Omegas. It conveys things even our intentions might deny us. The slightest touch can deeply affect an Omega and, in turn, affect the one who reached out."

Hannibal considered it, thinking of Will's reactions to him.

"I have great difficulty imagining you could be so entirely thoughtless in your dealings with Will," she said, gathering herself for a stern lecture. "In some respects, you are incredibly and undeservedly lucky that Will Grant was clearly not raised as most Omegan children are, or he would already be far beyond your reach... or the reach of any other Alpha."

Filled with discomfort and guilt, Hannibal restlessly reached for his own teacup and took a sip. He honestly wished it was something stronger, but no matter how uncomfortable or odd this meeting would no doubt become, he was determined to see it through.

He had to find a way to reach Will.

He had to find a way to both understand his Omegan nature as well as give Will the opportunity to explore it himself, instead of forcing him to restrain even the least of his instincts.

"Your father should have taught you."

"You know he did not," Hannibal said, avoiding her gaze. "Rather, what he taught me instead."

"And by the time you came to Grandfather, it was too late to... undo the damage regarding your instincts," she observed, and exhaled a soft, heavy sigh. "I can only inform you, Hannibal. I cannot make you understand at the level a child's acceptance grants us."

"If I am informed, I can make my way from there," Hannibal said, meeting her gaze directly. "I offend him. Without meaning to, I blunder gracelessly into places we both are unaware of and neither one of us knows how we got there or how to get back out again without bloodshed. I need to understand how to connect with him. I need to understand where I am going wrong."

Bedelia considered, then reached out to pull the velveteen cord next to the fireplace, still watching him.

The Fernhill butler turned up with near immediacy, silent and attentive.

"Lord Clarges will be staying for dinner," she said, a slight smile appearing. "We will take a tray here for two. Please inform mother we do not wish to be disturbed."

"Yes, my Lady."

"We have a great deal of work to do, Hannibal," Bedelia murmured, settling in with cat-like satisfaction. "I do hope you've come prepared."

Hannibal thought of Will, of Miska, of the Omega who had raised him and her entourage which had shaped the entirety of his perception regarding her gender.

His voice was firm and steady when he told her, "Yes. I am entirely prepared."

⌘⌘⌘

It was a relief for Will to get back to his routine, however little his husband and grandfather wanted him doing his work. Francis rode with him, silent and unobtrusive but watchful in a way that left Will with no doubt that Mina had confided her fears in him. It made him feel slightly less vulnerable, but not more safe.

He could only rely on himself for that.

They rode his rounds, and Will had to ignore the weighty knowledge this was all just a breath away from being lost to him along with the life he had managed to build here.

Things, he was forced to admit, were *already* being lost to him. The tenants and farmers were all polite to him. Far too polite, truth to be told. The loss of their prior easy camaraderie forcefully brought home the fact that Hannibal's efforts had managed the desired effect.

He was no longer Mr. Grant, land agent and employee of Hartford House.

He was William Ledford, Marquess of Clarges, equal in rank and importance to his husband and, thus, pushed beyond the boundaries of their comfort with him.

"Mr. Grant," Francis said, so softly Will almost did not hear him over the cheerful chirping of birds. He looked over at the Alpha riding a proper distance away, his brows rising in inquiry.

"Your thoughts look heavy," Francis said.

"They are," Will said, and hesitated. He longed to confide in someone, to confess his fears, and there was no one in Hartford House with whom he dared do so, not even Jimmy. Roland was likely complicit in whatever had befallen the former Lady Clarges, and that lost him his most powerful ally. Though he did not doubt the strength of Grandfather's affection for him, he knew it would never outweigh the love he had for his grandson, nor should it. If Hannibal managed to send him to an early grave, Roland would move to conceal it.

And who would mourn his loss?

The thought prompted him to confirm, "Did my sister speak to you of my situation?"

"Yes," Francis said, his blue eyes turning back to their surroundings, restlessly flicking as if searching for danger even on such a benign, relaxed, late afternoon. "Did you tell anyone about your saddle?"

"No," Will said, somber. "It wouldn't have done any good."

Francis frowned, considering, and said, "Mr. Grant, you know your sister loves you very much. Should anything happen, she would not let the matter rest."

"I appreciate that, Francis," Will said, offering him a smile. "I would rather not give her reason, however. I would prefer no more accidents befell me."

"We wouldn't like for anything bad to happen to you, either," Francis said, his cautious tone plucking at Will's nerves. "Lord Clarges is back now and we're all... worried."

Will blew out a soft breath, trying to gain control of himself. "I find myself worried as well, Francis. I am afraid I am somewhat better informed than I previously was."

"The former Lady Clarges?" Francis asked, looking back at him again with piercing intensity.

"You know about her?" Will asked, startled. "Francis, *how* do you know about her? No one speaks of her here."

"Plenty spoke of her at the time, Mr. Grant," Francis said, breaking his gaze to shift in his saddle, his voice gruff when he added, "And Lady Rathmore had me find out about her some months ago."

Some months ago.

Will's eyes narrowed, uncomfortable suspicion squeezing around him. Trying to allay it, he asked, "Francis, why was Mina asking after the former Lady Clarges months ago? She has had six years, after all, to sate her curiosity... why now?"

"She did not say," Francis said, and that had to suffice. "Only that she was concerned for you and wanted to know what he had done."

Will nodded stiffly, patting the mare when she shifted in response to his unease. "And did you find out, Francis? Do you know what happened to Melinda Ledford?"

"No, Mr. Grant," Francis said, chastened. "Just that she was young, and married but a short time before her death, and the talk in Duxbury was of his guilt."

"No more than I know, then," Will said, disappointed and feeling rather ill. "I hate to admit it, Francis, even to myself, but I am... frightened of Hannibal."

Mina's conversation with him at the Garden Party, Molly's tearful and angry recounting of her sister's sad fate, the letter he'd received, his saddle being cut— all of it forced his Gift to focus on the understanding that Hannibal was entirely capable of doing what he'd threatened to do six years before. He was the only one who could benefit from Will's death, after all. Will had never known anyone well enough or long enough to offer such a grave offense that someone would seek his life. Though he tried to deny it, over and over he came to the same conclusion, and each time he did so, his bond gave a mighty tug within him, a physical pain that caught him by surprise each time.

"Mr. Grant," Francis said, earnest. "If you need anything, anything at all, you can rely on us. I am here to watch over you. Your sister will be here soon. We will protect you."

"Thank you, Francis. It is reassuring to know I am not without friends. However, I do not intend to make a target of myself here, where I am no longer able to be the person I once was. As you have seen for yourself, news of my affiliation with Hartford House has already reached the four corners of the earth," Will said, huffing a sad, frustrated little laugh.

"It has, but it's clear no one cares for the way he's dealt with you, Mr. Grant," Francis told him, rather forcefully so. "No one cares to have a master who treats good, kind folk as he's treated you. What sort of man invites his mistress into the home he shares with his spouse?"

Will flushed and looked sharply at Francis, asking, "What are you talking about, Francis?" He knew full well no one could know of Hannibal's intentions to bring Miss Blume and their daughter to Hartford House, as the issue had been spoken of when they were alone. Nor had anyone from Hartford Town been present at the Garden Party where that clueless friend of Hannibal's had confirmed it.

"I beg your pardon, Mr. Grant," Francis said, immediately contrite. "When I stopped in town to rest my horse, before that little boy brought your letter, I overheard talk from some... unsavory woman. Apparently, he has called for her and she's to meet him up at the manor house, right under your nose."

"Francis, please—" Will said, heart clenching and stomach sinking.

"I wouldn't lie to you," Francis said, stiff with offense on Will's behalf. "She was talking about it even to strangers, crowing about it to everyone she saw how she's going up there to be with him. You don't have to stand for being treated so, Mr. Grant—"

"*There is nothing I can do!*" Will said, appalled at how sharp his voice was, but bitter in his anger. He softened his tone, took a deep breath, and said, "I have no means to change anything, Francis. I am powerless in that regard."

Francis' pale blue eyes flashed then with something Will was entirely too familiar with and recognized at once—a capacity for violence only just restrained. It was a dangerous gleam, and it accompanied dangerous words.

"You are never powerless. You have friends here now, Mr. Grant. Perhaps someone wanted to hurt you by cutting your girth strap. Perhaps someone wanted to kill you."

Will's heart roared in his ears, the noise of it trying to remind him that this was his life, however worthless it must seem to some, and he was terribly vulnerable to the man he'd bonded to.

"Wouldn't it be a relief, Mr. Grant, if you knew you had friends who could take care of that someone for your sake? Friends who gladly *would* take care of it?"

Will swallowed hard, trembling at the inference.

"Had I such friends, Francis," he said, careful with his words, almost calm to be faced with something so familiar as the threat of violence. "I would be grateful for them to wait such dedicated acts of loyalty until such time as I could fully appreciate them."

Francis smiled. It was nearly as unsettling to see as the sudden intensity that had gripped him. The strange gleam retreated, sequestered away once more behind the diffident, shy man he presented to the world.

But Will saw cracks in his mask, and what looked out at him breathed sulfur, testing powerful wings to strain the seams of the man before him.

It was deeply disturbing to think people could hide themselves so thoroughly, but deep down in his soul, in a place that would defiantly break before bending, Will realized he wasn't surprised at all. Everyone had a dark hidden heart, he knew, even himself.

Not all of them showed it as easily as Hannibal Ledford.

"Then I'll say nothing more about it, Mr. Grant," Francis said, inclining his head with a slight, secretive smile. "And be relieved to know you understand me."

"Oh, yes, Francis," Will said, thinking of the fall he'd taken, the dead Lady Clarges, the corner he was being backed into. "I understand you very well, indeed."

⌘⌘⌘

They returned home to a second round of chaos.

There was an unfamiliar coach in the drive Will only briefly noted was piled high with luggage before Francis murmured, "Your sister has come."

"Mina!" Will urged his mare into a trot, eager to reach his sister.

He heard her before he saw her, her voice raised with indignant outrage at how the footmen were handling her trunks.

"—my Lady, I am merely trying to convey that we are even now preparing a place—"

"*My brother has invited me!*" she said, and when Will hastily dismounted and reached the front door, it was to find his petite sister standing with her hands on her hips before a flustered and repentant Mr. Hawkes.

"Mr. Hawkes," Will said, inserting himself into the fray and drawing Mina back by her arm. "I do apologize, I had no idea my sister would arrive so soon. It was badly done of me to not inquire for the sake of the staff."

"*Will,* you don't apologize to *servants,*" Mina said in a scandalized whisper.

"Mina, please, hush," Will said, taking both her hands in his to offer Mr. Hawkes a smile. "Please, Mr. Hawkes, have Mrs. Henderson send the girls to prepare the Victoria Suite." He looked back at Mina, telling her, "It is close to mine, Mina. The best suite in the house aside from my own and Hannibal's."

Moderately mollified, she glanced around and asked, "And where is Hannibal?"

"I really couldn't say," Will admitted, drawing her inside, Francis and his strange behavior almost forgotten behind him.

"Heavens, how little regard he has for you!" Mina complained, allowing Will to escort her to the drawing room while her trunks were taken upstairs. "What a horrid man he is!"

"Mina, please," Will said, hoping none of the servants had heard her. "He is well-respected and a man of importance. It is not wise to disparage him in his own home."

"You mean *your* home," she corrected, flouncing down onto a settee with Will next to her and dragging her hat off with a sigh.

Alarmed, Will asked, "How did you know of that arrangement? I was given to know it was not made public."

"Oh, *darling*," Mina sighed, laughing. "It was the biggest to-do in town when it happened! *Everyone* knew about how he'd left Hartford House in a fury with his ancestral home handed over to his new spouse! Goodness, the chatter could've burned the ears off a devil!"

Will frowned, feeling rather ill again, his temperature rising once more, a light sheen of sweat appearing on his upper lip and brow.

It was little wonder Hannibal wished to kill him. He had no idea how a man as proud as his husband could stand for such gossip for six whole years.

"Is Francis tiring yet?" Mina asked, unaware of his silent reflection, choosing instead to fuss with her dress. "He is so dogged in his tasks, I felt I should never get rid of him!"

"He isn't bothersome in the least," Will told her, his smile fading somewhat when he recalled Francis' threatening words spoken in an offer of assistance. "It is a relief to have him here, to have both of you here beside me."

Mina's smile was bright and wide, a painful reminder to Will of how his own smile might have looked had things gone differently. But there was some measure of satisfaction to be felt in seeing a face so similar to his own so entirely happy and without cares. It was the law of his life with his sister—if he could not be happy, then she should be, and a part of him would feel it through her.

"Ah! You will not introduce me to His Grace in such a state, I hope!" she said, alarm coloring her features with a pretty pink blush. "My maid will need a day, at least, to get my wardrobe presentable! I cannot face such a great man as I am, Will!"

"No, Mina, I would never insist and neither would he," Will assured her, smiling at her fussing. "He has been reclusive these last few years. His health is not what it could be and he sleeps more than he would prefer, but he has earned his rest."

"No doubt your husband hopes it to be eternal!" she said.

"Mina! That is entirely inappropriate!" Will scolded. "He may despise *me*, but Hannibal has nothing but love for his family! Honestly, the things you say!"

He stood, agitated and uneasy, the mention of his husband reminding him of what else Francis had said—the Widow Reynolds and her bragging, making lies of Hannibal's assurances they were not and would not be lovers. He wanted to believe it was nothing more than a stupid woman making a thoughtless play for advantage, but in his current dark frame of mind, he couldn't help but dwell on it, wondering if it was true.

Will turned his eyes to the window, worry wrinkling his brow, thinking that Hannibal might even now be in Hartford Town with her, plotting how best to manage his murder.

"I am so dreadfully tired, darling," Mina said, heaving a hefty sigh. She craned a look at him, assessing him with her own shrewd intuition. "It's such a long ride from the Capital and I got such an early start to get here before dinner."

"I know, Mina," Will said, pulled from his thoughts to soothe her, a smile curving his lips. "I am sorry. I had no idea when you were arriving and Francis could not tell me."

"Well, it's all worth it to be with you," she said, delighted to have his attention once again. "How glad I am that I came, Will. You will surely need me now, with your husband home with such intentions. How lucky we both are I could arrive so quickly, aren't we, darling?"

"Yes, Mina," Will said, as he knew he must. "We are both of us lucky."

His sister smiled like a lively, lovely mirror, reflecting his best back at him, well pleased.

⌘⌘⌘

Will escorted his sister upstairs once her suite was ready and visited with her there as Gretchen, her maid, unpacked with the help of the Hartford Staff. Despite her insistence she was near dead from exhaustion, Mina kept up a lively stream of chatter on the current events in the Capital and Will was desperate enough for distraction to simply listen. It was an easy, impermanent escape, imaging the world as she saw it—glittering and bright, full of sights and sounds and smells that were all uncharted territory for him, meeting people from distant lands and famous public personalities. It was a world in which Mina absolutely belonged, and a world which Will knew he himself would never see, never *fit*.

He had never fit anywhere. Not even here at Hartford.

"But darling, you just let me go on!" Mina scolded, emerging from her washroom pink and rosy from the heat of her bath, which she'd taken with the door standing wide, as was her habit.

"I enjoy hearing you speak of your adventures in the Capital, Mina," Will said, moving from the open doorway to the dressing room, where he'd stood with his back to her just for the sake of propriety, idly watching Ms. Spark arrange Mina's vast and surprising wardrobe. "But how is your husband? You have said nothing of him."

"He is as happy as a man can ever be," Mina sighed, pushing past him to vanish within. Will was relieved when Gretchen closed the door to dress her mistress, though he could still hear Mina's vibrant voice saying, "He drinks, he gambles, he buys jewels for his mistress, and he bores me to tears on those rare occasions when we happen to speak. I am glad to be parted from him, darling, I assure you."

"I had worried you would miss him terribly," Will said, situating himself in the little chair next to the window, looking out at the scenery again, the familiar boundaries of his world for the past six years. "I wish you were happier, Mina."

"I am far happier than you are, Will," she said, and there was a long pause filled with her cursing at her maid softly before she emerged in her undergarments and dressing down, flushed but smiling. She sat across from him, watching him with a small smile. "But you must tell me everything, Will. That letter of yours was appallingly short and we had no chance to truly speak."

"What would you like me to tell you?" Will asked, tearing his gaze away from the window to rest on her face, his eyes meeting hers.

"Everything," she said, shifting forward just enough to take his hand and kiss it before squeezing it in both of her own. "What was it like when you got here? What happened to make him leave? How have you spent the last six years, dearest? You can confide in me, Will. We are twins, are we not? Surely, after all this time, alone and friendless in this ghastly place, you must long for someone to talk to without hesitation? I am that person for you, Will. I have always been that person, haven't I?"

"Hartford House is not *ghastly*, Mina! It is beautiful and I have spent these many years comfortably enough. It is only my experience with Hannibal that has been... unpleasant," Will breathed, uncomfortable just thinking of it. "But perhaps it is relevant, Mina. Six years ago he threatened to have me killed."

She remained silent, simply holding onto him, her cool little hands warming in his.

Will searched her face, took a deep breath, and he told her everything.

It took longer than he thought, and was harder than he imagined it would be, but once the words started, they flooded out of him like a dam had broken. His memory replayed every instance with such accuracy that he could, word for word, recount to his sister every exchange he had with his husband from the moment of their meeting, and she listened with wide-eyed attentiveness.

By the time he finished catching her up to date, she was even more convinced Hannibal was the one behind the incident.

"I am so profoundly relieved I am here with you, Will," she breathed, kissing his hand again and pressing it to her cheek. "To think I might have lost you! He could come into this room at any moment and do you to death in your bed! Goodness, how frightful! What a terrible cloud to live under, being hated in your own home and so deeply reviled! What an awful, unkind man he is, to keep you trapped in this marriage when all you wish is to go away!"

"I have made arrangements, Mina," Will said, her words carrying a barb he hadn't expected to feel. "I will be leaving Hartford House. I will give you notice, however, so you and Francis may join me when I do. I wouldn't expect you would prefer to remain here with Hannibal as company."

"Heavens, Will, I should rather fling myself out of the window!" she said, letting go of him to surge to her feet. "But look at the time! Goodness, how long we've spent here speaking of your misfortune! I find it has all quite drained me, darling. Please, allow me a little time to rest and order my thoughts before dinner?"

"Of course, Mina," Will said, standing and touching her shoulder. When she glanced back at him, he gave her a soft squeeze and said, "I truly am glad you've come. I have so longed to see you."

"I have come and I will stay," she said, the intensity of her words somewhat surprising him. "I will stay until this all is settled, Will."

He let go of her and dropped his hand, strangely uneasy, and retreated a pace.

"Thank you, Mina," he breathed, and excused himself from her suite.

He headed towards his own set of rooms with the intentions of dealing with some built up estate correspondence, hoping it would help to settle the odd alarm his sister had raised in him. He was stopped at his door by Mrs. Henderson on her way up the stairs with a tray for his sister.

"Ah! Mr. Grant! His Grace wishes to see you before dinner," she called, pausing on her way to address him. "I do hope the menu will suffice?"

"Oh, yes, Mrs. Henderson, it will serve very nicely," Will assured her, smiling to allay her worries. "My sister tends to speak before she thinks and can be particular in her tastes. Please let Mrs. Pimms know it is no reflection on her skill and her efforts are always above and beyond what we expect or deserve."

Mrs. Henderson gave him a soft, knowing smile and said, "I will, Mr. Grant! And thank you for being so thoughtful of us."

Will left her with a smile, making his way to Grandfather's suite and entering after a soft knock. He found Grandfather settled with a tray in his bed, Zeitler at close, if rather lax, attendance.

"You wished to see me, Grandfather?" Will asked, moving closer but not sitting down.

Zeitler was snapped from his idle inattention by Roland angling a hard look at one of the chairs placed nearby. The good-natured valet hastily retrieved one and placed it for Will to sit, gesturing gallantly at it, which only earned him another dark look from Grandfather.

"You cheeky little brat, go make yourself useful somewhere and leave us in peace!" Roland said, and Zeitler took the order with a wide grin and an irreverent, "Of course, Your Grace."

"That boy has never taken a thing seriously in his entire life," Grandfather complained once he had gone, inspecting his tray with a weary sigh, as if even the prospect of eating was tiresome. "What unfortunate luck I was so very fond of his mother!"

"Are you feeling unwell, Grandfather?" Will asked, concerned by how pale he was. "Would you like me to read to you?"

"No, no, Will," Roland said, smiling at him with genuine fondness. "No, I only wished to see you and tell you personally to pass along my excuses to Lady Rathmore, I am not quite up to being at table this evening."

"I am sorry, Grandfather, that I did not consult you—"

"Will, this is your home," Roland said, solemn. "Your family is welcome here, I only wish they had come before now so you were not so lonely all these years."

"I have not been terribly lonely, Grandfather," Will said, thinking of the nights he'd spent reading book after book to the aging Alpha before him, trading musing thoughts and listening avidly to Grandfather's recollections of distant lands he had visited as a boy. "I prefer my own company, or the company of just a few."

That won a wry smile from Roland, who said, with a touch of amusement, "I am not calling off my little dinner party, Will. But I do wish your dear sister had given you and my grandson some time to get to know one another again."

"I know Hannibal as well as he ever wants me to," Will said, feeling the soft pulse of his husband's breath against his mouth, the light touch of fingertips drifting down his throat.

The sickening shock of his saddle breaking free to send him falling helplessly to the ground.

"Will?" Roland asked, concerned when he jumped as if someone had pinched him. "Are you quite all right?"

"Yes, Grandfather, I'm sorry, I just... it is nothing," he said, summoning a smile. "I suppose it will be for Mina and I to entertain ourselves, as Hannibal has gone."

"Only to Fernhill," Roland supplied with suspicious haste. "He had something or other to speak with Bedelia about and he is an ungodly impatient boy."

Will nodded, but an entirely unhelpful part of his mind quickly reminded him the road to Fernhill ran through Hartford Town and it would take little effort on Hannibal's part to stop there, with even less effort on the widow's part to accompany him back to Hartford House.

"You look as if you do not believe me," Roland gently said, cocking his head. "Has something happened? I was told you rode to Duxbury, Will. Have you found something there which you would like me to clarify?"

It was the first time Will truly doubted the older man who had been so thoughtful of him for the past six years. It was a frightening, ugly feeling that left him hollow, but he knew better than to give voice to it.

Calmly, carefully, with composure honed in the fire of his father's temper and perfected to an art, Will said, "No, Grandfather. I merely wanted to pay my respects."

"You are far too intelligent to have gone for no reason, and far too shrewd in your own counsel to confide it in me," Roland said, and raised his hand in a staying gesture when Will looked as if he would protest. "No, Will. You are a young man who is wise beyond his years. Trust your instincts. If you trust nothing else in this world, trust yourself to know what is true."

Moved, Will impulsively reached out and grasped Grandfather's papery, warm hand in both his own, swallowing hard against emotion that tried to break the seal on his control.

"You are my pride and joy," Roland said, covering Will's hand with his free one. "You are strong in ways most people are never pushed to become, and despite the circumstances that have affected you, you have never once complained or lost your capacity for compassion and caring. Never forget that, Will. That is who you are, and nothing and no one can ever take that from you. Not myself, not your father, not your sister, and certainly not my grandson."

Will smiled, and managed a small nod, fingers clenching on Roland's when the old Alpha gave his hand a squeeze.

"Now, off you go," Roland said, releasing him. "And send that useless boy back in here to read to me. He might as well do something to earn his wage."

"Yes, Grandfather," Will said, and did as he was told with his heart lighter, a little more confident he could fight whatever fate might have in store for him.

He had survived his father for eighteen years, after all.

He was not about to be done in by the likes of Hannibal Ledford.

⌘⌘⌘

It was full dark by the time Hannibal returned to Hartford House, his head still swimming with newfound information.

He should have learned it as a boy from his stepmother, or from his father, but all his father could ever tell him of Omegas was that one day he would understand how a man could lose his wits for one.

And she... that creature...

'I love you, mother!'

'I'm not your mother, little fawn. Never, never call me that...'

'I love you anyway!'

'And what is a boy's love worth, hm? It doesn't make my life better, does it? You give it to me one day, Hannibal, when your love is worth something...'

Hannibal flinched still all these years later, the child in him who had never survived that encounter clinging to the memory of what had harmed him.

She had taught him, oh yes, all too well.

She had taught him Alphas were monsters to be controlled, that there was nothing too small it couldn't be bartered and bickered and haggled over, that someday an Omega would play with him like a puppet on strings, as she had with his father.

She had taught him that affection was trivial and love had a price, that some love was worthless, that strength and stoicism were to take the place of his need for attachment if he ever wanted to survive in a world which would never have a care for him.

She had rebuffed and refused and hardened him to suspicion until he trusted nothing from her, nothing at all. She had surrounded herself with Omegas who embodied the worst qualities of their sex, giggling and stupid things who teased him, their behaviors impressed on his malleable young mind, the only examples he'd ever had. There had never been a reason to imagine others were not the same.

But Will...

He smiled, thinking of his mate on his first day home, asking, '*Are you trying to* insult *me, Hannibal?*'

His sharp-tongued, shocking, vibrant, violent little spouse was her polar opposite, calm and capable even when goaded into a temper. He was a fascinating mixture of simplicity and complexity with whom Hannibal could never seem to communicate properly.

But that, hopefully, would change now, with Bedelia's thorough instruction.

At least now he could keep from unintentionally suffocating his spouse with his inexpert and accidental intrusions onto his person.

Hartford House was dark but for a few lamps up in the servants' quarters, and the lantern of the night guard wobbling off on his rounds. Hannibal stabled his horse himself, reluctant to go wake Peter or one of the stable lads so late. He half expected to be locked out, but the door swung open on cue as he approached it.

"Mr. Hawkes, you should've made one of the younger ones wait up at this ungodly hour," he said, grinning at his butler's dignified performance, not affected in the least by the time.

"I take my duties to Hartford House very seriously, my Lord," Mr. Hawkes reminded him, closing the door and locking it up tight behind him. "The Butler is the gatekeeper of a great House. It is a considerable responsibility and an even greater honor."

Hannibal reached to take a taper to get him upstairs and paused, testing the air for the faint scent of perfume still lingering.

"Have we had guests this evening, Hawkes?" he asked, wrinkling his nose.

"Lady Rathmore has arrived, my Lord," Hawkes said, politely not acknowledging Hannibal's soft, sour curse. "She is in the Victoria suite at Mr. Grant's request."

"Forewarned is forearmed," Hannibal said, and cast his eyes heavenward. "This does complicate the situation more than I would like. How long is she staying."

Much to Hannibal's dismay, Mr. Hawkes said with steady, bland serenity, "She has made no mention of leaving, my Lord."

Heaving another sigh at this unexpected bump in his path to get to know his spouse, Hannibal put an end to his day and went upstairs for some much-needed sleep.

⌘⌘⌘

Something woke Will sometime in the night, rousing him from his fretful, horror-laced sleep, confused and far too warm. He couldn't place at first what had drawn him from slumber and waited for a long, tense moment, straining to hear anything strange.

Just as he settled again, he heard a creak on the landing outside of his door and a soft thump.

Alarmed, wondering who on earth was outside of his door this late, Will crept out of bed, dragged his robe on, and opened his door.

The hallway was black as pitch, the lower level a lighter darkness thanks to the high windows. He could just make out the shadow of a figure at the head of the stairs and called out softly, "Jimmy? Is that you?"

The figure turned and darted down the stairs as if startled.

Concerned, Will started after them, his hand reaching for the banister to feel his way.

Rough hands shoved him squarely between his shoulders and Will cried out as he tumbled head first down the stairs, smacking into the carpeted risers as he rolled down, bouncing from the railing and striking his head on the floor when he landed, the world swimming in dizzy chaos.

Chapter 19

Will lay where he landed, taking stock, his head flaring with pain where he'd struck it. He groaned, the ache in his skull sharpening, wincing as the impact made itself known all over his body.

"Mr. Grant! Mr. Grant!"

"Will! Oh my goodness! *Will!*"

The voices of Mr. Hawkes and Mina reached him through the thundering in his ears and Will opened his eyes, finding the butler, the housekeeper, Jimmy, and Mina looming over him by lamplight to help.

"What on earth happened?" Jimmy gasped, helping him sit up. "We heard you all the way upstairs!"

"Will! Are you hurt, dearest? Oh my gods!" Mina fretted, pale and frightened, her fingers fluttering over him like butterflies, uncertain where to land or what might pain him.

"There was something on the landing," Will said, biting his lip slightly in discomfort as her questing fingers skimmed over his rib cage, waking a flaring ache that stole his breath. "I-I tripped over it. I was just clumsy..."

Mrs. Henderson rushed up to check and Will heard the low drone of Hannibal's voice when he spoke to her, a soft purr accompanied by the growing strength of his scent as he was drawn by the ruckus.

Will tried to recall if he'd caught Hannibal's scent in the hallway, but it permeated everything to such varying degrees and he couldn't be sure if he had or hadn't. The hands that had pushed him, too, he couldn't quite recall being large or small, it had all happened so quickly.

Hannibal's suite was right next to his, yet the servants in the attic had heard the commotion and responded before Hannibal had. Will stared at Hannibal and wondered with cold dread if his husband had found an opportunity yet again to deal with him as he had his first wife.

"Will?" Hannibal called, standing at the top of the stairs in his dressing gown and nightshirt, his hair mussed from sleep. He started down and Will tensed, earning himself a sharp, suspicious glance from Jimmy. "What on earth happened?"

"He's nearly broken his neck!" Mina said, concern sharpening her voice to a knife's edge. She turned on Hannibal, half blocking Will behind her as if to protect him.

"I was clumsy," Will said, recalling the feel of quick hands pushing him. "I fell."

"Fell? Down the *stairs*?" Hannibal asked, incredulous, bewildered by the whole episode and especially bewildered by Lady Rathmore's trembling outrage.

Will stared up at him as if he was a deranged stranger and Hannibal could only look back at him in confusion, his concern doubling with the sight of a lump rising on Will's pale forehead.

"He is shaken up, my Lord," Mr. Hawkes said, straightening and attempting to diffuse the tension when Will refused to answer.

"He woke half the house! How could you have slept through it?" Mina demanded, nostrils flaring and mouth taut. "He might have *died*, Lord Clarges! Little though *you* would care!"

"*Mina*," Will sharply said, and winced with pain as Jimmy helped him to his feet, supporting him under his arm.

"Lady Rathmore, I am not in the mood to have a guest in this household shrieking at me in her nightclothes," Hannibal said, the set-down coming out more sharply than he intended due to his concern, but at least hushing her wild accusations. "I will attribute that comment to an excess of nerves and forgive it."

"Come along, Mr. Grant, let's get you back to bed, shall we?"

"Let me examine him," Hannibal said, true worry gnawing at him. The scent of Will's fear agitated him, the sensation of it in his gut and chest waking a primal desire to comfort him. He wanted nothing more than to pluck the slender Omega from Jimmy's grasp and carry him off someplace safely within reach.

Will's fear spiked palpably when Hannibal reached for him and Hannibal immediately dropped his hand, alarmed by it. Will's voice was thin and cold when he said, "No, thank you, Lord Clarges. I assure you, I am fine."

"*Will*, you've just fallen down the stairs! You might've broken something!" Hannibal said, his mate's resistance only making him more worried. This was not the first time Will had behaved and responded as if he was afraid, but never to this level of absolute terror and he could only put it down to what had just happened. "I understand your fall has frightened you, but you might truly be badly hurt! Please allow me to examine you before you try to take the stairs, or else let me carry you up! You might have broken a bone, for the gods' sake! At the very least, you've hit your head—"

"*Leave him alone!*" Mina said, nearly a shout, her fear more obvious than Will's but no greater.

"Jimmy can see to me," Will said, moving away when Hannibal stirred closer in response to his upset. "*Do not touch me.*"

Jimmy waited, looking anxiously from Will to Hannibal until Hannibal gave him a short, sharp nod, settling for saying, "Check him thoroughly Jimmy. If anything is broken, get me at once."

It was immensely disturbing to see Jimmy and Mina helping Will up the stairs, knowing he was hurting. It was even more disturbing to think Will was quite tangibly frightened of him for no reason he could discern, and his mind could only find one answer as to why.

Duxbury. Melinda. The shadow of his first wife and the circumstances of her death that Hannibal, even in the face of Will's distrust and fear, was at a loss or an opportunity to explain.

"My Lord!" Mrs. Henderson hurried his way, her white nightgown billowing around her slim ankles.

"There's nothing there, m'Lord!" she whispered, casting a worried glance at Will as he hit the landing with Jimmy's help, Mina lingering behind to glare daggers down at Hannibal before flouncing off in a huff. "Nothing at all!"

"He tripped over nothing and nearly killed himself rolling down the stairs?" Hannibal queried, worry gnawing at him. "He has never once been clumsy."

"He seemed frightened, my Lord," Mr. Hawkes said, shielding his bare lamp from the breeze of their movements. "It is possible he tripped in the darkness."

"What on earth was he about this time of night?!" Hannibal asked, deeply unsettled. He'd felt such a gut-wrenching stab of worry when he'd heard the commotion and seen Will mounded at the foot of the staircase like a discarded rag doll it still twinged in his stomach, sour and heavy. Thank the gods the noise had finally penetrated his heavy sleep, else he would have had no knowledge of the event at all.

"Perhaps that is a question best asked come breakfast, my Lord," Mr. Hawkes said, delicately pointing out it was late and no time for harsh feelings.

"Of course, yes, back to bed with you both," Hannibal said, waving them off towards the servants' stairs as he slowly made his way back to his suite. He lingered at the top of the stairs, searching the black-on-black darkness for any sign of what could have tripped Will into his fall but there was nothing he could see.

'*Clumsy*,' he'd said, and the air still smelled of his fear. It brought a rough, involuntary chuff from him, tugging him again to check on Will and ensure he was calm now, no longer so frightened or threatened.

'*It is natural*,' Bedelia had said, firm in her instruction of him in all sorts of surprising things. He wanted to go to him, to see if he could ease him as Bedelia had insisted was possible, to try establishing a connection and soothe the fear Hannibal had all but tasted on him.

He was not, however, such a cad that he could not recognize what Will would make of it—namely that he was taking advantage of his vulnerability. Unwilling to risk engendering any of Will's righteous violence, Hannibal returned to his suite instead, knowing he would be awake, sleepless in his bed, until the wee hours of morning wondering how on earth he would manage to get closer to his mate when Will was so strangely, terribly frightened of him.

⌘⌘⌘

The aftershock of his fall left Will trembling as Jimmy and Mina eased him down onto his bed. The world seemed to sway sickeningly in one direction then the other, and he winced from the lamps as Jimmy lit them, every bone in his body protesting with each breath he took.

"Oh, my darling," Mina whispered, sitting next to him to gently tease his hair from a place throbbing in time with his heartbeat. She grimaced as she did so, breathing, "A goose egg already, and you've bloodied it. Will, what happened?"

"Nothing," Will said, knowing she could feel his agitation as keenly as her own. When Jimmy vanished into the washroom to gather supplies, he quickly whispered, "I was pushed, Mina."

"*Pushed*?! But dearest, you must—"

She cut off, casting a nervous glance at the doorway when Jimmy passed across to reach the cabinet. Lowering her voice to a bare purr, she said, "Will, you must tell someone."

Will shook his head just slightly, cringing against renewed discomfort. Swallowing hard against growing nausea, he managed, "No, Mina, please say nothing."

Jimmy returned and carefully cleaned up the few places on Will's scalp still oozing blood, wincing as he did so.

"Well, no stitches required," he said, carefully dabbing some ointment on the open places. "So far so good, but no promises for tomorrow. Does anything feel really wrong? I'm no doctor, Mr. Grant, so I apologize for my ineptitude on this count."

"It's fine, Jimmy, you needn't examine me," Will breathed. "Hannibal was merely posturing before the servants."

Jimmy frowned, regarding Will in silence before he said, "You really should have let Lord Clarges have a look."

"How can you say such a thing?!" Mina asked, aghast, and nervously averted her gaze from Jimmy's questioning glance.

Will said nothing. Through the crashing pain in his head he kept feeling hands pushing him, just like in his dream. And he'd fallen, hadn't he? Fallen and been hurt, and the one who was supposed to protect him, to care for him, was in all likelihood the one who had pushed him.

"Mr. Grant," Jimmy said, finishing up and mixing some headache powder into a glass of water for him. "Did something else happen?"

Mina tensed beside him, trembling to burst into an admission but wisely holding her tongue.

Will shook his head and immediately regretted it when his skull felt fit to fracture. Closing his eyes to allay his nausea, he whispered, "No, Jimmy. I fell."

Jimmy sighed, pressing the glass into his hand.

"You can tell me, Mr. Grant," he insisted. "If you're frightened of Lord Clarges, I will make sure His Grace is made aware—"

"*No*," Will sharply said, fingers clenching on the glass. Softening his tone, he said, "No, it isn't that. I just fell, Jimmy. That's all."

The press of his mouth betrayed the fact that Jimmy knew he was lying and didn't like it one bit, but he patted Will's knee all the same and told him, "Well, drink that right up. It will help with the pain. Leave the glass on the nightstand, Mr. Grant, and I'll get it come morning."

"Thank you, Jimmy," Will said, barely more than a whisper.

"Goodness, the servants here are so familiar with their betters!" Mina said, glowering at Jimmy who, surprisingly, glowered right back. Wordlessly, he put out the other lights and left Will alone with Mina.

"We should write father," Mina said the instant the door was closed, turning to take Will's hands in hers.

"No, Mina."

"But, Will, we must do *something!*" she said, and cupped his cheek, her mirroring blue eyes searching his own. "What comes next? Hm? Will he come through that door and throttle you and allow everyone to think it was your fall that did it?"

Will dropped his head, wishing it didn't make so much sense, the pull on the muscles in his neck making him grimace.

His twin, however, had her own measure of his strange intuition and knew precisely where his fears lay.

"I will stay here with you," she decided.

"No, Mina, please," Will said, squeezing her hand. "He failed once tonight, he will hardly try again. Please, don't trouble yourself. Go back to bed and get some sleep."

"How on earth can I, knowing what I know?!" she hissed, glaring at the washroom door as if Hannibal might burst through and murder them both.

"Mina," Will said, taking a deep breath. "Please, I just want to get rid of this terrible headache. I will not be done to death in my bed, I swear it."

"You never imagined you would be done to death on your own stairs, either!" she flared, but after a long silence only pressed a kiss to his unhurt temple and said, "Very well. I'll turn out these lamps, dearest, and you try to get some sleep."

She rose gracefully and put out the remaining lamps, finding her way to the door in the faint moonlight. She paused there before leaving and told him, "I am only just beside you, Will. If you need me, call out."

Will waited for the quiet click of the door and eased back into bed. He tried to go back to sleep but he found he couldn't. Even after drinking the drugged water down, he lay awake wondering who that person was he'd seen fleeing downstairs. He could easily imagine it was the Widow Reynolds, attempting to skulk from the house, her purpose accomplished. He wondered if Hannibal had seen his opportunity and taken it, one forceful shove to end Will's life and grant freedom to his own. It would not, according to Molly and Mina and the world at large, be the first time he would have done such, Will knew.

It chilled him to the depths of his soul and left him nervous and out of sorts. He abandoned all pretense of sleep and rose to dress with excruciating slowness, using only the bedside lamp so as not to call attention to himself. The servants would be up if they knew he was and he had no desire to bother them.

He took his small, mostly-shuttered lamp to light his way and crept out onto the landing again. It took him some pacing, but he found the creaky board that had alerted him to a presence. It was between his door and Hannibal's, not beyond. Whoever it had been, they had come from the direction of Hannibal's suite, or else further down the hall.

Will's heart skipped, the beat of it echoing in his head, and he tamped his fear down firmly. It was an old acquaintance, after all, following him here from the house of his father and dogging his steps every day since his saddle had been cut. He would not allow himself to be controlled by it nor dissuaded by his instincts, which pushed him to seek safety with Hannibal.

Squaring his shoulders and fighting the pain that threatened to break his skull, he went to the stairs, recalling his angle. Whoever had pushed him had come from the deeper darkness behind him. Unless two strangers had somehow broken into Hartford House in a bizarre attempt to harm him, it was likely the person who had pushed him was Hannibal.

Will's breath left him on a shaky exhale and he took the stairs cautiously, clinging to the railing. It felt as if every joint in his body had been jostled loose, aching from the top of his head all the way to his knees, throbbing in time with his heartbeat.

He couldn't allow it to deter him, however. He resolutely caught his breath at the foot of the stairs and took stock, determined to figure at least part of this issue out.

The other person had fled somewhere when he'd called out to them. The stairs fed onto the main doors, the most likely escape. Will rallied and checked the locks by lamplight.

They were undone, the latches opened from the inside. Whoever they were, they had been here, inside the house before Mrs. Henderson or Mr. Hawkes had locked the doors for the night, and had fled through the front door in the confusion of Will's fall.

Trembling, Will hastily locked the door again, leaving no sign of an intruder to alarm the servants. He knew there were any number of ways to gain access to a house this size during the day and it worried him. Had it not been Hannibal's paramour, waltzed in on his arm in the dead of night, then it was someone with wicked intentions and no business being here. Grandfather's suite was on the main floor; he would make a rather tempting target, Will knew, if he himself was not the intended victim.

Shaking off the feeling of hands shoving him, Will carried his little lamp downstairs to the darkened kitchen and made a small breakfast of dry bread and cold tea to accompany more of the headache powder Mrs. Pimms kept in the cupboard. He sat alone at the servants' table in the meager light with oppressive darkness looming all around him, his thoughts turning to Hannibal.

He had applied himself to Hannibal's perspective since that day his Omegan nature had latched onto the man as the ruling and most dangerous Alpha to be pleased. It had been less of a struggle to suppress his point of view these last six years, but with Hannibal so close so constantly it was all too easy for Will to see what would suit him best.

Unfortunately, that was himself dead and removed from his problematic position if all other methods failed. After all this time, he was surely impatient to move on with his life and Will was nothing more than an obstacle to be overcome. There was no consideration for his feelings or understanding that he even had them. There was no concern for him in the least—he was in the way, and all this talk of accepting him and giving him a child was simply a means to get close enough to easily push Will off the nearest cliff.

It was frighteningly, perfectly reasonable.

"Mr. Grant! Goodness, you're up early, considering!" Mrs. Pimms declared, up and dressed and ready to start the morning meal for the servants who would soon rise. "Ah, you should've rang for me!"

"It's perfectly fine, Mrs. Pimms," he said, rising slowly to leave his barely-eaten bread on the table as she moved about lighting lamps. "I couldn't sleep. I'm sorry for invading your kitchen yet again."

"Pft, *invading*!" she laughed, sweeping the plate away. "Mr. Grant, after the night you had, you're due a little sleeplessness, and you're always welcome in your own kitchen, by rights."

"You heard?" Will asked, barely above a mute whisper.

"Mr. Hawkes informed us," she said over the sounds of the house awakening, servants milling, boots clicking on wooden floors, voices raised in whispered conversation as they filed downstairs. "Everyone woke at the hubbub and you know how he hates gossip!"

"Mrs. Pimms, I—Mr. Grant! This is unexpected!" Mr. Hawkes said, drawing up to a halt with a spill of maids coursing around him like water around a stone. "Are you unwell, Mr. Grant? Should I fetch Lord Clarges?"

"No, Mr. Hawkes, that won't be necessary," Will assured him, making room for Mrs. Pimms' assistants as they started their morning chores. "But I would like to ask if you could be vigilant for new faces coming in below stairs."

"New faces, Mr. Grant?" he echoed, a frown falling over his somber face. "Lady Rathmore arrived with only her lady's maid, Ms. Spark, I believe, and, of course, Mr. Doranhouse."

"I have an uneasy feeling, Mr. Hawkes, there have been individuals in Hartford House who have no true business here," Will said, feeling increasingly like a madman as he spoke, a sentiment Mr. Hawkes was too dignified to allow to show on his face.

"I will, of course, inform the staff to be alert," Mr. Hawkes said, indulging his requests as he must.

"Thank you, Mr. Hawkes," Will said, and made the laborious return trip upstairs where he supposedly belonged, wondering how on earth he could protect himself against an Alpha who saw him as nothing more than a weed to be plucked out by the root.

It was that thought which decided him and brought him to his little desk in his suite to write to his father's solicitor, Mr. Brauner.

In short, concise sentences, he explained everything that had happened and instructed Mr. Brauner to gather an accounting of his assets and all material worth. He wrote they should be given to Mina if anything was to happen to him, and she should use those funds to discover the truth of what might have happened to him.

'I am in a very precarious position,' he said in closing. 'I rely on your silence in this case, Mr. Brauner. No one in my family should be bothered by this unless I come to an untimely and suspicious end.'

Will's hands shook as he folded it into an envelope and sealed it against inquiry. It relieved him somewhat to have someone else in possession of what he

344

had learned. Should anything happen to him, at least Mina would be able to find out the truth of it.

He took the letter downstairs, panting softly against rising nausea, and headed directly for the door, starting like he'd been caught stealing when Mr. Hawkes politely inquired from behind him, "May I take that for you, Mr. Grant?"

"*No,*" Will clutched the letter to his chest protectively, embarrassed by the clear concern he saw on Mr. Hawkes' face at his strange behavior. He felt heat in his cheeks and sweat break out on his brow, enough that Mr. Hawkes' somber face fell into lines of concern. He cleared his throat and said with practiced calm, "No, thank you, Mr. Hawkes. I thought I might ride down to town and post it myself."

"You do not look at all well, Mr. Grant. It would be less trouble for you if I send a footman—"

"No, Mr. Hawkes, thank you," Will said, his smile tight and tense as he tucked the letter out of reach. "I will take it myself. I'm rather at loose ends now that I've been removed from my position."

"You have not been *removed* from your position," Hannibal said, his deep voice sounding as he came downstairs. "You are assuming your proper position, Will."

"And rightly *so*, my Lord," Mr. Hawkes confirmed, nodding sagely, extraordinarily pleased.

Hannibal moved towards him, fluidly graceful and strong, and the tug Will felt towards him from their bond brought an answering flood of fear and something else that felt frighteningly like the stirrings of his heat, though it was still too early by Will's counting.

Hannibal cocked his head, sensing it, his deep frown pulling on Will like a hook in a trout, bringing a fresh flush to his cheeks.

"You're up early," Will said, forcing himself to ignore the persistent dull throb in his head, the worsening ache spreading through his body from his fall.

"The military makes one an early riser," Hannibal said, his concern growing as he looked at Will. "I thought I might go for my ride. On any other day, I would ask if you'd care to join me, but you really don't look well, Will. Not surprising, all things considered. I do wish you would permit me to examine you. I'm certain you are not as hale as you believe you are."

"My apologies, Lord Clarges, but I was heading into town," Will said, wincing when the throbbing in his head took umbrage at his speaking, the pounding of it holding pace with his quickening heartbeat.

Hannibal noted how pale he seemed, and told him, "Will, I truly advise against it. You took quite a fall last night and I don't think you should be riding."

"I'm fine," Will said, desperate to finish his task. "It is only to the village and back, not clear across the country."

"Then I will ride with you," Hannibal decided, Will's reactions to his injuries lifting an irresistible urge to care for him, watch over him, keep him safe from harm. Hannibal didn't know if the instinct was due to his being an Alpha or a physician and he honestly didn't care—his mate was hurting, perhaps badly injured, and he needed to be near in case Will needed him. "I will not stand for you tumbling from your mare and injuring yourself further, nor do I want you to be found unconscious on the roadside."

"No doubt if I were, those who found me would consider it merely an Omega's foolishness and deliver me back to my proper owner," Will said, bitter with the harsh truth of his life. "Mr. Hawkes, please have Mr. Doranhouse meet me out front. He can accompany me to town in case my weakness overcomes me."

"Hawkes, you'll do nothing of the sort," Hannibal immediately countered, informing Will, "I am not allowing a man I have no knowledge of—let alone another Alpha—escort my spouse into town! There has been quite enough gossip regarding this family, as I have become painfully and thoroughly aware! The only thing overcoming you right now is that crack to your head, Will; *weakness* plays no part in it!"

Glowering at Hannibal, Will made for the front door hastily enough that Mr. Hawkes was not in time to sweep it open for him. The world quivered dangerously at the edges of his vision, but Will put one foot in front of the other with stiff-backed determination, heading straight for the stables.

"Will, I know for a fact you aren't feeling well if you're confounding the staff." Hannibal's voice followed him out into the brightening morning. His long-legged stride caught him up to Will in moments. "Hawkes nearly had an apoplexy at the sight of you getting the door yourself. He thinks you abused having had to do so."

"He needn't concern himself to such an extent," Will assured him, brushing past the startled stable lads and Peter, Hartford House's diffident groom, to reach his mare's box. Her ears were perked, already swiveled to the sound of his voice, and her bright, eager eyes eased his upset somewhat. "I have been put to much harder use than opening a door."

"Peter," Hannibal said, noting he looked torn between wanting to interfere and wanting to escape. "Please fetch your Lordship's gear, so he may not be abused on that count. And mind that you *check it*! I want no more accidents befalling my spouse!"

Will bristled but did not nay say him. Impressed that he held his tongue, Hannibal said, "Thank you for not arguing."

"Peter is sensitive to unpleasantness, as well you should know," Will said, slipping into the mare's box to lean against her neck and hide his face, already exhausted but not about to admit he was feeling dizzy and doubted his own ability to saddle his mare in his worsening state. "Contradicting you would only have upset him."

"Such a thoughtful master you are," Hannibal mused, frowning. Will still carried the scent of fear, but it was overridden by his pain. Hannibal could feel his awareness of it growing, plucking at his nerves. Frowning, he patted his stallion's nose, reaching out for its outstretched muzzle and avoiding its nibbling teeth from force of long habit.

"I am not the master here, Hannibal. I never have been," Will said, glad to have his mare's solid, sturdy body between him and the man he simply could not trust. "I am merely a placeholder."

"Will, you are married to a man who will eventually hold a precious title," Hannibal reminded him. "You are no *placeholder*."

"That is not what your social circle believes," Will said, pressing his forehead to the mare's warm neck, careful of the lump that had grown larger in the hours since his fall. "Nor what you have admitted. I am not welcome, or wanted, or needed here. I have only been a troublesome guest for the past six years. The staff have been kind enough to take care of me."

"Take care of you? They have hardly seen you!" Hannibal said, preparing to address the subject of Will's fall last night and, perhaps, open the way to telling him about Melinda. Before he could imagine a graceful way to do so, however, Peter and the stable boys returned with their gear.

Will took his chance to escape the uncomfortable conversation by allowing Peter to saddle his mare while he retreated to the yard, using any excuse not to look at his husband. He grew cold thinking about how provoking he had been, his frustration and the after effects of his fall pushing him past the bounds of common sense. It was not wise, he knew, to needle a man who wished to kill him.

Peter finished quickly and led the mare out into the growing sunlight, holding her bridle and soothing her when Will tried to mount. He could barely get his foot into the stirrup for the hurt it caused, and swallowed back a harsh cry at the scream of refusal from his back when he tried to pull up.

Peter, worried and uncertain, ended up boosting him into the saddle, casting anxious looks back at the stable as if willing Hannibal to emerge and put a halt to it.

Will settled in his saddle and for a chilling moment he was sure he *would* slide from the mare's back onto his face. The world tipped and swayed and his head hurt from the top of his skull in a flare of fire all the way down to his pelvis. It took every bit of his formidable willpower to remain upright.

It was the sound of Hannibal's voice that prompted him to move despite his injuries. Without waiting to consider the consequences, Will urged the mare onto the lane and gave her her head, the chill morning air cooling his flushed cheeks and mitigating the nausea his horse's movements caused.

There was a thunder of hoof beats behind him and a glance over his shoulder showed him Hannibal bent over the stallion's neck, crop flat to his side, urging the horse to stretch its long legs. It sent a deep jolt of terror through him and Will's mare nickered, responding by stretching her own gait. Will leaned over her neck and held on for dear life, his usual ease abandoning him to stiffness and pain, leaving him clinging to her back. He prayed he wouldn't be sick down her neck, he prayed he wouldn't fall off of her, and he prayed Hannibal wouldn't run him down on the lane where no witnesses would see what might befall him.

His mare picked up on his anxiety and hastened her pace, straining into a full-blown run. She was shorter than Hannibal's horse and didn't have as much speed in a sprint, but she easily outdistanced the high-spirited stallion's short-lived burst of speed, only losing her lead when they hit the outskirts of Hartford Town.

She slowed, unused to such concentrated effort, and Will cautiously pushed upright, hoping he was safe enough with the town's waking eyes to see them. He patted her damp neck with appreciation, releasing a shaky breath of relief when the cool air soothed his heated skin and the nausea that seemed to worsen with each beat of his heart. The world glimmered around the edges, wavering and indistinct, threatening him with dizziness he could ill-afford while trying to keep his seat.

Hannibal overshot him, slowed, and circled back, flushed with the cool air, the picture of a virile Alpha in good health. He seemed in tolerable spirits, Will irritably noted. But then, he had every reason to be, considering how close he'd come to killing Will last night. It was dangerous to be alone with him, mortally dangerous, and Will had the lump on his skull to prove it.

"You shouldn't have ridden so recklessly, Will," Hannibal said, concern overcoming him, his stallion's hide steaming in the cool air. "What if you'd fallen unconscious? You might have been killed."

"I am unfortunately resilient," Will said, giving him wide berth to continue towards town, almost unable to keep his seat. "As my various accidents and my father can attest."

"Your father?" Hannibal asked, the oddness of including a man Will rarely, if ever spoke of overridden by his worry when Will listed sharply and only just caught himself. "Were you prone to accidents as a child?"

Will hesitated, his breathing shallow. When Hannibal's stare sharpened, he merely said, "Yes."

"Strange," Hannibal said, treading lightly in his attempts to engage him as Will was in pain and nervous of him, that same fear from last night rearing its ugly head. "You have never once displayed a lack of grace, Will, yet you say you are accident prone and only just fell down our stairs and nearly broke your neck."

"I am sorry to have deceived you yet again, Lord Clarges, but I am exceptionally clumsy," Will said, taking a ragged breath and swallowing against the urge to be sick. "My father is a saint for his patience with me."

"I had imagined he held you quite dear," Hannibal said, falling in next to him as they rode towards the awakening town, alert in case Will *did* slide from his saddle. "The only son in a family of females."

Will skated a sideways glance at him, swaying more from his dizziness than his mare's gait. The ache in his head and down his back made him short in his answers and his voice was sharp when he said, "I was never the son he deserved, Lord Clarges."

"Still, I cannot imagine he was very pleased with your reception here, or the fact you took over as land agent," Hannibal said, unabashedly fishing for information on the man who had refused correspondence from his newly-married son. He angled more than one worried glance at Will, concerned by his obvious discomfort and distress. The doctor in him wanted to put a stop to this nonsensical ride this instant, but the newly-informed Alpha in him hesitated to do so.

"To the contrary, I am sure he was quite pleased. It is his philosophy that useless things are only fit for burning," Will said, closing his blue eyes down to slits as the sun intruded to further agitate his stomach. "Father insisted I apply myself to learning the intricacies of running an estate."

"He imagined he would one day leave his own in your charge?" Hannibal inquired, imagining how besotted Will's father must have been with him if he thought to challenge inheritance laws which treated Omegas the same as women. But it made little sense when compared to what Hawkes had said about the Earl being unpleasant to Will. Whatever the case may be, he clearly had not raised Will with any great affection, though Hannibal could not imagine why on earth he had restrained himself from doing so.

"Heavens, no," Will said, huffing a soft, scornful laugh, moving his mare away from Hannibal's mount, keeping enough distance between them to stay out of his reach. His circumstances drove him to impulsively say, "*No*, Lord Clarges. He knew I had no prospects for marriage and would need a livelihood if I did not wish to starve on the street."

Hannibal was slightly taken aback by his statement, sure he had not heard correctly. "Why would your father think you had no prospects?"

"I was unfortunately born both unattractive and Omegan," Will said without rancor, and a sharp glance showed Hannibal he was not uncharacteristically fishing for compliments. "After seven sisters, there was no money left to promise a dowry that could adequately compensate for the burden of my care. The best I could hope for was to earn my living. He was never hopeful I would manage to attract a mate or have a family, but he did the best he could for me under the circumstances, which was to see to my education."

"That is entirely perplexing," Hannibal murmured, decidedly aware Will was anything but plain or unattractive and wondering how his father had managed to convince him it was so, or why he would bother doing so.

He nudged his horse slightly closer to Will's mare when his mate slumped in his saddle, wincing. He hesitated, wanting nothing more than to ease him down from his mare and examine him, but in Will's current state of hurt and agitation, he knew he only risked being coshed for his concern. He settled instead for speaking, keeping Will focused on staying upright, and said, "I had always imagined you spent your days at your father's side being coddled and doted upon."

"You mistake me for one of my sisters," Will softly said, a sad frown bowing his mouth when he thought of his father and how dearly he loved his many daughters. Figuring his husband would praise his father's dogma, he swallowed back his growing sickness and said, "Coddling is dangerous for Omegas. It encourages weakness and dependence. It terrified him to think I would be enslaved by my biology. He used strong measures to ensure I would not be."

"Well," Hannibal said, digesting what he'd been told, his measure of Will's father finding sharp new corners that cut a much different picture than he'd always held. Yet, he could not tell Will's feeling for his father. His husband seemed defensive of his father, spouting rhetoric Hannibal saw the ugly shadow of himself within. Hoping not to offend Will any more than he already had, he could only offer, "He must love you very much to take such pains on your behalf."

"Pain is the very cornerstone of his love for me," Will said, the words bitter and harsh, dislodged from him in an excess of physical discomfort despite the presence of Hannibal so near him. "I was not always sure I would survive it."

The sobering seriousness in the way Will spoke gave him goose-flesh, made him wonder just what relationship Will had with his father that would make him honestly think he might not survive it.

Hannibal swallowed hard to force down the strengthening sense of unease Will had given him. He looked at his spouse, who seemed terribly fragile and terribly damaged there in the early morning sunlight, pale and clearly ill, his tired blue eyes ringed in dark circles, the lump on his head purple-red and angry.

"Will," he said, drawing his stallion to a stop, Will's mare pausing alongside him. "I cannot dance around this subject one moment longer and I cannot hope to guess your feelings in this matter. Will, tell me plainly, was your father... was he unkind to you?"

Will looked over at him, his blue eyes moiling with misery and deep, profound distress before they glazed over, giving Hannibal nothing more than the reflection of his own stern face.

"He was the only Alpha who cared for me," Will said, his voice faint and resigned and filled with a deadly kind of calm Hannibal knew all too well from

351

the battlefield, and it chilled him to his soul. "He would not have been unkind or cruel for no reason."

"Therefore, the obvious answer is that you gave him reason?" Hannibal asked, rapidly coming to the conclusion he immensely disliked Will's father, if only because of the way Will reacted at the mere mention of him.

"I suppose I must have," Will said, relieved they had stopped moving, though the world still swayed dangerously and he had tiny little spots dancing at the edges of his vision that in no way aided his equilibrium. He sat half-hunched in his saddle, burning with heat and regretting his rash decision to deliver the letter himself. There was every possibility he *would* end up in the ditch by the side of the road, perhaps not even due to Hannibal putting him there.

"Will... I am not your father," Hannibal said, realizing his spouse's family dynamic had not been at all what he once imagined and he may never have the truth of it. "Not all Alphas are the same."

Will stared at him for a long, silent moment, long enough Hannibal cautiously asked him, "What? What is it?"

"Not all Alphas are the same?" Will asked, and offered a mirthless laugh, the statement so absurd under the circumstances that he couldn't restrain himself, despite his survival sense warning him to tread with caution. "Yet all Omegas are. I wonder how that could be."

"Will—"

"I have known my father and I have known you, Hannibal," Will said, overriding him. "Suffice it to say, the majority of my experience is that you *are* the same in the most dangerous of ways."

Hannibal paled, uncomfortable to be categorized by Will in the same company as the man who had so clearly mistreated him.

"I find myself curious, Lord Clarges, how you will treat the child you insist I give you," Will said, his eyes open only enough to fix on Hannibal, picking him apart and finding him lacking. "Beaten for the smallest infraction? Gagged for laughing, perhaps? Would you break your son's fingers for touching things he should not?"

Utterly horrified and shocked, Hannibal said, "*Of course not!* What an appalling thing to say, Will! No one in their right mind would treat a child in such a way! Why would you even think of such things? Did he do such to you, Will?"

"It isn't my place to say. Blame it on my imagination, Hannibal," Will said, looking away so Hannibal would not read the illness and wretched sadness rapidly overcoming him. He felt out of resources, at the end of his strength and wits, vulnerable and friendless and with so little left to lose he wondered why he'd ever bothered to protect it. "It is, I've been told, my greatest fault."

"Honestly, who would speak of such horrors?" Hannibal breathed, grimacing at the images Will's words had conjured. He could feel agitation vibrating from his mate, a physical pain he clenched his teeth against the force of. Vastly disturbed, he said, "You can safely assume I would never do any of those things, if it even needs to be said. Any Ledford heir will know a life of contentment, I assure you. A proper son is the point to all of this, after all."

"A proper *son*," Will echoed, and laughed again, harsh and unhappy and grim.

"Yes," Hannibal said, wondering at his emphasis, at his strange behavior and a fearful *something* from Will he could sense that felt too close to despair. "That is what the two of us are required to provide my family, after all. I do not need another daughter. One is quite enough."

"You speak of children so easily," Will said, disturbed to an unsettling degree and driven to fearless imprudence with the force of his hurt. "Pretending your forced attempts to know me for your grandfather's sake are in pursuit of an heir when we both know well enough what you truly intend."

"Will, what do you think I intend?" Hannibal asked, noting how upset Will was, so tense, in fact, his mare sidestepped, which irritated his own mount. "Will! If you mean my goading about bringing my daughter here, let me assure you I have absolutely no intentions of doing something so callous!"

Will's mare tossed her head and Will nearly lost his seat, and that decided Hannibal, who said with an Alpha throb in his voice, "You are being foolish, Will, and I am putting a stop to this right now! You're coming down from there if I have to drag you kicking and screaming, which I am sure you are still up for despite your terrible state."

"Don't you *dare*!" Will warned him, clinging to the saddle, his breath hitching when the mare skittered to one side of the lane.

"I have no idea what on earth has gotten into you, but it is high time we settle this—" Hannibal moved to reach Will, who jerked the mare's reins with uncharacteristic roughness, causing her to rapidly turn, the words '*settle this*' echoing in his mind.

"Will! For the gods' sake, have a care!"

Will leaned over the mare's neck, the motion causing him to teeter on the cusp of actual sickness. He sensed Hannibal coming closer and snarled, "*Stay away from me!*"

Startled, Hannibal hesitated, Will's jittery fear and obvious hurt like a punch in his gut. Despite the warning, he couldn't help but try to get closer, concerned his mate might slide from the mare's back to the ground.

The sturdy little horse protested Will's treatment of her, unused to such handling, and broke into a trot back towards Hartford House and the soothing affection she knew waited for her there.

Will scrambled to sit upright, the world spinning and his heart thundering. He was terrified he would fall again, terrified Hannibal would keep questioning him, would force him down and throttle him right there on the lane and *settle* things after all.

"Will!" Hannibal shouted, deftly turning his mount in pursuit, rushing to reach him before he could fall as he had before. He overtook him and managed to grasp the mare's bridle, slowing them both to a stop. "Will, what in the seven hells is going through your mind right now? You could have been killed!"

"Isn't that what you're after?!" Will flared, pulling the mare's head away and breaking Hannibal's grip.

"What I'm after? Will—"

Will listed to one side and Hannibal caught his arm to steady him.

"*Don't you dare touch me!*" Will snarled, eyes wide, fear rolling off of him in metallic waves. The scent and taste of it hit Hannibal with the force of a cannonball, overriding him with an instinctive, aggressive need to shield Will from what threatened him. The unexpected shift in his mate was so abrupt Hannibal was breathless with it. Before he could react to the change, Will's other hand whipped around, his crop snapping across Hannibal's cheek in a white-hot flare of pain.

Hannibal jerked back in mingled shock and hurt, hand lifting to touch his cheek where blood was already beginning to well from the cut, his stallion sidestepping and loosing an unhappy whinny.

Will panted, cheeks flushed, eyes showing whites all around as if he was consumed with absolute terror. As much as Hannibal wanted to question him, the plunging depths of Will's fear made him realize something was very, very wrong.

"Will—"

"*Don't touch me!*" Will hissed again, the horse dancing beneath him in agitation. "You are *not my Alpha!*"

"*Will!*" he said again, calling out as the young Omega rode off like the Devil himself was after him, trailing the scent of terror and a strange, warm sweetness much stronger than his usual faint, sugary scent.

Chapter 20

Will's form was a small smudge in the distance by the time Hannibal collected himself enough to head home, terrified he would find his spouse lifeless in the lane along the way, sick and frightened as he was.

The staff assured him Will had, indeed, made it home in one piece, though he was so ill Mr. Prince and Francis had taken him upstairs at once, according to Mr. Hawkes' agitated recounting. It left Hannibal vastly relieved on that count, at least, knowing Will had made it home and was in good hands.

Grandfather caught sight of him as he came in and wheeled towards him from the east wing, shouting, "What on earth have you done to him now? You should be horsewhipped!"

"Will saw to that already," Hannibal wearily said, concerned by the state Will was in.

"Ha! Serves you right, you ingrate!" Grandfather scolded, angry. "*Someone* needs to take that arrogance down a few pegs!"

Hannibal scowled at him and took the stairs two at a time, Grandfather calling admonishments up after him. He could smell the faint, foul stink of Francis Doranhouse on the landing and it ratcheted his agitation higher, the presence of the other Alpha a threat Hannibal could barely stomach. It was all he could do not to barge his way into Will's suite and get some answers, but that would do more harm than good, he knew. Will was in Jimmy's faithful hands and that was, perhaps, the best thing for both of them right now.

He slammed into his room instead, stripping his jacket and waistcoat off, still shocked at how Will had flogged him away as if he'd been in mortal danger.

'*You could have been killed!*'

'*Isn't that what you're after?!*'

Terror. The scent-memory of it prickled Hannibal's sinuses, his heart rate picking up and his stomach tightening. Will's violence had always intrigued Hannibal, but even he knew Will striking someone with a riding crop was the last resort of a desperate kind of fear. He'd stank of blind fright and a sweet, elusive *something* that had acted like icy water on Hannibal's own reactions.

Something about him made his mate fear for his life and the fault, he knew, lay in himself. He had never taken the time to know Will, had never attempted to befriend an Omega or understand one—he was essentially as unschooled in Omegas as a toddling babe, his father's concubine and Bedelia's instruction notwithstanding. All he really knew was he had somehow goaded his mate into lashing out on the lane.

And he needed to know why.

A mute knock at the door admitted Berger, silent and leery and clearly expecting to find him in a temper.

"Fetch my bag down," Hannibal ordered him, moving to the mirror to inspect the damage Will had done.

It would scar, he knew, this livid, bruised and bloodied mark on his cheek. He was lucky Will had only used force enough to check him, else the damage might have cost him an eye. But he could hardly begrudge him, considering the scars he had left on Will. Marks on the heart showed in different ways than those on the skin, but were, Hannibal knew, no less painful a reminder of the injury that caused them.

Hannibal looked thoughtfully at the closed door to the washroom, aware of the faint sounds of water as his mate moved within and the light tones of Jimmy's voice as he assisted his master. It reminded Hannibal of when he'd burst in on Will and surprised him from the tub. He'd been as delicate and beautiful then as he'd been ablaze with righteous indignation and outrage on his horse, wielding his crop like a soldier with a saber, but no less beautiful.

Beautiful but terrified all the same.

"Would you like me to stitch you?" Berger offered.

"I would like to start this day over entirely!" Hannibal sighed. "Inform Jimmy that I wish to have a discussion with Will when he is dressed."

He dearly hoped by then they *both* would be a little more calm.

"In his suite, m'Lord or your own?"

"He can choose, it's no matter to me, but tell him I wish to speak with him immediately," Hannibal said, shooing Berger out on his way.

Trembling with the loss of the adrenaline that had flooded him, he collected his supplies from his bag and returned to the mirror, grateful for the pain of washing and repairing the wound on his cheek that forced him to pull himself back under control, to recall Will's condition and how he'd behaved.

Broken ribs, perhaps. Bruised, at least, and definitely a concussion. He knew too well how brutal even one of those could be, let alone a combination. He chafed to examine Will and settle his mind there was nothing terribly wrong, to have a chance to speak to him about what had happened, to hear him give voice to his fears so Hannibal could address them.

He took a deep breath and snipped off the thread before inspecting the small, tidy stitches holding his tanned skin together.

He carefully put his tools away, only half aware of Will in the washroom, only half aware his anxiety for his mate was tuning his senses towards him. But when the faint slosh of water was accompanied by a pained, nearly inaudible noise of distress, that very awareness sent Hannibal bursting through the door before his mind caught up with his immediate response.

Will, teetering in an attempt to get out of the tub, immediately dropped back into the sudsy water up to his chin, his blue eyes wide and alarmed and fixed on Hannibal with sharp anxiety. His voice came out with a harsh, sharp edge when he said, "Do *not* come any closer, Lord Clarges!"

"I heard you cry out," Hannibal said, guilt clawing at his gut when Will looked up at him, blue eyes wide with mingled fear and fury. "You're dizzy, aren't you? And it's getting worse?"

"Please, leave me alone," Will said, his breathing shallow as he fought the nausea his abrupt movement had inspired, the walls of the washroom seeming to tilt and run together quite alarmingly.

"And let you lose consciousness in the bath?" Hannibal asked, grim. "I will embarrass both of us before I allow that, Will."

"Hannibal, I am warning you—"

"Considering there is little within reach you can fling at me," Hannibal said, kicking the small bathing stool over to settle on it next to the tub, "I believe this is my opportunity to expect you to behave rationally and get some answers."

Will's cheeks colored and he glowered, wrinkling his small, perfect nose and once more lamenting the lack of locks on the doors. "You can hardly be said to have behaved rationally where I am concerned! I sought a hot bath to find some *relief*, Lord Clarges! Do not mitigate what little headway I've made by badgering me! *Get out.*"

He tensed in the tub, aching muscles screaming their reluctance, but he was not about to take any chances, vulnerable position that he was in. Hannibal, for all he knew, might just take it into his head to hold him under until the bubbling stopped and be done with it at last. *Settle things*, as he'd put it.

"When I said you might've been killed, you responded by asking if it wasn't what I was after—why would you say such a thing? Why were you so frightened of me?" Hannibal demanded, entirely ignoring the jibe, all grace and good manners abandoned to the Alpha urge to unearth the source of this problem and deal with it. He tasted Will's fear like ash on his tongue, the sharp scent of it strengthening despite his being immersed in water, and said, "No, allow me to amend that, why *are* you so frightened of me?"

"I am not—"

"Don't you *dare* lie to me now when you never have before," Hannibal said, cutting him off. "I want the truth of it, Will. You were terrified of me. So terrified, in fact, that you whipped me with your crop—something I know even a violent termagant such as yourself would normally hesitate to do! Did you honestly believe I was going to hurt you?"

"You grabbed me! I have no idea what you are capable of," Will told him, stiff with tension. His hands rose to grip the sides of the tub, knuckles turning white with force as if bracing for an attack. "I only know what you have shown me."

"Which has not been kindness?" Hannibal finished for him, chuffing a short, sharp bark of unhappy laughter. He spied Jimmy peeking in through the washroom door, but the valet closed it again under Hannibal's dark glare. "Will, I am being entirely serious with you. I want to know what I have done to make you so fearful of me!"

Will looked down at the water, the goose egg lump on his forehead painfully stark where his wet hair parted around it. Not all of the tension around his mouth and eyes came from his fear, Hannibal knew. He was in a good deal of pain and Hannibal wanted nothing more than to soothe it from him.

"Will," he said again, softening his tone, wishing he could convey his sincerity to his spouse as bonded couples were said to do. "Please... you spoke of my intentions towards you. Have I given you some reason to believe I mean you harm?"

"Shall I list the ways in which you have shown yourself a less than caring spouse?" Will asked, his blue eyes lifting slowly with great respect for the worsening headache he risked. "Or even remind you that you have treated me abominably?"

"My memory is not lacking in that respect, Will. I am aware of how badly I've treated you," Hannibal said, having the good grace to blush. "Yet, I've hardly threatened to kill you."

Will's eyes rounded and he drew into a little ball of outraged fury that made Hannibal stare at him with growing shock.

"*Will*," he pressed, unable to believe his young spouse had reason to think he might actually do him deadly harm. "When have I ever threatened your life?"

Will's chin tipped up, familiar stubborn tenacity rising to the fore. With a tone that spoke of resignation to circumstances, Will said, "You told His Grace, '*Take him off of my hands before I arrange an accident for him.*' My first night under your roof when you were forced to share a table with me."

It was Hannibal's turn to be speechless. He gaped at Will, who gazed up at him with glittering assessment in his dark blue eyes, and he uttered a sharp, aghast laugh at how foolish it was, how ridiculously misplaced Will's fears were.

"What a lot of silly nonsense," he decided, shaking his head, another harsh, unhappy laugh escaping him. "Where has this come from so suddenly? Will, you're far too intelligent to make a mountain out of that particular molehill! I was speaking out of anger! *Six years* have passed since then! You can't expect me to accept *that* could make you believe I would actually *kill* you, Will. Honestly—"

"There was nothing at all laughable or accidental about cutting the girth strap on my saddle!" Will said, the pain in his sharp tone bringing Hannibal's scolding to a cold halt. "Nor in pushing me down the stairs!"

Hannibal let the implications of that sink in. He stared at Will, who seemed very small and very vulnerable, braced in the bath as if expecting he might not ever leave it alive, his blue eyes large and mournful in his flushed, lovely face, the wet tips of his curls dripping water down his cheeks.

"Excuse me, what did you just say?" Hannibal managed to ask, the words a breathless, shocked whisper.

"Why pretend it didn't happen?" Will asked, his bare throat tight with tension and his full mouth curving in a smile absolutely divorced from happiness. It was rueful and broken and Hannibal never wanted to see such an expression on his face ever again. *Ever.* "We both know my girth strap was tampered with the day I fell in the hopes I would break my neck, and you know as well as I do that I didn't trip down those stairs."

Heat flooded Hannibal's veins and he surged to his feet, protective anger swelling in him fit to make him burst. It did not escape his notice that Will flinched from him, no doubt thinking he would drown him there in the tub.

"Will," he said, struggling to contain his growing upset and anger. "Are you telling me someone *sabotaged your saddle*?"

"*You* hardly need to be told such a thing!" Will shot back, the heat of his bathwater flushing his skin. "You barely waited a full day before trying to kill me!"

"*I did nothing of the sort!*" Hannibal bellowed, horrified. "Why in the seven hells would you even *believe* such a thing? What on earth gave you that idea?"

"I received a letter claiming to have been privy to the attempt!" Will said, pressed back into the deeper end of the tub both to hide his nudity beneath the cloudy water and make it harder for Hannibal to force him under. "And Matthew showed me the girth strap! I could see for myself it had been cut."

"*Cut*?" Hannibal echoed, swiping his hand down his face, pacing like a caged animal with the force of his growing agitation. "Why would I have ever done such a thing? *When would I have ever done such a thing*?"

"*You* tell *me*!" Will snarled, Hannibal's forceful Alpha posturing filling him, as if his husband's anger belonged to him. Perhaps it *did* belong to him, some portion of it. He certainly felt angry, felt enraged, felt ready to shout back just as fiercely as he was shouted at.

Let no one ever say Will Grant went down without a fight.

"You have loathed me from the day you set eyes on me!" Will reminded him. "It is not entirely outside of the realm of possibility that you have *twice* tried to kill me! But I warn you now, Hannibal, the third time you had better make certain you succeed or I will not answer for what happens next!"

"There will *be no third time*!" Hannibal shouted, the throbbing Alpha undertone of his deep voice bouncing off of the decorative tin ceiling and reverberating through Will's chest. He swung around and pinned Will with incredulous amber eyes, such perfect horror written in their depths that Will almost questioned himself. "There was never a *single time*!"

He took a dragging breath, struggling to control himself, and Will mirrored him, panting and tense.

"Even were I the kind of man who could coldly murder an innocent person in my home," Hannibal said, a harsh thread of true fear ringing in his voice like the somber tone of a church bell. "I did *not* sabotage your saddle and I most *certainly* did not *push you down the stairs*! I sleep like the gods' own *dead*, Will! Had the servants not come pounding down the hall, I might not have woken at all!"

"If it wasn't you, then *who*?" Will demanded, challenging him, his smaller Omegan fangs bared in a snarl. "I *saw* whoever was there in your room, Hannibal! I called after them and they ran. When I started to follow, *you came from the shadows pushed me.*"

Hannibal stopped pacing abruptly, asking, "Whoever was in my room? You think I had someone with me? *Absolutely not.* Whoever you saw outside of your room—"

"Outside of *your* room," Will corrected, bewildered by Hannibal's reactions. He could feel pure, unadulterated, protective rage swelling through his bond to Hannibal, so great, in fact, it was almost overpowering. It was as if every word he spoke merely goaded Hannibal to greater upset.

Upset that seemed, strangely enough, to be on *Will's* behalf.

It threw Will off kilter and that only worried him all the more, thinking his bond might be twisting his perception to favor Hannibal when he should do nothing of the sort.

"I cannot believe what I am hearing," Hannibal said, horrified. "I honestly *cannot believe what you are telling me.*"

Will took advantage of Hannibal's pacing to pull the plunger from the tub and reach for a bathing sheet as the cloudy water drained.

"Am I liar now, as well, Hannibal?" he asked, bundling himself into the smooth material of the sheet, hiding his bare body behind the shield of the tub's side while he did so. He trembled in the cool room from nerves and chill, his sudden movements making his whole body ache in outrage.

"*No*, you are not a liar!" Hannibal said, a dark laugh escaping him. "If there is one thing in this world I can rely on, Will, it's your brutal honesty. What I *cannot believe* is that you have kept this to yourself! Someone has tried twice to kill you and I cannot even *try* to protect you because you have said nothing! Even knowing there had been one attempt already to kill you, you still found it beholden upon yourself to confront an *intruder* in *our home*! *Why* for the sake of all the gods?"

"I have never had reason to fear for my safety inside of my own house before," Will responded, the sharp edge of his anger subsiding as Hannibal's panic receded, the smallest kernel of doubt taking hold. "Why shouldn't I go check when I hear someone creeping about in the hall?"

"It did not even occur to you to wake me?" Hannibal asked, pausing in his pacing to pin Will with a glare, his hackles rising at the idea of a stranger being in his home, in his territory, within threatening distance of his—

"Well, *certainly*, had you been sleepwalking when you *shoved me down the stairs!*" Will said, clutching the bathing sheet close when Hannibal advanced on him.

"I will say it once more, Will, I did *no such thing!*" Hannibal said. "*This* is why you are terrified of me? You thought I've tried *twice* to kill you and I was going to, what? Drag you from your mare's back and squeeze the life out of you on the lane to Hartford?"

"*Yes*," Will said, trembling but not backing down. "Why shouldn't you? It would certainly make things easier."

"Easier on *whom*, pray tell?" Hannibal asked, gesturing widely. "*What* would I gain by it? The probability you have left your worldly belongings to your father? The very real possibility of losing Hartford House forever, if we prefer to be as cold as you believe I am?"

Will stared at him, his pain-clouded mind seizing on what his husband had said, perfectly reasonable arguments he'd been too nervous and uncertain to consider before now. It cracked his surety like a shell and left him adrift on sudden, frightening doubt.

"This is entirely beyond my comprehension! You are only now telling me your saddle was tampered with! There was an intruder—no *two* intruders—*in our home*, one of whom pushed you down the stairs, no doubt fully intending you not survive! And when you *do* manage to survive, you *don't tell me about it!* Gods, I cannot remember ever being so angry! Why on earth didn't you come to me so—"

"*Because I didn't wish to meet the same fate as the* former *Lady Clarges!*" Will said, his anxiety and confusion putting a snarl in his words.

Hannibal drew back as if he'd been hit with something much more painful than a crop and Will felt his stomach sink, his bond to Hannibal giving him nothing but pain.

Hannibal's amber gaze fastened on Will, his eyes wide and horrified and showing profound hurt nearly as palpable as the bond itself.

"*Murdered*, you mean?" he asked, and his mouth curled in a wry, unhappy smile. "Do you imagine I drowned her in the bath, as you seem to believe I intended to do to you?"

Will swallowed hard, clinging to the tub with one hand, the seam of the sheet with the other, staring at his husband who seemed equally as devastated as he was hurt.

"I can only infer from what little I have f—"

"Which is *nothing*," Hannibal said, the echo of the Alpha growl in his voice dying in the resulting silence. Will sat still and alert but not cowering, not with that much steel in him. "What version of the story have you heard? That I seduced her? That I tired of her? That I threw her from the parapets in a rage?"

"You cannot blame me for listening to rumors when that is *all* I have to listen to!" Will flared, wincing when his head throbbed with more insistence from the volume of his voice. "I was never even told she existed, Hannibal! The world believes you killed her and I am left with nothing but... *pieces* to put together as they fit!"

"And they fit in the shape of my killing her," Hannibal said, and turned away, rubbing his face, weary resignation falling over him in a way that made Will's tension fall, in turn. "Shall I tell you another story? Hm? One to set your mind at ease, perhaps? Or merely confirm that I am, in fact, just the monster you imagine?"

Will shivered in the bath sheet, fingers so tight on the side of the tub that his knuckles blanched white.

Hannibal swung back to face him, the stitched wound on his cheek livid against his skin, his amber eyes unhappy and angry but filled with something else Will's gut told him was guilt.

"Or perhaps it is suitable you imagine me precisely as I am," he said, hollow and cold. "A man who sends his young spouse out alone in his nightclothes with no protection, a man who has killed as many men in a war as he has saved, and a man who gutted his first wife like a felled doe in our marriage bed."

Will flinched from the statement, from the brutal picture it brought to his mind—blood, fear, and anguished, frantic screams streaking across his imagination like fingers of lightning, a brief illumination of a possibility that shook him to his soul.

Yet, as it had with Molly in Duxbury, even hearing it from Hannibal's own mouth couldn't stem the sliver of hope that Hannibal was innocent and the world was wrong.

That his husband was, beneath it all, just a man like any other and not the monster he seemed or claimed to be.

"You're deliberately trying to frighten me," Will said, feeling it through his bond, latching onto Hannibal's words to find the holes he had left behind, gaping emptiness of events he'd pared away to leave himself culpable. "*Why* are you telling me this way? *What happened to her*, Hannibal? *Why do you feel so guilty?*"

"I *am* guilty, Will," Hannibal said, and stood trembling before him, fists clenched and chest heaving with his short, sharp breaths. The forceful maelstrom of emotion drained slowly out of him, leaving only abysmal grief and a terrible sense of wrong. "You *should* be afraid of me."

"*Don't* lie *to me*," Will said, clenching his teeth against the pain in his head as it shot down his shoulders, aching and deep. "I have *never* lied to you, Hannibal, and you will not lie to me, in turn! Tell me the truth—"

"What possible difference could it make, now? The worst has happened and you have nearly been killed because you fear me," Hannibal said, dropping his gaze to the floor, his fists unclenching. "Once again, I have failed someone I should have protected. At least you didn't die because of it. I suppose that makes you a rarity of *one*."

Hannibal crossed the washroom in three quick strides and wrenched open the door to Will's suite, intent on his plans to keep his mate safe. He shouted for Jimmy to go fetch Berger, the boom of his voice loud enough it was entirely likely Mr. Berger heard him without Jimmy having to do so. The valet, very wisely however, did as he was told.

Will stared at him through the ache in his head, reading his pain and his upset, reading the deeper guilt which seemed to permeate him, at odds with the bone-deep regret saturating his bond.

"What happened to her, Hannibal?" Will asked, the shiver from the cold giving way to feverish heat and an unsettling lurch from his stomach. "Tell me what really happened to her and I will give you the benefit of the doubt. I want *answers*. I want you to *talk to me*."

He swallowed hard at the startled flare of hope he saw in Hannibal's amber eyes, at the sudden surge of it he felt through his bond, and said with less force, "You should have told me long before now."

"When? Over tea and scones? During all of the many long hours we've spent together?" Hannibal scoffed, and snorted with disdain, still chuffing with protective fury. "Believe it or not, Will, I did plan on telling you, but I certainly won't do so in the middle of your bath while there is a killer lying in wait for you! Regardless of your current feelings for me, you are my spouse and your safety is my foremost concern."

Will watched Hannibal move back through the washroom to his own suite, feeling less sure of his suspicions and more sure Hannibal was genuinely and deeply distressed by what he'd told him. The understanding that his fears might have been mislaid untangled a twisted jumble of isolation and hopelessness inside of him, filling him with a relief he couldn't quite keep out of his voice when he called out to him, "You truly do not wish I was dead?"

"*No! Gods* no!" Hannibal bellowed, frustrated and angry because too much time had passed now to properly figure out who actually *had* rigged Will's saddle or violated the safety of their home. He yanked the bell pull by his bed for good measure and returned to the washroom to stand in the doorway, eyes blazing. "Had I any idea you had been so threatened in our home, Will, I would have packed you away from here in a heartbeat! When I find out who is responsible for this—and I *will* find out—I cannot guarantee I will hold my temper! They are certainly going to pay in full for the pain and fear they have caused you, I can promise you that!"

The weight of the entire world lifted from Will's heart. Such simple words with such profound effect accompanied by Hannibal's protective Alpha anger made Will feel safer than he had in years. The dark, ugly knot of sick fear and distrust uncoiled from Will's heart in slow degrees of relief. He had no one but this Alpha his instincts had formed to so long ago, and the knowledge that Hannibal tried to kill him had hurt Will in ways he couldn't bear to address.

But now he was no longer standing alone against an unseen enemy with no resources and nowhere to turn.

Hannibal was there with him, with all of his Alpha strength to lend in his defense.

"We shall have to take measures," Hannibal said, thinking aloud, distracted and frustrated and practically growling. "It is unacceptable that we are not safe in our beds! Everything about this is unacceptable!"

"I asked Mr. Hawkes to be more vigilant with who had access to the house," Will said, eyes sweeping closed with the force of his relief, the enormity of it eclipsing even the pain he was feeling, if only for a moment. "I worried your grandfather would be in danger."

"Yet you were not worried for yourself?" Hannibal asked, and laughed again, humorless and resigned. "Don't answer that, please. I would only be burdened by it."

Will said nothing, still absorbed in the growing understanding that Hannibal was not intent on seeing him dead, by the hope that he *hadn't* murdered his first wife as everyone assumed, though Will had a good many questions on that count.

"I cannot *fathom* what you were thinking! Your mind is such that I have great difficulty believing you could ever be remotely thoughtless, yet thoughtless you have been!" Hannibal said, hands on his hips, beside himself with disbelief and surging, protective anger. He was at a loss, uncertain how to protect Will when Will refused to be protected—worse, when Will thought *he* was what he needed protection from. "Where the *seven hells* is he? I refuse to tolerate this!"

"I suppose there's nothing to be done about it now," Will said, fumbling the bathing sheet around when his words drew his husband's agitated, unsteady attention. He managed to cover himself from nape to ankles but he did not try rising from the empty tub. He did not at all trust himself to get out of it now. He'd nearly gone head first into the floor trying the first time.

"Noth—*have you taken leave of your senses completely?*" Hannibal asked, looking fairly fierce as he glared down at Will, who managed to gaze back up at him with that damnable composure of his, glassy-eyed and woozy. "You will—*no, I have no reason to explain this to you."

"Hannibal?" Will called, wary when he strode from the washroom once again, leaving the door to his suite standing wide. He clutched the side of the tub and leaned over, calling, "Hannibal! What are you going to do?"

367

"I cannot trust you with your own safety!" Hannibal shouted, and yanked fiercely on the velvet call rope by his bed much more vigorously than he had before, no doubt waking a clamor downstairs loud enough to scare the dead in Duxbury. "You are reckless and thoughtless and haven't a care for yourself! If I leave you to your own devices, you'll be dead by the end of the month! *Nay!* By the end of the *week!*"

Will subsided, a thoughtful frown on his face. With force enough to be heard over Hannibal's dark, angry muttering, he said, "I don't like the sound of that!"

"I am entirely disregarding your preferences in this matter, Will!" Hannibal said, appearing in his line of sight looking quite unsteady and angry, his scent a flagrant warning he was in full flush to fight and damn the consequences. It teased Will's nose and pooled in his belly, making his fingers and toes curl, as if the scent was something he could wrap around himself and delve into quite happily. "I am your husband and you will do as I say!"

The words acted like cold water on that warm feeling and Will drew up, offended. Before his better sense could catch up with his temper, he shouted, "Like *hell* I will!"

He rose like Venus from the sea and those playful little spots at the corners of his eyes unhelpfully converged on him all at once.

Hannibal saw the blood drain from Will's face and saw him start to buckle. In an instant he was there, rushing to catch Will up and swing him from the tub, bulky wet sheet and all.

"I am going to be sick," Will said, in the cautious, quiet tones of someone who very much meant it, his back and shoulders flaring with pain, even as gentle as Hannibal was with him.

"It's that damned knock you took!" Hannibal said, careful not to raise his voice, his anger evaporating to deep concern. He eased Will down next to the basin and held him there. When Will bent his head to the porcelain, Hannibal took the chance to smooth his damp curls back and take a closer look at his head. He was distracted from his inspection by Berger coming in at last, and called, "Berger, have Cook make some weak tea and porridge and bring it up with some ice as quickly as possible."

"Please, don't trouble yourself," Will said, the urge to be sick passing in increments now that he wasn't moving so rapidly. He felt the warmth of

Hannibal's body around his and relaxed slightly, some of his pain easing with the loss of his tension.

"I will trouble myself and everyone else all I like, thank you very much," Hannibal informed him. "Considering how little trouble you are most times, I think we can manage well enough just now. Do you need to be sick?"

"No, I think it passed," Will said, still understandably cautious.

He growled softly when Hannibal scooped him up, his brow furrowing with irritation as he was carried into his husband's suite.

"The nausea is brought on by movement," Hannibal said, depositing Will neatly against the pillows, half sitting up in his bed. "As you have undoubtedly realized. You need to lie quietly. Keep your eyes closed as much as you can."

Will didn't. He slit his eyelids against his better judgment to see Hannibal moving from window to window, drawing the heavy drapes closed against the brightening sunlight, leaving the room in near total darkness. The flare of a match was followed by the sharp scent of sulfur as Hannibal lit a lamp and turned it down to a low, bare flame still achingly bright in the darkness.

When he returned to the bed, Will unconsciously clutched the bath sheet tighter and closed his eyes again, wincing as the bed shifted with his husband's weight.

Callused fingers brushed softly against his brow as the lump was again exposed, followed by the unexpected brush of Hannibal's thumb over the wrinkle in his brow which accompanied the gruff admonition, "Being cross won't help your headache."

"I am not cross," Will said, eyes fluttering open with less pain than before. "I am thoughtful."

"*That* is certainly true," Hannibal admitted, seated alongside Will's hip, his fingers moving to linger in Will's curls, warm and gentle. "Try not to be too terribly thoughtful, Will. Rest is what fixes this particular problem. I've seen these types of injuries before."

"I know," Will said, swallowing hard. "I've read your contributions to the Capital Medical Journal. Not that I am any wiser, mind you. For an entry occupying so many pages, it offered surprisingly little insight into the matter of concussions."

Hannibal chuffed a low laugh and told him, "See? You're already more yourself."

Will offered a rueful, reluctant chuckle, resisting the urge to turn his head against Hannibal's touch. Those long fingers moved softly against Will's scalp, lifting goosebumps on his skin. He was checking, Will knew. Checking for other lumps, for other cuts, yet even knowing the intent behind the touch didn't lessen the effect. It eased him, reaching deeper than the surface to find the tension that had hardened him since childhood. It annoyed him something so insignificant could make such a profound difference without Hannibal even being aware of it, and he summoned a glower to look up at his husband.

Much to his surprise, Hannibal gazed down at him with an expression he'd never chanced to see before. Softness, perhaps. Fondness. Concern. Worry. Will had no idea how to interpret it.

He'd never had to do so before now.

"Most of my observations into such injuries were made on the battlefield," Hannibal said, and when those ugly memories assaulted him, as they so often did, he found the heat of Will's skin and the soft, soap-sweet scent of him made them lose their sharpness. He checked Will's eyes, noting the reaction of his pupils, murmuring, "War is not all gunshots, impalement, and cannon blow back. I've seen a good many knocks such as this, though recovery vastly varies and war is hardly conducive to proper observation."

A slight, amused smile curved his mouth, the light gleaming across the stark height of his cheekbone and just barely lighting the edges of his lips as he said, "Knowing your resilience, Will, you'll be back on your mare come morning."

Will laughed softly, a light sigh escaping him when Hannibal's thumb traced the arch of one eyebrow. He cleared his throat to cover it and reminded him, "It is important to be useful."

"Believe me, you have been a tad more than useful," Hannibal told him, dropping his hand, but with great reluctance.

Berger returned then, bearing a lovely tray with the requested weak tea.

"The porridge takes a bit of time, m'Lord," he said, cautiously pouring a cup for Will. "I'll bring it up as soon as it's done."

"Berger, tell Mr. Hawkes I wish to speak with him on the subject of House security," Hannibal said. "And tell Peter I expect to see him directly after."

"Hannibal, no," Will protested, groping to put a restraining hand on his husband's arm, imploring, "There must be some reasonable explanation, there is no cause—"

"You have been hurt, Will, which is all the cause I need to do what I feel is necessary to secure your safety," Hannibal said, thinking anxiously of what he'd been told. "And considering you think *I* am the culprit, I am not going to rely on your definition of *reasonable*. Berger, do as I say at once."

"Yes, m'Lord," Berger said, immediately on his way.

"*Thought* you were the culprit," Will murmured, accepting the teacup cautiously when Hannibal handed it to him.

Hannibal blew out a soft breath of relief and asked, "Do you believe I am not at fault?"

"I think you are at fault for a good many things, Hannibal, but I no longer think you tried to kill me," Will offered, wincing as his shifting pulled on his back. "Your reaction alone reassures me. Even you must surely lack the guile to perform with such conviction."

"In which case, will you allow me to examine you?" Hannibal asked, his amber eyes flicking over Will's sturdy little body there in his bed, his worry clear in the weight of his gaze. When Will's brow furrowed up again, he hastened to say, "At least let me make sure you haven't broken any bones. You must be bruised to an inch."

"My inches are not up for inspection," Will warned him, taking a sip of his tea, eyes closing as his aches and pains warned him he might not be as well as he wanted to be. With caution and hesitance, he said, "It might be wise to allow you to offer your professional opinion... on one condition."

Hannibal's mouth quirked at the corners, the barest hint of a smile. "Name it."

"Tell me about her," Will said, setting the teacup aside. "As you intended to, Hannibal. The whole truth of it. You owe me that."

Hannibal reached out and smoothed his hair, the heavy uneasiness in him lessened somewhat by the strengthening scent of Will's skin, by the silken feel of his curls, by the gentle readiness for acceptance he could sense.

"I owe you far better than you've gotten from me so far, Will. You have a vast capacity for goodness in you that I lack," he said, fingers falling to Will's neck, lightly stroking his skin. He pulled away with a sigh and folded a cloth over the ice Berger had brought him. "I do not wish to test that. My behavior regarding Melinda does me no credit."

"Your willingness to speak of something which shames you does you credit, Hannibal," Will breathed, eyes closing when Hannibal gently pressed the ice pack to the lump on his head. A deep breath gave him Hannibal's Alpha scent, the sharp warning tone softening as he calmed. It brought another warm ripple to his lower belly, slumberous and faint but potent. "Truth has many sides, and we each prefer a side of our choosing, but I would hear yours in this matter."

"May I ask first how you heard about Melinda?" Hannibal asked, letting Will's slender fingers replace his own on the pack. He moved down to Will's long feet to bare his legs to his knees, wincing at the smattering of purple bruises he'd gathered on his shins and knees.

Will toyed with the lip of the sheet with his free hand, nervous as Hannibal began at his toes, gently testing the digits. His skin tingled, foot twitching in response to the ticklish touch as his husband's capable hands moved firmly over him, seeking any sign of tender response.

His own curiosity if Hannibal intended to move up his entire body in such a manner brought heat flaming into his cheeks, making him doubly grateful for the ice on his head. He blurted rather than said, "I met her sister, Molly, in Duxbury. She was kind enough to tell me her story."

"Molly Forester," Hannibal murmured, thinking of that young blond woman Will had lunched with. He laughed once, short and sharp, trading one foot for the other, Will's curled and unharmed little toes forsaken for his delicate ankles. His physician's mind cataloged the movement of bones and ligaments, but the Alpha in him marveled at the solid feel of his mate in his hands, an intriguing mixture of delicacy and honed muscle that woke an unusual itch in him for more. "She was barely four years old at the time! Perhaps less, even. She was born while I was away at medical school. She couldn't possibly recall much of what happened."

"She didn't, but gossip and conjecture filled in the details she lacked," Will said, subsiding against the pillows under Hannibal's gentle touch. He lay unresisting as his shins were inspected, each delicate brush of Hannibal's fingers on his skin vibrating through his nerves like a plucked harp string, thrumming and true. "She told me you broke Melinda's heart. That you swept her away when she was barely grown and eloped with her. That within a month she was dead and in the ground, her death a mystery quieted with your grandfather's money."

"The lauded opinion of a child not quite five years of age," Hannibal said, and sighed, his attention shifting to Will's bruised knees, finding them tender but not displaced, and fairly painless upon movement. He got up and went to his medical bag, still there on his vanity, and dug out his salve. He searched Will's young face as he returned to his place, taking in his sleepy expression, his woozy blue eyes, his tousled, damp curls and the aching vulnerability that had always been there before him.

He'd just been too blind to see what Will's strength was protecting before now.

"I had hoped, once, to never have this conversation," he murmured, dabbing the salve on Will's bruises with light, soft strokes. "I was a fool to think the former Lady Clarges would remain a secret, but now that I have the chance to tell you, I hardly know where to begin."

Will took a steadying breath, preparing for the worst, the specter of his father in his dark heart whispering the truth would crush even so tentative a faith as his, that Hannibal was everything Will feared he might be and he would always be disappointed, always be betrayed.

But deeper still was something his father had never been able to pare out of him—*hope*. Ugly and awful and frightening in its capacity to grow, heedless of all consequence. Whatever the outcome, he knew he had to abandon expectation and simply seek the truth.

After everything that had happened, they *both* were owed a little honesty.

"Molly's story was true, in most respects. Melinda and I were best friends from childhood, inseparable despite Grandfather's disapproval. I would not heed him. You must find it hard to imagine such a thing," Hannibal said, uttering a low, wry chuckle, concentrating on applying the salve to Will's bruises. "I went away when I was sixteen, packed off for early entry to medical school. I wrote her every single day. Even knowing my grandfather had a contract with yours, I promised myself I would marry her and we would be terribly happy and nothing would ever trouble us again..."

Will's heart ached for him, seeing Hannibal there in his imagination, young and happily in love, doting on a young blonde much like Molly. Finding hope in life after the terrible loss of his family, starting a new career as a doctor with a bright future ahead of him. The potential made Will's throat constrict with emotion, a life yet unlived, memories yet unmade, the promise of things that never came to be.

If there was anything Will could understand to its depths, it was an unfinished life.

"I returned earlier than planned on holiday to surprise her," Hannibal said, lost in his memories. He smiled sadly and said, "She surprised me, instead."

"Hannibal," Will said, blinking hard against threatening tears, feeling too keenly through his bond the things Hannibal's ingrained stoicism would never reveal. He barely noticed when Hannibal tucked the sheet up to bare one long thigh, grimacing at the bruises there. "If you truly do not wish—"

"It is far past time I say it," Hannibal said, careful to keep Will's groin covered as he checked both of his legs and hips, satisfied he had no palpable fractures, only deep bruises he began to cover with salve. "Perhaps it will help you see me more clearly."

Hannibal's hands on his thighs bled into Will's awareness, bringing blushes in their wake. His husband's professionalism made it less embarrassing, but Will still shifted and tried to sit up straighter in an effort to not feel so exposed. The movement rippled down his spine from his nape to his tailbone, terrible pain that made him wince and prompted Hannibal to gently touch his waist, warning, "This may pain you, Will, but I suspect you might have broken a rib or two."

"No, it's just an ache," Will said, a bit breathless when Hannibal shaped his torso through the sheet, carefully feeling his way up Will's body, testing and gentle. Will winced, relieved when nothing shifted, and Hannibal seemed satisfied, though reluctant to pull his hands away.

"You're remarkably resilient, not a break on you. Jimmy should bind them during the day. I'll let him apply the salve for you," Hannibal said, placing the little jar on the nightstand. "Here, let me check your spine."

Will followed his lead, letting Hannibal shift him around on the bed onto his belly, a pillow hugged underneath him to cradle his bruised ribs and head, the ice pack propped carefully so as not to press on the painful spot.

Hannibal settled at his side, a warm, weighty presence next to him, one hand on Will's nape in a gentle pressure he shifted to soft kneading, his sensitive fingers finding the ache with unerring accuracy.

"It will help the headache," Hannibal said, not wishing to be misunderstood. There had been entirely too many misunderstandings between them already.

Will focused sharply on the warm, sure hand kneading his nape with such gentle caution, not in an attempt to control him, but to heal him. It bothered him that even so well-intentioned and impersonal a thing could affect him with such deep immediacy, and he found himself confounded by his Omegan nature yet again, unsure how to counter it, uncertain if he even wanted to.

So many long, lonely years without comfort made it difficult to resist.

Hoping to distract himself, Will whispered, "How did she surprise you, Hannibal? What was it that set such sad circumstances into motion?"

Hannibal smiled, a taut and unhappy smile he used to cover all manner of disquiet. "It was to be my last year in medical school. I managed to escape a few days ahead of schedule, and when I came home, I went straight away to a place where we always met in secret in the hopes of finding her there," he said, the words coming out a low, throaty purr. "And she was. I discovered her naked in the arms of her lover."

Will flinched, the image hitting him like a slap in the face.

"I cut off contact entirely, naturally," Hannibal said, leaning over him, moving both hands to Will's shoulders to knead away the pain. "I left her behind, spent a sorry few weeks with Grandfather, then returned to finish my schooling and resign myself to the understanding I had made a serious error in judgment. She wrote to me for months afterwards, letter after letter I returned unopened until one day I received one from her father telling me Melinda was about to give birth to my child and demanding some action on my part."

Will remained silent, feeling Hannibal's anger like a burning brand within him, but it was overshadowed by the rupturing hurt it tried so desperately to hide. This girl, this child-bride he'd had such hope in, had landed him a blow that had fractured him down to his soul.

"I read the next letter she sent me, begging me to rescue her from her thoughtless actions, pleading for me to remember our fast friendship and extend my protection to her," Hannibal said, sightless eyes fixed on Will's soft and tousled, damp curls, but seeing only the damning words on the pages she had written. "Her lover abandoned her, as they so often do, so she chose to lay it all squarely on my shoulders, trusting our friendship would save her."

"You did save her, didn't you? Rather, you tried," Will softly said, feeling the tension crawl down Hannibal's arms and settle in the hands on his body. "You loved her too much to leave her in such wretched straits."

Hannibal's shoulders slumped, the barest sign of defeat. "Did I? Perhaps I did. Perhaps that was it, what compelled me to return and hide Melinda and her coming child beneath the blanket of my position.

"When I came for her, I found she had tried to rid herself of the baby through... unspeakable means but only gained an infection from the attempt," he murmured, cautious in his anger not to hurt his little mate, tenderly easing his hands down the ditch of Will's spine and up again, chasing the tension away with his inspection, the unevenness his hands encountered lost in the texture of the sheet as it shifted and bunched. "She was so very ill. The infection had gone into her blood. She was in great pain when I reached her, and I feared the damage done to the baby through her rash actions."

"She was frightened," Will breathed, feeling the panic of her situation, the future stretching ahead of her in abysmal loneliness, shunned by her neighbors and shamed for her youthful indiscretion. The only reason it didn't entirely overcome him was due to the gentle pressure of Hannibal's hands on his shoulders and back. "It is such a harsh price to pay for such a trespass. Her parents knew of the attempt?"

"That is how they discovered her circumstances," Hannibal said, focusing on the feel of Will's body beneath his hands, the warmth he gave off, the suppleness of his muscles. The more he touched him, the more aware he became of his own calm. He knew from an intellectual standpoint it was a natural occurrence between an Alpha and Omega, thanks to Bedelia's instruction, he just hadn't expected to feel it so keenly or so deeply, as if merely touching Will was an action he could continue forever and feel perfectly completed by. It made it less painful to continue confessing his sins, and he drew a deep breath to say, "I told Melinda I would rescue her reputation on the condition she admit to her mother and father the child was not mine.

"She did so, eager to be unburdened, eager to find a way out of the mess she had found herself in. They were stunned but quickly saw their livelihood was at stake," he went on, recalling their faces. "They were simple people with good, simple lives and her conduct shocked them but they were grateful for my intervention. I took her north and married her."

'I thought she was a princess and he was taking her away to a royal castle...'

"Grandfather was furious, of course," Hannibal said, a dark chuckle escaping him as he went to work on Will's fragile neck again, smoothing his thumbs up to

376

the base of his skull. "He threatened to disown me on the spot, raged about the contract he'd made, demanded I annul the marriage. He was far too wise to think the baby was mine and accused me of throwing away my future for childish fantasies. We eventually agreed I would send her and the child to the south and never set eyes on either of them again, but he needn't have worried. She succumbed to her infection just a few days after her sixteenth birthday."

He fell silent and Will took a deep, shuddering breath, feeling the warm weight of Hannibal's hands slide down to his shoulders. He wanted to weep for him, a disillusioned youth still so deeply in love he would risk the ire of his family and his very position just to rescue her.

"I had to... I had to cut her open to save the baby, a little girl," Hannibal whispered.

Will's heart lurched with his quiet statement, a world of horror pared down to such a simple sentence, describing something even Will's vivid imagination had difficulty wrapping around—cut into the body of a loved one or else lose two instead of one.

"Did she live?" Will asked, hoping she had, knowing if she hadn't, it made Hannibal's necessary action even more upsetting.

"She lived," Hannibal said, resuming his gentle massage of Will's back, remembering when he had held her, his fingertips brushing the soft, round cheek of Melinda's newborn daughter. "There wasn't a mark on her, though she was weak from the state her mother had been in."

"What happened to her?" Will breathed, grateful for Hannibal's warm touch as he worked both hands down the loosening muscles of his back, firm but tender. It eased the sharp bite of his imagination, somehow both calming and feeding the warmth within him as if such soothing attention could hold it at bay. "Is she close?"

"No... I honestly don't know," Hannibal whispered, his deep voice raw and unsettled when he said, "Grandfather had to step in; I was too... I was useless with shock and grief. He sent the baby away to be raised when the Foresters could not take her. At my insistence he gave her family a settlement to lift them from poverty and allowed Melinda her place in the family cemetery. I left the moment I could get away, fled to the military and left the country, the only thing I could think to do to get as far from her as possible."

"She hurt you," Will whispered, knowing there was something more, something Hannibal had still not told him. His flight tasted of guilt and anguish and soured adoration, an overpowering wave of oppression flooding him to foreign shores.

"She begged me for my forgiveness," Hannibal said, all tone and inflection leaving his voice. His hands slid to the wings of Will's scapulae and paused there, fingers curving just beneath his arms, the tips smoothing absently against his sheet-covered skin. "As she lay there in pain, striving to last long enough to bring her daughter into the world, she confessed she had wronged me, that she had been frightened and had turned to me because she trusted me and I had never failed her. She begged me to forgive her... and I refused."

Will's head came up and he turned slightly, just enough to see Hannibal's handsome face set in lines of pain and self-reproach.

"She wept and pleaded for me to forgive her and I *refused* her," he said again, trying to make it solid in his memory, in his heart. That had been the start of it, Will knew. That was what had made those walls go up, thicker and stronger than before. Melinda had been the first to breach them after Lady Minamoto, after losing Miska, and her betrayal had taught an impressionable young man that the lessons he'd learned as a child were all true.

They were the very same lessons Will knew to their depths—there was nothing good or honest in the world, no kindness left unpunished, no feeling left unspurned, no way to take back what was said or done or say the things that should have been said.

It was little wonder this man was before him, divorced in so many ways from what others took for granted, lashing back at the world while Will removed himself from it. Two vastly different responses, each as destructive and unchecked as the other.

"She died mere moments after I did so. I stole her hope and let her die thinking I hated her," Hannibal whispered, seeking the comfort of touching his mate without realizing it, the brush of his hands changing to a caress that twined up into Will's fragrant, silken curls. "She was just a child, just a frightened, silly child, and I let her go in such a terrible way—"

"You were little better than a child yourself, Hannibal," Will said, his understanding of his husband finding a broad new wing where the weeping shadow of Melinda Ledford drifted. "She was in a hopeless situation that grew more desperate by the hour and you did what you could to mend it. When we are wounded and cornered, we strike out. We strive to walk in the footsteps of saints and martyrs, but we are merely human, Hannibal. You had no control over her decisions."

"No, I didn't, but had I been a better man, she would never have sought such disreputable company," Hannibal said, moving his hands to the base of Will's spine. "Had I come at her first letter, she never would have sought out a back alley butcher. Had I returned sooner, I could have cleared the infection she contracted from it. Had I put aside my anger at her, she might have found the strength to survive."

Will's mouth tightened and his throat constricted, even as his heart fluttered and ached with the guilt rolling off of Hannibal in waves of self-loathing. "Looking back at what might have been is a dangerous pastime, Hannibal. We have all been in situations where we wish things might have gone differently, fantasies where we change the course of our world through one correct word or one right action. It is a fiendish torture. There is no return to what has been. There is no reversing time to bring teacups back together again, however much we lament their shattering."

Hannibal flinched from his soft, quiet statement, Will's surety in man's stagnant nature sliding like a knife between his ribs. Melinda was dead and gone from him and all the mistakes he made lost to a past that would vanish with his own death.

But Will was before him, with his keen understanding and valiant strength, not so far from his reach that he could not touch him, not so lost that he could not win him back and make amends for what had passed between them.

If there was anything to be learned from shattering a teacup, it was to be more careful the next time around.

"I am as foolish now as I was then. The lessons she taught me I could not bear to benefit from," Hannibal quietly admitted, brows drawing down in a frown when his soothing hands felt a knot out of place on Will's back. "Her last moment on this earth was spent trying to reach me and I would not be reached."

"It was a terrible thing," Will said, thinking of the rumors and lies following Hannibal like a shadow for sixteen years, unchallenged by him because to vindicate himself would be to expose Melinda's secret. "I wish it had not happened to you. I wish... none of this had happened to you."

He, too, was a problem pushed onto Hannibal's hands, a marriage forced despite his wishes, a spouse with burdens he neither asked for nor wanted.

"I understand now why you were so livid," he breathed, lost in the reflection of Hannibal's perception, feeling the experience of their first few days of marriage from his husband's point of view all over again, but with a few facet. "Home from the horrors of war eager to see your family and start your life all over again, and your grandfather punished you for your disobedience by giving you *me*. Twice married by circumstances outside of your control, both times to people who gave you grave offense."

"You do not offend me," Hannibal whispered, brushing his hand down Will's spine and back up to his shoulders.

Every bit of Will seemed to freeze in the wake of that soft statement. Even his heart seemed to skip a beat, rattling to find a new rhythm that such a thing might be true.

"You... confound me. You amaze me," Hannibal said, feeling Will's tension fall to yielding beneath his sensitive fingers. "You infuriate me and sometimes you even cosh me, but you never offend me."

Will bit his lip, eyes closing against the tender touch, against the softness of Hannibal's words, against the way he turned the smallest flicker of light on the darkness of Will's isolation that had drained him slowly but surely, the steady drip of his soul from the cracks left behind in the wake of his father's and husband's careless handling.

Hannibal concentrated on rubbing Will's back, tracing the strange knot chasing across Will's skin in a most unusual fashion, palpable even through the bunched material of the bathing sheet. He slipped his fingers into the lip of the sheet, intending to tug it down only far enough to have a look, saying, "I'll right it in a moment, Will, there is something that isn't—"

He cut off and Will froze, heart pounding as the sheet was slowly drawn down to his hips. It pulled from his nerveless fingers, turned back to bare him all the way to his pelvis, the air lifting goose-flesh on his exposed skin.

"Will," Hannibal breathed, and Will squeezed his eyes closed, taking a shallow, stuttering breath, knowing what his husband was seeing.

Scars.

Scars crossing and recrossing the fragile expanse of Will's skin from his shoulders to the dimples above his bottom, all shapes and sizes, some stretched out of true by time, a map of cruelty testament to treatment Hannibal had never dreamed he might have been dealt.

"Gods in heaven," Hannibal whispered, sitting back until his mind could make sense of it, this history of Will's childhood laid out in a pattern of layered, trailing pain like brands on his skin.

Will moved to pull the sheet up but stilled when Hannibal touched his back, naked fingertips to bare skin. The touch was faint, a tracery of his scars so light he barely felt it, respectful of the pain he'd endured to bear them. Will trembled, aching with upset, confused by the relentless press of grief he could feel through his bond to Hannibal—horror and outrage and blazing, righteous indignation. His deep, secret heart was profoundly shaken when his husband leaned towards him, when both callused hands settled with exquisite tenderness on his shoulders and traced the scars with care.

"When you came to me that first night, Will, I remember seeing the marks on your sides," he whispered, his voice filled with husky sorrow. "I could not imagine what they were. I could never have imagined... *this.*"

Will swallowed hard, skin prickling beneath the touch as Hannibal took stock of him, seeing for himself the value his father put on an unwanted Omega.

"I would take these from you," Hannibal breathed, and Will shivered when he felt the heated puff of Hannibal's breath against his skin.

The faint, reverent kiss between his shoulders forced Will's eyes to fly wide open, rapidly filling with tears he refused to let fall. "I would take all of these from you and bear them myself, Will, if only I could."

"Hannibal..."

Hannibal pressed his forehead to the place he'd kissed, one hand on Will's shoulder, exhaling softly over his skin.

"It was your father, wasn't it?" he breathed, lifting his face enough to press another kiss to the base of Will's neck right on the knob of his spine, soothing and full of regret, as if the tenderness of his touch could somehow erase the suffering such wounds had caused.

"Yes," Will said, his voice throaty and low. A shiver flowed through him when Hannibal eased back, one large hand sweeping his skin from his nape to his bottom.

"I find I am capable of murdering someone in cold blood after all."

The flat, quiet fury of his statement was as startling to Will as the words themselves.

"W-what?"

"You heard me," Hannibal whispered, stroking Will's skin with both hands, taking up a soothing caress as if those horrid scars didn't inspire the disgust Will knew he surely must feel. "I would murder him for what he's done to you, Will, and *gladly.*"

Will said nothing, completely taken aback by his response.

"Any person, man, woman, or Omega, who puts their hands on you ever *in your life* will answer to me," Hannibal said, the words delivered without flourish, a flat statement of fact that made Will's eyes widen with surprise. His traitorous heart kicked with a sudden lurch and he brought his hand to press against his mouth, stifling the sound threatening to erupt. "Be it your father or this unknown person trying to harm you, Will, I promise you that. And I always keep my promises."

Will shuddered, resisting everything in him that pulled him towards the Alpha touching him, tender and filled with regret. The same Alpha who had once scoffed at his responses, called him repulsive and stupid and sickening, who had followed in his father's footsteps and managed to wound him in a way his father never could by forging a bond that could never be broken, a mockery of what might have been.

Will wet his lips and tugged at the sheet, attempting to cover his back, attempting to find what dignity was left to him now that Hannibal saw him as he truly was—damaged, weak, and insignificant.

"You needn't concern yourself, Hannibal," Will said. "You have always been very clear on your regard for Omegas, myself in particular. I will take care of myself. I always have."

"Will, I have treated you with unreasonable and unforgivable disregard," Hannibal said, slowly sliding his hands away, attuned to Will's deep turmoil. "Please believe me, had I known your circumstances, things would have gone much differently."

"For what reason? Would it have made me less Omegan? Or would you have thought it fitting to see me so shamed? Whatever feeling this moment has inspired in you, Hannibal," he whispered, sliding the sheet up to hide the proof of what he was, "please extinguish it. I am not what you think I am."

"I would not have you be *less Omegan*, Will. I would not have you be anything but the person you are, and I would never wish to see you shamed or believe any such treatment is *fitting*," Hannibal said, smoothing the sheet up over Will's shoulders, those scars imprinted on his memory, burned into his mind's eye along with the horrible understanding of what Will had suffered. "What do you imagine I think you are, seeing what has been done to you?"

"Weak," Will said, his voice cracking on the sharpness of the word, a single syllable filled with loathing and fear, as if speaking it aloud begat the possibility of truth. "I cannot bear being weak, Hannibal. I cannot bear being... *what I am*."

"Abused?" Hannibal asked, dropping his hands entirely despite the urge to soothe him, Will's growing distress pulling on his instincts in a way nearly impossible to resist. But *instinct*, he knew, was the heart of this matter, and he softly asked, "Or *Omegan*?"

"Is it such a difficult thing for you to imagine?" Will asked, breathless with the force of his upset, the lessons of his life and the origins of his bond to this man coming to bear on him, forcing the words from his mouth despite the pain they caused him. "I have spent the entirety of my life lamenting the gender of my birth. It took my father years to make me understand how offensive I and other like me are to the world. Did you think that it was my dream to end up with someone who loathes me and everything I am? That I hoped to leave my father's house as I was and find myself just as despised, faced with a different type of violence that was no less painful?"

Hannibal flinched, hands clenching into fists in his lap, the memories of his first days with Will stark and harsh.

"I *earned* those scars. Every one of them is proof that I was not betrayed into my nature. Each one is a moment of weakness that my father recognized and curtailed," Will said, teeth clenching to hold back the waver in his voice. "He could not change my gender, but he ensured I would not fall victim to it. I am... *grateful* to him, Hannibal. It is only due to his firm instruction that I am not a mindless bundle of instincts clinging to an Alpha for succor."

Hannibal heard the words but, more, he heard the meaning behind them and knew he owed his fair share of blame. He had no idea how to ease him but he wanted to. Will, however, was so deeply averse to his own nature that he would resist it, fight it, make himself sick rather than accept it, and he was far too ill already. Hannibal had condemned Will's Omegan gender as if it had been a choice made to spite him rather than a natural state of being that could not be changed. He had unwittingly adapted Will's burgeoning Omegan nature to mirror his own prejudice, making him resentful of his own instincts, impatient with the qualities that made him who he was, and deeply disgusted with the way Nature had designed him.

"I earned those scars," Will stiffly said again, refusing to cry, refusing to be weak, refusing to be those things his father had claimed to be beating out of him. "Every single one of them is a lesson learned."

Scars on the inside, Grandfather had said, and Hannibal saw just how devastating that could be. He wet his lips and pitched his voice low to say, "Then I disapprove of your education, Will."

"The last thing I need is your *pity*, Lord Clarges," Will said, moving to escape the acceptance those words hinted at, or perhaps what his own nature hoped to trick him into believing was there. He got to his feet and stood swaying in place, the force of his pain threatening to tip him into darkness, but he refused to give in to it and clenched his teeth on an exhale.

"That's a relief, as I would never pity someone who has risen so admirably against expectation to manage what you have managed," Hannibal told him, standing to steady him, his touch gentle and cautious but there all the same, ready to offer support should Will find himself wavering. Will's upset eased somewhat at the gesture, just enough for Hannibal to tentatively offer, "I understand now why you asked what you did. Believe me, Will, I would never treat any child of ours with the... *horrific* cruelty and disregard that your father has treated you. That anyone could treat another human being with such callous sadism, let alone the precious gift that is their own child—it infuriates me. Hanging is too good for him. Drawing and quartering is too good for him. There is no amount of suffering he could endure that would purge him of his sins against you. A child is a treasure, our only true legacy. I cannot fathom the legacy he wished to leave in treating you this way, but our children will be deeply beloved."

Will stared at him, his chest tight with something he could not recognize, Hannibal's sincerity finding the cracks in his walls and scaling them, threatening to breach the very thing meant to keep him at bay.

Hannibal tipped his head up, sensing or scenting it, one, and Will blushed, suspecting Hannibal's nearness and the stress of his situation was pushing his heat closer despite the tonics he took. It would be typically Omegan, he knew, to react to so much constant dread with a call for an Alpha.

"Why do you want a child so badly?" Will asked, his intuition warning him there was something he simply wasn't seeing, something which had brought his formerly-reluctant spouse back after six years, determined to bed him.

"Why do you not?" Hannibal asked, because he simply could not tell him, not now. Not ever, perhaps. How could he ever admit to what he'd agreed to? If he had his way, he never would, not at the risk of losing Will all over again. His voice was barely better than a whisper when he asked, "What kind of father would you be, Will?"

Will blinked, taken aback by the question, but answered without hesitation, "I would be a good father."

"I think so, too," Hannibal said.

Will stilled, unresisting when Hannibal slowly eased closer. The tightness in his chest grew as his husband folded around him in a blanket of heat and scent, a surety of strength promising a support upon which Will feared he could not rely. The cliff of his nightmares threatened to surface, the roar of his blood in his ears becoming the crash of the waves on the rocks, hungry and waiting for him to be foolish enough to fling himself into the unknown.

Hannibal's arms tightened around him and Will closed his eyes, the first tense touch of being held to his husband's chest giving way to slow acceptance. A sigh escaped him as Hannibal embraced him, his hunger for even so small an affection ravenous and frightening in its strength.

Hannibal cradled Will to him, one arm around his narrow waist, one arm sliding behind his shoulder to cup his head, urging Will to rest against him. He drew in a breath sweet with Will's scent and closed his eyes, Will's heart pounding against his own, a faint tremor coursing through his taut body. He stroked his hand through Will's curls, nose buried against his unhurt temple, and simply held him.

"I promise you things will be different, now. I *promise* you. Please stay, Will," he breathed, careful not to squeeze him, careful not to overwhelm him, wishing he could reach back through time and shield him from the men who should have protected him, starting with himself. "Please stay."

Stay here in this room.

Stay here in this house.

Stay here with me.

Will could feel... *something* through his bond, something in the softness of Hannibal's words and the gentle caution of his touch. His arms trembled when he lifted them, the pain of his fall forgotten, forsaken for the overwhelming pain of his father's ugly truths being challenged by the last man in the world he imagined would do so.

He settled his hesitant hands against Hannibal's back and nodded, the barest concession.

He wasn't prepared for the kiss on his temple, faint and brushing and tender. He wasn't prepared for the light squeeze of arms around him or the soft exhale against his ear when Hannibal breathed, "Thank you."

They stood there in each other's embrace, warm and uncertain but reaching, peering through the murky waters of their past together at a future that seemed impossible, all things considered. Eyes closed, tentative and raw with wounds from a battle yet far from over, Will found it was just as much his own strength being sought as it was Hannibal's, that his husband's tense body eased in his arms with every breath, that there was as much giving in both of them as there was taking.

They drew apart by degrees, and Will could feel Hannibal's reluctance to do so as he eased back. He gazed at his husband with confusion, trying to reconcile this moment with his bond, with everything his experience knew to be true.

Hannibal merely cupped his face, smoothing his cheeks with a crooked smile before pulling away entirely. Will watched him, bewildered as he moved to his wardrobe and plucked out a nightshirt, which he brought to his uncertain little mate.

"It will nearly swallow you, but it's better than that damp sheet," Hannibal said, noting the glassy look in Will's eyes and knowing he was still in a good deal of pain. "You must be chilled to your bones by now. It was thoughtless of me not to offer sooner."

"Thank you," Will said, automatic good manners bumping him out of his momentary stupor. He ducked slightly when Hannibal draped the nightshirt over his head and let it fall into place, dropping the bath sheet as he fed his arms through the voluminous sleeves.

It wrapped him in soft, cool folds that quickly warmed to his body, cocooning him in Hannibal's comforting Alpha scent in a way that made Will want to curl up into a ball and purr himself to sleep.

"I'll get you something for the pain while the girls build the fire up," Hannibal said as he knelt to pull the bath sheet away. He tugged the nightshirt down where it hung nearly to Will's slender ankles. He couldn't resist smoothing it, brushing his palms over his mate's pale, perfect calves and the small knobs of his ankles, even down to his feet, which turned in ever-so-slightly in a way he'd never noticed before but found profoundly charming.

Will looked down at him, the odd tightness in his chest never lessening, the pressure, perhaps, of the wind atop that dark cliff, luring him towards the drop. He never imagined being so close to the edge would feel like this, like promise and hope and potential.

"Thank you," he said again, barely an exhale.

Hannibal's only answer was a gentle, relieved smile.

Chapter 21

True to his word, Hannibal had one of the housemaids build up the fire, and when the porridge arrived he had Berger set up a tray for Will where he sat curled up in Hannibal's chair, snug beneath a lap blanket.

"Be sure you eat slowly," Hannibal cautioned, shifting things around for him to easily reach. "And drink as much tea as you can hold, fluid will help with the ache. I'll give you something stronger for the pain."

"I can handle discomfort, Hannibal, in order to have my wits about me," Will breathed.

"I insist on at least one dose for your head," Hannibal said, busying himself preparing it, saying, "It will make you sleepy, but it will ease the pain and we will make sure you are well protected."

He mixed the dose into a cup of tea and handed it to Will, watching him to ensure he drained the entire cup.

"Thank you," Will said, feeling immediately better for it, well enough to become absurdly aware that he was in his husband's suite wearing only Hannibal's nightshirt, thick and bundled though it was. "You should have taken me to the Duchess suite."

"I hadn't realized," Hannibal said, brows rising over his amber eyes. "I came here from habit. There is nothing improper in your being here, Will."

He took the cup and poured another for Will and some for himself. Berger bustled about unobtrusively, taking care of the damp sheet and going to tidy in the washroom. Hannibal could hear soft conversation as he spoke with Jimmy, both men exchanging information to make service run smoothly.

"Will, is there anything you can recall about your accidents that might help us discover who has done this?" Hannibal asked, sitting in the chair angled next to his, elbow on his knee and fervent eyes on his mate.

Will almost shook his head but caught himself, saying in a quiet murmur over the lip of his teacup, "Everything happened so quickly, I don't have anything clear to grasp hold of. It was all... it was motion and light, more feeling than memory."

Hannibal thought of Will sprawled at the foot of the stairs in his nightclothes, wounded and dazed. "A frightening experience," he said, his voice a low purr of displeasure.

"I was too surprised to be frightened at first," Will admitted.

"I would say you needn't be frightened now," Hannibal said, tucking the blanket higher up over Will's hip. "But I can tell you aren't. Not anymore."

"No, I'm not," Will said, and huffed a soft laugh. "I am, however, incredibly annoyed."

"Gods help us," Hannibal murmured, and grinned when Will did.

The light from the fireplace picked up the seam of the wound on his cheek, still ruddy from irritation.

"I apologize for striking you, Hannibal," Will said to him, studying the mark.

"Nonsense, you have nothing to apologize for," Hannibal said. "Considering the circumstances, you were justified. Even without the circumstances, you were justified."

Will gave Hannibal the steadiest stare he could manage in his state and said, "Justified, perhaps, but impulsive all the same. It must have pained you."

"It certainly woke me to the situation quite nicely, Will," Hannibal said, refusing to allow him to feel in the wrong for it. "Speaking of which, I would greatly appreciate it if you could eat that porridge and tell me everything you can remember."

They shared tea while Will ate and spoke of his fall, of what Matthew Dunn had told him, of the letter Francis had brought to him and the details of his accident on the stairs. Hannibal asked questions that probed Will's memory in ways that challenged him, pulling forth details his remarkable memory stored without his realizing it—scents, sounds, positions, environmental clues that might, when put together, form some piece of a larger puzzle.

"It is still a paltry sum," Hannibal said after, filling Will's teacup again, noting the way his lids drooped, the lines of pain easing around his firm, full mouth. "Yet I am better informed all the same. I will speak with Grandfather and tell him of everything that has happened so far. With the whole of Hartford House watching, it will be much more difficult for anyone to harm you."

"Difficult," Will said, wetting his lower lip as he put his teacup down, resenting the slight tremble of his hand. "But not impossible."

"They shall have to get through me," Hannibal warned. "And if that isn't ruckus enough to put you on your guard, I'm not sure what would be."

"It is troubling," Will mused, frowning, and when he caught Hannibal's raised eyebrow, he clarified, "My fall from the stairs, not your ruckus. They could not have known I would hear them or come out. It makes me wonder what their true purpose was."

He subsided with a soft exhale, his blue eyes glassy as he fought the much-needed rest that threatened. Hannibal got to his feet, his smile soft as he tucked the blanket up around Will's shoulders.

"We'll pick it apart after you've had a chance to relax some. Meanwhile, I'll go speak to Grandfather and make sure your sister is informed you're recovering," Hannibal murmured, pleased that Will smiled up at him, woozy and relaxed. "She's probably wondering where you are by now."

"I doubt that," Will said, freeing one hand from the blanket to rub absently at the base of his skull where the pain had dwindled to a dull throb. "Mina has never risen before two, and always takes her first meal in bed."

"I cannot imagine being in bed until such an hour," Hannibal said, straightening.

"She is accustomed to late nights," Will said, wiggling around in the chair to rest his head against the padded side. He closed his eyes and relaxed, yawning, only half aware of Hannibal reaching down to stroke his hair. "I always imagined her at parties until dawn, dancing holes in her slippers and meeting exciting strangers."

Hannibal smiled sadly, and asked, "Is that something you wished for, Will? Company? Dancing until dawn?"

"No, don't be ridiculous," Will said, perhaps a bit too quickly, a blush rising on his cheeks. He tossed his head, a slight resistance to the gentle touch that drifted to his nape, but went liquid beneath the firm squeeze that chased the last bit of ache from his skull. "That sort of life is... not for me."

"I disagree," Hannibal told him. "I think it would suit you."

Will's only response was a soft laugh, but he ducked his head to offer more of his nape, sighing when Hannibal obliged him.

"M'Lord, Mr. Hawkes and Mrs. Henderson are in the hall," Berger said, pitching the words low so as not to disturb Will.

"Thank you, Berger. Did you tell Jimmy everything you heard here?" Hannibal asked, releasing Will's nape with a final, lingering squeeze.

Berger nodded, mouth set in a fierce frown and looking impressively irate.

"Mark me, m'Lord, first one even dares raise a finger to him, Prince and I will flatten him."

"I trust that you will," Hannibal told him, brows rising, reassured when he saw the soldier surface in his longtime valet. He cast a look back at Will as he headed towards the door, telling him, "I'll be back shortly, Will. If anyone at all comes into this room, I want you to beat them senseless with that end table and ring every bell you can reach."

Will roused himself from his half slumber, preparing to very sensibly argue that no killer was likely to risk being caught by coming into Hannibal's suite after him, but when his eyes met Hannibal's the words somehow bottled up behind that tightness in his chest. Instead, he smiled and said, "I will, Hannibal."

"Berger?" Hannibal called, and when his valet looked over at him, alert, he said, "You remain here until I return. No one comes in with the exception of myself and Mr. Prince. Understood?"

Berger nodded, puffing up like a bullfrog in preparation to trounce anyone who threatened Will.

Satisfied that his mate was, for the time being, not directly in danger, Hannibal let himself out, pleased to find Mr. Hawkes in the hallway, as requested, with Mrs. Henderson in close attendance.

"Go lock Will's suite for me, please," he said, closing the door firmly behind him and waiting for the worried housekeeper to do so. If anyone was going to come into his room after Will, they were going to do so through the door of his choosing, not go sneaking up behind him through their washroom.

"Is Grandfather still up?" Hannibal asked, knowing the elderly Alpha took frequent naps due to his arthritis medications. He headed for the stairs with both Mr. Hawkes and Mrs. Henderson in close attendance, his agitation causing both of them to exchanged concerned, wary glances.

"Yes, my Lord, he is in his study," Mr. Hawkes said. "His Grace is feeling rather better today."

"Good," Hannibal said, making short work of the stairs and striding down the hallway to his grandfather's study. He rapped sharply on the door and when Grandfather called entry, he said to them both, "Come with me."

Uneasy and showing some slight alarm at the unusual request, Mr. Hawkes dutifully gestured Mrs. Henderson ahead of them and followed Hannibal within.

"Grandfather," Hannibal said, his worry for Will channeling to impatient pacing. "I have no idea where to start and there is no way to soften this, so I will tell you all plainly—there have been two attempts to murder Will in the time since I've returned."

"My *Lord*!" Mr. Hawkes said, aghast, and Mrs. Henderson gasped, her eyes widening with surprise.

Roland, old and wise in ways even Hannibal had no true knowledge of, paled to a frightening degree but absorbed the information, thoughts churning behind his amber eyes.

"Do you recall his accident?" Hannibal asked, pausing to face his grandfather, his hands on his hips and his shoulders tense.

"Of course I do," Roland said, the softness of his voice no indication of his inner turmoil. "I was told the saddle had a defect."

"*Cut*, Grandfather," Hannibal corrected him, including Mr. Hawkes in his uneasy gaze. "Someone tampered with his saddle, Will told me of it himself."

"Why did he not tell us?" Roland asked. "Who on earth has done such a thing? *Why* would anyone do such a thing?"

"He did not tell us because he thought *I* was the one who cut it," Hannibal said, ugly guilt filling him when he thought of how easy he had made it for Will to come to such a conclusion.

Roland stiffened in his chair, caught off guard and deeply disturbed, while Mrs. Henderson shook her head slowly with disbelief, struggling to make sense of it.

"Just as he thought *I* was the one who pushed him down the stairs," Hannibal said.

"*Pushed*?" Mrs. Henderson gasped, utterly shocked. "He assured us he had fallen, my Lord!"

"He was attempting to protect himself, Mrs. Henderson," Hannibal said, somber and grim. "He was, understandably, uncertain whom he could trust. Knowing now that I was *not* the one to push him, he has confessed that he saw someone on the landing in the darkness and pursued them. That is when someone else came from behind him and shoved him down the stairs."

"Why am I only hearing of this accident *now*?" Roland asked, concern sharpening his voice.

"It was *only* an accident as far as any of us knew, Grandfather," Hannibal said, rubbing his hand over his face, frustrated by how powerless he felt. "I had no idea it was more until this morning. Will is concussed, Grandfather. When he went riding off to town this morning, it triggered his symptoms and he mistook my attempts to help him for another attempt on his life."

Mr. Hawkes was at more of a loss than Hannibal had ever seen him in his life, and when he gestured for him to sit, Hawkes did so without argument, mutely holding Mrs. Henderson's hand on his shoulder.

"That is why he cut you with his crop," Roland said, his hand trembling as he plucked his spectacles from his face.

"It pains me to see you so upset, Grandfather," Hannibal said, calming somewhat as he ordered his thoughts. Just confessing to those he trusted most made him feel more in control of this ghastly situation. "But you, and the staff as well, need to know what danger he is in. Either instance could have resulted in great harm to him, if not killing him outright. I have no idea who has done this, or why, but I need your help solving this issue. That someone was able to gain access to this house unnoticed is concerning enough. Knowing they did so and harmed a member of this family is intolerable."

"Mr. Hawkes and Mrs. Henderson will rally the staff," Roland said, trembling hard. "If any one of them know anything at all, they will find it out, won't you, Mr. Hawkes? I imagine the locks will be changed before nightfall?"

"You have my solemn promise, Your Grace," Mr. Hawkes said.

"We will do everything in our power to protect the family, Your Grace," Mrs. Henderson said, her trademark fortitude rising in the face of adversity.

Hannibal pinched the bridge of his nose, his cheek stinging where he'd stitched it. He was unable to shake the nervous tension that rose with every thought of the danger Will had faced alone, thinking he was friendless in the house that had been his home for over six years. The comfort he found in his mate's company dissipated rapidly beneath the weight of his worries, leaving only a black hole of potential dangers.

"At least two people, Grandfather," he breathed, dropping his hands to clench his fingers into fists. "At least *two* people were in this house!"

"Two people familiar enough with Hartford to find their way without lamplight, Your Grace," Mr. Hawkes observed.

It was Mrs. Henderson who softly suggested, "Else *one* in where he shouldn't be to see someone already here."

Hannibal hadn't had the heart to say such a thing in front of Will, but he, too, had considered it and knew it was only a matter of time before Will landed on that thought himself.

"Whoever they were, at least one of them recognized Will in the darkness and did not hesitate to push him," Hannibal said, glowering. "He has theorized that their intention was not to murder him, Grandfather. It was an opportunity, but not the goal. Had that been their aim, they would have gone into his room after him."

"Then what does he believe was their purpose here?" Roland asked, watching him.

Hannibal shook his head, feeling helpless and powerless and entirely frustrated. "We can only guess. But I will not play games with Will's safety. The timing of this is altogether too convenient."

"It would seem, my Lord, that there is an intention to discredit you," Mrs. Henderson said, her eyes heavy with concern. "He was six years alone here, yet upon your return he has twice nearly died."

"You make a tempting scapegoat for anyone who wishes to remove Will," Roland said, gazing steadily at his grandson.

"But why would anyone wish to remove him is the question," Hannibal said. "Unless he has instructions set aside elsewhere, his belongings would revert to me on his death. At the risk of sounding every bit the self-absorbed Alpha I am, I also cannot help but wonder if this is someone who merely wishes to paint me a murderer, with Will as my victim and his death incidental to their purpose."

They all considered it in silence before Roland admitted, "The circumstances would be perfect for such. And Will is not a man who easily makes enemies. Even those rare few he offends with his honesty respect him enough to value his opinion."

"And Mr. Vorgert is still in prison, Your Grace," Mr. Hawkes said, looking anxiously from Roland to Hannibal. "He is, to my knowledge, the only one who might hold a grudge against Mr. Grant."

"Yes," Roland said. "There were other charges levied against him that will ensure he will not soon leave."

"Mason is still absent from the country as far as my sources know," Hannibal said, not elaborating further on why he kept close tabs on young Vorgert. He furiously tried to think of anyone else who might have a reason to hurt Will, anything to ease his mind from thinking that Will might've nearly died in an attempt to send Hannibal to the noose. "Who on earth else is left who might want to hurt him?"

"Whoever they are, I am determined to bring the full weight of the law against them," Roland said, his face clouding with his own temper. "Aside from being your husband, he is the grandchild of my dearest, most beloved friend. I would never forgive myself if anything happened to him."

"I would never forgive myself, either, Grandfather," Hannibal murmured. "I will find these people and deal with them. If there is some grudge they have against Hartford, against either one of us, I will not allow Will to stand as collateral damage."

"Where is he now?" Roland asked, groping for a small tin on his desk to fish out a tiny pill, which he promptly swallowed dry.

"He is in my room," Hannibal said. "He will not be fit for some time, Grandfather. He took quite a fall and that blow to his head will not resolve overnight. I want to keep him as close as possible until we find out who has hurt him and to what end."

"We will speak to the staff immediately!" Mr. Hawkes said, rising with indignant fury that anyone should harm any Ledford in his charge, only belatedly adding, "With your permission, of course."

"Please do, Hawkes, especially Jimmy," Hannibal said. "He is closest to Will. If there is anything about any of it that he can recall, any strange acquaintance, any new gossip in town regarding Will, have him come to one of us straight away."

Mr. Hawkes and Mrs. Henderson both nodded firmly and left to do just that.

Once they were gone, Roland ventured, "Why would Will believe you wanted him dead, Hannibal?"

Hannibal dropped into a chair with a sigh and rested his face in his hands, wincing when his stitched cheek began to ache afresh.

"His memory is appalling, Grandfather," he admitted. "Every single thing said to him, he recalls with uncanny accuracy. The night I chased him away from the table, I said I would arrange an accident for him."

Roland was silent for a long, somber moment. "That alone would not be enough, surely."

"Someone wrote him a letter claiming I was the one who had rigged his saddle," Hannibal said with a humorless laugh.

"The culprit himself, perhaps?"

"Who else?" Hannibal asked, and sighed again, slumping back in the chair and tipping his head back, eyes closed. "It doesn't help that he went to Duxbury to see if the rumors of my previous wife were true and ran into Molly Forester."

Roland started and said with a tremble in his voice, "I did my best to keep any gossip of that nature from reaching him, Hannibal."

"Perhaps you should have told him?" Hannibal asked, eyes slitting open.

"I didn't wish to frighten him," Roland said, guilt filling his eyes. "I wanted nothing unpleasant to touch him here. He has had unpleasantness enough in his life, and Melinda has always been your responsibility to explain. I *still* do not understand it!"

"I did explain. Badly, but I explained all the same," Hannibal said, thinking of Will's soft expression and how fragile he'd felt under his fingers. "All the bitter truth of her death and my guilt."

"And what did he say?" Roland asked, watching Hannibal restlessly clench and unclench his hands.

"He asked about the baby," Hannibal breathed, and smiled a sad, strained smile. "All of that, and his worry was for the child... "

"Will has a very large, good heart, Hannibal," Roland said.

Hannibal frowned, then, and quietly asked, "What did happen to her, Grandfather? What happened to Melinda's daughter? I know you could not place her with the Foresters—"

"No, they wouldn't have her," Roland said, grim. "They were distraught and barely able to accept Melinda's loss. Her mother couldn't even look at the baby. I arranged placement with a family of landed gentry, Hannibal, and assume she is doing well, as you should."

"That is sad recollection of her fate, Grandfather," Hannibal said, unsatisfied by the news he'd just received. "Were circumstances different, I would demand an accounting of her whereabouts, but I have larger worries on my mind, all things considered."

"We will find who this person threatening Will is, Hannibal," Roland said. "We *will* keep him safe."

Hannibal stared at the ceiling, his thoughts jumbled and agitated.

"I believe it might be a good idea to take Will away from Hartford House," Roland suggested.

"To the Capital?" Hannibal asked, thinking of the Seasons he'd spent in the ducal townhouse without his little mate.

"Perhaps," Roland said. "Will has never traveled and it would do him good to be away from Hartford House. When he is well enough, the two of you should take a trip. Go to the seaside or to another estate, someplace unexpected."

"Tell the servants to pack our trunks and simply go?" Hannibal mused. "Eluding whoever this person is?"

"While we do some investigating here at home," Roland said. "It will take some time to hire detectives in to assist in the situation."

"Unpredictable movements would stymie them, whoever they are," Hannibal said, and sighed heavily. "I wish it were not under these circumstances, but you're right, Grandfather. It isn't safe for Will here and new surroundings would do him some good."

"I will write to the Capital directly to inquire about an investigation," Roland said. "We will take steps, Hannibal. Between all of us, he needn't ever be alone and vulnerable to any unknown menace."

After a long, weighty silence, Hannibal said, "He thought I wished him dead, Grandfather. He truly believed I tried to murder him."

"But he knows now you did not," Roland pointed out, gentle with this child who had always been closer to a son than a grandson.

Hannibal didn't acknowledge his statement. The guilt that had plagued him since his return had found good, fertile ground and its roots reached deep, all the way to the pit of his stomach.

"Have you any idea how he was treated in his father's house?" he whispered, those terrible scars appearing behind his closed lids.

"Yes," Roland quietly said. "Jimmy has always been discreet, but he felt it was necessary to inform me."

"Some of those scars he has couldn't be more than a few years old, Grandfather," Hannibal said, disturbed and upset. "He was beaten like an animal until the day he left that house for this one."

Roland remained quiet, watching his grandson struggle with his newfound knowledge.

"The things I said to him," Hannibal breathed, and cut himself off, unable to finish.

"You had no idea how he was mistreated."

"That is *not an excuse*," Hannibal said, sitting up and gaining his feet. "Even had he been treated as a prince in his father's house, it would not excuse it!"

"It would not," Roland agreed. "But Hannibal, *I* am not the one who needs to hear you say it."

Hannibal was startled into looking at him, realization dawning in his amber eyes.

"If you feel you have wronged Will," Grandfather said, offering him a slight smile. "Then tell him so. Just... just tell him, so."

Hannibal's jaw clenched. Just *tell* him, as if it could ever be so easy as a few words. As if he could take six years of Will's life from him and erase the pain of it with *words*.

As if words could ever strip away those scars laid over his skin or the beatings that had put them there, brutal and harsh and unthinkably cruel.

Shaking with the force of repressing his emotions, Hannibal tightly said, "I want that Addendum destroyed."

Grandfather went still, but his amber eyes glittered with growing tears.

"I want it destroyed," Hannibal said again, moving to the window, looking out at a landscape that he never even saw. "Hartford House is to remain in Will's name. I want him to have it, no matter what happens between us. This is his home and there are other places I can go if he does not want me here."

"He will want you here," Roland said, almost frightened to say anything lest Hannibal change his mind. "There is a goodness in him, Hannibal, that nothing in his life has ever managed to extinguish. He will want you to remain here at Hartford."

"What needs to be done to get rid of it?" Hannibal asked, turning to pace before his grandfather again, restless energy returning at even the thought of someone lying in wait to hurt Will.

"I will write to Mr. Buddish requesting all copies of the document be returned to me," Roland said. "And then we will ensure they are destroyed."

"How many copies are there?" Hannibal asked, realizing there was much more he needed to take care of before he could even dream of making his home here at Hartford.

"The original, which the two of us signed," Roland said, "And the clerks always make a copy to send back to me, which has not yet arrived."

"I need to take a short trip to Galley Field," Hannibal decided. "I will stop in the Capital on my way and ensure that they receive your correspondence and send them back to you."

Roland was silent for a long, thoughtful moment before he said, "You are not being thoughtless, Hannibal, are you?"

"No," Hannibal said, taking a deep breath to calm himself. "No, I'm making a decision, Grandfather, not swanning off for an assignation with my mistress while Will is here facing an unknown threat! I will leave tomorrow morning and be back sometime in the night."

"That is a long distance to cross in so short a time," Grandfather reminded him. "You might spend—"

"I will not give him reasons to doubt me," Hannibal said, grim.

"Then you will stay here at Hartford and be a man worthy of calling Will his spouse?" Roland asked, watching the affect those words had on his grandson.

Hannibal's gaze snapped up to his, the fire in his eyes fading slightly when he said, "I will stay as long as he will have me, Grandfather, but I doubt I can ever be worthy of him. If life was truly fair and there was any justice in the world, then he would never have to see me again in his life, or any member of his family."

"Hannibal—"

"Excuse me, Grandfather, I need to speak to Peter," he said, subdued, and left his grandfather's suite still struggling to reconcile what his little mate awoke in him with what he knew had yet to be done.

⌘⌘⌘

Hannibal headed directly out to the stables once he left his grandfather's suite, intent on getting some answers or at least satisfying his urge to do *something*.

Peter was out in the paddock, attempting to shoo a peacock that had managed to gain entry to the grassy area and was strutting about without a care in the world. He straightened when Hannibal called out to him, his pleasant expression clouding with worry.

"Mr. Grant asked me, Lord Clarges," he stammered, gamely accompanying Hannibal into the stable to survey the situation for himself in the wake of close questioning. "My memory i-isn't so good sometimes."

"I know that, Peter, and I do not ask to trouble you," Hannibal said, judging the security of the tack room to be entirely too lax, considering. "I admit I am not surprised to find that Will was already asking, I only hoped to find out something more."

"You worry for him," Peter said, and smiled shyly. "He needs people t-to worry for him. He won't worry for himself."

"No, he certainly won't," Hannibal agreed, somewhat surprised by the sheer amount of gear they had even after six years of not entertaining. Hartford House was ready to accommodate a hunt at any given moment and kept both horseflesh and gear enough to do so without trouble. "Will's saddle is not particularly more worn than the others, is it, Peter?"

"No, Lord Clarges," Peter said, his diffident manner of speaking not tangling him up as much as his nerves began to settle.

"It would require familiarity to pick it out," Hannibal mused, mouth pursing. "Besides yourself and your stable hands, Peter, I would say there are few who deal much with the tack of our House."

"Not directly, Lord Clarges," Peter confirmed. "Of course, Mr. Grant i-is riding a lot and p-people see him, so..."

Hannibal nodded, realizing at once that Peter was right. Will's saddle was remarkable simply for its lack of embellishment. A working man's saddle, always near the front of the tack room, seen often by everyone in the surrounding area who had daily dealings with him.

The culprit could be literally anyone.

Aggravated that he was no closer now than he had been before, Hannibal said, "Be sure you keep the tack room locked up, Peter, and the keys on your person. I know it's inconvenient for the staff, but we will all manage for Will's sake."

Peter nodded, blinking owlishly, his brow furrowed as if he was troubled.

"Peter?" Hannibal prompted, noticing it. "Have you remembered something?"

He shook his head. It seemed hasty and emphatic, but realization dawned when Peter said, "H-how long before he's okay again?"

"There is no way to tell," Hannibal said, deflating when he realized he wasn't about to get any further information on Will's saddle. "It could be days, or weeks."

"He'll miss it," Peter breathed, more to himself than to Hannibal, who only looked at him with raised eyebrows, waiting clarification which Peter gave, nervous again. "Mr. Grant wanted to be told when A-Athena starts to whelp."

"Athena?" Hannibal asked, drawing a blank, though the wording told him she was a dog. "Will has an interest in puppies?"

"Mr. Grant loves dogs. He takes Athena with him on his rounds sometimes," Peter said, smiling. "He said he'll help me find homes for the pups. M-Mr. *Vorgert* always got *rid* of them."

"Mr. Vorgert was a menace and a monster," Hannibal said, glowering with dislike at even the mention of his name. "But, unfortunately, Will is much too ill to come all the way down here just now and I wouldn't risk his scolding to carry him. By the time they are big enough for new homes, I am sure he will be right as rain."

Peter's brow wrinkled up just shade, and his voice was soft and hesitant when he asked, "S-so you don't mind?"

"This is Will's home, Peter, and if he's told you that you may keep the lot of them, then I suppose we'll have ten new dogs, though the hunting hounds will no doubt object," Hannibal said. "Whatever makes him happy is perfectly fine by me."

Peter seemed vastly relieved on that count, tension sliding from his lanky frame.

"As Mr. Grant asked, Peter, please come to us if you remember anything at all that might help," Hannibal said, preparing to go back and check once more on Will.

"I-I will, Lord Clarges," Peter said, twisting his fingers into his loose pants, a habit that was familiar to Hannibal from his earliest memories of Hartford House, even before Peter's accident. "I p-*promise* you both. I just... my memory."

"I know, Peter, it's no fault of yours," Hannibal assured him, and clasped his bony shoulder once, warmly, in a gesture he rarely used. "Will's safety is my highest priority now and I need everyone's help."

Peter nodded and quickly ducked his head, leaving without another word to return to the paddock and the bawling peacock.

He absently watched Peter, still musing on the fact that Will apparently liked dogs, but the thought quickly lost out to the urge to check on his mate.

⌘⌘⌘

Hannibal heard a commotion before he saw one, and hit the landing to find a small gathering in the hallway. Jimmy Prince stood blocking the doorway to Hannibal's suite with the tenacity of a bulldog, refusing to allow either Lady Rathmore or her Alpha accompaniment, Francis Doranhouse, access.

"And *I* am telling you that I couldn't give two *figs* who you are, Mr. Grant is not to be disturbed and *no one will disturb him*!" Jimmy said, and with admirable ferocity, no matter the outrage he incited.

"Now you *listen to me*—"

"Lady Rathmore, the populace of the neighboring county is listening to you right now, willingly or not," Hannibal said, wading into the fray with a dark look at Francis, who bristled like a fighting dog and just barely fell back, the brimstone tang of his scent heavy and revolting to Hannibal.

"What have you done to him?" Mina demanded, looking suspiciously well put together for still being in her dressing gown, which she clutched dramatically at her throat. "*Did I not tell you, Francis*? He has *killed him*!"

"Lady Rathmore, I have never murdered anyone on this country's soil," Hannibal informed her. "Pray don't make me regret it."

She drew up, affronted, and hissed, "And now you will *threaten* me?! How *dare* you!"

"Your brother is suffering a concussion from that nasty fall he took," Hannibal said, rapidly out of patience with her. "What that means, my dear, is that noise and light and movement all provoke nausea and pain. Currently, you are manufacturing a good deal of noise, so if you value your brother even a *pinch* of what you seem, you will *be quiet*."

"My brother is precious to me, Lord Clarges," she said, but did lower her voice to a harsh whisper. "I fear for his safety every *second* he is in your care!"

"And did you fear so much for him in your father's care?" Hannibal asked, satisfied to see a vivid blush fill her face, which was altogether too like Will's for his comfort. It was a wonder to him that two people could share such identical faces and yet be so vastly different.

Jimmy only removed himself from the doorway when Hannibal stirred to go in, and even then he did so reluctantly, clearly suspicious of both Will's sister as well as Francis.

"I cannot believe you would treat a gentlewoman with such disrespect!" she said, retreating a few steps. "I am a *lady*, Lord Clarges!"

"I can only take your word for it," Hannibal said, but the anger that flashed across her face made him regret being so sharp with her. She was Will's sister, his twin, and regardless of her father's sins, she cared enough for him to challenge Hannibal in his own house.

With as little hostility as he could muster, he said, "Forgive me, Lady Rathmore. Your brother's accident has me at less than my best in my worry for him. You are his sister, and by extension you are *my* sister. Please accept my apology."

She tipped her chin, a subtle version of Will's mulish expression on her face, but gamely said, "I accept your apology, Lord Clarges. As you can imagine, I am extremely concerned for my dear brother! I wish to be informed the moment he wakes!"

"Of course," Hannibal said, watching her flounce back the way she had come just to make sure she did, in fact, return to her suite.

Francis, however, lingered on the landing, not quite managing to look at anyone, but not quite managing to be less menacing.

"Mr. Doranhouse," Hannibal said, leveling a flat look at him. "You are dismissed."

"I've been tasked to look after him," Francis said, the deference in his soft voice at complete odds with his looming presence. "My Lord."

Hannibal had little difficulty seeing why Jimmy disliked him.

"You have no cause to fear for Will's safety here," Hannibal said. His full mouth pursed with thought then, and he added, "Unless you know more than you're telling."

Francis met his gaze, a brief, hard glance that skirted the edge of a challenge and raised Hannibal's hackles in a way he thoroughly hated.

"He's spent all his life with Alphas like you," Francis said, and ducked his head again, a show of contrition that did not quite carry over to sincerity. "I only wish to keep him safe."

Hannibal blinked, doing his best to remember that Mina and her servants had been invited to stay at his mate's request, no matter their behavior.

"I understand your sentiment, I even share it," Hannibal said, getting another furtive flick of those dangerous blue eyes. "But I am Master in this house, and you will obey me. Go make yourself useful downstairs, Francis. Will is *my* mate, and I *will* ensure his safety."

Reluctant and nearly defiant, Francis backed towards the servants' stairs and only settled there to glare at them, hands crossed before him. Hannibal darkly considered thrashing him for his disobedience, but in all honesty it wasn't his place and if the watchful, menacing Alpha would even marginally help keep Will safe, then he would strive to tolerate him.

"Well that peeled a good ten years off me, I'll tell you," Jimmy quietly breathed, fanning his nose as if he had caught that sulfuric scent himself, though Hannibal imagined it was more a visceral reaction than a scent-based one.

"Thank you for holding the door, Jimmy," Hannibal told him. "Will is sleeping?"

"*Was*, by now, my Lord," Jimmy said, back to brisk business. "I imagine the clamor woke him. If he's hurting half as bad as I imagine he is, he'll be grateful rather than angry you sent her off, my Lord."

"I certainly hope so," Hannibal said, feeling as if he might have an ally in Jimmy, if only because of their common ground regarding Will and his safety. He angled a meaningful glance at the servants' passage and the hulking, glowering Alpha stationed there, "Keep an eye on him, if you would. I don't trust him."

"I know *precisely* what you mean, my Lord," Jimmy said, straightening his jacket. "If Mr. Grant needs anything at all, please allow me to take care of it. He gets *very* uncomfortable around strangers and that valet of yours is all elbows and feet."

Hannibal chuckled softly at that, duly warned, and sent Jimmy on his way.

Berger was on high alert just inside the doorway when he made his way inside, Hannibal was pleased to see. He closed the heavy wooden panel quietly behind him and asked, "Any problems?"

"None, m'Lord, though his Lordship's sleep ain't what I'd call peaceful," Berger whispered, nodding in Will's direction.

Will was fast asleep in the chair Hannibal had left him in. He made his way over to his sleeping mate, smiling at the way he lay slumped to one side with one arm dangling, the muscle of his forearm firm and solid to the graceful curve of his wrist. He looked picturesque but not the least bit comfortable.

Hannibal dismissed Berger back to his duties and the valet closed the door silently behind him.

"Let's get you settled," Hannibal murmured, delving beneath the blanket to find his tucked-up legs, managing to hook him behind his knees and heft him up, blanket and all.

Will murmured something in his sleep and curled against him, nuzzling against Hannibal's throat and subsiding with a soft sigh that brought a smile to Hannibal's mouth.

Silently, he carried Will to his bed and eased him down where Berger had turned down the covers, laying him onto his side with care not to pain him. It was impulse more than intention that prompted Hannibal to sit there next to him, absently combing his fingers through Will's silky hair, thoughtful and pensive.

"Grandfather is right," he murmured, careful not to wake him, though he doubted nothing less than an ecstatic parade band could if Lady Rathmore's screeching had not. "*You* are the one who needs to hear it."

But it wasn't just for Will, he knew.

All of his life he'd treated every Omega who crossed his path as nothing more than an inconvenient annoyance, an effigy of the woman who had ruined his father, not as human beings with feelings that could be hurt and fears that could be realized.

Or pains that could be borne privately and silently and with extreme bravery, from the battlefields across the sea to the violence done in the one place a child should be safe—their parents' keeping.

Hannibal knew too well the effects an unstable household could have on one's person. He never dreamed that he would share such unhappy common ground with his little mate.

Will flinched in his sleep, rolling onto his side towards Hannibal, balled fists tucked beneath his chin. A ferocious furrow wrinkled his brow, his dreams, perhaps, not as pleasant a respite as they should be.

"I have soundly wronged you," Hannibal whispered, sliding his fingers to Will's damp and heated nape, rubbing the base of his skull until Will sighed, the furrow smoothing. "I would very much like to get to know you, Will Grant."

He could only hope, after everything, that Will would wish to know him in return.

⌘⌘⌘

Will could hear the ocean again, an angry roar like flames, consuming everything flung into its greedy maw. The wind plucked and tugged at his hair painfully, but it wasn't nearly as painful as the tightness in his chest.

'Give him what he wants,' his father said, shoving him towards the edge.

Will caught himself there, toes curling on the sharp rock, the black ocean and frothy caps roiling against the jagged stones below.

'Father, please don't!' he cried, his balance threatened by the hand pushing him from behind. He turned and was a child again, looking up at the man who seemed to fill the world with his presence.

'You've been in your sister's things again!'

'I haven't, father!' Will cried, denying it, terrified because he hadn't. He hadn't. *But when he looked down, he was wearing Mina's favorite day dress, the dress he'd been married to Hannibal in.*

He looked up to explain himself, but it was Hannibal there before him, the sheer disgust on his face making Will's tight chest ache.

'You are vile to me, disgusting. *Get out. Out of my sight. Out of my house. Out.'*

His hands shot out and shoved Will, sent him tumbling backwards off of the cliff where that tightness in his chest burst open, an unwanted rupture Will's frantic hands could not contain.

'Will...'

'I'm sorry!' he said, gathering up the pieces of the teacup he'd shattered. Blood dripped on them from his chest and he trembled, sobbing, 'I can't make them fit. They won't fit. I'm sorry, I can't fix it...'

"Will..."

They wouldn't go back together, no matter how he tried...

"Will?"

He woke, realizing that someone was calling his name. For a moment he did not recognize the room he was in and he sat up too fast, wincing slightly at the protest in his spine that seemed substantially better for his rest.

"You were having a nightmare," Hannibal said, drawing Will's attention to the fireplace where his husband sat with a book open in his lap. It was so like the night that he had routed Will from the House that he flinched, dropping his gaze from Hannibal's inquiring one.

Hannibal closed his book and put it aside before rising.

"How do you feel?" he asked, crossing the short distance to the bed where his uneasy mate was sitting, twisting and untwisting the sheets in his long, pale fingers, still half lost in his dreams. "You woke once and I gave you some painkiller. Has it helped?"

"Yes," Will said, cautious not to nod in case it should wake the slumbering ache in his neck. "It seems to have. Thank you. What time is it?"

Hannibal checked his pocket watch, turning the face towards the firelight before saying, "Nearly four. Grandfather and your sister will be taking tea in the garden, if you feel well enough to join them. The fresh air would do you good and there is plenty of shade, as you know."

Will hesitated, then asked, "Will you be joining us?"

"I wouldn't intrude if you'd rather I didn't," Hannibal said, easing down at the foot of the bed, one hand idly dropping to rest on Will's ankle, his warmth discernible even through the layers of sheets and blankets. "I've been tending to some estate business while you were resting. There is plenty more to do there."

"There is always plenty more to do," Will breathed, smiling ruefully.

"I could have Berger bring it in to tea," Hannibal suggested, heartened when Will did not immediately accept his absence. "You could tell me what should be done."

Will's brows rose. Surprised, he asked, "Instruction from an Omega, Hannibal? However will you survive it?"

"You know a great deal more about it than I do," Hannibal said, his grin baring his sharp Alpha fangs. "I'll ring for Jimmy."

"Thank you," Will said, watching him pass through their shared washroom to pull the call bell. He worked his feet out from beneath the heavy nest of blankets and gingerly stood, much relieved when the world held still for him and the movement did not pain him.

The bright afternoon sun spilling in from the Duchess suite dimmed as he made his way through the washroom, toes curled against the cold tiles. He found Hannibal drawing the drapes just enough to make the light less invasive.

"I've instructed Jimmy in regards to pain medicine," Hannibal said, tugging the last drape into place. The room was still fairly bright, but he noted that Will was not flinching from it, which was a good sign in his book. "You need to let one of us know when you start hurting. Don't wait until it's too much to bear, or it won't be as effective."

"It's already much improved," Will said, and when Hannibal began to glower, he added, "But I will do so, Hannibal, thank you. I have no desire to indulge my aching head. I cannot bear to be incapacitated. Idleness is intolerable to me."

"It doesn't much suit me, either," Hannibal, lingering next to the window as if reluctant to leave. After a long silence, he finally said, "Will, there is something I need to tell you—"

A knock on the door interrupted them, at once an inconvenience and a relief to them both, as Hannibal did not relish confessing to Will the things he knew he needed to.

But he knew it was necessary. There were a great many things he needed to tell Will, not the least of which was that Hartford House would always be his home, no matter what, that nothing and no one would ever take that away from him.

Hannibal moved to unlock the door and Jimmy came in. The pleasant, smiling valet immediately froze, asking, "Is it a bad time?"

"No, Jimmy, please come in," Will said, bewildered by what had just happened and wondering what could cause such concern to cross Hannibal's handsome face. He sent an inquiring glance Hannibal's way, brow furrowing, and his husband briskly moved past him, saying, "I will wait and escort you down to tea."

Will turned, frowning as the washroom door quietly closed behind Hannibal, wondering what on earth his husband had been about to say and why he felt so strangely reluctant to hear it.

⌘⌘⌘

Roland did not particularly like Lady Rathmore.

To be honest, he hadn't tried that hard. He'd seen people like Mina come and go in his long lifetime and had little patience for the wide-eyed innocence she attempted to offer, a veneer of gentility cracking over the scaly green-eyed dragon of jealousy which lay beneath.

She glanced at him from beneath her lashes and took another dainty sip of her tea.

"It is very good of you to come keep your brother company, Mina," he said, and added with a smile, "I do hope you don't mind me using your given name? After all, we are family through your darling brother, whom I have come to love as much as my own dear grandchildren."

The veneer cracked wider at that.

Roland smiled and sipped his tea.

"How dreadfully dull you must find the country, Your Grace," she said, politely skirting the issue of her name. "Cooped up at Hartford for six years. Your grandson has been having such fun in the Capital in your stead."

"I am very happy here at Hartford, young lady, so long as I have Will's company," Roland said, finding that for all their similarities the two of them were no more twins than they were friends. "I wouldn't wish to put my grandson to shame by joining him in the Capital. He should have some time in the spotlight without me outdoing him, hm?"

She absorbed that, thoughts flicking rapidly across her face in a minute play of expression. Roland took another sip, just waiting to see what she would use to fill the silence.

"Your Grace, I would never wish to betray my brother's confidence, but I fear things are not at all well with him and I worry so terribly much about his state of mind," she said, settling her teacup into its saucer and summoning a woeful look that Roland paid prompt, polite attention to. "You see... I am afraid Will believes your grandson is trying to harm him."

Roland's brow rose. He, too, put his cup down and steepled his fingers, wondering how much rope she would need to finish herself.

"I would never wish to alarm you, but I worry that he might... react badly," she breathed, looking the very picture of frail dismay. "Will has always been so unpredictable. If he feels threatened—"

"I expect he will beat me with a poker," Hannibal said, emerging from the shadow of the conservatory doors and moving towards them with a swift, sure stride, his wry and amused gaze fixed on Mina. "Seeking counsel with my grandfather, Lady Rathmore?"

She had the good grace to blush and hastily picked up her teacup again.

"I do not fancy myself a gardener, as I lack Will's talent for multitasking," Hannibal said, settling at the grand table the servants had set up in the shade for their tea. "But for the sake of nipping buds, Will and I have already spoken at length about his various accidents which I have, in turn, conveyed both to Grandfather as well as the staff."

She cleared her throat and said with a soft smile, "I was merely expressing my worry for Will. You did mention he was violent with you."

"I never said it was unprovoked," Hannibal said, waiting for his cup to be filled.

"Is Will joining us?" Roland asked, amused to see Will's sister stymied in her scheming, though he couldn't imagine what she'd hoped to gain with it.

"Yes, I had hoped to go over some estate business but I don't think he should be pushed," Hannibal said, settling to his tea. "He got a little dizzy while dressing. He insisted Jimmy would bring him down momentarily."

"Perhaps he should stay abed?" Roland asked.

"Only if you're the one to tell him so," Hannibal said, smirking. He gestured at his stitches and added, "I have no wish to match my other cheek."

"I meant to inquire earlier, Lord Clarges, what on earth happened to your face?" Mina asked, turning her attention to Hannibal.

"Ah! Here he is now," Hannibal said, excusing himself to meet Will on the path.

Roland silently watched the consternation fill Mina's face, her personality so vastly different from the twin whose features she shared.

"You seem bewildered, Mina," he said, cocking his head to smile at her.

"Yes, Your Grace," she admitted, her delicate brows drawing down. She realized he was watching her and summoned a soft smile in return, admitting with a becoming blush, "I was so frightened for him all these years, Your Grace, considering my father sent you the wrong child."

"Oh, allow me to set your mind at ease on that count," Roland said, dropping a wink at her. "He sent me precisely the child I wished for."

She flushed to her hairline so floridly that Will, upon his arrival, asked her if she was ill.

"I am afraid the doings at Hartford House are something of a surprise for your dear sister," Roland said, delighted to see Hannibal escorting Will with appropriate attentiveness, taking pains not to overwhelm him. It gave him painful, deep hope that all would yet be well between them, though he would never dare give voice to such.

"If you will excuse me," Mina said, surging to her feet. "I do not feel at all well."

Will stared after her, puzzled by her abrupt retreat. Hannibal barely noticed her departure, and certainly missed the look she cast back over her shoulder, a slight glimpse to see if her exit had been marked.

No, Roland most decidedly did not like Lady Rathmore.

But he never had been much for dragons.

⌘⌘⌘

The warm breeze in the shade and the soft twittering of birds in Hartford's overhanging trees proved to be more refreshing than Will could have hoped. He seated himself at Grandfather's right, surprised when Hannibal moved to push in his chair, but not minding it. He wondered if it was the knock on his head working on him, but he honestly wasn't sure. There was something... compelling about Hannibal's concern, and it certainly made a pleasant change from their usual battles.

"My dear, you are a sight for sore eyes!" Roland said, lightly kissing Will's knuckles as he often liked to do.

Hannibal settled across from Will and motioned for service, trying to unobtrusively keep an eye on Will for signs of strain.

"I am glad I could join you, Grandfather," Will said, smiling at the gesture and murmuring thanks to the servant who filled his cup. "I wish I felt well enough to pour for you."

"Nonsense! The staff can handle it!" Roland assured him.

Will's brow furrowed when he looked at Mina's conspicuously empty seat. Concerned, he asked, "Did my sister make mention of anything that might be troubling her?"

Hannibal's mouth pursed and he, too, looked at her empty seat, saying, "Ah! I hadn't realized she'd gone; I thought she was being unusually quiet."

"*Hannibal*," Will said, disapproving.

411

"Nothing you could sort for her, Will, I'm afraid," Roland said, tucking into his favorite little sandwiches. "I dare say she will get over what is ailing her."

"I hope it is nothing serious," Will said, not sure if he was up for the dramatics that usually accompanied Mina's illnesses.

"I believe dying of envy is a manner of speech, rather than an actual demise one may meet," Roland said, amused by the spasm of confusion that marred Will's brow. "Your sister is fine, Will. Her understanding of the world has developed contours she doesn't understand. She most definitely will live, as we all do with such realizations. Now, I've been informed your accidents have a more sinister purpose than I was first led to believe. Shall we discuss that? I do feel it is more important, in the grand scheme of things, than the lovely Lady Rathmore."

"All of you go inside, please," Hannibal said to the staff, pushing Will's teacup a bit closer and adding a few little sandwiches to his empty plate.

"In the matter of my spill down the stairs," Will said, putting out a protective hand to prevent Hannibal from adding a third. "I did mention to Hannibal my thoughts that whoever pushed me down the stairs took advantage of an opportunity. They had no way of knowing I would wake and confront them. I cannot venture a guess as to their purpose, but it was not my death."

"We were discussing just the same thing," Hannibal mused, plucking a few sandwiches for his own lovely plate. "The question is, what were they doing on the family floor that would align with potentially killing you? No tryst is worth murdering witnesses over, and no servant would dare come down to our rooms for such a thing."

"I have a difficult time imagining any member of Hartford's staff would wish me harm," Will said, blanching to think of it. He took a shallow sip of his tea, but it didn't settle well.

"You *shouldn't* think such things," Roland said, patting his hand. "There is no member of this household that would wish to hurt you, Will. To that end, Hannibal and I have concocted a plan."

"A plan?" Will echoed, lifting his weary blue gaze.

"With your permission, of course," Hannibal said, hastening to assure Will he would not pluck him up and cart him off.

Will's head turned slightly to include him in a stare that was rapidly growing glassy with exhaustion.

"When you are well enough to travel, I think it would be wise to remove to another estate," Hannibal said.

"Steal away in the dark unnoticed?" Will asked, arching a disapproving brow.

"Something of that sort," Roland said, dabbing at his lips with his napkin. "I propose that on the morning Hannibal deems you fit enough to travel without aggravating your condition, the two of you simply instruct your respective valets to pack your trunks and leave as soon as possible, telling no one your intended destination."

Will sighed softly, disliking the necessity of such a thing.

"And how will that solve the issue of who is behind it?"

"I will be looking into that matter," Roland said. "Mr. Hawkes and Mrs. Henderson are thoroughly interviewing the servants as we speak for anything they might have seen or heard."

"I should be the one sorting this," Will said, frustrated.

"As your husband, *I* should be the one," Hannibal interjected. "But since we cannot put our heads together here and do so without keeping you at risk, our leaving is the only viable option."

"It feels dishonest," Will said, nibbling at a sandwich. It was delicious enough to goad him to do it justice in a few small bites.

"There is nothing dishonest in strategy, Will, as you well know," Hannibal said, adding another sandwich to his place, which earned him a glower but no protests. "Grandfather is sending to the Capital for detectives to assist his efforts in our absence. They will be running down leads and investigating these accidents to find out how they connect."

"I will need the letter you received," Roland said. "It might yield something useful."

"I will see that you get it," Will told him, absently rubbing at his head, a fine sheen of sweat rising on his skin. He put the remnants of his second sandwich down and took a few swallows of his tea, hoping it would all settle. "I have no idea if he can offer any additional insight, but Matthew Dunn is the one who informed me my saddle had been tampered with."

"I will be sure they are told of it," Roland said, and urged them, "Come, now, children, do this fine service justice! Mrs. Pimms will be beside herself if her efforts go to waste!"

413

"You may mark this date for posterity, Will, because I agree with Grandfather," Hannibal said. "You need to eat, and to drink as much tea as you can."

"I would like to do so but my head is disagreeing," Will said, taking a shaky breath. He resisted the urge to rub his aching neck, but knew his stiff posture was betraying him to Hannibal's practiced gaze. "Mrs. Pimms' porridge was very satisfying."

"Then I will ask—"

"No, thank you," Will said, uncertain if he was up to the task. "I can wait for supper, Hannibal... but my head is beginning to bother me again."

It was such a small thing, his quiet offering of that information, but Hannibal couldn't help but feel glad that Will had done so.

"Grandfather," he said, wiping his mouth and rising. "If you'll excuse us, please?"

"Please don't miss your tea for my sake—"

"Yes, yes, both of you do whatever you need to do to take care of that headache, and I will pray for a speedy recovery for you, Will," Roland said, delighted when Hannibal moved to Will's side, ready to steady him should he grow dizzy. "I will put a dent in these little darlings and Mrs. Pimms will never know the difference. If you would ring Zeitler for me, please?"

"I will, Grandfather," Will said, his relief to be going inside almost palpable. "It's the least I can do for disrupting your tea."

"You've done nothing of the sort, just get some rest and feel better," Roland said, watching them as they made their way back inside, his memories transforming them for an aching heartbeat into himself and Charles. He was so lost in his musings he didn't realize that Zeitler had arrived until he plopped down at the table and started serving himself.

"Brat," Roland sighed, taking a few more sandwiches for himself. "Be useful and pour my tea."

Zeitler poured for them both, grinning at the chastisement.

"Have you been looking into matters, as I asked?"

"Don't I do everything you ask?" Zeitler shot back, poking a small sandwich into his mouth. He swallowed it virtually whole and chased it with a swig of his tea. When he looked back at Roland, it was with the steady, no-nonsense gaze

Roland knew meant he was finally being serious. "I still don't get how you knew he was coming here."

"Zeitler, I am an old man who once had many enemies," Roland said. "*Once.* It took very little effort to realize that if Lady Rathmore was asking Anthony about Will after six years of silence, she was up to no good. It is always wise to be in possession of the facts."

Zeitler's brows shot up and he smirked. "You never cease to amaze me."

"I am not doing it for your benefit," Roland reminded him, and rapped the table with his fingers. "Out with it."

"Francis Doranhouse got chased out of the mills up north," Zeitler said. "Not sure why yet but I got somebody working on it. Guess where he was before."

Roland picked his cup up and fixed Zeitler with a repressive look. "You know very well I don't like guessing games and I despise not knowing things. It's why you're allowed to get away with murder, you scamp. You're just a hair more useful to me than you are a thorn in my side!"

Zeitler grinned and ate another little sandwich, but in actual bites this time.

"He was a stable hand at the Grant place. Lived with his grandmother until he was in his teens; she was the family housekeeper, a real battle ax."

Another sandwich, another sip of tea. Roland waited patiently, knowing how Zeitler enjoyed testing the patience of everyone around him.

"There was some kind of accident there, no one would give the girl I sent any specifics," Zeitler finally said. "Mr. Grant got hurt and Francis left, did a stint in the Navy overseas. Never made it back for granny's funeral."

Roland frowned. "I thought he might have been a military man. I wish it laid my fears to rest."

"Well, it shouldn't," Zeitler said. "He earned a dishonorable discharge and a prison sentence. Somebody at port didn't like the way he looked, Doranhouse rearranged his face for him."

"That certainly settled it," Roland said, feeling even more uneasy now than he had been, and his initial unease had been bad enough.

"I'd say so; he rearranged it all the way off, nearly killed him," Zeitler said, beating Roland to the last sandwich. "He tried the mills after his release but didn't last there, either. Lady Rathmore tracked him down after and he's been her constant companion ever since."

"*Companion?*"

"No proof," Zeitler said, and added with a grin, "*yet*. But I'm working on it."

"I know, you're a good boy, Zeitler, appearances notwithstanding," Roland said, earning a guffaw from his valet.

"Oh, another thing—you're going to love this—he got himself a big tattoo on his back while he was in service," Zeitler said, and waggled his brows with a grin. "It's your favorite."

"A dragon?" Roland asked, annoyed by Zeitler's delighted nod. "Of course it would be. Tell me, my boy, what do you make of him?"

Zeitler shrugged. "He's big and he's dangerous and I don't like him."

"I couldn't agree more," Roland said, frowning. "But then I never have cared much for dragons."

Chapter 22

Will thought that Hannibal would take him back to the ducal suite.

'Please stay...'

It was a possibility that was as daunting as it was compelling, and the closer they got to the doors, the more pensive Will became.

Hannibal could feel the tension humming through Will's slender body, even just through the light touch he kept at the base of Will's spine. It wasn't hard to guess the cause. As much as it disappointed him to do so, he escorted Will to the Duchess suite and unlocked his door, swinging it wide to admit him with a slight gesture.

Will exhaled softly, relieved and oddly disappointed, but knowing it was for the best. He was ill and tired and in no state to be tied into nerves over such trifling things when his defenses were so badly unprepared.

'Only an Omega would worry about being bedded at a time like this...'

The thought sounded far too much like his father's words in his father's voice for Will's comfort, and he took a step away from Hannibal's lingering touch to gather himself. The fact that he wanted to stay close to his husband was reason enough to call for distance. His illness made him far too vulnerable to his own nature—he could not trust himself not to make more of Hannibal's attentiveness than was actually there.

Hannibal watched him, feeling Will moving further and further from him in a way that had nothing to do with rooms or cities. The feeling of Will's warm, bare skin tingled on his fingertips, branded there and seared into his memory, and he clenched his hands around it as if he might lose that, as well.

He steadied himself, not wishing to push his presence on his husband, and moved instead to Will's vanity where a second bottle of headache medicine had been placed by Jimmy Prince, conveniently next to a pitcher and delicate little cup.

"It's fairly early still, so you should have another before you go to bed for the evening," he said, his voice vibrating in the silence between them, low and husky.

417

He mixed the medicine with the ease of long practice and brought the cup to his contemplative mate.

Will took it with murmured thanks and sipped it, grimacing at the bitter flavor.

"The headache will, unfortunately, be fairly nagging for some time," Hannibal warned, making sure he drank the entirety of it down. "But the more you drink, and rest, the better it will go for you. Be sure to let me know if you start feeling dizzy when you stand up."

"I will, thank you, Hannibal. I am clear on the restrictions," Will said, the words breathed softly so as not to tempt the ache back to life. "I only hope this subsides quickly."

Hannibal made a gesture at Jimmy when he poked his head in, sending him to Will's dressing room where the valet fetched fresh nightclothes and Will's robe.

"Jimmy will get you settled," Hannibal said, taking the glass from Will and putting it on the nightstand. "Is the binding on your ribs adequate?"

"Yes," Will said, touching his side where the bottom of the binding reached. "It did make a substantial difference in the pain. Thank you for suggesting it."

"I am a doctor, Will," Hannibal said, a rueful smile curving his mouth. "I should hope after this long I would give sound advice on medical matters."

Will smiled, tight and perfunctory, too many questions swimming in his large blue eyes, the tendrils of distrust creeping in to steal away the warmth that had built between them. That uncanny mind of his was working, Hannibal knew; dissecting what he had learned, what he had shown, and trying to establish where he fell on the scale of Hannibal's perception. The fearful, abhorrent *weakness* again, as if Will could ever be such a thing.

"I will be in my suite working on the estate business that's built up," Hannibal said, searching for any sign that the small kernel of trust between them was not altogether lost, merely dancing out of reach.

Will just offered a cautious, "Yes."

Hannibal took a deep breath, weighing his options, his Alpha nature at war with itself. He wanted to reach out, to soothe the pain he could feel in his mate, to be near him and protect him. But just as strong was the need to give Will the room he was so clearly asking for, the space to draw an easy breath and think, to respect his right to his privacy.

Lingering in one last attempt to reach his mate, he asked, "Is your neck bothering you again?"

"Some," Will said, moving another step away from him towards the covered window.

"If you were comfortable with such a thing," Hannibal said, aware of Jimmy noisily fussing in the dressing room to give them privacy. "I could wait for you to change and work on your back and neck again. It might help chase the pain away sooner and help you sleep."

He could sense Will considering it, haunted by the shadowy presence of Will's father there between them as if the man himself had slipped into the room, cruel and baleful, coaxing Hannibal's mate into believing that the basic human need to be cared for was nothing more than an embarrassing display of bad behavior.

Will didn't turn around. It didn't surprise Hannibal in the least when he said, "You're very kind to offer, Hannibal, but I can bear it."

It took him a long moment to whisper, "Is it preferable to bear that pain rather than my touch?"

Something shuddered and ached within him when Will said nothing, only ducked his head, his long curls shifting over his neckerchief and collar.

Hannibal nodded, even though Will couldn't see him. It was the only reaction he could manage before manners took over.

"I have overstepped, Will. I apologize. I'll be just next door if you need me," he said, moving to the washroom door, doing his best to conceal his disappointment. "I will have guards posted outside of your door for your safety. Please don't mind them."

Will felt him hesitate there, felt the weight of Hannibal's amber gaze on his back. The urge to call him back was so strong that he clenched his teeth, eyes sweeping closed to squeeze hard. He heard the quiet click of the washroom door and released a shuddering sigh, wishing that he could have accepted that invitation without risking his nature responding.

But it was too dangerous and his father's lessons had taught him too well that he could ill afford to allow his Omegan instincts the slightest outlet. He had been drawn alarmingly far down the path already in the midst of his pain and vulnerability with Hannibal.

419

'Given so much as a pinch of wiggle room,' his father had said, slapping his belt into his palm for emphasis, *'you will fall down the road to ruin and end up nothing more than a harlot begging in the street!'*

"Mr. Grant?"

"Yes, Jimmy," Will said, startled out of his thoughts by his valet urging him into his dressing room.

He was thoughtful and weary and uncertain as he was helped out of his clothing into his nightclothes. Jimmy kindly did not attempt to make conversation, merely helped him change, mindful to put more salve on his bruises with gentle care.

Before Jimmy left, Will said, "There was a letter in my jacket from this morning, Jimmy. Do you know what happened to it?"

"Yes, indeed, I meant to ask you what you'd like me to do with it," Jimmy said, settling Will on his bed and vanishing back into the dressing room. He returned with the letter, wrinkled and bent from its ill-fated journey. "Would you like me to post it?"

"No, Jimmy, thank you, just bring it to me, please," Will said.

Jimmy handed it over with a soft, "There we are! Will there be anything more for now, Mr. Grant?"

"No, that will do, thank you," Will said, clutching the letter tightly and stifling a yawn. "I'll ring you if I need anything. I think I might need to nap again."

"You get all the rest you need, Mr. Grant," Jimmy said, smiling at him. "We're all here to watch over you!"

He let himself out and Will sighed in the ensuing silence, his aches already fading beneath the strength of the medicine Hannibal had given him. He idly rubbed at the envelope in his hand, and was only just considering shredding it when a soft knock came at his door.

"Yes, come in," he called, rubbing his temple opposite where the goose egg rose. He dropped his hand, surprised to his sister admitting herself, and asked, "Mina, is something the matter?"

"I wanted to check on you," she said, teary-eyed and pale.

"I should have checked on *you*," Will said. "It was remiss of me not to do so. You left the table so suddenly, are you unwell?"

"I apologize for leaving so abruptly, I was just so frightened for you, Will," she said, trembling there just inside his suite, as if unsure she had the right to approach him. "I had an attack of nerves when I saw your husband go to you, pretending he has a care in the world for your safety! He would not let me see you —"

She cut off, pressing a lace-edged handkerchief to her face.

"Mina," Will said, and patted the bed beside him. "Here, come here."

She crossed the room with small, frantic steps to sit next to him and Will covered her trembling hand in his. He rubbed her fingers with his own, sitting with her in uncertain silence.

"What is this?" she asked, her voice thick with tears. She plucked at the corner of the letter idly, toying with it.

"A letter I wrote to Mr. Brauner this morning... so much has changed since then. I asked him to see to it that my death was investigated, should anything happen to me," Will said. "I'm relieved I didn't make it to the post. It would be terribly embarrassing trying to explain my fears now."

"Send it!" Mina insisted, trying to pull it from his fingers, but Will held fast, refusing. "Heavens! Send one to everyone you know! There is no telling what might next befall you!"

"Mina, stop! I'll do nothing of the sort!" Will told her, moving it out of her reach to place it on his nightstand. He took both her hands in his and said with every bit of honesty in him, "Hannibal and I have had a discussion regarding my accidents. He is not responsible on any count, Mina."

"That's absurd!" she said, pulling her hands away to stare at him, aghast. "Will! Honestly! You confessed you knew his plans and he told you he was not responsible?"

"Yes," Will said, careful not to nod. "He was greatly surprised—"

"Surprised you *knew*, you mean?" she snapped, upset. "And what? He gave you his word he had done nothing?"

"Mina, even Hannibal could not manufacture such a response," Will said, his tenderness for her rapidly wearing beneath the weight of her suspicions and the lingering pain of his aching head, neck, and back. "Please trust that I have spoken with him and judged that he is telling me the truth."

"Trust your judgment, Will?" she breathed, turning to cup his face. "When I know your bond to him would drive you to defend any horror he might visit on you?"

Will blinked, pained by that statement, and asked in a strained whisper, "Why do you distrust him so, Mina?"

"Because I love *you* so, Will," she answered without hesitation. "I cannot believe, considering his past, considering what he is capable of, that he would be above lying to you. When I tried to check on you this afternoon, he insulted me and turned me away. When Francis attempted to stay in order to protect you, he sent him packing off like a mongrel dog. He means you harm, Will. I will never believe otherwise."

Will drew a deep breath and sighed softly before standing. Leading her by the hand, he took her to his dressing room, telling her, "If you ever feel you need to see me, Mina, or that I am in danger and you cannot reach me, then here is a way that will not fail you."

"Will, what—" she cut off, eyes fastening on the little panel that swung open onto the dark, spare passageway within the wall. "What on earth?"

"Hartford House is riddled with such passages," Will said. "I came upon them when I was studying the architect's notes for some repairs to the load-bearing walls. They were added in a revision during the Inquisition, a means of escape from persecution at the height of the terror. All of them are still sound, though dark and close. No one uses them or knows of them, that I am aware of. Except, perhaps, Grandfather, and he has no reason to do so."

"These passages connect most of the rooms?" she asked, pulling back when Will took a step towards the inky darkness within.

"The entire house, from the attic to the cellar," Will said. "There is an identical panel in all of the dressing rooms. I admit I use them more than I probably should. It is a very convenient method to get from one place to the next without having to explain myself or engage in conversations I would prefer not to."

"So I can just wiggle into the wall like a rat and come see you?" she asked, wrinkling her nose in a way that made Will smile, knowing very well she had already discounted it.

"Yes, if all else fails," he said, squeezing her hand. "Mina, I appreciate your fear for me, but Hannibal is not the one who wishes to kill me. Whoever they are, will you please keep an open mind and be watchful for them?"

"Darling," she said, her gaze fastened on the panel as it swung back into place, hiding the passage as if it did not even exist. "There is nothing in this world I would not do for you."

She folded him into a warm embrace, careful to be gentle with him, and cooed softly to him as she had when they were children. The sweet scent of her skin and the familiar softness of her touch made Will smile, and he silently thanked his lucky stars that his sister was as deeply devoted to him as he was to her, in turn.

⌘⌘⌘

Doors were locked and trusted guards were stationed at the entrance to Will's suite, securing him against an all-out attack. Though Will's aggressor seemed to prefer more subtle methods, his husband was taking no risks with his safety.

Hannibal bent his attention to the estate work that had built up without Will's careful attendance and made moderate headway before he was interrupted by Berger bearing a missive.

The note was from Grandfather, a copy of a letter even now on its way to Mr. Stammets, detailing Mr. Doranhouse's history and requesting all pertinent information be forwarded to the constabulary in the Capital as a matter of record along with a request for an investigation into the matter of Will's accidents, the accounting of which was as thorough as they could manage with such limited details.

Francis' past military service didn't put Hannibal any more at ease than it had Grandfather, but it did make Hannibal reassess the simmering violence that crept beneath the surface of Doranhouse's flat, unblinking eyes.

"Berger," Hannibal said, lifting his eyes from the note, tracking his valet bustling about getting things set to rights. "Have you done much talking with Mr. Doranhouse?"

"Try not to, m'Lord," Berger said, a rare expression of true distaste on his weathered face. "He's an odd sort. Doesn't talk to anybody, doesn't look at anybody, just... glowers. He's a right nasty bit of business, m'Lord. Got that hard look about him."

"He was a serviceman," Hannibal murmured, thoughtfully folding the note up and placing it on his desk. "A seaman."

"Explains a bit about him, but in all honesty, my Lord, he gives the girls a fright and the servants are all shy of him," Berger said, falling back into the old

423

habit of being frank with him, as they'd been in the field. "No one is used to having an Alpha belowstairs. It ain't natural, is it? Alphas ain't meant to be servants, it's against their nature."

"Not everyone is born to circumstances which support their nature," Hannibal said, his thoughts turning to Will and those terrible scars. The note had mentioned an accident. An accident involving Will, after which Francis had left the Grant estate for good. "Is he outside?"

"Won't budge from the door," Berger confirmed. "No one really knows what to do. Can't properly order about an Alpha once their mind is set, hm?"

Hannibal's mouth pursed in thought, recalling what Francis had said to him on the landing earlier, 'He's spent all his life with Alphas like you...'

He got up, ignoring Berger's questioning look, and let himself out into the hallway where, sure enough, the two guards outside of Will's suite were nervously flanking the stony-faced and rigid Francis Doranhouse.

"You," he said, abrupt, an uncharacteristic Alpha growl under the words that he couldn't quite control. "Come with me."

Francis stirred slightly before he stopped himself. The low, soft whisper of his voice was as agitating to Hannibal as his sulfur and brimstone scent when he said, "I swore I would protect him."

"I appreciate your dedication, but I require answers from you, and as you are in my house, you will obey my orders," Hannibal said, standing expectantly in his doorway. He opened the door wide and said again, "Come with me."

Hannibal had never clashed with another Alpha in any ungentlemanly way, but he felt quite certain that it was an instance like this which prompted those deadly rows that sometimes made the papers with their violence. He had always imagined himself above that sort of nonsense.

Standing in his doorway smelling the scent of hot ashes with those pale, fierce eyes boring into him, Hannibal clearly and instinctively knew that one of these days he would be forced to prove beyond a shadow of a doubt to Mr. Doranhouse just which of the two of them was the better Alpha.

Bristling, he deliberately followed Francis into his suite, pleased when the man's shoulders tensed in response to giving Hannibal his back.

"Berger, go check on Will," Hannibal said, and took a seat, indicating that Francis should stand in front of him. "It is my understanding that you are more acquainted with my spouse than I first realized."

"Yes..." Again, that telling pause, testing and pushing despite his submissive posturing, "my Lord."

"In what capacity did you serve the Earl of Reddig?" Hannibal asked, his eye contact direct and steady when Francis would lift his gaze.

"I was a stable hand," Francis said. "... my Lord."

"It amused him to put you in the role of servant, did it?" Hannibal mused, frowning.

Francis bit back a retort, took a steadying breath, and said with dull deference, "He was Master there. It was his choice."

Hannibal tapped his fingers against his thigh, weighing how much truth he'd get out of Doranhouse and how much would be Mina's influence.

"What happened the day when you left?" he asked, pleased by the startled look he got in return. "Answer me, please. Something happened to my spouse and I want the truth of it."

Francis shifted, shoulders squaring, chin tipping up as he braced. "I'll not entertain you with talk of his *pain, Lord Clarges.*"

"Do I appear amused?" Hannibal asked, his voice sharpening to a snarl. "Does any part of my countenance imply that I anticipate taking pleasure in what you will tell me, Mr. Doranhouse?"

Those glittering, cold eyes wavered and dropped, his tense posture subsiding.

"Well, then," Hannibal said, brusque with him but unable to help it. "Out with it. I find myself in possession of facts I was ignorant of for nearly seven years and I refuse to remain ignorant a moment longer."

After a long, considering silence, Francis softly said, "When Lady Rathmore and her brother were little, their elder sisters would play with them like dolls, dress them up to match, play like children do."

Hannibal felt a small, hard knot of dread in his stomach, a knot that was fed by the obvious way in which Francis was disturbed merely speaking of his past.

"Lord Reddig forbid it, of course," Francis said, his eyes catching the flicker of flames from the fireplace, glittering with anger that had long been pressed down and confined. "Whenever he ever caught them at it, he would go on a rampage."

Francis looked to one side and said with harsh hatred, "It was Mr. Grant he always punished for it, never the girls. Even as a little one, he'd have servants hold him down and beat the dresses off his back. I can still hear it sometimes when I'm sleeping, his screaming; still see him struggling."

The image of it was sharp and immediate, painfully forceful as if his heart had ruptured in Hannibal's chest. He knew from the sight of those scars that Will's childhood held terrible horrors, but the truth of it from a witness was almost more than he could bear. He swallowed hard, and said, "That must have been very difficult for you, both as a child and as an Alpha, hearing an Omega in such terrible distress."

"Not as difficult as it was for Mr. Grant," Francis said, anger oozing from every nuance of his posture, every crack in his whispered words. "It never stopped Lord Reddig. It never stopped any of them. He'd heal, and they'd do it again."

"He was just a toy to them?" Hannibal said, thinking aloud, piecing together what little Will had mentioned of his sisters. "Not a brother, not a person, merely a doll to be played with at their convenience."

"It was a game," Francis said, the words escaping him on a hiss of disgust. "They saw the result but never the violence; it was meaningless to them, with no connection. Their father's anger was ephemeral, never harming any one of them, and Mr. Grant never spoke of it. So they made a game of upsetting Lord Reddig. How often could they get away with it? How far could they push their father? Lady Iris went too far. She dressed them to match, two little angels in beautiful frocks, and the lot of them rode on ponies down through town in a small parade."

Hannibal took a deep breath to control the pounding of his heart but it didn't help. He could see Will in his mind's eye, frightened atop his pony, terrified of being caught by his father while his sisters laughed around him, enjoying their little game. The casual cruelty of children trained to believe that one among them was lesser than they, expendable in emotion and flesh.

A way to pass the time.

"I saw them riding back," Francis said. "I tried to get to him first because he was coming, he was already moving towards them, and I just couldn't—"

Francis paused, fury and upset shaking the whole of his impressive build from head to toe. Hannibal trembled in his chair, leaning forward to brace his elbows on his knees, his face in his hands and his stomach churning with sickened anger.

"I didn't make it." Francis' voice was flat, emotionless, fearful in its intensity. "He took hold of Mr. Grant's leg to drag him off his pony but he got hung up on the sidesaddle. There was this... this horrible sound, it... it *popped*. His leg, it... He didn't even scream. He *couldn't*. He just... he fell to the ground and his sisters started screaming for him. They'd never seen it for themselves. It terrified them and they all started to-to *panic*. Lord Reddig shouted at him, telling him to get up, and Mr. Grant tried, he just... he couldn't stand, and... I couldn't bear it anymore."

Francis looked back at Hannibal, simmering with outrage, eyes blazing with challenge as if daring Hannibal to interject a single word on the subject.

"I pushed Lord Reddig out of the way and carried Mr. Grant home," he said. "He'd dislocated his hip, pulled it completely out of place. He wasn't even six years old at the time. Just a baby, just-just a *baby*..."

Hannibal swallowed against the bile that wanted to rise, his heart breaking for Will and filling with deep, swelling anger for what he'd been put through. He'd never felt so ill and wretched in his life as he did in that moment, hearing just one tale of Will's pain from a lifetime of it, one bare glimpse into the terrible abuse that had defined his life in his father's house.

"Lady Rathmore later told me it took a doctor in from the Capital to set it right again, but it was never whole as it was before," Francis said, shuddering hard, hands clenching into fists at his lean thighs.

Hannibal blinked hard, mouth pressed in a thin line of pain for his mate. Struggling to maintain his composure, he whispered, "She *later* told you?"

"You asked about the day I left. *That* was the day. I couldn't bear to stay a moment longer," Francis said. "I couldn't protect him. I couldn't keep him from suffering, not then."

There was fire in his eyes and a dangerous promise of violence in his deceptively soft voice when he said, "But *now* I can, Lord Clarges. I won't make the same mistakes as I did then. I'll protect him from whatever might hurt him, even if that's *you*."

Hannibal's head whipped up and he surged to his feet before he realized it. Trembling with barely-suppressed rage at what he'd been told, he said with clipped, harsh anger, "You will never have any reason to protect Will from *me*, Mr. Doranhouse. But despite your story, your history of violence and your unhesitating use of it makes me understandably wary of having you anywhere near my mate. That you arrive now, when he is in such peril, only makes me all the more suspicious of you."

"I arrive now *because* your mate is in peril," Francis said, his gaze unwavering. "*My Lord*. Mr. Grant has suffered enough in his life, first at his

427

father's hand and now at yours. I'll not add to his woes. I only wish to keep him safe from harm. I will protect him."

Hannibal took a step closer, looming into Francis' space, watching the Alpha bristle in response.

"*You* are dangerous and your intentions seem cloudy at best," Hannibal said, taut with tension, grimly staring at Francis and holding those dead, pale eyes. "*Protection* is a very loose term, after all, and I am not sure our definitions align. As you are here at his request and under his sufferance, I will not interfere or undermine his authority in this house, but I promise you this, Doranhouse, if one curl on his head—*one single hair*—comes to any manner of harm, *you* will be held accountable."

Francis stared at him, unblinking, unwavering.

"I appreciate your actions on his behalf in the past, but be sure your actions are on his behalf now," Hannibal warned, staring him down. "I am going to find whoever has tried to harm Will. I am going to see to it that they pay, either by the law or by my own hand. I can promise you that, Francis. And I *always* keep my promises."

Francis blinked, his tension thick enough to cut.

"Keep that in mind as you maintain your vigil," Hannibal said, gesturing him towards the door, "and see to it that your loyalties lie where they will best preserve your life."

⌘⌘⌘

Deeply disturbed by what he'd managed to get out of Francis, Hannibal declined to attend dinner, choosing instead to continue his work on the estate business with a decanter of brandy.

It didn't help.

It didn't erase or even numb what he'd been told and he found himself over and again in front of the washroom door, staring at the panel and debating intruding on Will. He grew more anxious as the hours passed, irrationally worried that someone would manage to find their way through the measures they'd taken and somehow snuff Will out like the bare flame on a candle.

Resigning himself to bed and the hope that morning would bring him some improvement in his disposition, Hannibal finally did go through to check on Will once more.

His spouse was sleeping soundly when Hannibal moved to check the locks again. The bolt was thrown, of course, but he was compelled to check anyway, and turned from the door to look at Will's sleeping form.

He was all but lost in the bedding, his dark, curly-haired head resting on plump pillows, the purple lump on his forehead stark against his pale skin but already beginning to subside. One arm was atop the covers, his slender wrist curved, his fingers lax. Hannibal reached out and slipped his own fingers beneath them, feeling the calluses of hard work and the strength there that was as much dogged determination as it was his nature. He slid his fingertips to Will's palm, thumb brushing over the top of his hand, and felt a pang when Will's mouth twitched in a slight smile.

Hannibal crouched next to his bed and smoothed Will's curls with his opposite hand, thoughtful and sorrowful. Everything he learned came to bear on him and he trembled with the force of it. In the quiet, moonlit darkness, he clasped Will's hand tightly, bowed his head to the mattress, and silently wept.

He wept for the child Will had been.

He wept for the boy who had come to his home with the promise of a new beginning and found only the same disregard his father had always shown him.

He wept for what Will might have been, and for what he had managed to be despite everything—stalwart, honest, *good* to the very core of himself in ways some people could never hope to achieve.

He wept for the role he'd played in continuing a lifetime's worth of uncertainty and fear.

But in the end he wept for what might have been, the potential he'd wasted for both of them, the hope of happiness he'd rejected, and all the time they could never get back.

He almost didn't realize at first that Will was stroking his hair, fingers soft and gentle in their petting of him. He stilled beneath that touch and the soft exhale of, "Sh..." that came from his little mate.

Hannibal lifted his face, finding Will still sleeping, brow furrowed in slight distress.

"Sh..." Will sighed, his hand falling away but the fingers still trapped in Hannibal's hand squeezed him softly.

"Will," Hannibal whispered, wiping his face against the fresh tears that threatened just knowing that, even asleep, Will couldn't bear another's suffering. "How can I ever make any of it up to you?"

He couldn't. It was the simple and ugly truth.

"Will," he said again, a soft smile overcoming his sorrow when Will squeezed his fingers again, murmuring something in his sleep that Hannibal couldn't make out. He leaned closer and Will's eyes fluttered a bit, bleary and glassy. Hannibal smoothed his curls again and whispered, "I didn't mean to disturb you. I only wanted to check on you."

Will blinked slowly, as if his eyelids were too heavy to raise, partly the late hour, partly the concussion, and partly the painkiller Jimmy had given him before bed.

"If you need anything," Hannibal said, moving to stand, "please call out."

Will's fingers tightened on his unexpectedly and he sighed, "Don't..."

Hannibal's smile faded and he stood, reluctant to let go of Will's hand but knowing he had no right to stay when Will didn't want him to. "I apologize for intruding on you. Please, go back to sleep, you need your rest—"

"Don't go," Will said, rolling onto his side with Hannibal's fingers trapped against his chest. He snuggled into the pillows with another weighty sigh and relaxed.

Hannibal hesitated, and gently eased his hand out of Will's. He considered leaving. He knew he *should* leave, all things considered.

But part of him—a part that was growing stronger by the moment—wanted to stay, not for any nefarious purpose, but to keep him safe, to watch over him, to give him some small measure of comfort the people in his life had denied him from his earliest awareness.

So he moved to the opposite side of the bed and eased down atop the covers next to his mate's sleeping body. He moved closer cautiously, careful not to disturb Will's sleep. Hesitance made him graceless but he folded one arm over Will's side, settling against the warm curve of his body and tucking close.

Will uttered a soft, coaxing chirp in his sleep and, when Hannibal's hand came to rest against his chest, he wrapped his smaller fingers around Hannibal's and clung tight.

"Go back to sleep, Will," Hannibal murmured, curling around him as best he was able, considering he was atop the covers and Will was tucked beneath them.

He nuzzled his nose into the crown of Will's head, his soft curls tickling and fragrant, and sighed softly at how good it felt, as if some part of himself he'd never known was missing had clicked into place. He blinked in the darkness, drowsy and content, and pressed a soft kiss to Will's head. "I won't let anyone hurt you again, Will, not even myself. I promise."

And Hannibal always kept his promises.

⌘⌘⌘

Will felt much improved the next morning, waking from a peculiar but pleasant dream of being held through the night. It felt so real that it surprised him to wake alone, though there was honestly no reason it should.

He rang for Jimmy, rubbing the sleep out of his eyes and sitting up with only a twinge of the pain he'd felt the day before. He hated to admit it, but Hannibal's methods and medications worked, even if it made him sleepy.

He just felt awake enough to brave standing when Jimmy came in, bright-eyed and chipper and smiling, as always, calling a cheerful, "*Good* morning, Mr. Grant!" as he snagged Will's robe to bundle him up. "Do you need help to the washroom?"

"No, Jimmy, I think I can make it, but do you know what happened to that letter?" Will asked, troubled to see that it was no longer on the nightstand where he'd left it.

"No, Mr. Grant, last I saw it was when I handed it to you," Jimmy said, concern wrinkling his brow. "I doubt any of the maids took it, but I'll ask all the same."

"Thank you, that would be very kind," Will said, making a mental note to write Mr. Brauner as soon as he could, just in case some well-meaning someone had put it to post.

"We'll check for it when we clean, of course," Jimmy called, watching him hawkishly as he made his cautious way to the washroom. "Will you be going down to breakfast?"

"No, thank you, I'll have a tray," Will told him, preferring that to facing conversation at the breakfast table he simply wasn't up for.

Much to his surprise, when he emerged from relieving himself of his excess tea, Jimmy informed him that Hannibal would like to join him at his small breakfast.

Will agreed before he realized it, and in the few moments it took to relay his assent, Jimmy set him up at a small table near the window in the dappled morning light, comfortable and snug in his robe.

Hannibal knocked, coming in when Will called entry. He stopped just inside the door and smiled, a slight curve of his lips that caused Will to look away hastily. It made him acutely recall the comfort of his dream last night, the warm closeness that had allowed him to sleep without nightmares to plague him. He wondered if perhaps Hannibal hadn't come in late last night to dose him and it had somehow translated to his dreams. Or perhaps his imagination—or the painkilling powder—was playing tricks on him altogether.

"You look much improved this morning," Hannibal said, moving to take the seat opposite Will. "Is the light too bright?"

"No, thank you, it's perfect," Will said, reaching for the teapot.

Hannibal reached as he did, both of them at once, the slight brush of his fingers over the back of Will's hand unexpectedly pleasant. "Please, allow me."

Will withdrew, blinking against the after effects of the medicine. Hannibal poured them both a steaming cup and turned Will's handle around to towards him.

"There we are. I thought we might try a small outing today and test how you're feeling," Hannibal said, not quite able to hide that he was assessing Will for signs of strain.

"To where?" Will asked, stirring his porridge without appetite.

"Down to the stables, perhaps? Or to your office," Hannibal said, content to simply sit opposite Will and sip tea all day, if all else failed. "I don't want you to overexert yourself, but some light exercise can often do more good for you than anything."

"The stables," Will said. "There is something there I need to check on and I'm not sure I could make it all the way to my office. How did the work go last night?"

"Slowly," Hannibal said. "I haven't your affinity for it, but I managed. Regretfully, I missed supper. I do hate abandoning my defenseless old grandfather to your sister's hands."

"*Hannibal*," Will said, keenly disapproving.

"That glower was nearly up to snuff," Hannibal said, Will's scolding something he relished.

"My sister is a lovely young lady," Will told him. "And your grandfather is hardly defenseless. I certainly hope Mina was on her toes last night."

"He has an uncanny habit of keeping people dancing to his tune, so I imagine so," Hannibal said. "Are we settled then? Breakfast, then a walk to the stable."

"Yes," Will said, unable to resist smiling. It faded some, uncertain at the edges, and his voice was quiet with concern when he asked, "Why are you being so kind to me recently, Hannibal?"

Hannibal gazed at him for a long moment, and then turned his head to look out the window, his profile severe and beautiful, so like that statue Will had first compared him to.

Yet this stone did not seem so cold as it had before, nor so immovable.

It seemed... reachable.

"The instant I first laid eyes on you, Will, I saw everything that was good about the country I had left behind, a breath of fresh air after the scourge of war. I saw beauty and youth and innocence and the potential for happiness," Hannibal said, and forced himself to look back at Will, to acknowledge what he had done and accept the judgment that would weigh in Will's sorrowful blue eyes. "A heartbeat later, I caught the scent of your skin, warmth and sweetness calling out like a siren song, a lure no Alpha could resist."

Will swallowed hard, and managed, "*You* resisted."

"Yes, I did," Hannibal said, mouth tightening. "But at what cost, Will? Everything you showed me in your attempts to appease my unjustified treatment of you, I saw as something else entirely and threw back into your face. I confused you, child that you were. I twisted every honest effort of yours into motivations not your own and turned them back on you with a sharpened edge meant to wound."

Will dropped his eyes to his porridge bowl, his chest aching to be reminded of the few short, awful days of their first acquaintance.

"There are a great many things I would change if I could, Will," Hannibal said, the soft rumble of his voice purring pleasantly through Will's chest. Despite himself, the young Omega responded to him, to his scent, the gentle tone of his voice—all those things his nature craved that he firmly rejected.

"You're an Alpha," Will said, his voice barely above a whisper. "When you change your mind, you change people's lives. It isn't something you should do lightly."

"No, nor do I," Hannibal agreed. "But I do think of what might have been had I done things differently."

"Then you are a fool, Lord Clarges," Will said, the sad surety of the words conveying how often Will had said those same words to himself.

Hannibal considered that statement in all of its resigned, unspoken pain, and drew another soft breath, tasting Will's faint scent on his tongue.

"I have caused you quite enough pain, Will," Hannibal said, and Will's eyes shot up to his, surprised and sparkling. "I have been needlessly cruel to you, wasted years of your youth I can never return, abandoned you to the gossip and opinions of people not fit to lick your boots, and I am sorry for it. To the very core of myself, I am sorry for it."

Will flinched when those words hit him, a physical ache in his heart that felt as if it might stop altogether.

"I am not being kind to you, Will, or even giving you your due," Hannibal said, distressed by his distress. "I am merely treating you with the respect and courtesy you deserve."

Will swallowed hard. "As an Omega?"

"As a *human*," Hannibal said, immediate and firm. "I have lived my life with the singular goal of never apologizing for myself or my actions. After Melinda, I swore I would never regret anything ever again. But you... *you*, I do regret. I regret how I have treated you. I regret what I have done to you. I regret the part I played in taking an aspect of yourself away from you and crushing it so thoroughly it might never recover."

"And what aspect was that?" Will asked, unable to look at him for fear Hannibal would see for himself how deeply his confession was affecting him.

"There was a heart in that youth I tried to destroy," Hannibal said. "It has had more hardship than any heart should ever have to bear."

Will took a shallow, shuddering breath, and whispered, "It isn't your responsibility to tend it, Lord Clarges."

"It *is* my responsibility, but not my right," Hannibal told him, his hand trembling slightly when he fiddled with his cup. He looked out of the window again, blinking hard and trying to regain control of himself, but his voice was unsteady when he softly added, "I would mend it if I could."

Will laughed at that, a short scoffing sound. "There are things which cannot be mended, Hannibal. There is no moving backwards and time does not reverse.

Teacups remain shattered, words remain spoken, and everyone lives with the consequences as they must."

"You are made of stronger stuff than a teacup, Will," Hannibal said, earning a soft, indrawn breath from his mate. "With a kind of strength that bows in the face of adversity like a willow tree in the midst of a storm, bending without breaking and rising up stronger than the force which tried to change you."

Will met his gaze, his eyes sheened with unshed tears. When he saw the mirroring gleam of tears in Hannibal's own eyes, he clenched his teeth to resist weeping right then and there, for he had never dreamed—even with his vast imagination—that Hannibal Ledford would ever show him such a thing.

"I will never forgive myself, Will, for ever making you question why I am being kind to you," Hannibal whispered, and reached across the small table for Will's lax hand, slowly enough to give away his intention and allow Will to reject it.

He didn't. He held still and let Hannibal's warm fingers brush over his hand and curl against his palm in a light squeeze. He blinked, dropping a few traitorous tears, and quickly brushed at them with his free hand.

"I apologize, I am not as well as I imagined—"

Hannibal shifted and wiped the tears away with his opposite hand, still holding tightly to Will.

"It has been a very trying few days," Hannibal said. "You have more right than anyone to a tear or two, Will. Gods know we all have our fair share at times... I wish I could wipe away the cause as easily."

Will struggled with himself, trying to parse out just what he was feeling and why. With Hannibal's gentle fingers on his face, he met his husband's gaze and whispered, "You *hurt* me."

Hannibal flinched, the shimmer in his eyes spilling over, but he never blinked, never turned away from the accusation; he didn't even react to the tears trailing down his cheeks, as if they were right and proper, justified somehow in ways that Will could not allow himself to feel.

"I did," Hannibal said, his low voice softly breaking with emotion. "And I have to live with what I've cost you, and so many others, Will. I hurt you, and I can only beg your forgiveness, though I do not expect or deserve it. I wish I could take it back."

"Would you strive to bring it together again, Hannibal?" Will asked, recalling his nightmare and how desperately he had tried to heal what had been broken.

"I can only try with everything in me," Hannibal told him. "And if it takes the rest of my life, I will never stop trying, Will."

Will drew a soft, unsteady breath and closed his eyes as he tried to control the shaken, aching vulnerability that Hannibal had awoken with his heartfelt words. He felt silly and stupid for having let those tears escape, but the longer Hannibal soothed them away, the less awful he felt for showing a weakness his father had always despised, a weakness Hannibal had no qualms in showing. His bond to to his husband hummed with the resonance of his feelings and his honesty in what he had said. He truly, in this moment, genuinely offered Will his regret, and the understanding of it nearly jostled loose another spill of tears.

Hannibal just kept gently brushing his fingers over Will's cheeks, long after the trails of his tears had dried to silvery salt on his pale skin. The touch was tender and attentive, soothing, and helped him to calm his anxiety somewhat.

"Shall we make ourselves presentable and take our walk?" Hannibal asked after a long, comforting silence. He turned his hand against Will's cheek and cupped his face, brushing his thumb beneath one weary blue eye and offering Will a soft smile when their gazes met.

Will hesitated, torn between wanting to retreat to his bed to rediscover his embarrassment and wanting to enjoy the ceasefire for a while. Before he could answer either way, a knock came on the door and Jimmy let himself in, agitated and flushed.

"Jimmy?" Will asked, his fingers clenching on Hannibal's in reaction to his valet's distress. Hannibal immediately dropped his hand, fingers trailing beneath Will's chin in a soft caress as he did so.

"Lord Clarges," Jimmy said, holding out a sheet of paper as he approached them. "I thought the two of you needed to see this immediately."

Hannibal gave Will's fingers a soft squeeze and let go of his hand to take the paper. Will wiped at his face, composing himself, grateful for the interruption for giving him a chance to feel less exposed.

"It was tacked to the doorway," Jimmy said, wringing his hands. "No one saw anyone about! His Grace has men on it now, my Lords, but there is so precious little to go on."

"Will," Hannibal said, handing over the paper with steady, somber seriousness. "I think we will be leaving immediately."

Will turned the paper over, a simple double-creased letter without a seal.

Next time you won't be so lucky, Mr. Grant. You'll never be safe again.

Will paled, but anger bubbled up in him just seeing it. It took him a moment to realize not all of his upset was solely his own—Hannibal was quietly furious, mouth pursed with anger, clenching and unclenching his hand into a fist as if imagining himself engaging this nameless enemy.

"Jimmy," Will said, gingerly gaining his feet and going to his jewelry box. He opened it and pried up the lining to fish the other letter out and handed both of them to his valet. "Run this down to His Grace, per his request, and then inform Mr. Hawkes that Hannibal and I will need our trunks."

He looked back at Hannibal, who was watching him with something that bled through his bond as fear—fear for him, fear for his life, for his loss.

"Light or heavy?" Jimmy asked, perking up considerably at the prospect of escape.

Squaring his shoulders, Will firmly said, "Heavy, Jimmy. We're leaving Hartford House."

⌘⌘⌘

Continued in Volume 2

437

Made in the USA
Lexington, KY
21 April 2018